Death Has A Thousand Doors
Patricia W. Grey
Proverse Hong Kong

DEATH HAS A THOUSAND DOORS is set in the little-known Pyrenean country of Andorra in the late 1990s. Family complications abound. Jane Burns, an Australian accountant, is a recovering alcoholic with a troubled past. When she receives a letter inviting her to visit Andorra for the winding-up of her grandfather's multi-million dollar trust, she jumps at the opportunity to leave her humdrum life and troubles behind. She expects to stay with her half-sister, Pearl, a photo journalist who moved to Andorra to escape an abusive marriage, but on her arrival Pearl is missing without explanation. The only clue to her whereabouts is an unlikely welcoming gift to Jane of a bottle of champagne.

Jane and Pearl's father, Charles, an aloof historian, becomes Jane's ally in the search for Pearl. In a twisted web starting from the founding of the family trust after the Second World War, and involving financial misdoings, kidnapping and tobacco-smuggling, Jane and Charles try to discover which threads will lead them to Pearl, and which are simply the detritus of her daily life as an investigative journalist. On the way, Jane meets a sympathetic village policeman. She also meets Pearl's lover, a prominent Andorran politician. But are these two men helping or hindering the investigation?

PATRICIA W. GREY was raised in Perth, Western Australia. In 1976 she and her husband established the first underwater pearl farm in Australia, pioneering unique growing methods for pearls. They retired in 1996 and moved to Andorra, where she is a member of the Andorran Writers' Circle.

Proverse Prize Finalist 2010

Death
Has A Thousand Doors

Proverse Prize Finalist 2010

Patricia W. Grey

Proverse Hong Kong

Death Has A Thousand Doors
by Patricia W. Grey
Revd Ed pub. in pbk by Proverse Hong Kong, April 2017.
ISBN: 978-988-8228-76-8
Copyright © Proverse Hong Kong, April 2017.
Available from https://www.createspace.com/6929883

1st published in pbk in Hong Kong by Proverse Hong Kong, 22 November 2011.
Copyright © Proverse Hong Kong, 22 November 2011.
ISBN 978-988-19932-6-7

Enquiries: Proverse Hong Kong, P. O. Box 259, Tung Chung Post Office, Tung
Chung, Lantau Island, NT, Hong Kong SAR, China.
E-mail: info@proversepublishing.com Web site: www.proversepublishing.com

Moral Rights: The right of Patricia W. Grey to be identified as the author of this
work has been asserted by her in accordance with the Copyright, Designs and
Patents Act 1988.

Cover photograph by Mr. Jan Roelof v/d Aa, Soldeu, Andorra. The door pictured
can be seen from the main road from Canillo to Ransol, near the village of Aldosa,
Principality of Andorra.
Page design by Proverse Hong Kong. Cover design by Artist Hong Kong Company.

DISCLAIMER: This novel is entirely a work of fiction. Names, characters, businesses, organisations, places
and events are either a product of the author's imagination or are used fictitiously. Any resemblances to
actual persons, living or dead, or to events or locales are entirely coincidental.

Proverse Hong Kong

British Library Cataloguing in Publication Data (for the 1st edition)

Grey, Patricia W.
    Death has a thousand doors.
    1. Australians--Andorra--Fiction. 2. Photojournalists--
    Andorra--Fiction. 3. Fathers and daughters--Fiction.
    4. Missing persons--Investigation--Andorra--Fiction.
    5. Andorra--Social conditions--20th century--Fiction.
    6. Detective and mystery stories.
    I. Title
    823.9'2-dc22

ISBN-13: 9789881993267

Dedicated to my mother
Eileen Margaret Grey (née Lacey)

"Anyone can stop a man's life, but no-one his death; a thousand doors open on to it."
– Seneca the Younger, *Phoenissae*.

CREDIT EUROPA
EDIFICI APEX. EL CENTRO   ESCALDES-ENGORDANY
ANDORRA

21 June 199-

Sra. Jane Burns
Sentry and Parker
P O Box 39
Fremantle Western Australia 6959

Personal

Dear Señora Burns:

The Charles Barclay family trust, set up by your grandfather, is due to be wound up as of September this year. Under the original terms, the trust was to run for fifty years to provide an annual disbursement to the beneficiaries for their education and general wellbeing.

Your presence in Andorra is requested for the day September 4 at which time we can discuss the formalities required before we pay out the remaining capital. Although a representative with a power of attorney would be acceptable, we urge you to attend the meeting in person. Please organize your flight details to suit and advise us of the cost for reimbursement.

The trustees look forward to meeting you, and to welcoming you to Andorra.

Yours sincerely

Señora Julia Menendez -Trustee

PROLOGUE

Jane kicked the gate shut as she simultaneously juggled her briefcase and the mail while keeping her blue heeler, Soda, from escaping into the busy street. Another long day at the office had left her jaded and now all she could think of was a run along the Swan River to the Bicton sand-spit. She hoped the sweat and the sunshine would distract the demon for one more day – the next meeting of Alcoholics Anonymous wasn't until Thursday.

The manila envelope with its exotic stamp and official seals stood out from the usual scattering of bills and she tore it open as she stood on the front step. A trip to Andorra in September? Why not? Tax season would be over by then and the office routine would have returned to some semblance of normality. Getting together with her freewheeling father and half-sister would be a bonus. Thoughts of a run postponed, she headed inside to email Pearl the news of her imminent arrival.

Soda pounced on her heels and tried his best to drag her by her left boot back towards the gate. She not so gently kicked him off. The boots had cost a small fortune. Retail therapy was yet another way to distract her from drinking. She often wondered if there would ever be a twenty-four hour period in which she didn't long for alcohol. Two years sober and she had yet to have that pleasure. "One day at a time," she mumbled to herself.

Her mobile phone vibrated. It was her mother, the only person likely to call her at this time of the day. She let it go to voice mail. Her mother's constant harping would definitely send her straight to the vodka bottle.

Pearl's return email suggested various alternatives for flights to Barcelona. If she chose the one through Hong Kong perhaps she could meet up with Charles and fly on with him from there. Sitting side by side on a plane for sixteen hours would certainly give father and daughter a chance to get reacquainted, although she wasn't sure if she was entirely comfortable with the idea of the enforced proximity. Charles just didn't seem to know how to act like a father. He told unseemly jokes and flirted with her. Here she was, thirty-eight, and the only person who ever flirted with her was her father. How sad was that?

CHAPTER ONE

"Anything to declare?" asked the customs agent without interest. "*Nada.*" Jane was anxious to put her night classes in Spanish to use, although she suspected they might prove to be a fruitless investment when faced with the rapid speech of the locals. Impatient passengers stormed the door marked "*Salida*" and swept Jane into the rose-pink marble arrival hall. She scanned the waiting crowd for her half-sister Pearl, whose high cheekbones, slanted eyes and waist-long black hair made her stand out in a crowd.

Three years before, Pearl had moved to Andorra, not entirely for tax reasons. Andorra frequently maintained that it was not a tax haven or fiscal paradise, arguing that the constitution sanctioned taxing its residents. Still, the official income tax rate was nil and the country had never imposed an income tax in its history, nor company tax. No estate tax. No capital gains tax; just a modest import duty on all goods. Jane's professional services as an accountant would count for very little in Andorra. There was something liberating in the thought.

Passengers were greeting family members in a fug of smoke from recently-lit cigarettes. Everyone in the airport appeared to be smoking – a culture shock after Australia where smoking was banned in public places and every packet of cigarettes carried the warning that smoking could cause death. As she watched the greedy inhalation of a hundred cigarettes, Jane wondered what percentage of them had been smuggled across the Andorran frontier.

The PA system squawked. "Would Mrs Jane Burns please make her way to the Lufthansa Airlines desk?" The crowd zigzagged past her as she struggled against the tide. She waited at the desk while a smartly dressed man reported his missing luggage to a clerk who seemed to think the loss was the passenger's fault. When the passenger stamped off, she announced that she was Mrs Burns.

"Message for you, *Señora.*" The clerk handed over a white envelope. Inside was the scribbled note:

Jane,
Sorry, a last minute problem. You'll have to catch the bus. It leaves
from between terminal A & B at 10.30am. I've booked you on it.

Show the driver my address and he'll take you right to the door. The concierge will let you into the apartment. Make yourself at home. See you soon. Pearl.

Jane sighed. She had been looking forward to seeing Pearl and catching up with her news during the three hour drive to Andorra, but she knew photo-journalists had deadlines to meet.

"A few more hours by bus. Great." she said under her breath. Just what she needed after the twenty-four hours it had taken her to fly from Perth. Thank goodness she had sought out the ladies room before collecting her luggage in the customs hall; otherwise the final phase of the journey might test her bladder. She had drunk litres of water while trying to ignore the liquor cart on the plane. She wheeled her suitcase out of the terminal onto the bus concourse and walked the two hundred-metre length between Terminal A and B.

It was ten in the morning, and a balmy twenty-four degrees according to the electronic signboard. No bus marked Andorra was waiting. Buses arrived and departed as she idly watched the passers-by, eavesdropping on their conversations. A large contingent of badly-dressed, sunburnt Brits with bandsaw accents from the Midlands trooped by. The Germans had better clothes. All were carrying large, flat boxes from Majorca that seemed to contain cakes. Straw hats were abundant as were shorts and sandals.

She was inventing a ten point system to identify nationality by fashion when a small bus with "*Viatges*" painted on the side and "Andorra" on the front pulled in. The driver sprang out and opened the luggage door. Jane pointed to herself and said "Señora Burns" and he waved her inside, throwing her suitcase into the baggage compartment with little care. Two other passengers appeared and their luggage was similarly tossed into the back. They all settled in to their seats and the bus drew away. The whole episode lasted no more than five minutes. It was only 10.20 and Jane wondered what would have happened if she had not sat outside to wait. Since the driver had not asked for tickets, or for names of the other passengers, she supposed a head count was all that was required.

Her seat behind the driver allowed a good view through the front window. Anonymous blocks of brick apartments dominated the streetscape near the airport. The bus was following signs that read

"Lleida" through surprisingly fast dense traffic. Half an hour out of Barcelona they went through a toll station where, in the distance, crenulated rock formations formed castles against the blue sky. An exit sign read "Bruc Roc" and she was thinking that her husband Bruce would have liked to see a landmark named after him as she fell into a deep sleep.

A voice spoke close to her ear, "*Lo siento, Señora!*" The bus was parked next to a modern restaurant set beside freshly ploughed fields. Each field was separated by ancient stone walls. The driver continued, "*Quisiera usted cafe o los servicios?*" She did indeed want coffee and the bathroom. She smiled and nodded, her Spanish momentarily deserting her. "*Gracias!*" she said belatedly to his departing back. The restaurant was a substantial building; spotlessly clean with tiled floors, wooden tables and chairs, a bar and a small shop filled with dusty souvenirs. She put a thousand pesetas on the bar and ordered coffee and a crusty ham roll. One of her fellow passengers, a short elderly woman in an unseasonable tweed skirt, was trying to pay the protesting driver for the fare. The woman spoke in English very firmly and loudly,
"I'm not Señora Fuente. I don't have a ticket."
The driver looked at the man behind the bar and shrugged. Jane supposed that Señora Fuente was still walking around the concourse wondering what the hell had happened to her bus.
"Do you know Andorra well?" Jane asked the woman.
"I've lived there ten years."
How was it possible to live in a country for ten years and not know enough of the language to communicate even simple needs? Jane wondered. The woman introduced herself as Lizzie Johnson and sat next to her as they remounted the bus.
"Perhaps you could tell me a little about the country? I'm visiting my sister Pearl, in Ordino," Jane asked.
"Not Pearl Wentworth? Lovely girl. She belongs to the International Club. I'd never take you for sisters; I thought she was from somewhere in Asia?"
Lizzie Johnson seemed only too happy to have someone to talk to. She was returning from visiting a daughter and grandchildren in England. "My husband and I moved to Andorra to avoid a capital

gains tax bill when we sold our business. We only needed to live away from Great Britain for three years but Roger liked Andorra so much that we stayed. Well, he liked not having to pay income tax, not to mention the duty-free whisky."

"And are you happy there?"

"I miss the family, plus we expats don't interact with the Andorrans much so I haven't made as many local friends as I expected. The Andorrans stick with their own kind. It's common for mountain cultures to be insular."

Jane winced. She supposed the other male passenger was Andorran and spoke English fluently. Pearl had said that she found the Andorrans to be worldly and sophisticated.

Jane turned to the man and asked hesitantly, "*Usted es Andorrano?*"

He looked sternly back. "*Si,*" he said in a drawn-out bass tone.

"Do you speak English?" There was a longer pause.

"No!" He looked out of the window, pointedly, to end the conversation.

"*Y Usted?*" she asked the driver.

"*Portugues!*"

So far, European men had a laconic bent, not unlike Australian men.

The bus continued towards Andorra. The road steepened into thickly wooded mountains and then wound beside a large dam displaying little water. Traffic was slow on the two-lane road and there were few overtaking lanes. The driver cursed each time he was stuck behind a truck. Then in a rush of bravado he would accelerate past; overtaking on a curve despite double lines that indicated passing was prohibited. The winding road and the sudden shows of bad judgement by the driver contributed to a queasy feeling Jane had from so many hours of continuous travel. They sped through a town too quickly for Jane to catch its name. Unpainted cement-rendered buildings with terracotta roofs pressed against the narrow road. More mountains rose in the distance.

Then at last they were at the border. There were no formalities. The bus simply charged through the Spanish and Andorran border posts and continued on to the town of Sant Julia where a wall of shops and hotels flanked the road. The buildings were now roofed in slate and faced with stone. A Mercedes showroom flashed by. The House of Cheese. A hotel advertising rooms for the equivalent of forty Australian dollars a night with breakfast. A phalanx of billboards advertised private banks. Jane realised she was reading and translating the signs without thought, although some of the Catalan eluded her. She grinned. The shops continued with barely a break until they reached a large field of tobacco, some cows, and then the adjoining village of Santa Coloma and more shops full of motorcycles and motorcycle accessories. More and more multi-storey buildings appeared as they approached the main city of Andorra la Vella. The pavement was crowded with shoppers carrying a multitude of colourful carrier-bags. It was like Hong Kong in the mountains – without the sea. The heavy traffic allowed Jane to window-shop as they crawled through the town. Escada, Louis Vuitton, Chanel, Gucci. All of the brand names were there. A glaringly modern, black glass pyramid pierced the dense barrier of shops.

"That's the Caldea. It's a luxury spa. Hot water is pumped into the baths from the underground thermal springs. The tourists flock to it." Lizzie Johnson had been pointing out the various highlights as they passed.

"It looks like the architect went mad. It is so out of keeping with the rest of the buildings," said Jane.

"Not really. When the mountains are covered in snow during the winter it represents a giant stalactite of black ice – or is it stalagmite? I always get them mixed up. The Andorrans are proud of it. It grows on one actually."

Mrs Johnson and the aloof Andorran man left the bus in La Massana near a hotchpotch of indistinguishable high-rise apartments – and more shops. Jane travelled on with the driver, leaving the bustling traffic of La Massana and soon entering the village of Ordino where an old church and its clock tower dominated the co-joined double- and treble-storied stone buildings. The buildings leaned on each other to form a rough semi-circle around a lushly planted communal vegetable garden. Two narrow cobbled streets bisected it. To the left a chicken coop protected hens from a clutch of cats sunning themselves on a wall. An elderly woman in black was collecting eggs and carefully placing them in a wide straw basket hooked over her arm. The bucolic scene was framed by steep mountains. Although Jane had seen photos, she exclaimed, "How beautiful!"

"*Si, es precioso*. You are right," agreed the driver.

He carried her suitcase past a gift shop and into the marble foyer of an apartment building. A heavy-set woman sat at the desk behind a counter. "*La Señora* Burns," he announced grandly after consulting his passenger manifest. He turned to go; Jane scrabbled frantically in her large shoulder-bag for a tip to discover she only had a 5,000 peseta note. Cursing her lack of forethought she awkwardly held her hand out to shake the driver's hand.

"*Gracias*," she said.

"*De nada*. It's nothing," he shrugged. Then he was gone.

The concierge, Rosa, had darting black eyes and a slight moustache. Without wasting words, she beckoned Jane to follow her into the compact elevator. They rode to the second floor, the lift giving an unpleasant lurch once or twice. Rosa unlocked one of two facing doors and led Jane into a gloriously coloured jewel-box. The room was small, but the walls glowed with filtered sunlight. It bounced off framed photos of autumn colours, fallen leaves and trails leading to panoramas of mountains and streams. Floor to ceiling windows overlooked the postcard-perfect village below. Colourful kelims, faded to terracotta where the sunlight beat on them, overlapped on the polished wooden floor. Tapestry cushions were thrown together on the leather sofa and its matching single armchair. A fringed cashmere shawl of faded ivory had fallen to the floor. Books tumbled in disorder on a glass side-table next to a shining brass lamp. A red and yellow striped Catalan flag was mounted oppressively high on the wall near the ceiling. The narrow balcony was lush with pots of ferns. Tendrils from a flowering creeper on a pale yellow trellis were making a break for the next floor. Red geraniums cascaded from the window-boxes.

The apartment was in startling contrast to the stark black and white portraits of war for which Pearl was known. It was as if she had over-compensated for the poverty and bleakness in her work by stuffing her apartment with as much colour as she could.

Rosa led Jane down a passageway to a bedroom at the back. A solid antique desk crouched under the shuttered window. On the night stand next to the double-bed, a metal lamp competed for space with a pile of magazines and a simple jar of perfumed freesias. "*Bienvenido*. Welcome." Rosa smiled as she turned the key to the old-fashioned wooden wardrobe empty of everything save wire coathangers.

The room was dark when Jane woke and for a moment she wondered where she was. The flashing red light of the bedside clock said that it was 10pm. She had slept for seven hours. A quick calculation, adding six hours, revealed it was 4am in Australia. Too early to call her mother and to say she had arrived safely. Her laptop battery light was blinking lazily, reminding her it needed charging. She had to unpack the contents of her entire suitcase before she found the right power converter. So much for her organised packing. The needle sharp pressure of a hot shower succeeded in waking her up. A long sleep had not been the best way to adapt to the local time zone. After methodically hanging up her clothes, she padded down the passage in search of something to eat.

The kitchen was sleekly modern with granite counter tops and white lacquered cupboards. Stainless steel appliances gleamed. The coffee-maker on the counter top drew her to the beans and grinder. Nothing beat the smell of freshly ground coffee. She opened the fridge hoping to find the makings of a sandwich but instead found prominently in the middle of vacant shelves a bottle of *Veuve Clicquot* tied with a ribbon, and a card with flowery writing attached.
"*Jane. Welcome to Andorra!*"

CHAPTER TWO

Jane looked at the champagne bottle and felt sick. Pearl knew Jane had not touched a drop of alcohol since the accident. It was inconceivable that she would leave alcohol in the house for Jane to find, let alone address a bottle to her. Taking a deep breath, she reached into the fridge and gingerly freed the card. The letters danced before her eyes. Leaning on the wall, Jane made her way to the bedroom where her shoulder-bag hung on the arm of a chair. Inside was the mail she had collected from her post-box on the way to the airport. A postcard from Pearl postmarked Sofia from fourteen days before was on top of the pile.

I've been in Kosovo doing a story on orphans – the product of war. It's tragic to see so many children without parents. They long for normality and a family. The older I get the more I understand that family is the most important thing. It will be great to see you in Andorra, it's been too long. So much to tell you. – Love Pearl

The writing on the note attached to the champagne was different to that on the postcard. In particular the extravagant loop on the L was missing. Jane reached for her phone and speed dialled Pearl's mobile number. A voice fired words at her that she could not translate, but understood to be a recording saying that the phone was either turned off or was out of the transmission area. She returned to the kitchen to pour a cup of coffee. If she deducted five hours to find the time in New York, at 4pm Pearl's editor, Gary Cohen should be at his desk.

"Gary, Jane Burns speaking, Pearl Wentworth's sister." She waited while he thought about this. Gary was a hyper New Yorker who juggled ten thoughts at once so it only took a moment.

"Jane, nice to hear from you. Are you in town?"

"I'm in Andorra, trying to contact Pearl. Do you know where she is at the moment? Have you spoken to her recently?"

"She's turned down all the assignments lately in order to deal with this family trust thing. Aren't you supposed to be staying with her?" A note of impatience surfaced in his nasal delivery. Cohen was easily bored with trivia.

"There was a bottle of champagne for me in the fridge to

celebrate my arrival." This got Cohen's attention. He'd taken Jane to meetings of his local chapter of AA when she was in New York recovering from her breakdown.

"I'll make some calls." He was gone.

Jane speed-dialled her father's hotel in Paris. Her plan to travel to Andorra with him had been scuppered when she found he was spending a month at the Crillon before the meeting of the trust. His habit was to be out until the small hours of the morning but she left a message to call her no matter how late the time. She unfolded the note she had been given at the airport. It was headed by the Lufthansa logo and was clearly a standard piece of stationery for taking telephone messages.

To: Jane Burns pax ex Frankfurt flight.
From: Pearl Wentworth. Time received 9am.

Obviously an employee had simply taken a note. Perhaps if she examined the apartment in more detail she would find something.

Her sister's bedroom was similar to the guest bedroom, with dark wooden furniture in the Spanish style, cream coloured walls and a patchwork quilt. A sepia photomontage of family members hung on one wall. It showed Pearl's grandparents – Japanese, Aboriginal, and European – Jane and Pearl's father Charles, Pearl's mother Elsa, Pearl's half-sister Polly with her legs in the braces she had worn since diagnosed with cerebral palsy, and Jane standing with her arms around Pearl's twin half-brothers.

Jane opened the drawer to the bedside-table to find a packet of condoms and a partially used tube of KY jelly. A battery-powered vibrator was packed into a neat travelling pack. The wardrobe held mostly jeans or loose-fit trousers and T-shirts plus a warm anorak, polar fleece sweaters, pastel shirts and a smart navy jacket; the comfortably casual clothes of a professional journalist. A little black dress. Crushed silk trousers. Shoes. Stuffed in the back corner of the bottom shelf was a pair of scuffed heavy-duty Gortex-lined boots and a small daypack. This proved to be empty of everything save a scrunched up rain-slicker and an empty water-bottle. There was no camera-bag.

Her desk provided the usual array of power bills, bank

statements, credit card transactions and registration papers found in any home. Jane ran a professional eye over a sheet claiming travel expenses but could see nothing untoward. There was no computer or electronic organiser but alarmingly, her Australian passport was there, tucked into a leather folder. Had Pearl subsequently got an Andorran passport? She had never mentioned it.

The en-suite bathroom revealed a panoply of vitamins and headache remedies. One shelf displayed her preference for Chanel perfume. Another had matching soap, beauty products, hairbrush and a packet of birth control pills. The last pill had been taken on Saturday. It was Thursday.

The phone rang. Her father was on the line, sounding good-humoured and slightly blurred. "Jane, sweetheart, good to hear from you! Safe and sound in Andorra, are you? Trip go alright?"

"Charles, have you spoken to Pearl recently?" she answered. Her father took a minute to adjust to the abrupt tone.

"Why? What's happened? Where are you?"

"I'm in Andorra. Pearl didn't pick me up at the airport and there's something fishy about it." She explained about the champagne. "Her editor thought she was here, so she's not on assignment."

"Ask around the village in the morning. I'll contact her mother and call you back if she knows anything. If nothing turns up I'll come down there early."

The meeting to wind up the trust wasn't for six days.

"There's nothing you can do at the moment except get some sleep."

Sleep. Jane didn't think so. She went to her computer and clicked open a file called "P-ltrs" and scanned through the letters she had received from Pearl since her sister had moved to Andorra, jotting down names as she went. She put a stroke by each name every time it appeared; figuring that the more times a name occurred, the more significant the person was in her sister's life. When she had finished there were remarkably few names.

Pearl generally called to chat, and had only written to her on birthdays or Christmas with funny stories about her problems with a new language, and comparing life in Europe with that of New York and Australia. Here was one she had written her four years earlier…

Dear Jane,

I must thank you for your letters, which have been a wonderful lifeline to what is happening, back home. The newspapers in Europe don't carry anything on Australia. Mum isn't much of a correspondent (so much of her day is taken up with looking after Polly and taking her to doctor's appointments) and neither are the boys. I'm sorry my reply has taken so long. I think of you often, but life has been busy.

Moving to Andorra is one of the best things I've ever done. I love it here and can't wait for you to come to visit. It's been fun getting used to living in a small village again after the years in New York. I'm gradually meeting more people. I wouldn't say they were friends yet, but the possibility is there. These things take time and I'm in no particular hurry. I've always been pretty self-contained. Having to look after the twins when they were young meant that I learned to appreciate my solitude. I miss the family though, and the sense of belonging somewhere.

Of course my lack of language skills makes it hard to really get to know the locals. Few Andorrans in their thirties speak English, although they speak Catalan, Castilian and French fluently. Europeans are so cavalier about language. They speak several and wonder why the English make such a fuss about it. I'm going to the free classes in Catalan given by the Comu, or local council. It's difficult. The pronouns and verb constructions are a nightmare. Only six million people speak Catalan, here and in greater Catalunya, so sometimes I think I should switch to learning Spanish. I'd be able to use that in South America as well. On the other hand if Andorra is kind enough to give me a home, I ought to do my bit to help keep their language alive. Plus I suspect that until I am fluent in Catalan my access to locals will be severely limited.

It's intriguing to live in the centre of Europe and to watch the European Union at work. The French still hate the English, who reciprocate. The Germans despise the Turks although they have long had a guest-worker programme for them. The Spanish aren't keen on the French. Barcelonians don't like Madrilenians ......and so on. The level of mistrust is based on centuries of invasions, wars and small skirmishes. Memories are long and unforgiving. Regional differences are very marked within a country, so imagine how *different the country next door can be. I travel around with several phrase books, electronic language translator, maps and a guide book for each country and several envelopes full of cash for the different currencies. I'll be pleased when it's 2002 and I can use the Euro everywhere.*

You ask about my love life – well, I'm having the odd encounter; nothing significant as yet. One lives in hope! So far I like the interaction between the sexes here. They are equal but "vive la différence". The women are much less aggressive than those I worked with in America. There is not such a cult about health although few people are obese Most women seem to smoke to keep their weight down, and then eat anything they like at mealtimes, but don't snack inbetween. Apart from smoking, there seems to be no excess in the culture. People have one or two glasses of wine with a meal but it is rare to be offered a glass of hard liquor and I have yet to see anyone who is drunk. The other day I was sitting next to a group of teenage boys in the plaça and they all ordered coffee – even though they could have had a beer if they wanted. Can you imagine that ever happening in Australia? I nearly stood up and cheered.

The women in the gym all wear gorgeous lacy underwear regardless of their body shape, which makes my sensible white cotton look pretty redundant. They're careful about their appearance and it's rare to see them rush out of the changing-rooms with wet hair and no makeup, something I used to do all the time in New York. It is teaching me to slow down and take more care of myself.

How about you? I was sad to read in your last letter that the in-vitro programme did not work out. It must be a big disappointment for you and Bruce. You would both make such great parents. Reading between the lines, I can see that the whole process has been very draining, both financially and emotionally. Still, you are both young and there is plenty of time for this to turn around. Why not come over here for a holiday? Perhaps if you took some time off together and relaxed, you would feel under less pressure? I'd love to see you both, and the spare bedroom is always made up ready for visitors.

I've been thinking about the letter from Dad telling me to look you up once I got to Perth. I was nervous when I first called you, but you sounded pleased to hear from me and you gave me such a lot of support while I was studying. You've always encouraged me to go out and accomplish as much as I could and not to set limitations on myself. I'd love to be able to repay that one-day. It has meant a lot to me. Meanwhile – forgive your busy sister for her delay in writing back. For a journalist, my writing skills aren't always what they should be. Photos are my medium, and since a picture paints a thousand words, I'll enclose a self portrait. Me in my new home – you can judge for yourself how happy I am.

Lots of love – PEARL

Jane sat by the window overlooking the village thinking about Pearl and occasionally dozing. When the dawn light crept over the mountain she put on her jogging shoes, crammed a cap over her short, blonde hair and left the apartment block. One of the many things she had learned at her Alcoholics Anonymous meetings was that exercise was a better way to deal with stress than reaching for a bottle. She could better organise her thoughts while she ran.

An unusual perfume dominated the air as she ran northwest, up the road to the village of La Cortinada, 3kms, according to the sign. After a while she realised it was the fields of tobacco. How beautiful and innocuous tobacco smelt while it was freshly growing. This time of the morning was always a gift. Normally she rose early and ran with Soda before going to work in the small accounting firm that she had joined after leaving the high-powered firm of Ernst and Young. The run, and cooking the evening meal, were the decompression stops she had deliberately inserted into her busy life. She enjoyed shopping for groceries each day and loved to cook but found it harder to entertain now that she couldn't keep alcohol in the house. When she married, she had cooked elaborate dinner parties for friends every Sunday, preparing everything from scratch. They would start the evening with several stiff drinks then enjoy a different wine with every course. Monday morning they would wake up, hung-over and sick, and drag themselves off to work. She didn't see many of the old crowd now.

"I believe that I am powerless over alcohol, and that with it my life became unmanageable." She began Step One of the twelve steps by which AA members meditate. Maybe she'd call her sponsor when she got back to the apartment. He'd been a huge force in her life since she had joined AA. There was not a day that went by when she did not count herself lucky to have him as her mentor. It was hard to imagine that this sixty-five year old man had burned so many bridges in his days of alcoholism that his children barely spoke to him. He was more a father to her than Charles had ever been.

Jogging back down the road and into the outskirts of Ordino, Jane saw the large sports centre was already open for early morning business. Jane's stomach growled – sweaty or not, she was ready for breakfast. Walking into a café alone still felt awkward despite years of travelling to audit company books. In those days she had usually ordered room service and drunk the mini-bar dry.

"*Un café con leche, tostada y mermelada por favor,*" she asked at the bar, feeling diffident about her accent. Coffee, toast & jam duly appeared. Jane wondered if she should start her sleuthing here. "*Conoce usted a mi hermana Pearl que vive aquí en Ordino?*" she asked the waitress, but all she got in reply was a quick shake of the head. She carried her breakfast on a tray to one of the tables by a glass wall overlooking the pool. Watching the early morning swimmers doing their laps was soothing.

A man at the next table leant over and said in accented English. "You are the sister of Pearl?"

"Yes."

"You do not look alike," he said doubtfully. His dark eyes were searchlights sweeping over a well-kept moustache.

"We're half-sisters." Jane wished that she had ten dollars for every time someone had mentioned that she and Pearl were not alike.

"I am Juan-Antonio Ribera-Batista," he stood up and walked over to her, holding out his hand. When she stood up to shake it she found that she was several inches taller.

"Jane Burns," she introduced herself.

"May I?" he said indicating the spare chair, and when he sat down the waitress immediately brought him a *cortado*, a small glass of strong coffee that was half milk.

"Where is the beautiful Pearl this morning?" he asked. "She does not run with her sister?"

Jane had practiced asking about her sister, but had not thought of a scenario where she would be questioned. "She's not here at the moment." It was best to be ambiguous.

Juan-Antonio repeated. "She's not here at the moment …and yet her sister has just arrived from far away. Australia is very far away is it not?"

Jane wondered how he knew she had come from Australia. "Twenty-four hours," she said.

They sat there in silence for a while contemplating such a long journey, thoughtfully sipping their coffee. The waitress brought refills without being asked.

Finally Jane asked, "How do you know Pearl, Juan-Antonio?"

He smiled a cheerful smile and tapped his nose. "How? I am the village policeman. I know most things that go on in this parish. *Bon dia*. Have a nice day."

He tossed the hot coffee down an asbestos-lined throat and walked away. Under the khaki shirt, he had the heavy shoulders and barrelled torso of a weight-lifter. He was light on his feet and moved silently on what Jane now recognised as police-issue rubber-soled shoes. She wondered if she should have said anything more, but decided not. Pearl wouldn't thank her for raising the alarm without sufficient cause. Pearl had fought hard to be taken seriously in the male-dominated world of war-correspondents and was proud of being able to look after herself, asking for no favours. She expected to be recognised for ability not gender. Her considerable good looks might sometimes open the door, but her professionalism kept it open.

No, for the time being, it was better to make discrete enquires and to wait.

CHAPTER THREE

"Pearl talked to Elsa last week. She was looking forward to your visit and spending time with you." Charles called in the middle of the Andorran siesta time. He always referred to Elsa as the great love of his life. She was the only one of his many loves who had left him for another man. Jane thought it typical of her father that he idealised a failed relationship. "She didn't mention plans to travel anywhere before you arrived, in fact she said she was worn out and needed a rest."

"I spoke to several people in the village." Jane consulted her notes. "Rosa, the concierge, hasn't seen Pearl since she asked her to prepare the spare room for me." Jane didn't mention how long it had taken to solicit this information with her halting Spanish. "The woman in the gift shop downstairs, who speaks good English, rarely sees Pearl unless they both happen to be in the elevator together. I introduced myself at the general store but apparently Pearl buys her groceries in Andorra La Vella. The post-office said that mail is delivered daily, not held. I haven't found out anything. Maybe I'm being too subtle, but on the other hand I don't want to say 'Do you know where my sister is?' either.

"I made a list of names from her letters to me, but there aren't many, and they don't come with surnames, addresses or phone-numbers. It's mainly just casual references like 'Had coffee with Conchita'. But who is Conchita and how do I find her? There's no address book. Do you remember meeting anyone in particular when you were here?"

Charles had helped Pearl settle in, and then returned six months later on his way to a sailing jaunt in Majorca.

"Not really. I remember meeting one of the ministers in the Government who was helping her get her local driver's licence. He seemed like a nice chap – suave and good-looking." Neither Jane nor her father felt it worth a comment that a minister would be involved in such a minor matter. Pearl was beautiful.

"Well, what was his name? I have to start somewhere."

"No idea. Just look for a handsome politician." Her father seemed to think that was an oxymoron.

"Maybe all Andorran politicians are good-looking," Jane said.

Her father snorted. "This one would stand out in any crowd."

"Can you remember anyone else?" Jane persisted

"A short motherly-looking woman with a hooting voice. Well endowed. She was English. A Danish woman – thin, late sixties. The poof next door. That's about it really. She was coming and going for most of her first six months so she didn't have much time for making friends."

Jane rang off, promising to call again the following day. They agreed to give it another twenty-four hours before reporting Pearl missing. Jane hoped the trail wouldn't go cold by delaying. She checked her email for the third time that day and sent off another email to pearl@andorra.ad

"Where are you? We're worried." Suddenly she had a flash from years before and a night out with Pearl in Perth. Two sisters out on the town and a drunken conversation, "Does size really matter?" and Pearl's laughing assertion that she used the password "6inches" to access her email. Once connected to the Andorran ISP webmail she keyed in pearl@andorra.ad and the password 6inches. Bingo. She trolled through the spam until she reached four recent messages, three from her and one from Gary Cohen asking her to contact him ASAP.

Perhaps something was recorded on Pearl's answering-machine. The light wasn't blinking but sometimes people neglected to erase their messages. She pressed the button for replay. After a few seconds of silence and some beeps signifying hang-ups, she discerned a muffled message consisting of two discernable words *"Portella Blanca"*. The rest of the message had been erased. It was hard to know if the message was recent. "White Portal?" What did that mean? She opened the local telephone directory. Maybe it was a bar or a business? Nothing. She keyed the words "White Portal" and also *"Portella Blanca"* into her search engine but came up blank.

Taking the elevator to the ground floor she rang the bell on the desk.

"No sé nada de Portella Blanca – pero soy Portuguesa!" Rosa wasn't any help.

Back in the apartment Jane pressed the telephone redial button and copied the number from the liquid crystal display panel. The number rang with no answer.

At 3.30 when the banks reopened for business, Jane called the Credit Europa Bank and asked to speak to Señora Menendez, the trustee who had signed the letter. A clause in the trust deed specified that one of the three trustees must be a woman. She wondered why her grandfather had insisted on this.

"*Buenas días,* Señora Menendez. It's Jane Burns speaking. I have just arrived in Andorra and my sister, Pearl, is away. I wondered if she had been in contact with you regarding next week's meeting of the beneficiaries."

"I spoke with her last week to confirm that it would be held at the office of the lawyer, Riccardo Castillo in Andorra La Vella on Thursday at 5pm. Señora Wentworth assured me you would all be there. Is there a problem?"

"No problem. I'm just double-checking that there has been no last minute change to the venue or time. I look forward to meeting you then."

"You are aware that all of the beneficiaries must be present, or send a proxy with the correctly authorised papers?"

"Yes. I am aware of that." Jane rang off.

She sighed and started to page through the credit card accounts in the desk drawer. Working from Pearl's bedroom made her feel closer to her sister. A faint trace of her perfume still lingered in the air: Restaurants, department store purchases, nothing from "*Portella Blanca*". A beautician in La Massana. Jane would make an appointment to have a facial. Sometimes girl-talk at a beauty salon was surprisingly frank.

An hour later, having walked the two kilometres to La Massana, Jane was trying to relax while Conchita massaged her neck and shoulders. At least that was one mystery solved. She had found Conchita, and her English was very good. She was still marvelling at the difference between the two sisters.

"…but your skin is lovely too, *Señora*…"

"Do you know if she's been seeing anyone special lately?" Jane asked

"Your sister is a very private person," Conchita hesitated, "but of course I know she is in love with a married man. There are few secrets in Andorra." She started to apply a seaweed mask to Jane's face. "I can see the attraction. He's a handsome man. Still, it's a great shame for everyone concerned... the family, his wife, and Pearl too, because divorce would obviously not be possible in his situation."

"What situation is that?"

"Well, as a possible future *Cap de Govern*, the voters would not appreciate him leaving his family. He must be seen to be trustworthy and stable. He has ambitions for the future you see. It would be unthinkable for a future Head of Government to divorce in order to marry a foreigner. As it is, his wife is not Andorran but she is Catalan from Lleida, so that is acceptable."

The daily newspaper *Diari d'Andorra* was on sale at a kiosk opposite the beautician. Jane was thumbing through it at the bus-stop trying to make some sense of the Catalan when she heard herself being hailed. She turned in surprise to find Lizzie Johnson with a thin elderly woman.

"We've just come from playing bridge at the Hotel Rutllan," Lizzie boomed. "Do you have time for a coffee? I'd like you to meet my friend, Greta."

Greta's handshake was firm and belied the years shown in her weathered face. They entered a cheerful café with checked tablecloths and a wood-fired oven. One wall was taken up with racks of red wine. Jane felt she would give a year's salary for a glass. Luckily Greta ordered for them all. "*Tres cafes americanos.*" Her accent made the waiter wince, as if chalk had squeaked on a blackboard. They chatted desultorily, Jane trying to duck their questions about why Pearl wasn't with her.

"Greta knows Pearl rather well. When I pointed you out, she wanted to meet you."

Greta's blue eyes snapped at Lizzie. "I was hoping to talk to Pearl about our little business arrangement. You see, I'm not, strictly speaking, allowed to work in Andorra. Work visas are rationed and they go mainly to the young who are willing to do the jobs that Andorrans don't want to do themselves." She signalled vigorously for another coffee.

"I teach English, privately, in my flat to a few young Andorrans. The Immigration Department turns a blind eye to that. However under the new Passive Residence Laws, people can live in Andorra only if they lodge a security deposit." Greta stopped and looked enquiringly at Jane to see if she was following. Jane nodded, knowing this from Pearl's decision to move to Andorra.

"My pension from Denmark is modest but because I immigrated to Andorra before the new laws, I expected to be grandfathered, so to speak. Even so, the law is retrospective and I'm worried that, if I can't post the deposit, they'll ask me to leave. Since my apartment has two parking spaces attached to it, Pearl offered to rent one to give me more income."

"Why would Pearl need a second garage space?" asked Jane.

"She wanted to turn the storeroom into a darkroom; not all her photos are digital. Plus the car bay is fully enclosed, so Pearl also stores her old removal boxes there. I suppose they are full of things she didn't want in the apartment.

"The thing is I'm a bit short of money right now. My son needed a loan to get himself out of a legal problem back in Denmark and I was hoping for a few months' rent in advance."

Jane reached into her shoulder-bag for her Credit Europa chequebook. "Do you have a spare key?" she asked.

CHAPTER FOUR

The devils pursued her as she ran. Jane felt the hot breath of the past on her neck and she ran faster and faster trying to outpace it. "I believe that a power greater than myself can restore me to sanity." She intoned Step Two of her daily AA meditation. She had been awake since three, reading the pile of International Club newsletters stacked beside her bed, and waiting until it was light, and safe enough to go out. The literature said Andorra was a safe country. There was little crime. No homicides. No rapes. No break and enters. There was very little theft except for the theft of opportunity, such as skis taken from a ski corral during winter or items taken from a car. One newsletter said teenagers had stolen a car that was left running with the keys in it, but they were stopped at the border. Their parents let them cool their heels in the local jail for twenty-four hours to teach them a lesson. An isolated house had its satellite dish stolen. What would one do with a second-hand satellite dish? Jane wondered.

Bruce had always impressed upon her that she should be careful with her personal security…"Take the dog with you when you run. Don't open the door to a stranger. Leave the chain on the door, and double-lock it, even during the day. Most rapes happen in daylight. Be careful where you go. Don't wear provocative clothes. Pull down the shades at night." Thoughts of Bruce filled her head today.

She ran up the hill towards La Cortinada in the veil of rain that had drifted across the country during the night. The light wind-proof jacket above her running-shorts did a reasonable job of keeping half of her dry. Cars passed with encouraging toots. The drivers smiled broadly to see her running in their headlights and waved in encouragement with calls of "*Vamos!*" Some of the toots appeared to be in appreciation of her short shorts. You had to love a country where men applauded cellulite. Jane waved and smiled back. She didn't feel at all threatened by the attention. No wonder Pearl said she loved Andorra. And yet the chances were that something had happened to her here. It had been too long without word.

Who had access to the fridge? Who had a key to the apartment? Not a comfortable idea since she was sleeping there on her own. She resolved to put something heavy in front of the door at night. She ran on.

The cost of casual use of the gym in Ordino was 700 pesetas; $7 in Australian currency. Jane stripped down to her Lycra two-piece workout suit and made sure that her shoes were dry so she wouldn't slip on the wooden floor. The gym was full of the latest exercise machines. In the corner, with his back to her, a heavily-muscled man worked relentlessly on the speedball. She picked up the skipping-rope and started doing spurts in rhythm to the sound of the regular blows. The memory of the many times she had worked out like this with her husband scorched her. She and the anonymous boxer began a syncopated duel – changing speed and rhythm but always in tune. Jane was grinning with pleasure when the boxer turned around to reveal himself as Juan-Antonio, the policeman.

Laughing, "Señora Jane.....do you box as well?"
Sweat dripped from his moustache. She flexed her biceps playfully and thought of her Tae Bo classes.

"You'd be surprised."

"Are you breakfasting here today?'
She had bought an avalanche of food supplies yesterday when asking questions around the village. "*Claro*," she replied, "I'd like to talk to you about something."

"I'll save you a chair," he said as he went off to shower. He had a sense of humour. Yesterday they had been the only patrons of the café. Jane finished her light free-weights routine and stepped in and out of the shower. Yesterday Conchita had tinted her fair eyelashes blue-black to accentuate her eyes. She only had to apply some duty-free lipstick. She felt OK, considering.

The policeman was sitting with his back to the room, watching the swimmers through the wall of glass. He had ordered a large platter of fruit, toast and ham. He was rubbing the toast with garlic and tomato in the manner he called *Pa amb Tomaquet*. A glass cruet of olive oil stood waiting to be poured on top. As Jane came in, the waitress brought over carafes of coffee and hot milk, and a dish of warm, hard-boiled eggs. Juan-Antonio smiled from behind his luxuriant scrubbing-brush moustache, smoothing it downwards with his thumb and forefinger.

"You must be hungry."

She was, and after thanking him she attacked the food with gusto. "I like to see a woman enjoy her food," he said.

She checked him for sarcasm. When she gave up alcohol, she found herself craving desserts and she was not happy about the weight she had gained. At 5 ft 10 inches and with what her mother liked to call a statuesque build, Jane was finding it hard to lose the extra pounds despite her regular trips to the gym. She often got unwanted comments about her height and weight. Australian men seemed to prefer their women shorter and thinner.

"Where is Pearl today?" Juan-Antonio's eyes met hers with an open and direct enquiry.

"I don't know where she is." There was no easy way to say it. "She's missing."

10am in Andorra was a good time to call home. Jane's mother picked up the phone on the second ring. "Jane dear, I thought you would call me before this. You left two days ago. Anything could have happened to you. How very thoughtless. I thought I had brought you up better than that." Her mother was the master of polemic. Or should it be the mistress of polemic? Jane felt guilty that she had delayed the call, and annoyed that she felt guilty. It was hard to escape her Catholic upbringing and its strictures on sin, guilt and remorse.

"I'm over twenty-one, Mum, and I'm fine. Sorry, I've been a little preoccupied. Pearl is away so I've been fending for myself"

"Really!" Her mother was now indignant on her behalf. "After all that way you travelled and she's not there." She was jealous of Pearl and tried to put the knife in whenever she could. "It's in the genes you know. Coloured people just don't have the same standards of behaviour that we have." Jane wondered if her mother had ever considered becoming a member of the Aryan Sisterhood. Charles said she had changed. "She used to be a golden girl. Always happy. A gorgeous blonde and quite a conquest. I was the envy of my peers."

Jane hadn't wanted to enquire further. Her parents' sex life was a definite no-go area. Her mother had shown no further interest in men since Charles left her. She was more excited by a new china catalogue in the mail.

"Hmmm," Jane hummed noncommittally, she'd heard it all before, however when in doubt, lie low, create a diversion, tell an untruth, or say very little. That was her childhood law and she reverted to it now. She was due at the police station to make a missing-person's report at 10.30 and wanted to get this chore out of the way first. It was often a chore to talk to her mother.

"You're not being tempted at all are you, dear?" Her mother might as well be a Methodist, with all the rigour she put into monitoring Jane's alcohol intake, instead of a hefty social drinker who had her first glass of liquor at 6pm. Jane wanted to say she hadn't been tempted at all until now, but that would have followed an age-old pattern in their relationship. AA was teaching Jane to recognise self-destructive behaviour and to change.

"How is Grandma?" she asked instead. Ever since her grandmother had become incapable of looking after herself, Jane had applied some of her income from the trust to pay the monthly fees for her nursing home.

"The same," Jane's mother sighed. "Some days she recognises me, some days not. When I went to visit her yesterday, a visitor was trapped in the lounge and couldn't get out. The nurses forgot to mention that in the Alzheimer wing the security code is printed above the door where the patients don't remember to look for it. The poor woman was nearly hysterical with claustrophobia."

Jane rang off, pleading the high cost of long-distance calls.

She pressed speed dial and reached her father in Paris. "I've got an appointment to officially report Pearl missing in half an hour. Then I'll call the Australian Embassy in Madrid to see if they can be of any help. Australia doesn't have a consulate in Andorra.

"Did I mention that I checked Pearl's answering-machine last night and there was a message about a *Portella Blanca* but I haven't been able to find anything about it."

"*Portella Blanca*," Charles repeated. "I'll do some research at the university to see if anything comes up."

Jane sometimes forgot her father was trained as an historian. He had a wide array of friends in his field and was always welcome to use the facilities of university libraries wherever he happened to be in the world.

"I'll check Pearl's *trastero* at Greta's this afternoon and call you again tonight," she said.

Jane checked herself in the mirror. She wore a simple, button-through navy dress, flat court shoes with matching shoulder-bag, in which she had placed Pearl's passport, the original note from the fridge, the postcard, a list of names gleaned from Pearl's letters, and copies of the letters themselves printed on her small travel printer plus the telephone number of the last call from Pearl's phone. She tried it one more time to no avail. Carefully placing a paper bag over the champagne bottle, she lifted it out of the fridge. She had read somewhere that plastic bags and fingerprints did not mix, and hoped she had got that the right way around. She fingered the key to Greta's *trastero* and put it in her bag, but she was not keen to relinquish it until she had looked at the contents herself.

The Ordino police station was a small room on the ground floor of an apartment building called Edifici La Font. It consisted of a counter and one oscillating pedestal fan placed equidistantly between two desks. Juan-Antonio urged Jane to sit at one side of the desks in front of a young man he introduced as Detective Victor Ignacio from Headquarters.

"*Su pasaport por favor?*" The detective put his hand out and flicked through her passport to scrutinise her Schengen visa for the European Union and entry stamp. He carefully copied out her details, repeating her name, age, date of birth and nationality. The office was bereft of photocopier, computer, typewriter or any modern convenience save two telephones and the four-bladed fan, which made an annoying click each time it changed direction.

"Let us begin. *Como se dice en Ingles*? Ah yes, two heads are better than one." Victor Ignacio nodded pleasantly at Juan-Antonio in deference to taking over on his home turf, and gestured for her to begin.

Jane thought that there were three heads in the room, but perhaps that was the pedantic accountant in her coming out. She ran through her story without hesitation, used to giving presentations in company boardrooms. As she ticked off the points in her narrative, she placed the evidence before them. Juan-Antonio sometimes translated into Catalan to clarify the position for Victor whose English seemed shaky. Victor wrote it all down.

"I'm a recovering alcoholic," Jane said, trying not to wince. "That's why I know Pearl wouldn't have left a bottle of champagne addressed to me in the fridge. I haven't heard from her since I arrived, and I'm afraid for her safety. Will it be possible to lift some fingerprints from the champagne bottle to see who left it?"

"We have a new police-headquarters in Escaldes with a forensic section and a state-of-the-art computer fingerprinting section – in fact all the latest equipment," Juan-Antonio assured her.

It surprised Jane to hear that the tiny principality of Andorra was better equipped than the huge state of Western Australia, where the police were constantly bemoaning the conflicting budgetary requirements of a state government with a social welfare agenda, and the ever increasing needs of law enforcement.

The men pored over the note and postcard, comparing the handwriting and obviously trying hard not to look sceptical; however when she mentioned the words *Portella Blanca* from the answering-machine, the policemen exchanged a quick glance and then gave her their complete attention.

"What?" she said.

"*Portella Blanca* is a mountain pass near to Pas de la Casa, on the border of Andorra and France on the GR 7 walking trail. Does Pearl like to hike?"

"Well, she mentioned hiking with a group called the Hash."

"Yes, Hash House Harriers is an international running club, but here they mainly walk, because the terrain is steep and many of them are elderly," said Juan-Antonio.

"Do many Andorrans belong to the club?" Jane asked.

"Mostly English, or English-speaking," he replied.

"How do you know about them?"

"It's a small country."

"We're policemen."

The two answers came at once. The policemen had deep voices. Since she had disembarked in Barcelona, every man, including the radio and television announcers, had a deep voice. No wonder bulls, and billboards of bulls, were prevalent in the Spanish culture. Jane felt guilty at this wayward thought while she was reporting her sister's disappearance. Still, it had been a long time, she excused herself.

Victor squinted at the telephone number of Pearl's last call, scribbled on a post-it note, then dialled. After twelve rings, the number disconnected. He tipped his palm up to indicate lack of success.

"Perhaps you could ask the telephone company to help, and also call the bus company to find out who paid for my ticket from Barcelona to Andorra?" Jane suggested mildly, knowing from experience that professional men often resisted being told what to do.

She remained sitting and studied her nails, which Conchita had not had time to address and which were in urgent need of attention. Juan-Antonio dialled the number of *Viatges Autobuses*. Jane recognised some of the simpler words and wondered why they were talking in Spanish instead of Catalan. Spanish conversations seemed to go on forever. Maybe it was because there was so much ambiguity in the language. One verb could mean many things and so more words were needed for the nuances to be understood. At least that was her theory. Her Spanish teacher had told her that Spanish had many more words than English and was an altogether richer idiom. Jane was sceptical.

"The booking was made on Wednesday by a man who said he'd deliver the money later that afternoon. An envelope with the correct amount of cash for a one-way ticket for Jane Burns was left with the receptionist. She found it on the counter. It was plain white with nothing unusual about it, and after removing the money she threw it away."

Jane handed over Pearl's passport and a copy of the registration details of her red jeep. "Would she have an Andorran passport?" she asked.

"No. You have to live here for twenty years and speak Catalan before Andorra grants you a passport."

Jane's heart sank. She had hoped that Pearl was finalising an assignment and for some reason had not been able to use a phone.

"And you, *Señora*? How do we reach you?"

Jane handed them her business card complete with mobile phone-number and email address. Juan-Antonio considered it:

"JANE BURNS, CPA, SENTRY AND PARKER," it said.

He ushered her onto the street, one hand on her back. "Leave it to us and try not to worry."

He hugged her politely and kissed her on both cheeks with old-fashioned courtesy. She noticed with surprise that she had hugged him back.

CHAPTER FIVE

On her way back to the apartment, Jane visited the Tourist Office. She collected each free brochure, and purchased a 1.50 topographical map of Andorra. She looked for Pas de la Casa near the French border; and below it near the ski station of Grau Roig she saw the GR 7 trail marked with red dashes and noted in the index that GR stood for Grande Route. She traced the trail to the border where *Portella Blanca* was marked at 2,517 metres. She left her finger there briefly, like a woman consulting an ouija board, but nothing came to her. She traced the winding trail back though the high plains, past lakes and peaks, to the Southern border with Spain. What to do next?

"Frank Daltry." The voice of the embassy official from Madrid was clipped and officious. He was a busy man. He punctuated Jane's stumbling story with, "Yes. Yes. Yes…," hurrying her along.

"Nothing much I can do," seemed to be his final verdict. "She'll probably turn up."

"Pearl is a highly regarded war-correspondent."

"Never heard of her," said Daltry, unimpressed.

"Look. Is there someone else there that I can talk to who has some experience in these matters?" Jane finally asked, exasperated.

"You've got him," he said with evident satisfaction.

"Would you please repeat the details, Mr Daltry. So I know you have noted them correctly," Jane insisted. "The police report number is WX5729. Please call me or Detective Victor Ignacio if anything should come across your desk." She was polite, although it was hard to imagine less co-operation than she had received, but it was pointless to antagonise someone who could possibly help her. "Would it be a good idea for me to hire a private investigator to look for her? Someone, who would know his way around Andorra and speak the language? Could the embassy recommend someone?"

"A private investigator in Andorra?" Daltry laughed a short bark. "Nothing ever happens in Andorra. He'd go broke in no time flat. They've only got fifty-five people in their prison at the moment. That's one of the lowest incarceration rates per capita in Europe. No, I'm sorry. You'll just have to leave it with the police and rely on their competence. If we hear anything we'll let you know."

Lizzie Johnson's phone-number was listed under her husband's name – Roger Peyton Johnson. Lizzie answered with a gruff, "Johnson".

"Lizzie, Jane Burns calling. Thanks for the coffee yesterday. It was nice to run into you. I was wondering if you were by any chance a member of the Hash?"

"I do the short Hash occasionally. Getting old you know."

Jane remembered Pearl explaining it was like a fox hunt. Two of the members, or "hares", laid a trail of chalk and flour for the "hounds" to follow.

"I can take you today if you like. It starts at 3 o'clock."

Jane thought of the key to Greta's *trastero* tucked away in her shoulder-bag. "Does the Hash do long walks, like the GR 7?"

"Oh no dear, that would be the Wednesday group," Lizzie said. "The fitter Hash members meet on a Wednesday and do a steeper and more strenuous hike, taking a packed lunch with them."

"Could you give me the name of someone in the Wednesday group?"

"You have some of the keenest hikers right next door – David and Lyn – although I'm not sure if they're here at the moment. I'll give you their number."

David and Lyn's phone rang out with no answer. Jane made a mental note to try again later. She consulted the street map she had picked up at the Tourist Bureau. Greta's apartment was only 2kms south of Ordino. She could easily walk there after lunch. The groceries on the kitchen bench stared accusingly at her as she turned to lock the door and headed for the Restaurant Armengol in the centre of the village. A 1,500 peseta daily menu boasting regional specialities and consisting of three courses with a carafe of wine was posted on the door. *A la carte* and a bottle of water would be safer.

She decided on salad and *brandade* – a delicious salt cod and mashed potato dish. The woman at the tourist bureau had said that tips were not necessary but they were appreciated. Two hundred pesetas seemed a reasonable amount to leave.

The waitress seemed to think so because she stopped to talk. "My family's from Morocco originally. We all speak English because of the English skiers who come to Ordino during the winter. We work long hours then, but in May we close and go to the beach for holidays."

"Do you know my sister?" Jane asked, showing her a photo.

"Of course. She comes in quite often, but I haven't seen her lately."

The morning's rain had disappeared, and a cloudless, sunny sky surrounded the mountain peaks as she set off for Greta's apartment. The walk took her past a riding school in the *pueblo* of Aldosa, skirted a large condominium development at the base of a steeply wooded mountain and continued to the village of Anyos. There the picturesque Romanic church of Sant Cristofol contained, or so the sign said in its quaint English, frescoes concealed under the present paintings.

Concealed frescoes? Interesting promotion. Imagine what one could promote that wasn't there. Concealed beaches. Concealed army barracks containing concealed soldiers. Jane was amused at the idea. The tourist brochure had said that in the 13th century Andorra had become the first demilitarised zone in the world, when France and Spain signed a treaty to stop pillaging Andorra in exchange for an annual tribute. Andorra in turn agreed to have no army, and to build no forts.

Jane strode on, checking addresses against her map until she came to Greta's apartment building. It was the usual stone clad building with red geraniums spilling forth from window-boxes. Access to the garage was easily gained by passing through a motion detector, which automatically raised the steel doors to the large underground car park. Each apartment had a fully enclosed garage. Motion detectors turned on overhead lights as Jane walked past them. She looked for the garage marked 4A. The side door opened into a three-metre by four-metre space with cartons of cardboard stacked tidily down one side. At the rear, another door led to a shallow storeroom and makeshift darkroom containing a four-drawer filing-cabinet, enlarger and shallow plastic trays set on a stainless steel bench next to a chipped, porcelain sink and tap. Bottles of chemicals were stacked on shelves below. A series of photos was hanging on a line strung along the back wall. Jane unclipped them and took them into the brighter light of the garage.

It was a sequential study of the planting and harvesting of tobacco. She paged through them. Workers with seedlings. Fields of lush tobacco. Workers clipping off the pink tobacco flowers or spraying insecticide. Some close-ups of weathered faces. A woman wearing a scarf, and a child running. An old man sitting on a wicker chair by an arched doorway, a slash of sunlight across his chest like a bandolier. Tractors hauling trailers full of harvested tobacco. Stone barns, smart enough to live in, housed bunches of tobacco hanging from the rafters to dry. A group of workers alighted from the tray of a tractor in front of a stone farmhouse. The photos were in colour, which seemed to indicate they had been taken for a magazine since Pearl normally worked in black and white for the *New York Times*. Few captions would be needed for the sequence. Jane clipped the photos back onto the line in the same order. Pearl was particular about her work.

The filing-cabinet was full of negatives filed into some incomprehensible order with the help of a numeric index, but there was no key to decipher the code. The cardboard removal boxes in the garage held the surplus of the move from Australia and New York. The lids were dusty. Inside, books from Pearl's university days were jumbled with a sheepskin car seat cover, a collection of kaleidoscopes and books on photography. An old photo-album with a moth-eaten, paisley cover floated to the surface as Jane rummaged around. She flicked through it. There was Pearl as a little girl growing up in Broome with her mother Elsa, even more beautiful than Pearl herself. The mixture of European, Aboriginal and Asian cultures in Broome's Pearling Industry had produced not only the best cultured pearls in the world but some of the most beautiful women.

Jane turned the pages, engrossed. Her own photo didn't appear until Pearl was seventeen and attending university in Perth. They had both been worried they wouldn't like each other when they first met. Luckily the awkwardness soon dissolved and a real friendship was born. A few pages later Pearl pirouetted in her ivory wedding dress. Five pages showed the riotously boozy reception, the handsome troubled groom dancing with the joyful bride. The faces of guests were a little out of focus as if the photographer had joined in the drinking. She saw glimpses of Bruce, in profile or with his back to the camera. Her own lilac bridesmaid dress looked very dated now, as did the uncomplicated happiness in her face. The following page was of Pearl's graduation from university eighteen months after her marriage.

A sound like a sigh prompted Jane to turn her head. The light went out. A hard push to the small of her back propelled her forward. Still holding onto the photo-album and without a free hand to protect herself she struck the concrete wall with the front of her head. She went down without a sound.

She woke to the darkness of the grave. No glimmer of light indicated where she might be. The floor beneath her was concrete-hard and so cold she was shivering. For a while she lay there trying to work it out. She remembered getting on the plane and arriving in Andorra, and then? She painstakingly put the past two days together. After what seemed like a long time, she pawed her way upright; leaned heavily on the rough wall, then slowly shuffled a few paces until her shins banged on a cardboard box. Bending down she felt around and behind it. There was another box, then another. She remembered Greta's *trastero*. Evidently she was still there. By trailing her hand against the wall she made her way around the small room until her fingers touched a wooden doorframe. She found the doorhandle and turned it. The door swung away from her, so she knew it was the door to the darkroom, not the one that led outside. She groped on the right-hand side of the wall next to the door until she found the light switch, but when she flicked it on nothing happened. A frustrated cry leapt out of her mouth but she quashed the sobs that were queuing behind it.

When she reached the tap she drank greedily in large gulps, trying to remember if it was OK to drink when you have concussion. She felt nauseous and disoriented and took several deep breaths before splashing water over her face and hands. The rough wall caught the material of her blouse as she slid down it, trying not to vomit, squatting with her head between her knees. She sat there with no idea of time passing. Finally she started another search, this time for the door leading out of the garage. She banged her shins on more boxes, probing around until she found the door handle. She turned it and pushed. The door stayed firmly shut. She pushed and pushed, putting her shoulder to the door. The door wouldn't budge. She was locked in. She tried the light switch without result.

"Help me!" she screamed. Her fists pounded on the door. She screamed and screamed, and banged and banged – but nobody came.

The sound of the mobile phone clipped to her belt exploded in the darkness.

A calm voice said, "*Bon dia*, Señora Jane. We've checked with the hospitals and Pearl is not there. We gave the Spanish and French customs details of the jeep. The Spanish stop every car unless they are very busy; the French only stop cars at random but I'm sure they would have stopped Pearl anyway. No Frenchman would allow such a beautiful woman to pass by unnoticed. We've rung the airports and Interpol…"

"Juan-Antonio!" she shrieked, cutting him off in full flight.

It was another half an hour before he came, but he kept her on the line all the while, talking to her in his composed voice, and telling her what he was doing.

"I'm driving up from St Julia. I've radioed for a locksmith to meet me."

"Couldn't you just break down the door?"

"I'm in Andorra La Vella now. No, I don't have a siren."

The key was in the lock on the outside of the door. The locksmith waved away any offer of payment with a calculated, "*de nada*."

Juan-Antonio regarded her thoughtfully in the glare of his giant torch. "You have a very large bruise on your forehead."

She squinted at him. He cast the beam around the room, noted the boxes and walked into the darkroom where he opened the drawers to the filing-cabinets. Then he stamped out to peer into boxes, rummaging through the contents in a hopeful fashion. As he pointed the torch to the ceiling he noted that the light bulbs in both the garage and the *trastero* had been removed from their sockets. Calling the locksmith back, he told him to fit a new, secure, altogether more serious lock. He shone the torch along the walls until it lit upon a large switch set at head height. As he pressed this, the automatic garage door rose up, to Jane's mortification. Because she had not come by car she hadn't thought to check for a control switch. Nor had she remembered her mobile phone until it rang. What an idiot.

"Sorry," she mumbled.

"*Vale*," he replied. "It looks as if whoever did this just wanted to slow you down not to keep you imprisoned. Is anything missing?"

Jane shrugged. Who would know in this mess.

"Señora Jane," Juan-Antonio added, "I thought I told you to leave the investigation to us. Until we establish what has happened to your sister, we are not sure if you are completely safe. Why did you not tell us about this *trastero*?" He put a guiding arm around her and helped her up into the twilight and settled her into his car for the trip home.

"Not to the hospital," she had insisted, although her voice wavered a little. He wagged his head, but in the end he said nothing and turned the Land Cruiser towards Ordino into a sea of oncoming traffic. The road was far too narrow to accommodate two lanes so they proceeded in fits and starts whenever a car pulled over for them. The cars were decorated with floral wreaths and the drivers all waved gaily at Juan-Antonio.

"It's a very jolly funeral," Jane said, wondering if etiquette demanded that they wave back. Juan-Antonio laughed.

"The priest is blessing the vehicles today as part of the annual festival."

Outside Pearl's apartment they parked in the no-park zone and then took the lift to the second floor. Juan-Antonio kept a taut arm around her. She leant against him gratefully, her legs shaky. As the lift door slid open she again protested that she would be fine and had no need to see a doctor. His hand cut her off in mid sentence.

"Quiet!" he said.

The front door to the apartment was open.

CHAPTER SIX

Juan-Antonio motioned for her to stay where she was. He slipped into the apartment on his soundless rubber-soled shoes.

"*Dios Mio!*" he said weakly. Jane rushed through the door, forgetting caution. A young girl stood on the balcony. A large marmalade cat was draped over one arm like a handbag. In the other hand she held a yellow watering-can. Her skin was translucent, setting off wild ginger curls and big green eyes. Jane guessed that she was about ten or eleven years old.

"Who are you?" the young trespasser asked.

"Who are *you*?" responded Jane.

"Mary. After Mary Queen of Scots you know. I'm staying next door"

"Next door?"

"With Dad and Dave."

Jane wondered if this was an hallucination. "Dad and Dave" was the name of a popular Australian radio series in the 1950s.

"...and your Dad is?"

"Lyn. Lyn Pingelly. I'm here on holidays. Dad and Dave picked me up from the airport yesterday."

The penny dropped; the men next door, the "poofs" as her father had called them with his customary lack of political correctness, the Wednesday walkers, Dave and Lyn.

Juan-Antonio had been watching this exchange. Now he said, "How did you get inside the apartment, Mary?"

"Pearl keeps a spare key in the umbrella stand in the hall. Everyone knows that. I saw Trevor crawling along the balustrade onto Pearl's balcony.

"And Trevor would be?"

Mary indicated her inert fur muff. Trevor's ear twitched but he kept his eyes firmly shut. Mary threw him over her shoulders like a shawl. His claws extended and then slowly retracted.

"He wouldn't come back when I called so I came to fetch him, then I noticed the pot plants hadn't been watered. That's one of my jobs at home. Pearl lets me do it when I'm visiting."

Juan-Antonio gloomily rang the locksmith and asked him to come and fit a new lock and a security chain to the front door. When he arrived the locksmith was wreathed in smiles.

"My cousin needs a work permit," he informed Juan-Antonio, speaking in English in deference to the general conversation. "He's from Lisbon and is an excellent carpenter. Do you know anyone in the immigration office?"

Lock fitted, and as Juan-Antonio departed, the phone rang

"You didn't call." It was her mother.

Jane's description of her day was highly expurgated. She didn't mention the blow to her head. "Tell me what you've been up to, Mum," she said instead, the thought of a mundane life being rather appealing at that moment.

"The spring flowers are out in the garden, it looks a picture. The jasmine is flowering outside the window and smells better than pie. I transplanted the kangaroo paws to the Eucalyptus grove. They look good there. You seem tired though, darling. I'll call you tomorrow."

The mostly incomprehensible Catalan on the television was a soporific white noise that seduced Jane into sleep until the phone rang again. It was Juan-Antonio.

"If you have concussion you shouldn't go to sleep yet. You are well?"

"Yes. OK," she yawned.

"Tomorrow I'm going down to Lleida." He pronounced it "Lerida". "My cousin Fernando has a country house there. I often spend Sunday with him shooting pheasants." He said "peasants", which made Jane laugh. "We have lunch. It's a pleasant day. I was wondering if you'd like to go? To keep you out of trouble," he added, but Jane's attention was on the TV where a strikingly handsome man was giving a speech to a gathering of journalists. The caption below read: Fernando Ribera-Lopez, *Ministre d'Urbanisme i Ordenament Territorial*.

"What's your surname again, Juan-Antonio?"

"Ribera-Batista," he replied. "Andorrans follow the tradition of using the father's surname followed by the mother's."

"Is Ribera a common name?" asked Jane.

"Not especially."

"I think I'm watching your cousin Fernando on TV right now?"

"Oh, he's always on TV. He's the rising star of the party."

"I'd love to go with you tomorrow. Will you have a gun for me?"

"I don't really think an *extranjera* suffering from concussion should be in possession of a shotgun."

"Even foreigners can be good shots. You'll see."

"*Mañana.* We'll talk about it. I'll pick you up at nine o'clock."

Jane dozed.

The phone rang. Charles, sounding rather self-important, said, "I've been at the university all day. *Portella Blanca* is part of an old smuggling route. Refugees and allied airmen used it during World War Two, escaping on foot through the mountains on their way to Spain and Portugal."

"I can't see how that helps us."

"The Andorrans didn't participate in the war beyond profiting from their smuggling activities you know." Charles was on a roll. "At one point Germany decided to invade Andorra, in the person of several soldiers in a half-track. The mountain men met the soldiers with an invitation to lunch, then escorted them back to the border at gunpoint minus the half-track. The Andorrans took a fancy to that and kept it. Apparently it's still in their automobile museum."

Jane stuck the phone between her cheek and shoulder and went into the kitchen to brew coffee. When her father had the bit between his teeth he was hard to corral.

"I've been researching your grandfather's life to write a memoir and by an extraordinary coincidence it seems he used the *Portella Blanca* route to get into Andorra after he was shot down over occupied France."

"You're shitting me!"

"Don't use coarse language, Jane. It shows a lack of imagination."

"Honestly, Charles, you're a relic."

"Getting back to my father; after the Battle of Britain, England was short of experienced pilots so my father was seconded to the British Air Force. On his sixth mission his plane was shot down. He survived and managed to contact the French Resistance who smuggled him out of France."

Jane didn't know which was more surprising, her work-shy father actually using his degree in history to research a book, or the connection between her grandfather and *Portella Blanca*. She decided against telling Charles about the attack on her.

"Keep digging," she said instead, "this might fit together

somehow. Meanwhile I'm on the trail of the handsome politician who was so helpful to Pearl. It seems he's related to my tame policeman. I'm hoping I can question him while he's relaxing at his country-home tomorrow." She didn't mention the possibility that Pearl was having a fling with him. Fathers should be spared any knowledge of their daughters' affairs.

The church bells woke Jane on Sunday morning. It was her first night of unbroken sleep. Pearl's picture-window framed a clutch of villagers returning from church via the bakery, the long, crusty baguettes tucked firmly into their armpits. It must add a certain flavour, she smiled. The men wore black berets and the women were in their Sunday-best. Groups congregated to exchange gossip. She could like it here if it were not for Pearl's disappearance.

At last she saw Juan-Antonio's dark-blue Land Cruiser turn into the roundabout and she hurried down the two stories to the no-parking sign where it was idling. Juan-Antonio looked ready for war, in camouflage trousers, khaki shirt, and a sleeveless vest with many pockets. Jane hoped her jeans, blue shirt and navy sweater were appropriate. She wore jogging shoes, and a denim cap to hide her bruised forehead. In her shoulder-bag were two bananas and a stainless steel thermos filled with thick percolated coffee. Not being able to remember Juan-Antonio's preference for sugar, she had brought some in a twist of paper. She had dosed herself with aspirin and had only a mild headache.

They drove south towards the border through thin traffic, but at the town of Sant Julia, Juan-Antonio turned left, up a steep and winding road, following signs depicting a skull-and-crossbones with La Rabassa emblazoned below.

"This isn't the way to the border," Jane said.

"Plenty of time."

They drove higher and higher, and Juan-Antonio pointed to the panorama of the twin parishes of Andorra la Vella and Escaldes-Engordany spread far beneath them. The road was paved but had no guardrails. An injudicious use of the accelerator could easily precipitate them into space. Finally they turned into an isolated compound surrounded by a cable fence topped with barbed wire. A large sign saying "*Camp de Tir*", under two crossed shotguns, marked the entrance. Extensive lawns surrounded a motley collection of buildings. Jane was curious. Was this some type of paramilitary base? Juan-Antonio pulled up beside what looked like a guardhouse and spoke in Catalan to a man with slit eyes and an inscrutable expression who exited the hut and walked around to the back of the Land Cruiser where he opened the tailgate and took out a bandolier full of shotgun shells. Juan-Antonio took two leather cases from under a blanket on the back seat and extracted two shotguns. After breaking them and checking the breeches, he handed one to the man and put the other over his arm.

"*Venga*," he said.

The three of them walked across the lawns and down a rise. Far below Jane could see thousands of terracotta shards of what appeared to be shattered bricks. The second man walked to a small lean-to on the side.

Juan-Antonio put the shotgun to his shoulder and shouted, "*Empuja!*"

Jane heard the sound of the shot. A clay pigeon shattered overhead. Juan-Antonio shot ten more times and six clay pigeons fell to the ground. The second man returned and handed over the other shotgun. Juan-Antonio checked it then turned to her.

"You are familiar?" Juan Antonio's English was not always perfect.

She nodded. She loaded the shotgun and raised it to her shoulder and fired – and missed. She fired and missed again; then smoothly reloading after each brace of shots, eight quick shots and eight on target.

"*Jesus!*" said Juan-Antonio.

"My husband was a policeman," she said, as if that explained everything.

A long line of cars waited to be searched in the large customs shed on the Spanish border. Juan-Antonio made no attempt to conceal the shotgun cases on the back seat. A swarthy customs officer with a flaming birthmark across one cheek lent in the window and conducted a staccato conversation with Juan-Antonio. He seemed more interested in checking the size of Jane's breasts than in the arsenal in the back. After punching Juan-Antonio on the shoulder he waved them through the border.

"My cousin," the policeman explained.

"Can you just bring guns through the border like that with no controls?" asked Jane in amazement.

"Andorrans go across the border to hunt wild boar nearly every weekend during the season."

"It would be a good place for ETA to smuggle arms into Spain then."

"Not really. The Basques don't want to aggravate the Catalans since they support them in parliament. Both states want more regional autonomy. There is a gentlemen's agreement not to implicate Andorra or Catalunya in ETA's struggle for independence."

"You think ETA terrorists are gentlemen?"

"A manner of speaking only."

"Didn't they bomb one of the seaside resorts South of Barcelona, somewhere near Tarragona? Isn't that in Catalunya?"

"It was Salou; but that was a mistake, not sanctioned by the main arm of ETA."

"I'm sure the victims' families would be relieved to hear that."

They drove past the town of Seu D'Urgell – where, since the 13th century Pareatges treaty, the Bishop took a bi-annual tithe of hams and cheeses from Andorra – and on down the narrow road towards Lleida. When they approached the outskirts of the town some two hours later, she saw a large hilltop fort dominating the landscape. It was visible from 20kms away and resembled the fairytale castle from Jane's childhood reading. On closer inspection however, Lleida had nothing magical about it. It was a college town with a rough, hard-edged quality to it. A number of African college students in colourful caftans lounged against street corners. The groups of men whistled at young women, who walked quickly by with their faces averted. A prominent sign proclaimed Lleida to be the snail capital of the world.

"They hold a snail festival here each August. Snails are prepared and eaten in over fifty different ways. It's very popular."

"I'm glad it's September and we've missed it."

"I have wonderful memories of collecting snails with my father after the rain and bringing them home for his mother to cook."

"I'll pass."

Next to the posters advertising the snail festival, *Independencia Ara* graffiti adorned many concrete surfaces.

"Catalunya already has a good deal of autonomy, but there are always those who would prefer independence." Juan-Antonio was a good travelling companion, telling Jane just enough about the surrounding countryside to keep her interested.

At one point Juan-Antonio said, "Your husband was a policeman?"

"A detective. He died." Somehow saying he died instead of he's dead was preferable to her.

"Are you married?" she asked, after another long silence.

"Divorced," he said. "I have a twenty-two year old son, Paco. He goes to Barcelona University and is studying to be an architect."

"Is it common to divorce in a Roman Catholic country like Andorra?"

"We got an annulment. My wife is from Barcelona and she never settled in Andorra. It was too quiet for her. Inbred, she said. Eventually she left to go back to Barcelona. Even for Andorrans the country can get very claustrophobic. Still, I wouldn't want to live anywhere else."

"I didn't know the Church would annul a marriage with children."

"It happens more frequently than you'd think."

A little later he asked, "How did you come to marry a policeman?"

"I'm an accountant. When you start with the big firms they really want their pound of flesh. You get worked half to death – really long hours, and if you're a woman you have to work twice as hard for promotion. After work, around 10pm or so, a group of us from the office would have a few drinks at a local bar, and kick on…

"Never mind," she said to Juan-Antonio's look of incomprehension at her slang. "Anyway, policemen are night-owls too, so we used to hang out with them and one thing led to another."

"They were a good bunch," she added, thinking about her husband's colleagues neglecting to breathalyse her after the accident. "There were a couple of bad apples of course," she continued. "Most police forces seem to have some corruption within the ranks. How is it here?"

"Bad apples – *Malas manzanas*. We don't say that in Spanish but it's very descriptive. Do you have children?"

"No. We would have liked children, but it didn't work out."

The silence between them was not uncomfortable, and they drove for miles thinking their own thoughts. At last they turned onto an unkempt stony thoroughfare. Large potholes followed by areas of deep dry sand made the road suitable only for four-wheel drives. When they reached the farmhouse, assorted SUVs were parked randomly outside. Four or five dogs milled around barking and nipping at each other. A group of men stood off to one side. Some of them were wearing camouflage, others were in khaki; all had guns. The men were not particularly tall but they looked tough, as if bred for hardship. There were no women.

"*Les presento a Jane*," Juan-Antonio introduced her to them collectively. The men acknowledged her by lifting their chins and without further discussion set off at a punishing rate. Jane and Juan-Antonio brought up the rear. Jane wondered if the men were testing her endurance or if they always pushed so hard and spoke so little. She clamped her teeth together so no involuntary complaint would escape her, and followed in their tracks.

CHAPTER SEVEN

The total bag was five pheasants and eight doves. The dogs flushed the pheasants from the bushes then retrieved them as they fell. The men and dogs had obviously hunted together on many occasions and the dogs responded obediently to hand signals and whistles. As the day wore on the men gradually relaxed around her. There was quite a bit of good-natured banter between them and Juan-Antonio – probably bawdy judging by the laughter, but since it was all in Catalan she really couldn't say for sure. As the day progressed it had turned quite hot and she had tied her sweater around her waist, rolled up her sleeves and pulled the shirt-tails out of her jeans. She was glad she had put on sunscreen.

It was past three o'clock before they returned to the farmhouse. A long trestle table was set under a shady tree. Behind it a large, stone-faced barbecue contained sizzling sausages and a cauldron of white beans laced with garlic. An ancient lady in black stepped out of a fly-screened swing door and greeted Juan-Antonio shrilly. He bent down to kiss her and then introduced her to Jane.

"*Yaya* – my grandmother."

"*Mucho gusto, Señora*," Jane shook her hand, but the old lady tilted up her wizened face to be kissed, so Jane kissed her on both cheeks European style. She took Jane by the hand and, squeezing it gently now and then, led her to a small bathroom where she could wash. Jane wished she could speak Catalan or even reasonable Spanish. She was tongue-tied.

The house was dark and cool inside, everything shaded in hues of brown. Large brown-glazed tiles shone on the floor. Outsized, darkly polished, wooden furniture lined the rooms. The walls were washed white, but small windows and a large overhanging roof did not allow much light to penetrate. Jane guessed that the thick walls and small windows kept the house cool in summer and warm in winter. It was unclear to her whether the house was occupied year-round.

When she returned to the garden, platters of food had been brought out to the table: The ubiquitous finely-sliced ham with frilled edges of creamy fat. Bowls of olives and a dish of broiled red peppers, eggplant and onions drizzled with olive oil and garnished with anchovies. A simple dish of green chicory. An aromatic metal tray of what proved to be snails. Loaves of freshly-sliced, crusty bread. Cold clay jugs of rosé beaded with moisture and bottles of red wine and fizzy water stood beside glasses. Jane was relieved to see the water. Painted stoneware plates were colourful on the rough-hewn table.

Juan-Antonio patted the empty place beside him and feeling young and buoyant, her worries set aside for a few hours, she sat down. After bringing out the food, the wives of the hunters had joined them and the table was noisy with chatter. Juan-Antonio introduced her to the people nearest to them.

"*Mucho gusto*. Pleased to meet you," she said over and over.

In deference to her, everyone began speaking in Spanish, but it was soon apparent that with her limited knowledge she could not keep up, so they lapsed back into Catalan. From time to time, Juan-Antonio would translate.

"The children learn English in school today, but my generation generally speaks only Catalan and Spanish. I had to learn English for the job. La Massana and Ordino have the largest English-speaking communities."

The lunch progressed in a leisurely fashion. Platters of stringy lamb chops and quail joined the *botifarra* sausages. It was well after six o'clock when Jane helped to clear the dirty plates and empty platters from the table. In her absence, Juan-Antonio joined a group of men playing *petanque* in a nearby raked gravel area. The clink of the metal balls rose above the constant chirping of crickets. A man would first cast a small coloured ball around ten metres away, then pace off the distance. Each player then had two metal balls, the size of tennis balls. The aim of the game was to get closest to the coloured target ball. The players took turns. If an opponent's ball was the closest, it was tactical to bowl it out of the way. After everyone had thrown their second ball, measurements were taken and the winner declared. Jane sat and watched from the shade of the spreading tree feeling relaxed and slightly sleepy from all the good food.

The women brought out glass decanters of muscatel together with platters of dried fruit and nuts. Spectators of the game rejoined the table. The man across the table from her picked up the decanter and lifted it into the air with the long spout about twelve inches from his mouth, then neatly poured in a thin stream of liquid. The decanter was passed around the table. Everyone was most proficient at drinking the muscatel without spilling a drop. Finally it reached Jane. She smilingly declined. The man on her left lifted the decanter and directed it towards her. Instinctively she clamped her mouth shut and the flow of muscatel hit her lips and flowed down her shirt.

The table was instantly quiet. Surprised faces looked at Jane. Juan-Antonio was walking back from the petanque game. The silence made him seek her out. She was sitting stiffly at attention, soaked in liquor, tears in her eyes. He was wearing his inscrutable policeman's face. He said something to the gathering. She recognised the word *enferma* and gathered that he was either telling them she was sick, or that alcohol made her sick. They clucked sympathetically. She pushed her chair back and headed blindly for the bathroom. Her former buoyancy turned to misery. Why couldn't she have a drink and know when to stop like other people?

She took her time to regain her composure, taking off her shirt and splashing her face and chest with cold water. The muscatel had not penetrated through to her bra. She put on her sweater. To calm herself she recited Step Three,

"I have made a decision to turn my will and my life over to the care of God as I understand him." She wondered if life would ever get any easier. After combing her hair and renewing her lipstick, she examined her face in the mirror. Only someone who knew her well would be able to tell she was stressed. When she left the bathroom she turned left and continued down a passage and through another door to the side of the house.

A young boy was kicking a soccer ball against the wall. As she stood and watched him, unobserved, he kicked with first his right and then his left foot, sometimes catching the rebound with his knee, never touching the ball with his hands. Finally he stopped and she applauded.

"*Muy bueno*," she said.

"Thank you," he replied gravely in English. "Would you like a game?"

They kicked the ball backwards and forwards for a while, until they were both rather hot and sweaty.

"My name is Pedro," he offered, drinking water from a goatskin, "and you are my uncle's friend, Jane. I heard them talking about you."

"Who were talking about me?"

"Oh – the women, and my mother. They thought it was ..." he searched for the word in English, "Funny? Strange?" – he tested it out – "that he should bring you here."

"Why was that?"

He shrugged, spreading his hands wide in the universal gesture men use when they don't understand women.

"Your English is very good."

"I had an English *ama* when I was small. Father says English is the most important language in business and I must learn to speak it well. Mother takes me to extra classes after school."

Jane looked up and saw Juan-Antonio standing at the door. A slight woman with ash blonde hair stood beside him. She was staring at Jane and the boy.

"Pedro!" she shrilled, followed by a string of fast, angry sounding words.

"*Perdon*," the boy gave a little bow. "My mother. Thank you for the game," and he ran off. The woman turned on her heel and disappeared into the dark interior of the house, but not before she threw one last angry look over her shoulder at Jane. Juan-Antonio came through the door and picked up the goatskin. He took a long drink of water, set it down and looked as if he were about to say something.

Instead he took her hand. "It's time to go."

Leading her around the farmhouse to the back garden, Juan-Antonio made their goodbyes. The hunters and their wives were regarding them with great interest. He squeezed her hand and met each man's eyes in what seemed to be a silent challenge. In the cool, flag-stoned kitchen, *Yaya* was bustling around the deep marble sink like a woman half her age. She hugged them both fiercely, spoke rapidly, and poked Juan-Antonio in the chest a few times. Then threw back her head and guffawed.

"She said I should bring you back here again," he said imperturbably.

Pedro's mother was drying dishes. She did not turn to bid them goodbye.

In the car Jane decided to explore a few ideas. "Is Pedro's mother related to you?"

He looked surprised. "Llourdes is the wife of my cousin, Fernando. How do you call that in English?"

"The same. Pedro called you his uncle."

"Well he calls me *Tio*, or uncle, because I am so much older, but we are second cousins. *Tio* is used rather loosely. Relationships are complicated in Andorra and Catalunya. It's often hard to describe how one person is related to another."

"Pedro said the women thought it was strange that you brought me today?"

Juan-Antonio shrugged. "They're not used to seeing me with another woman since my divorce."

Jane thought it was more than that. "Where was your cousin today? I assumed he'd be there. Doesn't he hunt?" she'd been waiting all afternoon for a chance to ask about him. He'd been the reason she accepted the invitation.

"Not often. He's a man of the mind."

"Who lives in the house then?"

"*Yaya*, and the men who look after the farm. Llourdes inherited the house from her father. She grew up in it, so she stays there rather more often than Fernando."

"Why does your grandmother live in Llourdes' farm?'

"She's Fernando's grandmother as well. Our fathers are brothers and she is their mother. She has a heart condition and cannot live in Andorra. The altitude is not good for heart problems. Llourdes is happy to have her there, minding the farm."

Juan-Antonio had some ideas of his own.

"What happens to this trust of yours if one of the beneficiaries does not turn up for the meeting to wind it up?"

"The trustees can postpone the meeting for up to ten days."

"And then?"

"I'm not sure. The trustees have considerable discretion."

"Tomorrow the contents of the *trastero* will have to be examined. Do you feel up to helping Victor sift through everything?"

"I suppose so," she sighed, feeling out of sorts for no clear reason.

"Do you have any other ideas of how to proceed?" Juan-Antonio asked. She did have some ideas, but she wasn't going to share them. They drove for a time in silence.

"You shoot very well." Juan-Antonio said at last.

"Is your cousin Fernando, Pearl's lover?" Jane contributed to the non-sequiturs that were flying back and forth.

He thought about that. "Did Pearl say so?"

"Pearl has had many lovers," she equivocated.

When he dropped her at the front entrance to the apartments, she declined his offer to escort her to the second floor.

"Victor will pick you up in the morning. His English isn't so bad."

"Thank you. I mean, thank you for everything. For inviting me and making sure I was comfortable and safe. It was a good day."

"I enjoyed it too." Juan-Antonio gave her the two-sided kiss that she had come to expect before pausing to examine her face, but all he said was, "Call me if you need to."

Jane pinged the bell on the front desk and Rosa materialised to confirm that "*claro*" each apartment had a *trastero*. She led Jane down some stairs to a basement area, where a series of steel doors were lined up side by side. Each door sported the number of the corresponding apartment on it. Rose unlocked Pearl's door with her master key and switched on the interior light, displaying a glorified cupboard. Firewood was stacked neatly on one side. An empty suitcase stood upright on a narrow shelf. Skis and a tennis racquet leaned against a corner. A wooden wine rack contained several dozen bottles of wine. Jane recognised labels from the Ribera del Duero regions of Spain plus a dozen assorted bottles from Bordeaux. One of Jane's many classes in self-improvement had been a master class in wine appreciation. Ironic when she thought of the addiction that followed.

"*Donde aparcan los coches?*" she asked Rose, who indicated an anonymous steel door, identical to the rest except lacking a number. It led to a largely empty, open car park. There was no red jeep.

"Did my sister have many close friends?" she asked

"*Si, muchos amigos. Todos le gustan.*"

"Anyone in particular?" Jane persisted.

It was not her place to notice these things Rosa replied slowly for the benefit of Jane's shaky Spanish. Jane decided to beat a few bushes and tell Rosa her sister was missing. Discretion had not paid dividends to date. Rosa looked worried. Jane supposed the news would ricochet around the village by morning. Perhaps it would flush out some information. Someone must know something. Today had been a washout. Her idea of confronting Pearl's lover at his farm had certainly come to nothing. Jane wondered about his wife Llourdes and her unconcealed hostility. Did that mean she was aware of the affair between Pearl and Fernando? There was no doubt that the sister of your husband's lover would be an unwelcome guest in your home. The phrase gave her a headache just thinking it. Jane wished Pearl's letters had revealed her relationship with Fernando in more detail.

Pearl's guest bathroom had only a tiny shower, which challenged Jane's elbows; however the master-bedroom's *ensuite* contained a commodious antique cast-iron bath. Jane eyed it hungrily. She was bone tired. While the water ran she checked her emails, and then Pearl's, but there were no messages. When she stripped off her clothes she considered herself in the full-length mirror. The bruise on her forehead was livid, accentuating her pale face. The newly-tinted dark brows and lashes stood out starkly against her fair skin and blue eyes. She pulled in her stomach and turned sideways. If she could lose half a stone she would look better. There was nothing wrong with her breasts. They were well proportioned and hadn't given in to gravity yet. Not having children had at least preserved her bosom.

She splashed bath-salts liberally into the bath and stepped in to soak. In the old days she would have played some music, lit candles and poured a glass of wine, but for now this would have to do. Lying back, she tried to relax. She rinsed out a flannel and placed it over her eyes. The water slowly cooled. Adding more hot water, she swished her hands around to froth up some non-existent bubbles. The bath-salts had no scent and no bubbles. Why bother? She lay back, letting her thoughts float but they kept snagging on a hidden rock – some ill defined sense of something out of place; however when she tried to reel the thought in, nothing surfaced.

She towelled off and put on the T-shirt that doubled as her nightie. Her headache, which had faded in the bath, came back energetically. How strange that something involving her head would immediately travel to her stomach and make her feel like throwing up. Jane hated to take medication of any sort. She worried that she would become addicted to sleeping pills, or pain medication, or anti-depressants and have to go through the whole process of rehabilitation again. Perhaps a cup of chamomile tea would help.

CHAPTER EIGHT

Victor rang her doorbell promptly at 10am. Jane proferred a Spanish-English dictionary. He, in turn, waved a copy of the day's *Diari d'Andorra*. Pearl's passport photo appeared on the front page, together with the caption *"Desaparaguda"* – missing person. The article said Pearl was due to attend the winding-up of the family trust so her disappearance was unusual. It did not go so far as to say suspicious.

Victor and Jane set off towards Anyos. It was another perfect day. Victor unlocked the side door to Greta's garage with the new keys, and screwed two 40-watt bulbs into the sockets.

Jane asked, *"Estuvo usted aquí ayer?"* Hoping she was using the right tense to ask if he had been in the garage and darkroom the day before.

"It should be undisturbed. Let us talk English."

"The photos on the tobacco industry are gone."

This news did not make Victor look happy. He tore a few pages out of his notebook and gave her a pen. "Write down what's missing," he said.

Greta appeared at the door at 11am. A wiry no-nonsense figure, her short grey hair was cut with little regard to style. Her tanned face advertised her love of the outdoors. "I saw you arrive in the police car, then read about Pearl's disappearance in the paper. Would you like to have lunch with me when you're finished here?"

Victor declined, saying his mother cooked lunch for him every day, but Jane gratefully accepted. At one o'clock she took the lift to Greta's fourth floor flat and admired its panoramic view across the roofs of Anyós to the Sispony Valley. Lunch was spinach soup, followed by chicken roasted with fragrant wild thyme.

"Did you ever watch Pearl work?" Jane asked, when their small-talk ran out.

"Sometimes she'd call me down to have a look at her latest photos. I'm a member of Amnesty International, so I'm a huge fan of her work. It's very political and anti-war, yet she also takes lyrical photos that wouldn't be out of place in an art museum. I tried to convince her to put on a one-woman show at the *Comu* art gallery in

La Massana. I'm sure her landscapes and photos of everyday people in Andorra would be very popular. Andorrans are almost as chauvinistic about their country as the French." Greta indicated a framed daguerreotype of an owl in snow. "That's one of hers."

Greta got up and opened a chest of drawers under the television, pulling out some 8 x 10 photos. "This was what she was working on last – a profile of the tobacco industry. These prints were slightly overexposed, but I kept them."

"What a bit of luck!" Jane flicked through them. They were identical to the missing photos. "I don't know how, but they could be important." She paged through them several times, but could find no indication of their significance.

"Do you think it's something to do with tobacco-smuggling? Or maybe one of the people in the photos is important in some way. Is a fugitive? Doesn't want to be found?" Greta asked.

"Have you told anyone about them?"

"There was no reason to."

Jane spread the photos across the table. Taking out her small digital camera she focused carefully on each one and took copies. "I'll keep a record of them before I hand them to the police. Just in case."

The rest of the day passed slowly as Jane and Victor painstakingly itemised the detritus of Pearl's former life crammed into dusty removal boxes. When they reached the bottom of the final box, Jane asked the detective again, "You haven't taken anything?"

"No, Jane, I told you I took nothing," Victor said.

Jane looked the word "album" up in the dictionary in case Victor didn't understand, then found it was a cognate – a word that is the same in Spanish and in English. She wished there were a lot more of them.

"There was a photo-album here yesterday."

Victor shook his head as if to clear it and wrote that down on his list with a question-mark next to it, as did she. A missing photo-album of Pearl's early life. Disappearances were becoming commonplace. What possible connection had an old photo-album with a series of photos on growing tobacco? Nothing made any sense.

After lunch Victor had taken the photos from Greta without

comment, thumbing quickly through them then putting them to one side. Jane had asked him what he thought but he just shook his head and returned to the job of listing the contents of the boxes until only the filing-cabinet was left. They were unsure how to attack it and decided to do one drawer each, then reconsider. Jane's drawer was full of negatives of the war in Bosnia. Her gut twisted to see the bloodied bodies, killed in a senseless sectarian civil war. Judging by Victor's sour expression he felt the same way. His hand was pressed against his chest as if to ward off indigestion.

"*Que tienes tu*?" During the day, alternating between Spanish and English, Jane and Victor had begun to use the more familiar *tu* form of Spanish. "What do you have?"

"*La guerra*. Always the war." Victor replied wearily.

How strange that war was a feminine noun in Spanish. Not many women started a war. Too many mothers lose sons in war for it to make any sense.

"You're not married, Victor?"

"Yes. I am married."

"Does your mother live with you?"

"No. But I see her for lunch every day."

"With your wife?" Jane was always curious about family relationships.

"My wife goes to the gym," Victor sounded defensive. "It's the custom here for mothers to cook lunch for their sons each day."

The job of cataloguing the negatives was overwhelming, so they agreed to quit for the day. When they arrived back in Ordino Juan-Antonio was in the street asking a tourist to move a car from where it was illegally parked. Jane waved, but he had on his policeman's face and he just nodded back. She walked through the town's narrow cobbled streets and stopped by an old stone barn tastefully converted into an antique store. "*Art i Fusta*" said the sign. The juxtaposition of old sleds and modern wrought iron candelabra arrested her gaze. A sign in four languages said that during the Middle Ages Andorra was famous for the iron works from its mines. That would explain the oxidised iron sculptures dotting Ordino.

"Can I help you find anything special?" asked the sales-lady.

"I was wondering if you know my sister, Pearl?" asked Jane,

producing the photo.

"Yes, I know her well. She often comes in to buy things for the apartment. I heard that she was missing. I hope they'll find her soon. Last winter a Frenchwoman disappeared from the Hotel Coma here in Ordino, leaving behind her clothes and her passport. They didn't find her until the next spring, near to Pas de La Casa. She must have fallen and hurt herself while hiking and then not have been able to continue...." After imparting this information, the woman's narrative ran down and she looked stricken, as she realised how this news would affect Jane.

"I mean to say that foul play is unlikely. Andorra doesn't have serious crime...." Again she faltered, her kind face flushed with embarrassment. "My English is not as good as I thought it was," she apologised, "I cannot say it properly."

But the result for the Frenchwoman in a country with no serious crime had still been death, Jane thought, and the terror that she had managed to keep imprisoned in her stomach flooded into her throat and tried to choke her. She walked quickly back up the street and sat at one of the outdoor tables and ordered a glass of mineral water. She felt dizzy with fear. Tears of frustration crept beneath her lashes and escaped from behind her sun-glasses. She dashed them away and took several long, deep, shuddering breaths. She mustn't give way in public. Showing any emotion to strangers had always been an anathema to her. They would find Pearl alive. They would! Jane repeated it like a mantra. She would never give up looking.

The sound of chamber-music drifted by. A black and white poster in the window of the general store advertised the Ordino music festival. A concert would take place that evening in the National Auditorium behind the café. Music soothes a savage beast. Or was it a savage breast? Was that Shakespeare? The waiter brought out a sweet crêpe she hadn't ordered and patted her on the hand sympathetically.

"Enjoy the music, *Señora*. No charge for the crêpe. They will find her."

It seemed that everyone in the village knew who she was now.

Dad and Dave's front door faced Pearl's across a shiny granite passage. When no-one answered the doorbell, she slipped a note under the door asking them to call her. She wanted to find out about the GR 7. As time passed she knew vital clues could be lost.

Later that evening she put on her jacket and went to sit on the bench outside the auditorium. As she listened to the music and the applause, she had never felt so alone. Her youth was slipping away, and despite her best efforts she had no life. Old friends had vanished after Bruce's death, wishing her well in a vague sort of way, but they were busy with their own lives. Long hours of work made it hard to make new friends. It was hard not to feel pessimistic about the chances of finding Pearl. People disappeared all the time. The music washed over her and threatened to drown her. She was engulfed in self pity.

The crowd surged outside during intermission and lit up cigarettes as one. She saw the ash blonde woman, Pedro's mother Llourdes, come outside. Her arms were linked through her husband's, the handsome politician Fernando Ribero-Lopez, and on her other side was Juan-Antonio. The woman was laughing up into his face. The trio looked happy and relaxed. They were all beautifully-dressed. Jane felt out of her depth and a long way from home. She was glad that they didn't look her way and see the orphan with her face pressed up against a window. It was the old outsider feeling. It had started in her private school when she realised she was one of the few children who had no father at home. No anecdotes to tell. No frame of reference. She didn't even know how to behave when other fathers were around.

She shrank back into the shadows and watched the happy crowd until the bell rang and they surged back inside the auditorium. The sweet strains of the flute were unbearable. She supposed she should wait to confront Pearl's lover but instead she fled home. Once the safety chain to the front door was secured behind her she felt more in control. Perhaps another bath might help her relax; it certainly helped her sleep the night before. She dumped more bath-salts into the hot water and sighed with pleasure as she sank into it. Simple pleasures were often best.

Cool water eventually forced her out of the bath. Out of nowhere a memory surfaced of an all-night party where a stranger chopped some white crystals into powder and snorted them up his nose. Dripping wet but not stopping to wrap a towel around her, she lifted the stopper from the jar of bath-salts. She sniffed, then wet her finger and dipped it into the white salts. She rubbed her finger on her gums and grimaced at the bitter taste. Her mouth went numb. Alcohol was her poison. Life with a policeman had precluded the recreational use of drugs, but she very much feared that this was cocaine. Was Pearl a user? Surely not. Pearl had done everything she could to help Jane kick her alcohol habit and had never confessed to a similar addiction or sounded the least bit knowledgeable about drug problems. Could cocaine have something to do with her disappearance?

Her mobile phone rang. It was Gary Cohen. "Wondering if there is any news?" he said.

"Nothing!"

"I've asked around, but everyone thought the same as I did – that she was having a break to sort out some personal business."

"Gary, did Pearl tell you anything about who she's dating now? You two got on pretty well together and she used to confide in you."

"Boast about her conquests you mean?" Gary sounded sour. "No. Not lately. She's been rather quiet in that department."

Pearl was surprisingly frank about her sexual exploits, turning her encounters into funny stories. It was not surprising that this made Gary wince since he had dated her briefly on her arrival in New York.

Jane took the plunge. "Did Pearl ever do drugs, do you know?" She could almost hear Gary's antenna quiver.

"Never. She was pretty anti-drugs as far as I could tell. What's the story?"

"No story. Just trying to cover all the angles. The whole thing's a complete mystery. I haven't even been able to establish who saw her last. No-one I've talked to knows anything. It's discouraging."

"Well. Keep me informed. I'll keep digging around."

After some thought, Jane took the bath-salts into the kitchen and poured them into the sugar basin. Then she left the empty glass jar under hot running water for twenty minutes, before squirting some detergent in it and scrubbing it inside and out. She dried it and, feeling somewhat melodramatic, carried it back to the bathroom wrapped up in a towel so as not to leave fingerprints. She felt compelled to shield Pearl from accusations of drug use until she knew more. Imagine how expensive the two baths had been! What a bad joke. Cocaine baths to take the sting out of life.

CHAPTER NINE

The night was full of dreams as Jane drifted in and out of sleep. Her subconscious was still struggling to capture an elusive memory. When the alarm rang she was tempted not to get up and go for her run, but her recovery plan didn't allow for any weaknesses of will so she got up and dressed anyway. She vowed to "make a searching and fearless moral inventory of herself." – Step Four.

Slowly jogging up the road she began to explore herself for weaknesses. She must look after her physical wellbeing and remember the Alcoholics Anonymous advice to avoid getting Hungry, Angry, Lonely or Tired, experiences that triggered relapses. She would be as honest and kind as she could be with herself and others. She would make amends to those she had hurt, and strive to improve herself. Keep learning Spanish and going to night classes. Her therapist teased her about the many self-improvement classes she took. He said she was always auditioning for life, not living it. That hurt.

The valley was covered in a mist of rain blurring the landmarks. Muffled footsteps followed in her wake as she ran. She wondered if she was starting a trend, and smiled to think of a line of well-fed Andorrans jogging patiently behind her, cigarettes in hand.

She ran on past La Cortinada to Arans, then stopped to stretch. As she stood on one leg stretching her quadriceps, her left leg bent behind her touching her buttocks, a hand grasped her shoulder. Instinctively she dropped her shoulder towards the asphalt and whirled on her right leg, kicking up hard with her left.

"Bloody Hell!" The voice was broadly Australian. A hand obscured the familiar, handsome chiselled features. "I think you've broken my nose, you silly cow."

"Harris!" Her knee hurt.

He gave her a mild shake. "What did you do that for?"

"Sorry. You gave me a fright. You shouldn't sneak up on people like that." The instructor in her self defence classes had been right. It was all about muscle memory. "What on earth are you doing here?"

"The trust meets on Thursday. Where's Pearl?" he asked, looking around as if she might materialise from out of the gloom.

"You tell me." Jane's voice was neutral.

"Don't start that shit again," he said, annoyed. "You'll be sorry."

"Don't threaten me." They glared at each other.

"Tell me where she is!" Harris gripped her arm tightly.

"Sod off."

"There you are." The quiet voice came from a barely visible figure ten feet from them, sheltering under the canopy of the Restaurant La Font D'Arans. It walked towards them.

"Juan-Antonio," he said politely – holding out his hand. Harris shook it with bone-çcracking force. Juan-Antonio gripped back. They smiled tightly into each other's faces, Harris's marred by a bloody nose.

"My brother-in-law, Harris Wentworth, Pearl's husband," Jane introduced them, trying her best to sound off-hand.

"Let's all run back together," suggested Juan-Antonio.

They stopped at the sports centre after a punishing sprint down the valley. Harris was out of condition in the 1,600 metre altitude and was breathing hard, but he had not allowed Juan-Antonio or Jane to pull ahead. Jane bent over and pressed her hand to a stitch in her side, gasping, "Where are you staying? I'll call you."

"Hotel Coma." It was right next door to Pearl's apartment. "Make sure you do." He moved away, leaving them standing alone on the *plaça*.

Juan-Antonio gestured towards the entrance of the *sportiu*. "Breakfast?" he inquired blandly.

"Why don't I cook for you this morning?" said Jane.

"Do you think my reputation can stand it?"

"Perhaps it will be enhanced."

They jogged up the stairs instead of taking the lift. Jane ground some coffee and put it on to percolate, then sliced onions and potatoes and threw them into a frying pan sizzling with olive oil and butter. Next she took some eggs from the fridge and began to beat them. Juan-Antonio folded his arms, leaned against the counter-top and watched her.

"*Tortilla*," Jane said, trying to impress him with her knowledge of things Spanish.

"Tell me about Pearl's husband. I didn't know she was married."

"They met at university and married when she was nineteen.

Harris was a year ahead of her, studying to be an anthropologist. It went OK for a while. They certainly made a spectacular-looking couple." Jane checked the progress of the onions and potatoes and added the beaten eggs. "The problem was that Harris was terribly possessive. He was always checking up on her. After a while he stopped studying and when she was at lectures he'd be sitting in the back of the auditorium. Marriage intensified his jealousy rather than making him feel more secure." She checked to see if Juan-Antonio was keeping up with her narrative, or if the flood of English was overwhelming him. He nodded for her to continue.

"They went to counselling and things improved for a while, but then it started up again. He became verbally abusive – then physically violent." She shuddered, remembering. "At the time she had a very close relationship with her tutor and they spent a lot of time together working on a special project. Harris thought they were having an affair. One night he broke into the guy's apartment when they were working late together and attacked them, breaking Pearl's arm and beating the tutor to pulp.

"The professor wouldn't press charges because he didn't want the scandal. Of course it didn't hurt that Harris has a prominent politician for his father. Pearl wouldn't charge him with domestic abuse either. She said Harris couldn't help it. He'd been diagnosed with bi-polar disease in his teens – which means he is manic-depressive. While he was on medication he'd be OK, but he'd stop taking it and without the lithium his conviction that Pearl was unfaithful would come back."

"Go on." Juan-Antonio was paying close attention.

"We all saw the bruises. How many doors can you walk into when you are a university graduate with 20:20 vision?" Jane slid the tortilla onto a plate and flipped it over, back into the frying-pan.

"In Australia doctors have to report all suspected domestic violence to the police, so after he broke her arm the police came to interview her and convinced her to take out a restraining order. Her father-in-law called to complain about the negative publicity. Can you imagine?" She put large slices of bread under the grill to toast. "Pearl moved in with me for a few months while she sorted herself out. I was dating Bruce at the time. He threatened to break every bone in Harris's body if he touched Pearl again...and said that being a policeman he would get away with it."

She pulled out knives and forks, rubbed the toast with garlic and tomato and poured olive oil over it, then slid the browned tortilla out of the frying-pan onto a serving-plate and cut it into wedges. As they sat down she poured two mugs of coffee and deftly moved the sugar jar out of reach, opening a packet of sugar lumps in its place. "The restraining order didn't work and Harris continued stalking her. We were afraid of what he might do. Fortunately at that point, the project Pearl worked on with her tutor paid off and she was given the opportunity to cadet overseas. Basically she never returned."

"Do you mind if I smoke?" Juan-Antonio asked, tapping his fingers on the table. Jane poured him a second cup of coffee then found him an ashtray. She wasn't his mother. He could choose a slow death by cancer if he liked.

"Three years later when Pearl surfaced with the *New York Times* using her own by-line, he started calling her again. He might call twenty times a night. She got a silent line but somehow he was always able to get the new number. Finally she moved to Andorra and started to freelance – although the *NY Times* still bought most of her articles. She continued to spend time in New York but everyone was sworn to secrecy so Harris couldn't find her. As far as I know, he hasn't been in touch or seen her since…but I guess he knew the deadline for the trust to be wound up and figured he'd find her here."

They ate their breakfast mulling that over. Juan-Antonio made noises of appreciation.

"The weird thing is that she never bothered to divorce him. She said it wasn't important since she would never consider marrying again."

"Do you think he has something to do with her disappearance?" Juan-Antonio lit another cigarette.

"Why would he ask where she was? He'd just stay out of sight. No-one knew he was here."

"Maybe he's trying to claim her inheritance from the trust, since they are still married. Would that be possible?"

"I don't know. I've never seen the trust documents, or a copy of Pearl's will."

"Would he try to hurt you? Try to get back at you for bloodying his nose?"

"He's never hurt me before. Pearl's his obsession, not me. I just reacted instinctively to protect myself when he scared me."

"Have you thought that Harris could have been the one who locked you in the *trastero*?"

"It's possible I suppose. We should find out when he arrived."

"You are a surprising woman – very logical. You shoot better than I do, and you can kick box! What else are you good at?"

Jane batted her eyelids at him.

He tousled her short blonde hair. "You're not a bad cook either."

The doorbell rang. A stranger with wild ginger curls, dressed head to toe in black leather biker's gear, stood in the passage. Large green eyes regarded Jane and Juan-Antonio thoughtfully.

"I'm Lyn, Mary's father." The likeness was unmistakable. "I got your message too late to call last night. We took Mary down to La Vella to see the Folk Dancing." His Scottish burr was thicker than his daughter's.

"Come in. Like some coffee?" Jane offered.

"Poison," he replied succinctly.

Jane reflected that if she gave up coffee as well as alcohol and dessert, life truly wouldn't be worth living. Juan-Antonio didn't look at all inclined to leave, but since Jane remained by the door waiting for him to go, he thanked her for breakfast and with a considered backwards glance, took the lift.

"Will the Wednesday Group be walking this week?"

"It will. We won't. Mary couldn't keep up. It's a pretty serious walk on the GR11 to the Pic de Coma Pedrosa – the highest mountain in Andorra."

"Don't you mean the GR 7?"

"That goes from Spain to France too, and it shares part of the GR11 route, but it's a different trail."

"Did Pearl go on many of the hikes?"

"Not many. Last year we went to Peramola and hiked for a couple of days. She came to that one." Lyn was skeletal and he fidgeted a lot. It made it hard to concentrate on what he was saying. Jane felt like she was looking through his skin to his bones.

"Did Pearl hike on her own, or bring a friend?"

"She hiked with the group as far as I know. Look, what's this all about?" Lyn's soft Scottish burr sharpened.

"I guess you don't watch the local news or read the newspapers? Pearl's missing. We have no idea where she is."

"Go on!"

"I'm serious. When did you see her last?"

"On Tuesday, the day before Mary was due. We went to Barcelona early to hit a few of the clubs."

"We're trying to figure out her movements. Who did she see a lot of?"

Lyn's fidgeting became more pronounced. "Well, they tried to keep it quiet but she was dead keen on Fernando Ribera-Lopez, the politician. I used to see him coming in and out of her place all the time. I joked that I wouldn't mind her leftovers when she was finished. She said as far as she knew, no Andorran politician was openly gay. It would be a death blow in the electorate."

Jane's mobile rang and she picked it up, expecting Charles.

"They've found her jeep," Detective Victor was succinct.

"Where?"

"Pas de la Casa. Juan-Antonio will pick you up in ten minutes."

CHAPTER TEN

The road to Pas de la Casa led northeast over the col, or saddle, of the bare mountain called Casamanya, which dominated the landscape behind the small village of Ordino. The bitumen road was shored up by intricate stonework and wound past natural springs and wooded forest before bursting over to the other side with a spectacular view of the second of two valleys of the Y shaped main road tri-secting Andorra. After a steep descent of 500 metres, it joined the road to France at the village of Canillo. Here hotel rooms and menus were advertised in francs as well as pesetas. The townscape of Canillo was dominated by both the ever-present sports palladium (this one advertising ice skating) plus the *Comu*'s latest project – an outsized four-storey building in which the ski resort's new gondola was to be housed.

"The shadow it throws reminds the local rate-payers of the size of the debt," Juan-Antonio said.

A cantilevered stone pathway hid the town's river, so the rushing water could be heard but not seen. Juan-Antonio kept up a running commentary, drawing her attention right and left. A series of colourful but dated posters advertising a country and western dance festival clashed with her belief that they danced sedate folk dances like *sardanas* in Andorra, but before she could ask, they were past the last of the posters and heading out of town.

Between the village of Canillo and the ski station of Soldeu a triangulated concrete sculpture reached skywards. Climbers were glued to its side.

"It's mandatory for Andorran school children to learn to mountain climb and to swim. No exceptions," Juan-Antonio continued. He pointed across the road to where tourists from two buses were lined up near a thirty foot waterfall having their photos taken. "We have a huge supply of pure underground water and bottle it for sale throughout Europe." The guided tour served to distract Jane from worrying about what finding Pearl's abandoned vehicle might mean.

The vivid green pastures etched into the precipitous mountains on either side of the road made her eyes ache. Australians rarely saw such a pure dark green. Herds of cows grazed contentedly.

Juan-Antonio had followed her gaze. "The government pays six thousand pesetas per cow a year to maintain the rural aspect of Andorra and to ensure landowners continue farming."

Bovine social security, thought Jane. Now I've heard everything.

Pas de la Casa was a sprawling ugly town with none of the charm of Sant Julia on the southern border. Tourist buses were parked in long rows by the multitude of shops advertising everything from hams to duty-free liquor and perfume. Couples bustled out of garish hypermarkets pushing shopping-trolleys piled high with sugar, pasta, and tobacco products, all highly-taxed items in France and Spain. If Pas de la Casa had any coherent architectural theme, it was one of raw commerce. The ski pistes behind the town were on a mountain stripped of trees. Across the border and into France, the countryside continued bare, bleak and forbidding. Jane thought of the lonely death of the French hiker in the midst of that moonscape of rock and experienced a frisson of dread.

The red jeep was backed into a corner of a large parking area attached to the local sports-centre, which was in the usual extravagant design. This one resembled a silver-plated armadillo joined to the street by a black glass bridge. The Caldea spa in Andorra La Vella and the Pas de la Casa *esportiu* had design elements in common. They both had all the charm of a finger poked in the eye. The red Jeep was unlocked, a parking ticket tucked behind the sun visor. Time of entry to the car park was 8.28pm the previous Tuesday. With so many people parking in the busy border town, it had remained there unnoticed for a week. Jane was vexed to hear that the local police had searched the jeep and rummaged around in it without wearing gloves. "What about fingerprints?"

Juan-Antonio was apologetic. "We don't have many unsolved crimes here Jane, so preserving a potential crime scene is not something that happens automatically."

Victor turned from the group of uniformed men surrounding him and spoke volubly to Juan-Antonio, who translated the outburst.

"They're waiting to look at Tuesday's tapes from the closed circuit TVs. The car park is kept under surveillance because of the number of thefts during the ski season. Many visitors are not as honest as we'd like."

One of the policemen opened the glove-box and began going

through the contents. A bottle of water. Cheap pair of reading glasses with a magnification of 1.5 available at any chemist. Hairbrush. Expensive pen. Jeep warranty book. Echinacea throat lozenges. The side-pocket held a well-organised map folder of Western Europe and the Eastern Block countries. In a 1.50 Andorran topographical map identical to the one Jane had bought from the Tourist Bureau, the words "*Portella Blanca*" were marked in yellow highlighter; but it seemed to Jane that if Pearl had been on her way there, she would have parked at the closer ski station of Grau Roig and have taken the map with her. The jeep yielded nothing else beyond small change that had slipped down behind the front passenger seat.

Victor led the way to the video room, where the security officer located the relevant tape, covering the time period between six and ten the previous Tuesday evening. Fast- forwarding to 8.24pm, they watched as cars trickled in and out of the complex. At 8.27pm the jeep turned in. A large scratch was evident on the right front mudguard. The driver wore sun-glasses and a cap. They froze the tape and enhanced the headshot but it was hard to establish any definition. A second tape from the cameras that scanned the parking area caught the jeep reversing before the camera panned away. The driver was on the offside of the car and reflection from the fluorescent lights bounced off the front passenger window, obscuring details of the car's interior. When the camera panned back it caught the back view of the driver walking towards the exit.

"*Páralo!*" called Victor. The security man froze the image. One of the policemen ran back to the parking area and stood at the same place. They compared the frozen image with the live, transmitted to the security booth. It was clear that the driver had been shorter than the six foot policeman.

"How tall is Pearl?" asked Juan-Antonio.

"Five feet six."

They considered what little they could see of the driver of the jeep. The hair was either short or tucked up under the cap. The leather bomber jacket over slim hipped jeans and sneakers was as anonymous as it was androgynous. They sighed, collectively.

"*Espera!*" The security officer targeted the driver's hand and enhanced the image. The nails were bitten to the quick. Not Pearl then. The driver was of medium height like nearly every person in Spain and Andorra and was not prone to manicures. It wasn't a lot to go on. Victor held out his hand for the tapes and confiscated them with remarkable lack of ceremony.

"*Algo más?*" Anything else? The security officer shook his head. As Jane reached out to shake his hand he instead embraced her, pressing her warmly to his considerable stomach in a gesture of solidarity. She found it hard to get used to this physical expression of feelings. Australians were thrifty with their body-language. This extended to barely moving their lips when they spoke. Stoicism was highly prized and a display of emotion was considered bad taste. People of her mother's generation had a dislike of touching people casually. A nod of the head usually sufficed for anything they might like to imply, and this economy had not changed to any measurable extent in Jane's generation. She wondered if the local policemen would hug her too, but with Victor looking on they were more circumspect, contenting themselves with handshakes and assurances of assistance, all in Catalan but unmistakable in their sincerity.

"What now?" she asked.

"We'll announce that we have found the jeep and ask for assistance," Victor frowned, thinking aloud. "Did anyone see the jeep before it was parked here and so on? Headquarters will send a helicopter to sweep the GR 7 and the hiking trails around Pas de la Casa including *Portella Blanca.*"

Jane knew they were thinking of the missing French hiker from the previous spring. Helicopters appeared to be used for a multitude of tasks in mountainous Andorra. She had seen one fly past the Ordino clock-tower towing a metal container on a steel cable. Juan-Antonio said it would be used to shelter hunters during the week-long Izard hunting season.

They walked back for one more look at the Jeep. Jane squeezed between the wall and the passenger's side and examined the scratch the video had revealed. The front indicator light was also smashed. The damage looked recent.

"Jane, would you drive the jeep back to Headquarters while I follow in my car?" Victor enquired.

"I'm sorry, I don't have an International Driver's licence."

"We're the police. We don't mind."

"I don't drive," she said more firmly.

He looked surprised. A modern woman who didn't drive was an anachronism.

"Anyway," Jane continued, "shouldn't you put it on a trailer and tow it? You don't want to complicate fingerprint or DNA analysis."

Victor rolled his eyes making it obvious he thought any outside intervention in Pearl's disappearance was unlikely, but he called back to one of the local policemen who agreed to organise a tow truck.

"I'll stay in Pas de la Casa and walk around a bit and take a taxi back to Ordino," she said.

"That will cost a fortune!" Juan-Antonio protested.

"I'll be inheriting a fortune sometime soon," Jane reminded him.

"How big a fortune?"

"I don't know exactly."

"Money is always a motive, no?" commented Victor.

Jane's thoughts were running in the opposite direction. "Will you be interviewing Fernando Ribera-Lopez today – or any time soon?"

"It's complicated," Victor replied shortly. Jane nodded coolly and walked purposefully away as if she had a specific destination in mind. She had to bite back a sharp comment about the reluctance of the police to interview a government minister. In business the better negotiator usually kept his temper, although, increasingly in the modern corporate world, sheer bad manners sometimes won out. Maybe she should lose her temper. Civility could well be a dying tactic.

The weather was a lot hotter than she had expected for autumn. The morning's rain had transformed the dry climate into a clammy fug, so her first stop was a small boutique where she bought a white T-shirt. She stuffed the jacket of her trouser-suit into the boutique's carry-bag and combed her hair forward with her fingers to try to cover the fading bruise on her forehead. A nearby café had extended its seating area by placing tables on a makeshift planked terrace over the road. The waiter was dishing up soggy pizzas. Not a good advertisement for the quality of the food.

Taking shelter from the sun under the restaurant's awning, she opened her shoulder-bag and drew out copies of the few emails she had received from Pearl. The last one read:

It was great to get your last email and to hear that you are doing so well at Sentry and Parker. Congratulations on the raise. Sounds like a good decision to move to a smaller firm. Wondering what will be next in your life? You have had two years to grieve for Bruce and your life together, and now it's time to look ahead. Making changes can be hard I know, but sometimes it's necessary. Look at me. I took a long time to get over Harris and that whole débacle, but leaving Australia for the cadetship then moving to Andorra from New York was the best thing I could have done. Being a journalist helps to put your own misfortunes into perspective. Having seen people lose their entire family, home and livelihood plus have their neighbours commit unspeakable acts that could never be forgiven in several lifetimes makes my own problems seem decidedly petty. Still, knowing that doesn't prevent me having the odd blue day.

Today's a blue day actually. The guy I've been seeing stood me up due to pressing family commitments. Andorrans are very big on the family. Normally I find this charming, but it's not so great when I discover that I come a long way down in the pecking order. I guess a lot of blokes would say I'm getting my come-uppance. So I rang my friend Conchita and we went out to dinner and a jazz club instead of staying home and moping. Always better to do something than nothing, don't you think? You'll be surprised but I've fallen madly (and probably stupidly) in love again despite vowing I never would. Why do I fall for such unsuitable guys (and don't give me any of that rubbish about deliberately choosing difficult people so I can avoid intimacy. I get that enough from Mum). I've tried to break it off a couple of times because he is married with a child so there is no future in it. I don't want to be responsible for breaking up his home; but then we run into each other somewhere and start up again. The sex is incredible. I'm addicted. I am trying to look upon it as a purely physical relationship without any need for ties. Men seem to be able to have non-relationship sex without angst. If I can manage it I will become truly European! Don't worry about me, big sister. I'm sure to get over it eventually....

Anyway – moving on – I've got an idea for an article I might freelance. It involves a bit of sleuthing and skulduggery. What set me off was a casual conversation at a dinner I had with friends Jean-Paul and Isabella. He's French, and he mentioned some unsavoury practices that took place here during World War Two. Isabella, who is Andorran, emphatically denied they were true. They nearly started World War Three arguing about it. A mystery is always intriguing. Following it up will be a nice distraction. Of course I don't want to wear out my welcome here by publishing anything too radical. I'll have to think this out a bit. Maybe I'll publish under your by-line (joking).

I can't wait until you're here. There's so much I want to show you. It will be interesting to see what you think of my "compañero simpatico". You normally have pretty good instincts. I could do with you vetting the men in my life to save me from any more major heartaches. I'm thirty-three and all of a sudden I am thinking about my biological clock. I always thought I didn't want children because it's not fair to play Russian roulette with genetics and I worry about the cerebral palsy. Polly and Mum's lives are pretty hard. But now I'm not so sure. I guess I've got to find myself a good man. Wow. I'm obviously becoming too introspective and need a new assignment.

See you soon.

Love Pearl

CHAPTER ELEVEN

Jane wondered if Pearl's disappearance had anything to do with the sleuthing mentioned. She should trace Jean-Paul and Isabella. Her thoughts were far away when her mobile phone rang with the call she had been dreading.

"Jane, it's Elsa – Pearl's Mum – here."

Jane and Bruce had spent a holiday in Broome with Elsa in the old family bungalow made of corrugated iron. Each morning they woke on the veranda beneath their bed's mosquito net and looked out of shutters onto a lush garden ringed with huge mango trees. The fragrance from the waxy white flowers of the frangipanni trees bordering the house mingled with the smell of coffee brewing. It was more like Bali than the sere desert of north-west Australia. The sun barely permeated the tangle of trees surrounding the house, so what little grass could grow was sparse. Elsa began each morning by raking the fallen mango leaves from the red pindan clay, leaving a flowing pattern of rake marks. She was a darkly beautiful woman, as exotic as her garden. Her body moved quietly in perpetual motion as she tended to her visitors and to her family's needs. She smiled easily and accomplished her daily chores without hurrying. The colourful batik sarongs she habitually wore did not disguise her youthful body, which displayed little of the stress of bearing four children. The contrast between Elsa and Jane's own tensely blonde mother was startling, and emphasized Charles's diverse taste in women.

"Elsa I'm sorry to have no real news for you, except we have found Pearl's jeep, but there is still no sign of her."

"Should I fly over?"

Jane knew it would be hard for Elsa to get away. Who would look after Polly? The twins were well-meaning, but unreliable. They spent a lot of time down at the pub. "I know you feel you should be here, but really at the moment there's nothing you can do. I don't think coming over will accomplish anything. If there are any developments, Charles or I will contact you immediately."

"The kids and I are worrying ourselves sick. It's not like Pearl to be out of touch for any length of time, no matter where she is in the world."

"Yes, I know. We're hoping someone will come forward with some information soon. Her disappearance is in the papers and on TV."

"Well, I'm glad you're there, dear. I know you'll do everything you can. Your mother called. She was upset you hadn't told her anything, so I said the police had instructed you not to." Elsa knew Jane's relationship with her mother was a troubled one.

"Thanks, Elsa. I just haven't been able to face the thought of getting the third-degree. I'll call her now – better late than never."

"Take care of yourself. Call you again soon."

The conversation had not been as traumatic as Jane feared. Elsa had the remarkable talent of putting the other person at ease, despite her own distress. Jane wondered if this empathy came with looking after a disabled child. She speed-dialled her mother's number and got the answering service. It was Tuesday; her mother would be at golf.

"Hi Mum, I just wanted to touch base with you now that the news embargo has been lifted." Years of experience in dissembling allowed her to lie to her mother smoothly, without rehearsal. "We've found Pearl's Jeep and the police are sweeping the hiking trails by helicopter in case she was hiking and had an accident. I'll call you again when I can."

That chore accomplished Jane went back to wondering if the jeep was a clue to Pearl's whereabouts or a red herring. The person who'd parked it definitely wasn't Pearl. Had she been in an accident that turned ugly? Road rage was becoming common. Or was she hurt on a hiking trail somewhere, hoping for rescue?

A small square of shade over a bench invited her to sit until a dusty blue bus pulled up to take her to Grau Roig, where the trail left for *Portella Blanca*. She thrust a handful of coins at the driver to preclude having to speak to him in Spanish. In her current emotional maelstrom her proficiency had dropped to zero.

The bus left her outside the ski area's vacant ticket office. A faded map of the area displayed a track leading to a lakeside restaurant at 2,300 metres. The GR 7 trail snaked past it on the north side of the lake and climbed to *Portella Blanca* at 2,530 metres. Judging from the scale of the map, the distance to the pass was around five kilometres. Her sandals obviously weren't adequate for such a long a trek but she could probably walk as far as the lake. She could have a cool drink, look around, and show Pearl's photo to the restaurant staff to see if anyone recognized her. She felt a moment's disquiet. Bruce would have said she was tainting the investigation but she set off anyway. Better to do something than nothing, she quoted to herself from Pearl's letter.

The unpaved gravel road was steep and unforgiving. As she walked with her head down, the sun reflected off the ground and scorched her cheeks. A small four-wheel-drive bus and several cars passed her, leaving her coughing in their dust. She was annoyed to realise that she could have caught a second bus to the restaurant; the tourist bureau had neglected to tell her that. By the time she breasted the rise before the lake she was hot and irritable, and surprised to find that Andorra had its share of the flies she had thought left behind in Australia. The postcard-pretty lake took her by surprise. A stone-clad restaurant fitted snugly into the hillside and overlooked a placid kidney-shaped lake that mirrored the rugged mountains behind. A dirt track wound between spruce trees and granite stones. The restaurant's sun-bleached terrace hung over the side of the lake and hikers sprawled on the plastic chairs drinking beer, eating baguettes and enjoying the view. A Saint Bernard dog frolicked in the shallows ignoring a small girl's shrill cries for it to return.

Ordering the *menu d'el dia* would give her an entry to question the staff. Two beefy young men strolled by, cigarettes drooping from the corner of their mouths. Their backpacks were festooned with mountain climbing regalia. Clips, ropes, and pitons hung in methodical disarray. Their cockney accents slashed through the confusion of foreign accents.

"I need some hair of the dog. Eh, Paul? Are you in? Was I pissed last night." There was no demarcation line between the stubble on their cheeks and the stubble on their heads. Designer stubble was now the accepted fashion of the hoi polloi.

Jane asked the waitress to remove the bottle of wine that accompanied lunch and bring her a bottle of water instead.

"*Que?*" enquired the waitress. "*Habla usted Francés?*"

It was disheartening to be asked to speak French instead of her carefully acquired Spanish. She tried to dredge up a French phrase from school days but in the end decided it was safer to persist in Spanish.

"Do you speak English? *Habla usted Inglés?*"

"*Inglés? No.*" The waitress shook her head.

Jane handed her the wine and said, "*Agua, por favor!*" and when the waitress returned she pulled out her wallet and the small photo of Pearl.

"*Comió aquí, mi hermana, la semana pasada?*" The waitress took the proferred photo and studied it closely, squinting in the strong sunlight.

"Jorge!" she yelled.

Jorge came from inside the restaurant. "Can I help you *Señora?*" His English was fluent and he confirmed without hesitation that Pearl had been there the previous week. She had sat outside and had coffee, saying that she was waiting for a friend. He wasn't sure of the day, but it was before lunch because they hadn't been busy and he was outside himself, having a cigarette.

"I thought she was from the Philippines until she spoke to me in Catalan. Many of the wealthy families here have Filipino staff. I didn't see her friend arrive because I went inside again.

"Sometimes I've thought about advertising for a wife from the Philippines. Better to marry a Spanish speaker than a woman from the Eastern Bloc. Plus Asian women are more likely to be family-oriented…"

"Jorge," Jane interrupted, "will you show this photo to the rest of the staff and ask if they saw her, or her friend, arrive or noticed anything else?"

He returned in a short while with a short, elderly man.

"*El proprietor.* Señor Molina," Jorge introduced him.

"*Mucho Gusto. Habla usted Ingles?*"

"*Lo siento. No.*" He indicated that Jorge would act as interpreter.

After some discussion, Jorge related, "Señor Molina knows your sister. She comes here quite often for lunch in winter when she skis. He saw that she had disappeared on the television news and wondered if he should mention that she was here last week, but he didn't think it could be relevant.

"He is reluctant to get involved," Jorge explained in an aside.

"Did he talk to her, or see her friend arrive?"

There was a pause while they conferred.

"They spoke a little of the weather. She asked after Señora

Molina who is not well and was going to the hospital for tests the following day. She must have been here on Tuesday, because of this. She said she might go hiking later if her friend arrived in time. The friend was an older man, about fifty, not the friend she normally comes here with. He was wearing a suit so Señor Molina thought they would not be hiking after all."

"Would you recognise him again?"

Señor Molina waggled his hand temporisingly. A rapid stream of Catalan revealed the man was average in height, average in looks, with nothing remarkable about him at all. Except, perhaps, that he could be English or German because they didn't kiss hello, they merely shook hands. And now he thought about it, the man's suit was badly fitted and shiny, so in fact he could well have been from Eastern Europe, even Russia – although those sly Russians usually arrived with bags of cash wearing the latest fashions. Many Russians were coming to Andorra now – the Russian Mafia – investing some of the aid money they had bilked from the International Monetary Fund.

Jane could see that Señor Molina and Jorge shared a tendency to stray from the point. "Aside from the suit, was there any other reason to think he might be from Eastern Europe?"

Señor Molina shrugged as if he felt the suit was enough to go on.

"Was he thin?" she asked, thinking of the man on the video, but Sr. Molina did not think him thin or fat, short or tall.

"Does Pearl normally come here with Señor Ribera-Lopez?"

Señor Molina looked uncomfortable at this forthright question. He tightened his already thin lips and scrutinised the sky, as if the answer was hidden in the clouds. The waitress, who had been listening to the Catalan side of the conversation, walked away and loudly asked for an order at a nearby table.

"*Podía ser*," Señor Molina reluctantly conceded he may be.

"What was Pearl wearing? Does he remember?"

"Such a beautiful lady! She was wearing khaki trousers and shirt plus hiking boots, and her long hair was flowing down her back." Jorge answered for them both.

Jane recognised the description of Pearl's ubiquitous working clothes. "Did you notice whether they drove away in Pearl's jeep?"

"No, we were both inside by then, serving the lunch-time crowd."

"Did they pay by credit card?"
"We only take cash."

CHAPTER TWELVE

Leaving a small tip for the waitress, Jane followed the signs to the GR 7. She forded a small rivulet by jumping from rock to rock then unbuckled her sandals and continued barefoot with the bottom of her trousers rolled up to stop them dragging in the dirt. There was very little rubbish by the trail, and she wondered who was responsible for cleaning it away. It seemed to be a fairly popular spot, and people being how they were she thought there would have been a greater build-up of old wrapping-paper and empty cans. It was another thing she would suggest the police should follow up. Like an audit, any small find could lead to a larger revelation.

Jorge had said the last bus to Pas de la Casa was at 5.30 so Jane continued to walk aimlessly along the track until she came to a grassed area under a large thicket of trees. The hot weather was soporific, and using her shoulder-bag and the carrier-bag from the boutique as a pillow, she lay down in the shade and tried to think in a logical fashion about what she knew so far.

Working backwards, she wondered what had happened to Pearl in the seven hours between having coffee at the Lake Pessons Restaurant with the unknown Russian/English/German man until someone parked the jeep in the car park. A lot could happen in seven hours.

How could she prompt the police to question Fernando Ribera-Lopez? They seemed unwilling. Was it so difficult to approach a member of the Andorran government in a police investigation? He was Juan-Antonio's cousin after all. Surely Juan-Antonio could have spoken to him informally about it, man to man, even though Victor was the investigating detective? ...and then there was the cocaine?

One moment she was trying to fit the pieces of the puzzle together and the next she drifted off to sleep, one arm thrown over her eyes. She woke to the sound of a branch cracking underfoot. A man was standing over her. With the sun behind him she was unable to make out his face.

"*Señora*," it was Jorge the waiter, "something else."

Jane sprang to her feet. "Yes, Jorge – what is it?"

"My *jefe* – my boss – said it was best not to get involved, but he thinks that the man who lunched with your sister was on Andorran television recently in regard to a big development project."

"Why didn't he tell me this himself?"

"He rang his wife in hospital, and I overheard him discussing it. I think she was advising him to leave it to the police. But I would feel badly if my brother was missing and people could help but wouldn't. I thought you should know. Family is the most important thing."

"Is there some reason Señor Molina is reluctant to give this information to the police?" Pearl had never said anything in her letters to imply there was corruption in Andorra, but this was Europe after all – what did Jane know about their justice system.

"There are families in Andorra who own and control most of the wealth. It is best not to question these people too closely. They are not above the law, but they are in politics and they make the law. Therefore they are the law."

"Your English is good. You express yourself well, with nuances."

"Thank you. I studied at Barcelona University and then did some post-graduate work in England. Political science major and English language minor."

"Heavens!" Jane swallowed her next question before it popped out. She didn't want to imply that there was anything unusual about a university graduate working as a waiter.

Jorge seemed to read her mind and continued, "There's no call for political science graduates in Spain right now. Catalan is my birth language, and although I'm not Andorran, I can work here without paying taxes to a government in Madrid whom I don't support."

"We rarely use whom in conversation these days," Jane said, the head-prefect in her coming out. She liked people to correct her Spanish so could see no reason not to return the compliment. "Why did Señor Molina tell me anything at all?"

"It's a way to cover himself if questions are asked later. However no-one could prove he watched a certain television programme."

"Won't you get into trouble if he finds out you've told me?"

"I don't think you need to reveal your sources." Jorge revealed his white even teeth. "I've finished work now. Can I drive you somewhere?"

They retraced Jane's steps to the car park and climbed into Jorge's battered aqua Seat Panda. As they clattered back down the rough road towards the highway, Jorge pointed out massive earthworks and explained there was an engineering project to tunnel from Grau Roig through to the French border, making the precipitous road from Grau Roig to Pas de la Casa obsolete during the snowy winter months.

They drove on towards Ordino, their conversation mostly satisfying Jorge's curiosity about Australian politics. Jane described an American friend who asked if Australia was a democracy, although she was an attorney and had graduated from law school *summa cum laude*. Australian politics had obviously not been part the course work.

The suspension on the little Panda did not make for a comfortable ride on the road over the col. The glove-box flew open when they hit one of the many potholes and emptied its contents onto Jane's lap. As she gathered everything together, a passport photo of an attractive Asian girl detached itself from the miscellany. She looked at it and turned to Jorge with an enquiring smile.

"An introduction service I'm using," Jorge explained; taking the photo and tucking it into his shirt pocket while single-handedly steering around a 250 degree turn.

People led complicated lives when a young, attractive man like Jorge needed to turn to a dating service to meet the right women, Jane thought.

As they drew up in front of Pearl's apartment block, Jorge confided that it was stimulating to have a fresh viewpoint. He rarely met a woman who was interested in social justice and politics. Jane suppressed the retort that a mail-order bride would therefore not seem to be the answer. Who was she to say? AA had taught her there was no perfect way to live a life.

"I'd like to help you," Jorge wrote his telephone number and email address on a scrap of paper and gave it to her. "If there is anything at all that I can do for you, please let me know. Anything! I mean it. Just call me. Family is everything."

Jane was touched again by how warm Latin people were, and how deeply they cared about family. There was a great kindness directed towards her; the stranger in a strange land. She drew a ring around her mobile number on her business card and gave it to him.

"Thank you, Jorge. Here's my number in case you hear anything else. It's great to know there's someone I can talk to who is not involved in the investigation. Where do you live? Have I taken you out of your way?"

"Not at all. I live in Encamp, it's not far."

As far as Jane could work out, Encamp was in entirely the opposite direction. Jorge gave her his beatific smile and pulled abruptly into the traffic, oblivious to kamikaze pedestrians stepping off the kerb and into his path. Through some miracle, no-one was run over. She was pleased that she didn't have to drive in these constricted streets.

Jane checked Pearl's mailbox and amidst assorted flyers she found a typewritten envelope addressed to her sister. The postmark clearly said "Paris", although the date was smudged and undecipherable. She ripped it open. The light in the foyer was dim and she had to peer at it, holding it at arm's length.

Jack Weinstein – Rue de la Réunion
Paris, France.
33(01) 47422365

22 August 199-

Mrs P. Wentworth
Cr. General, Ordino,
Principat d'Andorra

Dear Mrs Wentworth,

Thank you for your correspondence. I am very much interested in the matters your letter referred to. I would like to see you in person to discuss them further. Whether you come to Paris or I come to Andorra is not important to me. I travel a good deal in my profession. I am, of course, very keen to see the photographs. Please call me to set up a mutually convenient appointment.

Yours sincerely,

Jack Weinstein.

Jane was intrigued as much by the timing of the letter as by the letter itself. For Pearl to be selling photographs was not unusual, but the letter was obviously responding to a recent enquiry. She ran up the stairs and let herself into the apartment and impatiently dialled the number in France. The phone rang unanswered. What kind of a businessman had an office with no answering-machine, and a letterhead with no fax or email address, and typewrote envelopes instead of using printed labels? She could not imagine.

The Crillon Hotel put her straight through to her father.

"Dad, they found the jeep, and Pearl was at a restaurant meeting a middle-aged man the day it was parked. I don't know who he was yet, I'm just about to inform the police."

"Good work, Jane. I'll catch a commuter flight to Toulouse and drive down from there on Thursday. The meeting of the trust isn't until 6pm. If I leave early, I'll easily make it. I've booked a room at the Hotel Roc de Caldes. There aren't many five-star hotels in Andorra." – Her father wasn't happy straying too far from room service. – "I've been turning up some fascinating sources at the National Archives that date back to the Merovingian period." – Jane had no idea when the Merovingian period was and had a hard time catching up with her father's change in topics. – "Sometimes I get distracted, it's so hard to comprehend that Pearl is missing."

"Well, here's another distraction. Pearl just received a letter from a Jack Weinstein, in Paris."

She cringed as her father said unnecessarily, "Sounds like a Jew."

She interjected before he could say anything else, "He's not answering his phone. I wonder if you could visit his office in the Rue de la Reunion and talk to him, or at least find out something about him and what sort of business he operates?"

"I'll go first thing tomorrow. It's seven o'clock now, so it's unlikely his office would be open. The French keep regular hours, unlike the Spanish. *Rue de la Réunion*. Interesting address. Close to the *Cimetière du Père Lachaise*." Her father obviously recognised a certain quality in Jane's silence and continued, "It's a famous cemetery, Jane! Chopin, Proust, Edith Piaf and Gertrude Stein are all buried there. You've heard of them, at least."

"Well I hope an address close to a cemetery isn't some type of omen."

"Oh everything's a sign, Jane, historically speaking, when we look back with knowledge of forward events."

Jane wondered how many points you lost if you told your father he was full of shit. She took a deep breath and quickly counted to Step Six, reminding herself that she was "entirely ready to have God remove all of her defects of character," – including not honouring her father and her mother.

After she hung up she checked her emails and dealt with some mundane problems from the office, referring them back to Carol, her secretary. Having a competent secretary was rather like having a wife without the downside of emotional baggage, Jane thought.

She reached for the telephone directory. The number for the *Ministeri d'Urbanisme* was easily found in the government section in the front. Jane dialled, and when asked what her call was in reference to, she replied that she would like an appointment to see the Minister. The secretary immediately said that the Minister was not available for interviews this week.

"When will he be available?"

"I could not say, *Señora*. You could try calling next week."

Jane rang the operator and asked where the Ministry was located and wrote it down.

It was nearly eight o'clock before she remembered her promise to call Harris. They arranged to meet for coffee after dinner. Harris didn't sound like himself. He was monosyllabic. She wondered if he was taking his lithium.

CHAPTER THIRTEEN

A quick shower left Jane with time to kill. She wasn't the type to spend hours getting ready. It was enough to drag a brush though her hair, fluff it up and smooth on skin-toned moisturiser. A quick swipe of bronze highlighter on her cheekbones and a neutral lipstick and she was ready. Her style was to look neat and unthreatening. The girl next door, she mused. She was tall and tended to stand out in a crowd, which could be a disadvantage when you were an auditor. It was better to look unassuming and sneak up on companies unawares. Her promotion prospects also improved dramatically if she was seen as merely competent. A brilliant employee could threaten an incumbent's own career.

Looking around for something to do, she realised that she hadn't been as thorough in her examination of the apartment as she could have been. Jacket pockets for a start. She painstakingly went through all of Pearl's clothes, jeans, blouses, anorak, jacket, not forgetting to feel the hems and linings for items that had been tucked away. The small pile she accumulated contained tissues, a lip moisturiser with a sun protection factor of fifteen, small change and a business card that said, "Ramon Saboya *Advocat i Notario*," with a local telephone and fax number at an address in Escaldes. She wondered why Pearl needed a notary. There was also a credit-card slip from a local sports store for eighty thousand pesetas, which seemed like rather a lot to spend on a tennis racquet.

Feeling like a private investigator, she began to take out drawers from cupboards. She looked under and behind them to see if anything was taped there. This was where she had hidden her stash of birth control pills when she was still living at home with her mother and didn't want her to know she was sexually active. Her mother had no qualms about searching her bag, diary or any other number of intimate possessions to resolve her curiosity. Jane went to great lengths to frustrate this aim. When Jane started high school their relationship had morphed into basic guerrilla warfare with neither side giving quarter. Pearl, on the other hand, had an excellent relationship with Elsa and hadn't had to develop skills in dissimulation. There were no secret envelopes to be found. Perhaps there was a loose brick in the fireplace? This theory left her sootier but no wiser. She went to change again.

Fanning the leaves in the books stacked on the coffee-table and in the bookshelf yielded the brochure of a black and white photographic exhibition of Andorra, spanning the years 1930 –1960 currently showing in the La Massana exhibition hall, and a blurry photo of Pearl and Fernando Ribera-Lopez. The photo had been enlarged and cropped. Jane slipped the business card and photo in between the blank pages stacked in her travel printer, leaving a healthy few between. She rolled back the kilims and stood on a chair to feel the back of the wardrobes but found nothing more. It was a small apartment. She couldn't think of anywhere else to search.

Harris was leaning on the bar imitating one of the Blues Brothers. He was sporting dark glasses and his black suit had a latent shine the bar lights emphasised. He was nursing what looked like the latest in a succession of beers. As she approached, he straightened and kissed her on the cheek. She proferred the other side, now used to the European style of double kissing and there was an awkward pause before he pecked that one too.

"Sorry about this morning, I didn't mean to give you a fright."

"No worries," Jane replied with the all-purpose Australian comment. They gave their orders for coffee and made small-talk about Andorra and the weather until they were on their own again. Harris leaned forward. His nose was swollen.

"It's not what you think, Jane. I didn't come here to harass Pearl." He reached into his back pocket and drew out his wallet, flipped it open, and handed it over. Behind a plastic window Jane saw a photo of a pretty girl holding a chubby, dark-skinned toddler of about eighteen months.

"My son, Freddy," said Harris proudly, "and my girlfriend Melinda. We met when I was working at Balgo Mission. They're the best thing that has ever happened to me. I want to marry her and be a proper father to my boy. There are far too many illegitimate kids in the world.

"I came over to ask Pearl for a divorce. I knew that the trust was winding-up so she'd have to be here." He shrugged and looked glum. "I guess I should have approached her through a divorce lawyer but I felt I owed her an apology for the way I acted in the past. I wanted to be friends again and to thank her for the good times we had together. Not all the memories are bad you know."

Against all the odds, Jane believed him. "Step Eight. Make a list of all persons we harmed and become willing to make amends to them." She had travelled this route herself. It was hard to move forward in life dragging your past behind you. She saw the way he looked intently at the photo in his hand, and suspected that his obsessive nature was now firmly focussed on his son. She hoped this would be a good thing for them both, but wondered if too much interest in your child might not be just as damaging as not enough. She had grown up with a parent in each camp. A father who hadn't cared and a mother who invaded her personal space.

"Congratulations, Harris," she said, "I couldn't be more pleased for you, and I am sure Pearl would feel the same."

"What do you mean – would feel the same?" Harris noticed subtext.

"Pearl's been missing since last Tuesday. No-one has any idea where she is." Jane handed him the cuttings from the *Diari d'Andorra* and explained about finding the jeep, and the planned helicopter sweeps.

"When did you arrive, Harris?"

"Friday night."

The day after Jane arrived. She began to have doubts again.

"So you started following me on Saturday."

"Yes. I got Pearl's address from the bank. I made up some story they weren't even interested in; they just gave it to me without any questions. I couldn't understand why you were on your own and Pearl wasn't with you. It seemed like a conspiracy." Harris thought everything that happened or didn't happen in the world was a conspiracy materially directed at him.

"So you followed me over to Anyos after lunch on Saturday, and then…"

"You went into an underground car park and stayed there," he finished. Jane sensed there was more. She waited, saying nothing. Harris made a face, the lithium gave him the occasional tic, and continued.

"I was cautious about following you. I didn't want you to notice me and tell Pearl I was here before I spoke to her. I hung back – and just kept you in sight. There was another walker between us going in the same direction, and it wasn't until you turned into the apartment complex that I saw that he was following you too. He was pretty casual, but he had a good look around before he went after you into the car park. I played at being a tourist and turned my back and took some snaps of the Church. After that, I waited behind the wall in the cemetery and kept watch through the gate."

Jane interrupted, "You didn't get the man's picture, did you?"

"Well no."

Jane was hugely disappointed.

"Not then. But later he came out with some stuff and I saw he was looking through Pearl's old photo-album with the paisley cover. He took his time then threw it in the rubbish bin. I used the zoom lens to take a couple of shots of him. Then he called someone on his mobile phone and a black Mercedes came to pick him up, so I took a couple more shots. The whole thing seemed pretty strange. After they left, I walked over and fished the album out of the bin and then walked down to the garage but there was no sign of you.

"I thought you and Pearl had used the album with its crazy psychedelic cover as a decoy while you gave me the slip by going out another door. So I haired back to the apartment hoping to pick up your trail again and you turned up a couple of hours later with the policeman...although of course I didn't know he was a policeman at the time."

"Why didn't you simply ring the bell at the apartment, or call Pearl?"

"I was afraid she'd refuse to see me."

Jane was silent, thinking about the story. It was pretty off-beam, but it also didn't clash with the strongly-developed streak of paranoia Harris had. When he was in his manic phase he made amazing leaps of conjecture that seemed perfectly plausible to him. She supposed she was still unconscious and had not been screaming her lungs out and trying to beat the door down when he came down into the garage.

"Well, what did this guy look like – and who was driving the Mercedes?"

"He just looked like any middle-aged man. Nothing special. The person who was driving the car was wearing a cap and his face was in shadow, so I couldn't really see him."

"Can I look at the photos?"

Harris bent over and rummaged through a backpack on the floor before producing his camera and showing her the photos in the view-finder. Part of a man's profile showed the back of a dark head, an ear and a high cheekbone. He was dressed in jeans and white short-sleeved shirt and he was throwing something in a skip bin. A full body-shot showed him holding a large red plastic bag with "Pyrenees" written on the side. He had obviously turned just as Harris had pressed the button because his face was blurred and all that could easily be discerned was straight dark eyebrows. The small camera had its limitations. The black Mercedes was a S500 model. The Andorran plates showed the first three digits E05… the rest was in shade. A capped head inside the car was leaning over obviously opening the passenger door.

"We better send a copy of these to the police. They should be able to trace the car and maybe they can do some image-enhancing to help identify the man." Jane gave him Victor's email address.

"Done," Harris said competently. "I'll send you copies too."

Sometimes Jane forgot he was an intelligent man who just happened to have some odd thought patterns. Perhaps she should listen more closely to his ideas. Some lateral thinking couldn't hurt. Being an accountant made you think sequentially. Creative leaps of imagination weren't encouraged – except when it came to the numerous ways a client could cheat the Australian Taxation Office.

Explaining what had actually happened down in the *trastero* didn't take long, but Jane omitted details of Pearl's relationship with Fernando Ribera-Lopez. Despite the new girlfriend and protestations of change, she was afraid Harris would fall back on old habits where Pearl was concerned. She didn't want Harris up on a charge of aggravated assault of a government minister. Not that she was worried about Fernando's health. While she appreciated he was in a delicate situation, a concerned phone-call would have been welcome. Still, in fairness, for all she knew he could be onto the investigating detective every other moment.

"If the police trace the Mercedes it should lead them to the driver. Andorra's a small country. Pearl's photos of the Tobacco Industry should be easy enough to trace too." Harris suggested. "Someone is bound to recognise the location and identify the people."

Jane wasn't so sure. One stone-walled tobacco field looked pretty much like another as far as she could see.

"What can I do to help? Give me something to follow up. I'm not helping by just sitting around the hotel drinking," Harris said.

"Why don't you go down to Police Headquarters and introduce yourself to Victor? Get him to fill you in and ask whether finger-printing the car or the champagne bottle has turned up anything. See if the public have responded to the articles in the papers or if there are any reported sightings. Maybe they'd let you go on some of the helicopter sweeps. If so, pay particular attention to the GR 7 route that goes over *Portella Blanca*. I get the feeling that the police may not be as forthcoming about that as they could be. Since you and Pearl are still married, you might have authority to ask questions and to be included in the investigation. Only Harris, be aware that you could also be considered a suspect in her disappearance. They'll want to confirm when you arrived, and so on, so you should take your passport and airline tickets."

Harris nodded. It made sense to him. "What will you be doing?"

"Charles is arriving tomorrow or the next day, and then we have the meeting of the trust to prepare for. I'll call you tomorrow night and we can share information. Oh, and I'd like Pearl's photo-album back."

"I'll drop it off tomorrow." Harris nodded at the barman, "I'll have another."

The smell of the beer followed her home.

CHAPTER FOURTEEN

The morning dawned to a heavy squall of rain. A crash of thunder woke Jane. Flashes of brilliant lightning assailed her through the open window. Throwing a blanket over her shoulders, she crept out of bed to secure a loose shutter banging on the exterior wall. It was her birthday. She was thirty-nine years old. She went back to bed to snuggle into the still-warm cocoon. It felt like she was coming down with a cold. Many Happy Returns. In deference to the weather and in honour of her birthday she declared it a run-free day.

An hour later she went in search of comfort food. A packet of oatmeal caught her eye and she opted for porridge cooked in the microwave. She wasn't expecting her birthday to provide much else in the way of comfort. For as long as she could remember, birthdays had been a source of disappointment. As a child, her mother had bought her sensible clothes in lieu of a birthday treat. Bruce bought her flowers, perfume or lingerie. Although she had always expressed pleasure at him remembering, she wished he had put some thought into what would surprise or delight her – a special book, tickets to a show, maybe a surprise weekend away in the country, even a long walk on the beach at sunset. His gifts left her feeling like a generic wife. One year, while at a law and order conference in the Middle East, he'd bought her a fine gold chain linked to a word written in flowing Arabic script.

"What does it say?" She was thrilled.

"It's your name."

For months she didn't take it off, then one day a man approached her at the supermarket to ask if she was a Muslim. When she laughingly said no, he said, "but your necklace says Allah Akbar, God is Great." Bruce had never asked why she stopped wearing it.

She ate the porridge standing at the window and looking through a curtain of rain at the village. The gutters of the road were six inches deep and cars sluiced around the roundabout splashing early morning pedestrians who were battling their umbrellas in the gusting wind. More cars were lined up, idling by the no-parking zone next to the bus-stop, as parents waited inside with their children for the school bus. Windshields were densely fogged. Trucks trundled by on their way to construction sites.

She switched the television to CNN and, alternating with Sky, caught up on world events. Famine in Eritrea. More school shootings in America. Revolutionary new policies to encourage the long-term unemployed back into work. A drug bust in Miami. Same old, same old. She dozed until the phone woke her again.

"Hi Mum," she spoke over the refrain of 'A Happy Birthday to You'.

"I remember what I was doing thirty-nine years ago," her mother reminisced waggishly. "I've bought you a lovely nightie. I'll keep it until you get home."

Jane habitually slept in an oversized T-shirt. She couldn't imagine a less useful present. "Great, thanks, just what I needed," she said, wondering if her mother would ever give her something to treasure.

It was hard to summon the energy but eventually the day's programme had to begin. She called the notary Ramon Saboya's office, and made an appointment before carefully wrapping a brown paper package and placing it in a cloth carry-bag. Pearl's raincoat had sleeves a good two inches too short for her but it would have to do. The rain was coming down in sheets – in duvets, it was so thick.

"Escaldes," she said, giving the bus-driver the correct change. A passing car had splashed water over her shoes and she squelched her way to the back of the bus. Where she alighted, the street was dense with shops. Half the shopfronts looked like a parody of the 1950s, while the remainder were smart marble and polished wood. Entering the first in a line of electronic goods shops, Jane asked to see their smallest recorder. A palm-sized model was produced. She tested it and, making sure that the batteries and mini-cassette were included, paid the asking price without a quibble.

Her appointment with Saboya was not prolonged. Fortunately she had thought to bring her passport for identification purposes. It did not take him long to explain the nature of Pearl's business with him and to show her the official-looking documents complete with many crimson wax seals. He then carefully folded them back into their original long brown envelopes and placed them in his enormous walk-in safe.

The offices of the *Ministeri d'Urbanisme* were several streets away. She consulted the ground floor directory and took the lift up to the third floor.

"Señor Ribera-Lopez?" she enquired, proffering her wrapped package. The young receptionist held out a hand weighed down by multi coloured bracelets.

"*Eres su secretaria?*" Jane asked.

"No," the young woman waved her brightly manicured hand towards a door behind her desk. Each of her fingernails was painted in a competing colour.

Jane nodded, dazzled. "*Gracias.*" She let herself into a lavishly-appointed anteroom.

A middle-aged woman looked up from her computer. The light from the floor-to-ceiling windows bounced off her steely glasses. "*Si?*" her clipped voice enquired.

"Señor Ribera-Lopez?" Jane once again waggled the parcel. The woman reached for it, but Jane pulled it back. "*Es personal.*"

The secretary's radar blipped at the sound of Jane's accent. "He isn't here," she switched to nearly accent-free English

"I'll wait!" Jane sat down and took out a book, underlining her determination to stay until satisfied. The woman's eyes rested thoughtfully on her for a good five minutes before she spoke rapidly into the phone. Several minutes later two uniformed men walked in. The pockets of their grey jackets were embroidered *AAA Seguretat*.

In stilted English, the tall cadaverously thin man said, "I am with security. What's in the bag?"

"It's personal. The Minister wouldn't like you to interfere. Take my word for it."

The short fat man simply ripped the package out of Jane's hands, and held it to his ears. Nothing ticked. He shook it. Nothing rattled. He squeezed, then tore it open – unwinding yards of tissue paper to unveil the photo of Pearl and the Minister.

As he examined it in surprise, Jane said blandly, "My sister is missing in mysterious circumstances. She's a close, personal friend of the Minister. I believe the phrase is *compañera simpática*. I'm sure he would like a photo of them together to remind him of their intimate moments." She put as much insinuation as she could into the phrase.

The security man blanched, dropped the photo and wrapping-paper onto the desk as if scorched, and shouted at the secretary. He made it very clear that they did not wish to be involved in the matter.

As they speedily exited the room, Jane grinned. She had enjoyed the exchange. Sitting irresolute for a moment, the older woman then came to a decision and left the room. Going for instructions, Jane thought, and popped a throat lozenge in her mouth. Actually, this birthday was turning out rather better than she'd expected. After another five minutes the secretary returned and said, "The Minister has returned and will see you now. Please come this way."

The office was panelled in dark wood with several oriental rugs on the polished wooden floor. Lighted alcoves displayed a collection of ceramics with a blue and white patina. One complete wall held a series of photographs of the churches and bridges of Romanic Andorra. Jane wondered if they were Pearl's work. The man sitting behind the jarringly modern glass and brushed aluminium desk was dressed with subdued elegance in a tasteful suit. Silver graced the temples of his dark hair. His face was strong and sun tanned. She'd seen him before of course, both on the television and in person at the concert, but the animal magnetism and good looks were still astonishing.

He stood politely. "Please do have a seat." His English accent was as flawless as his appearance. He resumed his place behind the desk as Jane continued to survey the room.

"Are you Houdini?"

The urbane minister looked puzzled. "I beg your pardon, I don't…"

"Your secretary said you had just returned, but I came through the only door."

He didn't get it.

She shrugged. "Never mind."

She slipped her hand into her shoulder-bag to start the recorder, pulled out a tissue, and blew her nose. "Sorry. I'm getting a cold."

The regarded each other in silence for half a minute until she slid the photo across his desk.

"You haven't phoned me about my sister's disappearance."

Seemingly fascinated by her appearance, he said, "You're not at all alike."

"No we're not." She made no effort to conceal her irritation at this all too familiar remark. "You're hardly the caring lover I expected either."

He drew himself up, officious. "I assure you, I've been keeping abreast of developments through channels."

"Channels? What do these channels think has happened to your mistress?" Clumsy, but she wanted to get it on tape.

His eyebrows rose in surprise. "Mistress? That hardly describes my friendship with your independent sister. I am certain Pearl would never describe our relationship in that way." He laced his fingers together atop the desk. "Why, actually, are you here? For what purpose?"

Hot anger rose in her chest. "I'm tired of waiting! Tired of waiting for you to offer help, tired of waiting to learn of a police interview with you that never eventuates. I see now that it's up to me to find her. Just tell me this. When did you see Pearl last? What did you talk about? Did she say she was going somewhere? What do you think could have happened to her? Surely you must have an opinion."

His face showed nothing. "Our police will handle the investigation better than an intrusive foreigner."

"I don't agree. I'm told the police have not interviewed you. On Saturday I reported my sister missing, yet five days later – five days – you, Pearl's known lover have made no statement whatsoever."

He moistened his lips, ready to reply, when Jane forged ahead, heedless. "If this were anywhere else, you'd be a prime suspect in her disappearance. But here you are hiding behind your position and using your power to shield you from police inquiries."

Fernando regarded her soberly. "You are very headstrong."

"Not headstrong, persistent. Believe me. I won't go away until I am satisfied." She sat back and adjusted her bag, hoped that the tiny tape hadn't run out. The verbal fencing was taking too long.

His upper lip paled, faintly beaded with sweat. "I have not seen Pearl for quite some time. Our friendship" – he stressed the word – "was not so intimate that we saw each other regularly. I have no idea where she is or what, if anything, has happened to her. I hope she has come to no harm. She is a very special person."

"Special? She's more than special."

He shot his cuff and glanced at his watch. "Please accept my apologies for being so thoughtless. I should have called to express my sympathy and concern. The pressure of my official duties sometimes distracts me from good manners." He rose as if to dismiss her.

Jane remained seated. "I'll ask you again. When did you last see Pearl?"

He seemed amused by her question. "My sister, Jane, the bulldog."

"A dog is a faithful animal, unlike a rat."

"You are ill-informed, and prone to hasty judgements." He walked to the window and stared out, his hands in his trouser-pockets spoiling the line of his suit. "We had dinner together last month when she returned from Kosovo. The date's in my appointment book. We went to Versailles, a favourite French Restaurant nearby. We agreed to stop seeing each other. We both knew our relationship had no future." When he turned from the window his face was drawn, his eyes pained. "I have no idea what has happened to her. No idea at all. That night she said nothing of her plans, and we have not spoken since."

Hoping the recorder still ran, Jane challenged him. "I believe there were outstanding matters to be resolved between you." She waited for his reply as second by second passed.

"I don't know what you mean."

She would get no more. She stood up. "I'll let myself out."

CHAPTER FIFTEEN

Restaurant Versailles was two hundred metres up a narrow cobbled street flanked by art galleries and antique shops. The front door opened into a shadowy room crowded with five tables and a long, high bar. Jane stumbled down a hidden step and banged her shin. "Bloody hell!" she said, causing a waiter to materialise from the kitchen.

"We open at one."

"Thank you. I'd like to reserve a table."

The young man smiled and indicated two tables set for four against the shuttered window. She chose the one in the corner, furthest from the door and the tricky step.

"Thank you, it will just be for one person. *Me llamo*, Jane".

"It would be hard to forget you," he said.

The restaurant was close to a busy shopping precinct. As she meandered up the road, window-shopping, she came across a clutch of boutiques stocked with expensive couturier clothing. Impulsively, she entered one and bought a colourful shirt made of embroidered handkerchiefs sewn together patchwork style. The adjacent store offered a pair of castanets for her secretary's grand-daughter and an embroidered scarf for her mother. Jane wondered if unremarkable gift selection ran in the genes. She was sure it wasn't the done thing to go shopping in the current circumstances, but she couldn't think of what else to do. She bought an *International Herald Tribune* to read over lunch and the local daily, *Diari d'Andorra* to look for any mention of Pearl.

By the time one o'clock arrived, the rain had returned, pushed vertically along the street by a powerful north wind. Turning up her collar and holding the lapels closed with crossed hands, she scurried back to the restaurant where she burst through the door, and fell down the step again; bumping into the first table and spilling the occupants' soup. An attractive woman in leather trousers stepped forward and grasped her elbow to steady her.

"*Si?*"

Jane sank down at the corner table, "*Tengo una reserva.* I have a reservation."

The woman brought a dish of olives with the *à la carte* menu.

The daily specials were handwritten inside the front cover in Catalan.

"*Por favor*," Jane beckoned the woman.

"*Momentito*, one moment," the woman said, and disappeared into the kitchen.

The same young waiter reappeared to translate, carefully explaining each dish. "It's a family business. My father's the chef and my mother is the *maître d'*. Can I recommend a half bottle of wine from our home village of Corbieres?"

"Just mineral water, thanks, plus the oysters baked with *foie gras*, and then the *bouillabaisse*."

The young man nodded his approval of her choices. Before he could return to the kitchen, Jane pulled out Pearl's photo. "My friend recommended this restaurant. She said it was her favourite."

"Señora Pearl! A lovely woman. We see her quite often."

"Have you seen her recently? I've been trying to contact her."

The young man consulted volubly with his mother, who shook her head. "She came in with Señor Ribera-Lopez a few weeks ago, and left in the middle of the meal without finishing her sea bream. We haven't seen her since," he relayed.

This confirmed Fernando's story of their disagreement, but didn't mean the dinner had been the last time Fernando had seen Pearl.

The first oyster sailed down her throat on angel wings. As she reached for the second, her mobile phone rang.

"I missed you at the gym this morning. Where are you?" said Juan-Antonio.

"I'm downtown having lunch."

"Anywhere special?"

Jane listened for any tone of censure in his voice, sure that the family of a missing person should stay at home, waiting by the phone for news. She glanced at the beautiful restaurant and her plate of rapidly cooling oysters.

"No. Not really," she lied.

"I noticed it was your birthday today when we took the details from your passport. If you have no other plans, would you like to have dinner? It's a shame to be alone and worrying on your birthday."

"How kind," Jane said cautiously. "But I'm getting a cold and I really should have an early night." She wondered if Ribera-Lopez had called his cousin and the invitation was a prelude to warning her off.

"Well, I could come and cook dinner? Do you like fish?"

"I love fish. Thank you. It is difficult to spend your birthday alone." Jane felt like crying at the small gesture by the burly village policeman.

"I'll see you around nine o'clock then?"

Jane wondered what an early night constituted in Andorra, obviously sometime around midnight. "Fine," she said, smiling at four soberly clad businessmen as they walked through the door. One of the men was so captivated by her glance that he immediately fell down the errant step and banged into the nearby table, causing yet another spilt food incident. Jane was pleased she wasn't the only one lacking savoir-faire.

"Bye," she sang into her phone.

When the *bouillabaisse* arrived it was, if anything, even better than the oysters. She could see why this would be Pearl's favourite restaurant. She liked the European insistence on seasonal variety. In Australia foods were irradiated for long shelf life and most things were available twelve months of the year. Europeans seemed satisfied to eat only what was in season. She dragged her wayward thoughts back to Pearl and began to puzzle anew the unanswered questions surrounding her disappearance. The sequence of events danced out of reach and her headache returned. A taxi home might be a good idea. Was it "feed a cold and starve a fever," or the other way around? With Juan-Antonio's dinner still to come, she hoped it was the former.

The rain continued to teem down as she paid the taxi-driver and ran into the foyer of the apartment block. Mary was sitting glumly on the stairs by the lift with Trevor the comatose cat on her knee.

"Hi. What's up?"

Mary's face brightened. "Oh Jane, I'm so bored. Dad's gone out and our power's gone off so I can't watch TV."

Jane suppressed an inward sigh. She had been planning an hour or two in bed. "Come up with me then. We can play some card games or something."

"Great!' Mary's pale freckled face lit up with a hundred kilowatt smile. "Can we do some cooking too?"

"We'll see," Jane said, in unconscious imitation of her mother.

They climbed the stairs together, Trevor assuming the handbag position. He was such a fat cat, Jane wondered if he could actually walk. After letting them both in with her key, Jane noticed her power was off as well. The circuit breaker was just by the door and a power surge had flicked off the master switch. She turned it back on and heard the fridge motor kick in.

"Now I know how to fix ours myself," Mary said with great satisfaction. "Mum says I should learn to be independent."

They opened the cupboard in the kitchen and surveyed the stores. "What about scones?" asked Jane. "I learnt to make them when I was about your age." One of her happiest memories was learning to cook with her mother. It was the one time they were in harmony. Her mother cooked with great flair. On Sunday, after church, they would spend hours preparing a three-course meal. Out would come all the mismatched family antiques – bought at thrift shops and second hand stores. The table was a smorgasbord of Royal Doulton and Prince Albert china bracketed by sterling silver cutlery with a variety of hallmarks. "Anyone can have matching sets," her mother would say, laying the table with Gourmet magazines for placemats – for once impervious to social mores.

"The secret to nice puffy scones is not to pat them down too much!" Jane said as they slipped a tray of scones into the oven. They set the oven clock for ten minutes and Mary skipped around impatiently, counting down as if the scones were about to launch themselves into space. The scones came out doubled in size with golden tops. Jane mentally added up the calories she had consumed that day and thought about the dinner to come. When on earth was she going to get her appetite under control and stop substituting food for alcohol? Currently her only love affair was with lunch. How pathetic. Step Ten. Continue to take personal inventory and when wrong promptly admit it. Tomorrow she'd run further and faster and begin a new diet.

Mary had no such qualms and polished off two scones before contemplating a third. "Could I have the recipe so I can make some for Mum when I go home? She works hard and doesn't get much time for cooking."

"What does she do?"

"She's a social worker for the council. Mostly she counsels drug addicts."

"Do you think you'll do something like that when you get older?" asked Jane, curious to see if Mary wanted to emulate her mother.

"No way!" answered Mary. "I'd like to do something with animals. They're much nicer than people... although some people are very nice," she added quickly.

They heard the elevator doors open and checked the passageway. Lyn was putting the key in his door and talking over his shoulder to a well-muscled man with a striking head of dishwater-blonde dreadlocks. He lifted his eyebrows when he saw Mary and Jane framed in the doorway.

"Jane. Dave." Lyn introduced them. Dave had tattooed spider webs on each elbow. On the knuckles of his right hand, the word, "good", appeared. On his left, "evil". His leather jeans looked spray-painted on.

"How ya doing," Dave said in an easy-going, distinctively American drawl.

"Dad, the power went off," Mary broke in, "But Jane fixed it, and then we cooked some scones."

"Great!" Lyn said, nodding his thanks as Mary tripped ahead with Dave to open the apartment door opposite. "I hope she wasn't any trouble."

"No problem, Lyn. She's good company. I enjoyed myself."

She was surprised to realise this was true. The afternoon had passed quickly and there was still time for a short rest before Juan-Antonio arrived – but first she'd call Harris as promised.

CHAPTER SIXTEEN

Having been abandoned by Mary, Trevor the cat had in some mysterious way levitated onto the sofa without Jane seeing his feet touch the ground. He lay curled at the end of the couch, a big furry cushion. Jane carefully placed her bare feet against him. His warm purring vibrated through her soles and up her legs. She didn't think she would give him back; life had unexpected pleasures to be savoured when encountered. She sat blissfully for a full ten minutes before reaching for the phone. "Señor Wentworth, *por favor*?"

The phone rang endlessly before the receptionist asked if she would like to leave a message. She left her name and number then pulled the colourful pashmina from the back of the sofa and wrapped it around her, soaking up the warmth and feeling mellow. She didn't move again until nearly eight o'clock when Mary knocked on the door to reclaim Trevor. It was only then that she headed for the bathroom to shower and change for dinner.

She was surprised to find herself wavering over what to wear. The new shirt looked good, but since she hadn't noticed any women over thirty in Andorra wearing jeans, she settled upon a pair of loose, drawstring linen trousers. She fluffed up her hair, applied her makeup, sprayed a chiffon of duty-free perfume into the air in front of her and walked through the mist. A pair of pearl stud earrings from Broome, a present from Pearl, added the final touch. She touched both hands to her ears. The phone rang in time to interrupt her usual longing for a pre-dinner drink.

"Hi!" It was Harris. "I just got in. I went to buy some hiking gear after my appointment with the police. I didn't get anywhere with them. They already knew about the restraining order Pearl took out on me in Australia and viewed me with extreme suspicion. Actually, that surprised me. I didn't expect them to be so thorough."

Jane thought about her conversation with Juan-Antonio and had no doubt that he had passed the information straight on to Victor.

"After I gave them the photos there was a fair bit of consternation! I got the impression they knew exactly who owned the Mercedes, but when I asked whether they could identify the man in the street or the car, they just said they would 'look into it'. They obviously didn't want me to know anything and they kept talking back and forth in Catalan. It pissed me off."

"What about fingerprints?"

"They have all the latest computer equipment and it's linked to a forensic data bank. Impressive for a small country. They said the fingerprints on the champagne bottle didn't come up with any matches, then they grilled me for a bit, and checked my passport and entry stamps and car-hire documents. After they confirmed my travel itinerary they basically stonewalled. They wouldn't let me ride in the helicopter because of insurance concerns. It was just a bloody royal run around, so I thought I'd hike to *Portella Blanca* myself tomorrow, if only to satisfy us both that there is nothing to be found there."

"Couldn't you wait until Friday?" Jane asked, feeling a rising note of disquiet. "Then I could come with you. I can't go tomorrow because of the trust meeting."

"You really can't go anywhere, Jane. You have to be near to the police in case something develops. I'll check in by phone."

"Well, mobiles have a limited battery life. What happens if you get into trouble and you can't call? Or if the mountains interfere with transmission or something?" she said.

"If I don't check in every twenty-four hours you can send out the cavalry. It shouldn't take long to hike across to Porta. I've got a backpack and a rainproof jacket, and I'll take water and trail-mix. Aboriginal sacred sites are usually in isolated areas so I'm used to roughing it for long periods of time."

"It can snow in September in the higher altitudes," Jane reminded him, still not liking the idea of him going off on his own.

"Yeah. Yeah. Don't worry. I've got a polar fleece. You forget I've done lots of hiking in New Zealand so I'm used to changes of weather," he said, sounding fond of her.

"I'm not worried about your ability, Harris, I just wish you'd take someone with you. Apparently a French woman died last year after injuring herself when she was hiking on her own. What about taking Jorge, the young waiter I told you about? I could call him and ask if he'd hike with you. He was really keen to help and looks fit. He speaks Catalan and good English – so he could be handy."

Harris groaned. "You can call him if you like, but if he isn't ready early tomorrow morning, I'll go without him. It's been far too long already without any trace of Pearl. Tell him to call me at the hotel. I'll be here for the rest of the night."

Jane called Jorge immediately but got an answering-machine with an incomprehensible message in Catalan. She left a brief message. It was the best she could do. She hoped his offer of help hadn't been an empty promise.

The Crillon Hotel said her father wasn't in. She wondered what he'd discovered about Jack Weinstein. Hopefully they would have time to fill each other in before the trust meeting the following day. Maybe Charles's training as an historian would divine a pattern that was invisible to her. Just as she was considering logging on to her email, Juan-Antonio arrived, his arms festooned with bags of groceries. After he deposited them in the kitchen, he ceremoniously kissed her on both cheeks.

"Happy Birthday, Jane! You look pretty good for someone coming down with a cold." He flourished a bottle of what looked suspiciously like champagne, but turned out to be sparkling pear juice, putting it in the freezer with two glasses, and continued pulling things out of bags. Firstly a whole Dorado, then lemons, parsley, eggs, a large bag of salt, curly leafed lettuce, baby potatoes, olives stuffed with anchovies and a log of lemon-coated ice cream. He then started peering into cupboards and pulling out baking trays and serving dishes, all the while chatting about what he was doing. Jane sat at the kitchen table out of his way, enjoying the manner in which he was turning everyday cooking into theatre.

"First I will get the fish in the oven. Have you ever had fish baked in salt? You paint the outside with egg white then cover it with coarse salt and bake it for twenty-five minutes. This will be the most delicious way you have ever eaten fish. In Barcelona they sometimes cook a fillet of pork this way too. The potatoes just need to boil for a little while and I'll make a simple salad of lettuce. You have oil and vinegar of course?" He rummaged around and pulled out two cruets. "While everything cooks we will have olives and an aperitif of pear juice."

Jane was touched. "You are spoiling me, Juan-Antonio. Where did you learn how to cook?"

"Mostly from my grandmother. My mother didn't cook much, but my grandmother never stopped. She was in the kitchen from morning to night. It was warm and comfortable there, and she would give me little jobs to do for her to keep me occupied. Now I am a single man again, I am thankful for the training," he paused as if wondering whether to continue. "My wife had her faults, but I must say she was a very good cook. Her paella was magnificent."

He closed the oven door with a crash, making Jane jump. "Andorrans like good food. Once I was in Madrid with some friends and we went to several *tapas* bars. At about eleven o'clock we Andorranos wanted to know where we were going for dinner. Our Madrileñan friends said the *tapas* served as dinner and they went home; but we went on to a restaurant for a proper three-course meal!" He patted his paunch ruefully and rolled his eyes at her. She laughed, liking this man.

"Did you do any cooking when you were still with your wife?"

He shook his head. "No. We had a traditional relationship. She cooked and looked after our boy, and I went to work."

"Was that your idea or hers?" Jane was trying to get a sense of where the marriage had gone wrong.

"We never talked of it."

"Do you think if she worked, Andorra might not have bored her?"

"She doesn't work now," he answered.

They sat down with the dish of olives and sipped their pear juice. Jane produced an ashtray for Juan-Antonio. She could see it was bothering him not to smoke. He lit up immediately and smiled at her as he exhaled. "You notice small things. You'd make a good policeman."

"My job is a bit like being a detective. I follow clues when I audit a company's books. I have a memory that highlights any inconsistencies."

"Tell me about one of your cases."

Jane put her finger to her lips, "Don't ask. Don't tell," she said lightly. "I have to consider my professional ethics." She considered what she had just said, "but most Australians have an element of Ned Kelly in them and they don't think cheating the tax man is criminal... Ned Kelly was a famous Australian bush-ranger, or outlaw...." She broke off, realising that her explanation was becoming too complicated. It must be hard for a man and woman of different nationalities to resolve their differences without a common language and background.

"At one of the big companies I audited, they drank Grange Hermitage wine at $600 a bottle during board meetings while they drove the company into bankruptcy. I attended an emotional shareholders' meeting *post mortem*, complete with weeping widows who'd lost their retirement funds in a supposedly blue chip company. The board members didn't seem to think they had anything to apologise for." She shook her head. "There's a lot of greed in the corporate world but usually it stops just short of illegal activity. Tell me about one of your cases Juan-Antonio?"

"How many double-parked cars did I move on today?"

"There must be more to the job than that?"

He shrugged.

The fish looked delicious, light and delicate. Juan-Antonio cracked the hard shell of salt and carefully pulled the flesh away from the bones. Placing the boned fillets on two plates with a slice of lemon and the potatoes, he poured olive oil over the top and scattered some chopped parsley. The dish of salad he put in between them on the table.

"There's wine in the *trastero* if you'd like some," said Jane.

"It doesn't matter to me," he replied   "Do you miss it?"

"Yes, especially when I'm having a lovely meal like this."

"When did you know that you were an alcoholic?"

Jane hated to talk about it. "My husband and I were in an accident. I was driving. He was killed. Afterwards I had to confront the fact that my drinking was out of control."

"How terrible for you," said Juan-Antonio, his voice gentle.

"Worse for him," said Jane bleakly. The fish turned to ashes in her mouth but she chewed mindlessly for a while before continuing. "We were at a twentieth wedding-anniversary party. It was a Saturday. That afternoon a woman called. She came right to the point and told me Bruce was the father of the baby she was expecting. She asked what I was going to do about it." Jane paused and took a sip of juice. "I slammed the phone down and took the receiver off the hook so she couldn't call back. I had my first drink then, around three o'clock. By the time Bruce came home from golf, I'd had quite a few more. I was very calm. I think I was in shock. He walked in the door and I said 'Congratulations!' And he laughed and asked, 'What did I win?' I said, 'You're going to be a father.'" Jane stopped, took a deep breath, put a forkful of food in her mouth and managed to swallow it without gagging despite the lack of saliva in her mouth.

"Bruce thought I was pregnant. We had been trying so long to have a child. He looked pleased...happy...and said; when did you find out? And I said 'Mandy called me a few hours ago.'"

Juan-Antonio moved his chair closer and put his arm around her.

"Well, at first he didn't know what to say. He told me the affair didn't mean anything and that he truly loved me. He even said he would give Mandy money for an abortion. I couldn't understand how he could reject his own child. It was like I had been living with a stranger and our whole life together was a fantasy. I kept drinking. He kept saying, 'Why don't you cry, or hit me, or something. I'm so sorry.' I could hardly speak I was so distraught. He suggested that we make our excuses and not go to the party, but it was for his partner in the police force and he and his wife would be upset if we stayed away. I remember saying, 'At least I have good manners, if nothing else.' I was actually proud of how composed I was being."

Jane took another sip of her juice, and dabbed her streaming eyes with a napkin. Juan-Antonio hugged her encouragingly.

"Looking back I realise I had been a functioning alcoholic for a long time. I was used to drinking and hiding the effects so that no-one could tell. That made me pretty good at concealing my feelings too."

Jane could not bear to look at Juan-Antonio while she was telling him this so she kept her eyes on her plate and pushed the food around with her fork.

"We avoided each other at the party. Bruce drank quite a lot and, as usual, I had the keys to drive home. We left about two in the morning, so I'd been drinking for nearly twelve hours – although no-one seemed to notice when we said goodnight. His partner did come up to me at one point during the night to ask if everything was alright, and I said, 'Oh yes, brilliant. Lovely party!'

"In Perth, there's a problem with some of the aboriginal kids."

Juan-Antonio blinked at the apparent *non-sequitur* but she continued, "They have high unemployment and feel like they're not accepted. Life doesn't offer them much, so they sniff glue, and drink, and generally get into a lot of trouble. They steal cars and the police try to catch them. It's controversial, but the police say they'll abandon the pursuit if they feel there is danger to the public.

"We were nearly home when we heard the police sirens. I was driving through a green light at an intersection just two streets from home when the stolen car came through the red light and hit us on the front passenger side. Bruce was killed instantly. The kids all jumped out of the car and ran off into the night. The police cars were just a second or two behind them. There were two cars. The police in the first one ran off to search for the kids, and the other two came over to our car. I was still coherent and I said, 'My husband is Detective Bruce Burns. Could you please get him an ambulance straight away!'... But it was too late." She started to sob in earnest.

"But Jane," he whispered. "Then it was not your fault at all."

She wailed, "But I wanted it. I was an accident waiting to happen. I had no business driving that car. I wanted him dead. I was so angry. I've never been so angry. We started arguing in the car. I kept shouting that Mandy was expecting my baby. The one we had tried to have for so long, and he was willing to pretend the baby didn't exist; and the last thing I said to him – I'll never forget it. I screamed that I could never trust him again and I wished he were dead.

"Afterwards everyone thought I was the victim. They were sorry for me." Tears poured down her cheeks. She was taking deep gasps of air but there was not enough oxygen in her lungs. Finally she pushed her chair back and ran into the bathroom and vomited. Afterwards, feeling tired and spent, she rinsed her face, gargled then brushed her teeth vigorously.

"Wanting something doesn't make it happen." He was at the bathroom door, chewing his moustache. "Are you OK?"

Tears were still coursing down her cheeks. She sniffed and whispered, "It always makes me sick to my stomach when I talk about it." She turned down her mouth and shrugged. She guessed he would leave now.

"Life can be hard," he said.

"We had a prime minister famous for saying life wasn't meant to be easy.

"He sounds like a wise man."

"He was a politician," she disagreed.

They smiled. Juan-Antonio hugged her to him and gently kissed her on the lips.

"Careful," she said. "You'll catch my cold."

"I'll take my chances," he replied, and kissed her again.

CHAPTER SEVENTEEN

Juan-Antonio's body was wrapped around her, his arm across her shoulder, when Jane woke. The bed cover had slipped to the floor during the night and her feet were cold. As she stirred, he lifted one eyelid.

"Are we running this morning?" he asked, pressing closer.

"Hell no," she replied.

Later he came whistling out of the shower, a towel slung casually around his waist. He saw her watching him and drew in his stomach, then laughed at his own vanity and relaxed. She laughed too, feeling comfortable with him. She liked the look of him, solid and bear-like with hairy chest and shoulders.

"We can have the ice-cream for breakfast."

"I am as hungry as a wolf, woman. You'll have to do better than that!"

"How about a traditional English breakfast? Bacon and eggs?"

Jane cleared the debris left from dinner while the bacon sizzled in the pan. She was dazed by this unexpected development in her life. As a romantic start to an evening, on a scale of one to ten she would have rated throwing up after a man cooked her dinner as a minus one. Life was exceedingly strange and unpredictable.

The doorbell rang and Juan-Antonio popped his head out of the bathroom and raised his eyebrows at her.

"Yes or no?" Her hand enquired, tilting up and down. He shrugged and closed the bathroom door.

Victor stood at the door, two men at his shoulders.

"Is there news?" she asked, her heart pounding.

"No, I'm sorry, *Señora*. We are here to search the apartment for evidence," replied one of the unknown men. Victor nodded.

"What evidence?"

"Evidence. Clues. Whatever," said the young man.

"It's 8.30 in the morning. Couldn't you have called first?"

"We have other duties, and had to fit this in as well," said Victor.

Jane wasn't at all sure how Juan-Antonio was going to feel about this. As she opened her mouth to protest further Dave poked his unruly head out of the front door of the apartment opposite.

"Heard a commotion. Are you OK, Jane?"

"The police are here to search the apartment," she said. Dave passed the information inside to Lyn and Mary and all three of them came into the already crowded hall.

"We'll keep you company?" Lyn nodded meaningfully at her. "Make sure it's all on the up and up," and before she could say another word the three of them brushed past the police and trooped into the apartment. Victor followed hot on their heels, protesting. Mary went into the kitchen and took the pan of burning bacon off the flame, then came back to lean against Jane. Lyn stalked into the lounge and Dave stationed himself at the end of the hall where he could monitor the bedrooms and bathrooms. "Making sure they don't plant something," he said.

Jane was bemused. So was Victor when Juan-Antonio strolled out of the bathroom and into the chaos. Jane guessed the explosion of Catalan was Victor asking what the hell Juan-Antonio was doing here. Juan-Antonio was equally interested in what Victor was doing. Neither seemed inclined to answer the other one, they just kept shouting over the top of each other. Jane left them to it and went to brew a pot of coffee. It was all too much without some caffeine in her.

"Coffee?" she asked in general, pouring one for Juan-Antonio and handing it to him after stirring in the sugar. She broke open a new packet of sugar lumps and put it on the table. Destroying the cocaine would have been a good idea, she thought. She walked down the hall holding the coffee-pot in order to see what was going on. Dave was in the bathroom frowning at the policeman putting the few pharmaceuticals into a plastic bag. When Jane looked over the policeman's shoulder she flashed back to her inventory the first night of her stay. There were headache tablets, vitamins, makeup and birth control pills but she was pretty sure that there had been no jar of bath-salts. Someone had subsequently planted the jar filled with cocaine.

After taking a call on his mobile phone, Juan-Antonio left, saying that he would call her later. He kissed her on both cheeks and headed for the door. Jane sat at the kitchen table drinking coffee and prepared to wait until the policemen had finished. They were thorough, flicking through books and looking under carpets in what was an encore of her search two days before. Mary was in the lounge watching TV and peppering the young policeman with questions at the same time. She spoke a confusing mixture of English, Spanish and Catalan which the policeman had no trouble in deciphering. Not much time passed before Jane's phone rang and her father was on the line.

"Sorry, I didn't get back to you last night, but I came in rather late." Jane was pleased about that. "I'm calling from the rental car; I got an early flight. Thought I'd let you know that I went to Weinstein's address yesterday and his office was locked. It's an extraordinary building by the way, very Gothic, all turrets and gargoyles. I wouldn't have been surprised to meet Dracula on the stairs. Didn't have a wooden stake or any garlic on me either." As usual her father got waylaid by non-essentials.

"Anyway, I talked to his neighbours. Apparently he's some sort of Simon Wiesenthal. You know, the famous Nazi hunter? Did you ever read the book *The Boys from Brazil*? Gripping story-line."

Jane wasn't sure if this was a rhetorical question, or whether her father expected an answer.

"Well, it turns out that Jack Weinstein does the same sort of thing. Although rather than chase down the actual Nazis he's more interested in chasing down the funds and assets the Nazis stole and secreted away. I bet the gnomes in the Swiss banks don't like him much. They must have been shocked when they were forced to make reparation so many years after the event," he chortled.

"I bought one of those new fangled speaker phones so I can drive with two hands on the wheel and speak at the same time. I can hear perfectly through the earphones. Technology's amazing isn't it?"

Jane had a vision of her father tooling along the auto-route talking with both hands gesticulating wildly, rather than on the wheel where they belonged.

"There was actually an organisation called Odessa you know. Frederick Forsyth didn't invent it. They helped ex-Nazis escape from Germany via the Brenner Pass, and on to Spain or Latin America. Franco was always 'simpatico' to the Nazis of course. He'd wanted to join the Axis to share in the spoils. He had his eye on Morocco.

"Of course Hitler realised the Spanish economy had collapsed and he wasn't about to be involved in propping it up. It was only when Franco saw he couldn't get a deal with Hitler that he announced he had negotiated Spanish neutrality. What a load of codswallop."

"Charles, where are we going with this? You seem to have lost sight of Weinstein?"

"I'm getting to that. They estimate that two to three thousand Nazis escaped into Spain after the fall of Germany. Just before, or around, armistice a number went from Vichy France across the Pyrenees into Spain, through Andorra."

"What?" squeaked Jane incredulously, then quickly lowered her voice as the policeman in the kitchen looked interested. "What on earth has this got to do with anything?"

"I have no idea. I left a note under the door for Mr Weinstein explaining about Pearl and asked him to get in touch."

"Did the neighbours have an idea where he is or when he'd be back?"

"None whatsoever. Apparently he's often away for periods of time. He doesn't have a permanent staff, just volunteers."

"What's his involvement then, do you think?"

"We need more facts, Jane. No use in going off half-cock. I'll be in Andorra in about two to three hours. I'm just past Foix. I'll stop at Louis Durand in Tarascon and buy you some *foie gras*."

"Thanks Charles, but I really don't need the calories."

"I'd like to buy you something. Your mother called to remind me about your birthday." Jane wasn't aware that her mother still talked to her father. It just went to show that you could wallpaper a house with the things she didn't know.

"The police are here at the moment going over the apartment with a fine toothcomb. I'm not sure what they are looking for – hopefully for clues that will help them find Pearl." She was mindful of the policeman in the kitchen, looking through the cupboards and eavesdropping at the same time. He was very close to the sugar jar.

"I won't keep you then. I'll call you when I get to the hotel."

Jane jumped up and put some bread into the toaster and asked the policeman if he would like anything, successfully distracting him from the cupboard he was inspecting. She ate a piece of toast redolent with butter and told Victor that Harris was planning to hike the GR 7 to *Portella Blanca*.

Victor was exasperated. "I told him not to leave Andorra."

"Well, it's only for the day. He wanted to do something helpful."

"It won't be helpful if he falls and breaks his neck," said one of the other policemen gloomily.

"Is it dangerous?" she asked, surprised.

"It's steep for about two hours, and then it levels out again when you walk in the contours of the mountain. There is a drop off at the side, but the path is reasonably wide. From *Portella Blanca* down to Porta it's easy."

"Couldn't you call your French counterparts in Porta and ask them to keep an eye out for Harris. I don't suppose he wants to hike both ways."

"They aren't very keen to co-operate with us in Porta these days. An Andorran peppered their mayor's backside with buckshot in a territorial dispute during hunting season last year," said one of the young detectives, smiling. "We still maintain the Izard was on our side."

"What was the point in Harris going to Porta?" interrupted Victor, impatient with this ancient history.

"Well, the point is," Jane enunciated slowly, "That '*Portella Blanca*' is highlighted on Pearl's map and it also features on her answering-machine. In the absence of any other ideas, or clues…" – she stressed the last word sarcastically – "…it might be an idea to find out why."

"Why would she be interested in *Portella Blanca*?"

"She's a journalist. She's always investigating."

"There is nothing to suggest that the map was marked recently, and a fragment of a conversation on an answering-machine could have been on the tape for months. You are jumping to conclusions."

Jane paused and mentally regrouped, "Well, here's an idea. You could question Señor Ribera-Lopez and ask him about his relationship with my sister and whether he has anything to do with her disappearance."

"Have you any reason to think he might have?" asked the policeman.

"Pearl and Harris had an abusive marriage. This can be a pattern in a long-term relationship. Ribera-Lopez and Pearl were lovers. He says they broke it off sometime last month, but he's in a sensitive position being a married man holding a senior government position. You'd think he'd be worth talking to."

"You certainly talked to him."

"Gotcha!" Jane snapped. The policeman's reply had unintentionally revealed that her visit to the Minister's office yesterday had been quickly followed by a complaint to the police, and possibly prompted this morning's search of the apartment. "I did talk to him. I thought he'd be more concerned, since my sister is expecting his child."

"What!" exclaimed the policemen as one. Victor picked up the clear plastic bag into which the contents of the bathroom cabinet had been placed. He pointed out the birth control pills.

"What about these?"

"The last pill was taken on a Saturday. It doesn't say in which month."

"I caution you that this is a serious slander. Her letters don't mention pregnancy, nor did you say anything when you reported your sister missing."

"It was news to me too, when her notary told me yesterday. I was going to call you about it first thing this morning."

CHAPTER EIGHTEEN

It took the police another hour to finish scouring through the apartment. In the meantime Jane took back possession of the guest room and dressed in a grey suit for her meeting with her father and the trustees. Pearl's colourful Hermes scarf with the pattern of Spanish dancing horses peeped out from behind the lapels. If Pearl couldn't be there, Jane would take something of hers to represent her; a superstitious idea that took her by surprise.

Before the policemen left, Dave had pressed them to itemise the contents of the evidence bags. He was fluent in Spanish and eventually Jane held a list of oddly-assorted items. There was no discernible pattern to what the police had taken. She had given them Saboya's card and told them he was the source who would confirm Pearl's pregnancy. The bank statement and credit card transactions had been confiscated, but Jane had long since scanned copies of these into her computer.

Lyn wanted to know, "What's with you and Juan-Antonio?"

"What do you mean?"

Dave grinned. "Do you accountants charge by the word?"

"What's to tell?" she answered, weary of the day already. Tired of constantly being on edge and not at all inclined to explain herself to anyone let alone to a tattooed stranger. "You seem to speak Spanish pretty well. How long have you been living in Andorra?"

"Not long. I met Lyn when I was out here on a ski-holiday and he convinced me to stay." Dave's dreadlocks and tattoos in no way despoiled his all-American good looks of perfect teeth and square chin. "Love at first sight you might say. The old *coup de foudre*." His French didn't sound bad either.

"Why did you think the police would plant something? Have you had a bad experience with them before?"

"We were just being gentlemen," protested Lyn in his soft Scottish burr. In his white tracksuit and halo of red curls he looked like an exhausted angel. "Pearl's a good friend of ours and she'd want us to look after her sister."

Jane felt awkward at her churlishness. "Thanks, I appreciate it."

Mary gave her a quick hug as they left.

After the door closed behind them, Jane turned on her laptop and scanned the debit charges on Pearl's bank account to see if any of the names matched the doctors listed in the yellow pages. At last she found a match. "P. Ferreira 6,000 pesetas 3 July." She scribbled the address. She'd have to hurry to catch the bus. It was annoying not to drive. She started when she caught herself thinking this. Perhaps life does go on after all.

When Jane alighted at the Avinguda Meritxell she had the curious feeling of being followed. A swirling movement, possibly the edge of a coat, caught her eye. She dawdled to see if she could catch the reflection of someone behind her in the shop windows. Mostly it was a sense of someone or something moving just out of her peripheral vision. She browsed though several perfumeries. The shops were small and she carefully noted each customer who entered. No two customers were the same and there was no untoward interest in her. She drifted down the street, looking in the display windows until she reached the Escale department store, where she increased her pace and moved quickly through the crowds of shoppers and onto the escalator. As it ascended, she overtook the customers who were patiently standing to the left-hand side. She looked over her shoulder and tried to mark any disturbance below. A man was forcing his way through the *mêlée* of shoppers close to the escalator. His face was tilted towards hers giving the impression of a whiter than usual face with straight dark brows and a focussed, pinched expression. She had no time to register more before she reached the next floor. Taking a leap from the escalator, and startling all the nearby shoppers, she landed with bent knees and scuttled towards the back of the store, keeping her head down to disguise her height and stay out of sight from the moving stairs.

In the sportswear department she grabbed some shirts from a rack and dashed straight into a dressing-room with the surprised saleswoman treading on her heels asking if she needed help. Jane did.

"*Puede usted ayudarme? Un hombre me molesta.*" A man was bothering her and she needed help.

The saleswoman could not have been more than twenty. She had the complexion of someone who spent a good deal of time indoors watching television and eating carbohydrates. The unusual request for help elicited a mumbled response that ended with the word "... *policia*".

Jane waved her mobile phone and said "*Si, ya, lo hago.*"

She speed-dialled Juan-Antonio's number. "I think the man who attacked me in the *trastero* is following me," she said without preamble. "I'm in Escale, hiding in a changing-room. Could you ask the saleswoman to go and look for a man in a leather bomber jacket and jeans."

The young woman soon returned with a repertoire of shrugs which she translated into suitable Catalan for Juan-Antonio saying she could see nobody who looked like that. Jane pressed a credit card into her palm.

"Tell her I'd like to buy a few items."

This produced an immediate transformation in attitude and a conspiratorial wink. She was obviously paid on commission. In no time, a backpack, grey tracksuit, hiking boots and a black Nike cap appeared. Jane folded her own clothes and crammed them into the backpack with her shoes and changed into the new apparel, then she simply sat down on the floor with her back to the wall and prepared to wait.

At 1.28 she left the changing room – a lanky youth carrying a backpack – and joined the saleswoman on her way out to lunch. The woman casually lit a cigarette for her as they ambled towards the staff elevator and out of the store. Jane drifted with the crowd for two streets before deciding there was no discernible disturbance to the flow.

If Saboya was surprised at Jane's metamorphosis from the smart businesswoman of the previous day to sporty youth, he gave no sign of it. He was a corpulent man in his late sixties or early seventies, his face pitted with the old scars of some forgotten childhood disease. Tufty eyebrows bracketed a prominent nose. His well-cut three-piece suit was dignified with an old-fashioned fob watch and chain across his chest. Although his English was as antiquated as his choice of dress it was more than adequate. He ushered her into his office with great courtesy, calling for his secretary to bring coffee.

"At the meeting of the trust this afternoon, would you present the documents you are holding so you can answer any questions the trustees might have?"

"Of course, madam. That is for the best because the meeting will be in Catalan."

"Naturally," sighed Jane who had imagined no such thing. "Would you also make a call for me to a Dr Ferreira? I'd like to confirm that he was the doctor Pearl consulted about her pregnancy?"

"He is a obstetrician! Who else would she consult?" Saboya was amused. He flourished his handkerchief as if he was about to conjure up a white rabbit, but merely blew his nose with a mighty trumpet and reached for the phone. The discussion that ensued was rapid and loud. Jane tried to read the barometer of passing emotions on Saboya's face. Clouds formed and turned into storms and then blew away. When he hung up the prognosis looked sunny.

"I will fax him a copy of the power of attorney and he will fax me the medical report by return."

"Great. Now I'd like to make a notarised statement about everything that has happened until now, plus the fact, or...," she corrected herself, "the possibility, that I was followed this morning. ... In case something happens to me," she added by way of explanation.

Saboya looked mournful at the mention of so much work before lunch but he squared his shoulders and looked ready for battle. He lit a fat cigar and again called in his beautiful young secretary.

"We will make this statement in both English and Catalan."

After the dictation Jane used an empty office to change back into her own, now wrinkled, clothes. Saboya witnessed her signature with an impressive red wax seal. The elderly notary added one copy of the document to those in the safe while Jane slipped the other into a pre-stamped envelope. After some thought, she decided to send it to Pearl's mother in Australia. She addressed it and put it into her backpack without further discussion.

When the taxi arrived there was some initial confusion about the post-office. Which post-office? The taxi-driver wanted to know. The French or the Spanish – and did the *señora* know they were both closed anyway? They only opened in the morning. She pulled the envelope out and checked the stamps and asked for the French. She had forgotten that Andorra had no postal service of its own.

Pearl had always asked Jane to address her letters to her, "The

Principality of Andorra, via France", explaining that, "When they are not on strike – which seems to be a lot of the time – the French have the most efficient service…." She had also told Jane, "Would you believe that mail within Andorra is free? You can send a letter at either post-office to any address in Andorra without a stamp and it arrives there the next day! That has to go down as one of the most successful negotiations by any government in history. It works perfectly all year until Christmas, when all of a sudden the volume of mail increases so dramatically the two services become totally overwhelmed and they ignore all letters without stamps until the New Year."

The traffic was thin and, after a brief pause to post the envelope, the journey to Hotel Roc de Caldes took five minutes. The hotel was set back from the road and perched on top of an escarpment overlooking the twin parishes of Escaldes-Engordonay and Andorra la Vella. The deserted foyer was all Carrara marble and gilt mirrors. Smart wickerwork chairs with comfortable cushions were arranged in conversation groups. Because the concierge struggled to speak English, Jane broke out her Spanish to repeat her request to wait for her father in his suite. There was no trouble about getting the door key. What could be the harm?

The translucent curtains of the sitting-room were drawn to one side allowing the sun to bounce off the marble floor tiles with full force. Jane's eyes felt like they had been sand-papered by tiny pieces of glass, reminding her that she hadn't slept much last night. She kicked off her shoes and sank onto the sofa, wondering if it would be OK to call Juan-Antonio again. It was difficult to sort out the rules for dating these days. Ostensibly it was OK for either party to call the other, but Jane had a feeling that the old gender rules about the woman not pursuing the man probably still applied. She should also check in with Carol, although it was late to call her secretary at home. Still, it wasn't as if she'd wake the grandchildren. They only stayed on the weekend.

"Hi, it's Jane. Sorry to call so late. Anything I need to know about?"

"Are you OK?" An attractive redhead, Carol was ten years older than Jane and in the middle of a messy divorce. Now she was married to the job. As far as executive secretaries go, Jane had won the prize.

"I'm fine. We don't seem to be getting any closer to finding out what has happened to Pearl, but we're doing our best. Is there anything in the office I should be worrying about?"

"Well," Carol sounded hesitant to bring it up, "Talbot's been on the phone. The Tax Department is going to audit him. They've sent him a questionnaire to answer and he's panic-stricken."

Talbot bought and sold antiques. Jane suspected that he was running two sets of books and dealing in cash. She hoped that he hadn't been too flamboyant with his spending habits.

"Tell him to fax in the paperwork and we'll respond to it." Jane did not want her client's signature on a document that might contain false information. Tax fraud now carried jail time as well as financial penalties. "Reassure him that we'll ask for time to respond." The firm's normal response to a tax audit was to drag it out as long as possible until the tax department took a small settlement and moved on to a more lucrative target. Tax Department auditors had quotas to fill, just like traffic policemen.

"Anything else?"

"Just routine stuff. Everything's under control. The partners say they're happy to fill in until you get back." Jane reflected that moving to a smaller firm had definitely been a positive change in her life. She enjoyed the flexibility and the wider range of clients. When she was auditing the Top 100 Companies and travelling to Sydney and Melbourne, she worked fourteen hour days for weeks at a time. Now she worked a fifty-hour week unless it was the end of the financial year.

"Thanks, Carol. Again, I'm sorry to call you so late."

"No problem." Carol signed off.

CHAPTER NINETEEN

Charles entered the suite in a whirlwind of luggage. Two porters wheeled in suitcases and a trunk. As he simultaneously tipped them generously and kissed Jane on both cheeks, she felt the oxygen being sucked out of the room. She forced herself to breathe in and out. It was disconcerting that the sight of her father made her hyperventilate. His arms windmilling, Charles organised for the room to be rearranged around her. At last the porters left and Charles turned back and took her in.

"Jane, the short hair looks good. More sophisticated and it shows off your cheekbones. You look tired though. How have you been holding up? I really should have come down here earlier. It was too much of a burden for you to bear on your own."

The stream of words flowed on, and for the first time Jane wondered if her father was actually as nervous of her as she was of him. She took a deep breath.

"Charles," she started, and his body deflated as if that one word had pierced him like a pricked balloon. He began to cry. It was so unexpected that she had no idea of what to do. Tears fogged his glasses.

"A father's supposed to know what to do to keep his children safe from harm, no matter what their age. I've been coping by trying not to think about it. But now that I'm here, it's real."

"I know. I feel helpless too. Mostly I'm just trying not to drink and to stay calm. Sometimes that means I won't allow myself to think about what could have happened to Pearl and then I feel guilty."

Charles sat down next to Jane and gave her a hug. "Be kind to yourself. There's no reason for you to feel guilty. I hope we can help each other and share our feelings."

"God, Charles, that's very new age! I've never been comfortable sharing my feelings. I'm not sure what you gain by it."

"That's a man's way of dealing with problems. I thought women wanted men to be all touchy-feely these days."

"Not all women; plus it's the wrong time to be exploring my psyche with you."

"Let's stick to the facts then. What happened with the police this morning?"

"They searched the apartment and took an inventory. I'm not sure what they were looking for, but two nights ago I found some cocaine in Pearl's bathroom cabinet. I'm pretty sure it was planted after I arrived."

"Why on earth didn't you tell me this before? Maybe it's crucial evidence."

"I didn't want to muddy Pearl's good name. How could I prove it wasn't hers? And that's not all. Pearl's pregnant. She consulted a lawyer about custody issues. The father is Andorran and married. It's the good-looking politician you told me about, Ribera-Lopez. She also renewed a power of attorney for me to act for her, which she initially drew up in Australia. I guess she felt that now she was a resident of Andorra the Australian one might not be valid."

While Charles digested this, Jane continued, "I'm pretty sure I was followed from the apartment this morning. It spooked me."

"Did you call the police?"

"Ye – es...but not the detective in charge. I shook off whoever it was before I went to see Saboya, the lawyer. I am wondering if we could be in danger. First Pearl disappeared, then someone attacked me." She explained about the *trastero* and Pearl's photos.

"Maybe someone is trying to postpone the meeting of the trust," said Charles. He opened the mini-bar, ripped the top off a mini whisky bottle and drained it in one gulp. "Sorry Jane, I wasn't thinking."

"Drinking from the mini-bar used to be my forte. Guess it's inherited." She looked at her watch. "Harris should have reached Porta by now." She rang the number from memory. There was an amazing array of figures in her memory at any one time. She'd always had a facility for numbers. The call rang for a long time.

"It rang out. He promised to have the phone with him so we could keep in touch."

"Perhaps he's climbing and doesn't have a free hand."

"He said it was a steep hike, not a climb. And if he left first thing this morning like he said, he should be at Porta by now." She frowned and decided to try Jorge again but, as before, a recorded voice told her something quick and metallic in Catalan. "Now Harris is out of touch, God knows where."

Charles shrugged. "He'll be fine. Let's recap before the meeting so we're both on the same page."

They went over the sequence of events, jotting down a time-line until Jane was struck by a thought. "What does Jack Weinstein look like? Maybe he was the man Pearl met at Lake Pessons, and the person who parked her jeep at the sports centre?"

"I haven't seen him, remember? I could call the florist on the ground floor of his building, though, and ask for a description."

Jane might have known that, despite the circumstances, Charles would get the telephone number of any eligible woman who came his way.

Charles was busy looking through his filofax. "Here it is," he said, and reached for his mobile phone with evident pleasure. A rapid conversation ensued in French. Jane could tell Charles was exerting a great deal of charm on the person at the other end. It was disquieting to have a father who was an enthusiastic pants man.

He grinned as he rang off. "Weinstein's a German Jew, around mid fifties. Fit. Average-looking, but with a Semitic nose, a thin ascetic face and intense brown eyes. Not tall, not short. Careless in his dress. She says clothes aren't important to him – something the French find sacrilegious. Speaks French well, but with a slight accent. Perhaps he's our man. Let's try to find a photo of him in a news database. He's sure to have turned up in a media piece with the type of work he's doing."

It was Jane's turn to reach for her phone.

Gary Cohen's nasal New York accent came sharply down the line. "Jack Weinstein, Nazi hunter? I'll do what I can, but if this is a story, I want an exclusive!"

Charles was now drinking a glass of *Rioja* from a quart bottle with a screw top. "You probably could have downloaded the information on Weinstein yourself from the *NY Times* archives. I've got their web address. It's a handy site," he said.

"Well that's good to know. But let's allow Cohen to do the running around for us while we finish this. We've only got until 6pm."

"What time did Lyn and Dave see Pearl on Tuesday?" Charles asked.

"I assume they saw her in the morning, but it could have been later." Jane wrote a note so she'd remember to ask. "I'm wondering if Pearl had her camera-bag with her, because it wasn't in the flat or the jeep. Did what she was photographing have some bearing in her disappearance?"

Charles wrote "cameras?" next to "cocaine?" on the hotel notepaper. "Go on," he said.

"The night they found her jeep, I searched the flat and found Ramon Saboya's card. Yesterday he told me Pearl was pregnant. I went to Ribera-Lopez's office to question him and to confront him about her pregnancy but he missed my allusion to it entirely. In the end it was his lack of response that I found revealing. His story about going to dinner with Pearl a month earlier panned out, but we only have his word that it was the last time that he saw her.

"Is it a coincidence that shortly after I confronted Ribera-Lopez about Pearl's disappearance the police were on the doorstep? I have to wonder if he directed the police to search, and if so were they looking for something specific?"

"Like the cocaine, you mean. If you plant something it's usually with the objective of someone finding it again later. What did you do with it by the way?"

"Put it in the sugar jar. I thought I might have to produce it again for some reason, otherwise I would have flushed it down the toilet."

Charles checked his gold Rolex. "It's time to go. The trustees will be waiting."

CHAPTER TWENTY

The offices of the trustee Ricardo Castillo were on the third floor of the neon-green Credit Andorra building in the centre of Andorra la Vella. The conference room was on the south side of the building overlooking a wooden plaza and the river Valira. At one end of the room a raised platform housed a polished wood table and four chairs, behind which several framed pages of the 1993 Constitution of Andorra hung in a row. A tray of glasses and a crystal jug of water had been placed to one side of the table. Five rows of upholstered chairs faced the stage.

Jane and Charles seated themselves in the front row and checked their watches. It was 6.10 but the room was empty. Another ten minutes went by before the side door opened and a clutch of people surged in. A plump woman with unruly blonde curls split from the group and introduced herself as Señora Menendez, the sole woman trustee who worked at the Credit Europa Bank. Although her suit was impeccably tailored, her capacious figure would not be confined. The jacket failed to meet over her impressive jutting bosom. Diamante glasses, hung by a gold chain around her neck, drew attention to her décolletage. A large square-cut diamond flashed on her wedding finger. She gave the impression of a large personality barely holding herself in check in deference to her position with the bank.

"*Mucho gusto*. Pleased to meet you at last. I will introduce you to the other trustees," she said crisply, giving each of them a firm handshake.

She beckoned to the group of dark-suited men and two separated themselves from the group and walked over.

"Señor Alas is the trustee from Jersey."

Señor Alas was swarthy and short. He didn't look English and his slightly accented greeting bore this out.

"And this is Señor Castillo whose office this is; the third trustee."

"*Encantado*," and "a pleasure," they murmured in turn.

Señor Castillo wore the dark lawyer's suit common to those who appeared in court regularly. His eyes, one blue and one brown, were framed by horn-rimmed glasses. Jane wondered why he didn't wear a coloured contact lens to correct the imbalance. It was certainly disconcerting when you weren't prepared for it. Jane held his gaze a moment too long. He was watching her notice his eyes. He in turn appeared to be conducting a personal inventory. He took in Jane's understated suit and the colourful scarf that framed her tanned face. His strange mismatched eyes were level with hers.

He turned to Charles and gave him a similar slow scrutiny, saying, "My father knew your father well. We have acted as his trustees for many years. Father for father; and now, son for son. We do a lot of work that way. Our family has represented many generations of families. I'm afraid that I didn't meet your father personally, but I can see from the photos in the file that you resemble him very closely. It is not just your names that are the same."

Charles smiled back, grasping the other man's proferred hand in between his own. "I'm afraid I didn't know him very well myself. He died when I was eleven. I'd be very interested to see the photos. In fact, if you have any correspondence from him in your files I'd be grateful if you would allow me access. I am writing a memoir of his life and getting to know him at the same time. There are quite a lot gaps to fill."

"I'll see what I can do," the lawyer responded with crisp professionalism. "The meeting will start soon. I'm sorry we are not on time. My assistant will take notes to augment the audio transcript of the proceedings. As this is a small meeting we shall conduct it relatively informally. I shall chair it, and by that I mean I will conduct the preliminaries. Naturally you or your daughter may question any of the trustees individually, or ask questions to me as chair."

Jane and Charles nodded, and then turned towards the knot of people at the back of the room who had not come forward. A cluster of three men slid into the back row of seats, and the fourth man carried a tape recorder to the table, kneeling to plug it into the wall socket. Before Jane could ask to be introduced to the three spectators behind them, Riccardo Castillo moved to take his seat, motioning the two other trustees to either side of him. Then without delay he launched into a speech in Catalan. As Jane opened her mouth to protest, the door opened once more and Ramon Saboya rumbled into the room. His appearance served to stop the proceedings immediately, as he wheezingly introduced himself to Charles. Then, out of breath, and covered with ash from his last cigar, he lowered his considerable bulk onto a seat next to them, apologising in English all the while.

"Sorry. Sorry, Ricardo." This seemed to be directed at Señor Castillo. "I walked of course. It isn't far – but with my weight it wasn't wise. Just beginning, are you? Have I missed much?"

"Why are you here, Ramon?" asked Señor Castillo, to the point.

"I am here representing the interests of my absent client Señora Pearl Wentworth, and also having the honour to represent Señora Jane Burns." He made a small bow and smiled at Jane as he said this, his eyes twinkling. "Go on. Continue. I'll translate for Ms Burns shall I, or will you be repeating everything you say again in English?"

"I will of course be translating," Castillo snapped.

"Good. Good. Continue."

"As I was saying," Castillo switched to English, "We are here as trustees of the Charles Barclay Family Trust registered in Jersey. It has been our duty to administer the trust over the past years, and according to the conditions by which the trust was set up we are now convened to discuss winding it up and the dispersal of capital funds to surviving family beneficiaries. I note that the beneficiaries Jane Burns and Charles Barclay are attending in person. Now is the time to present proxies for absent beneficiaries."

One of the three men in the back row stood up and spoke for several minutes in Catalan. After this he proceeded to the trustees and set forth a series of documents on the table. Each trustee perused these in turn.

Saboya whispered to them, "The man is a lawyer from Lleida called Frederico Sanchez. He purports to represent two beneficiaries and is presenting their proxies for examination." Charles and Jane exchanged looks of consternation.

"We know nothing of any other beneficiaries. Will you please ask Señor Castillo their names and details?" Charles asked.

Saboya nodded and asked the question of the chair in Catalan. A lengthy exchange took place, with Jane and Charles getting increasingly impatient.

"The beneficiaries are called Llourdes Vendrell-Grau and Pedro

Ribera-Vendrell. It seems that Charles Barclay Senior had a son, Miguel, during his time in Andorra – that would be your half-brother, Charles. Miguel is subsequently deceased. But Miguel's daughter Llourdes and her son Pedro are beneficiaries."

While Jane and Charles were absorbing this in stunned silence, Saboya continued, "Señor Castillo has not drawn my attention to this fact, but it is generally known, and you should be made aware, that Llourdes Vendrell-Grau is married to Fernando Ribera-Lopez, the politician."

"What?" they chorused.

"Yes, I'm afraid so. It seems that our esteemed minister is married to one beneficiary and was also personally involved with another." Saboya sat back in his seat and blinked. His tongue darted in and out as he licked his lips. He appeared to be relishing the revelations.

"What proof of lineage do they have?" asked Charles.

"Miguel was specifically mentioned in the original trust documents. Your father acknowledged paternity and also made a generous provision to his paramour, Miguel's mother, Mari Angel Vendrell-Oliarte, for her life," Castillo replied, addressing Charles and taking control of the situation once more. Jane had never heard anyone referred to as a paramour before.

"I am sorry if this has come as a shock to you, Mr Barclay. We assumed that you knew about your half-brother and his family. There was no reason for us to mention it before," Señora Menendez said.

Frederico Sanchez spoke from the back of the room. "Señor Castillo, in view of the fact that the beneficiary Pearl Wentworth is not here today, and has been reported in the press as missing, should we not suspend the proceedings until such time that she is able to participate?" Jane nodded to Saboya who stood laboriously, then bent to open the briefcase he had placed on the next seat. He shuffled forward and put his own sheaf of documents before the trustees.

"I have here the correctly authorised papers from Señora Pearl Wentworth which give power of attorney to her sister, Jane Burns. Ms Burns is empowered to act in all legal, financial and family matters. There is a clause that specifically relates to trust matters. I believe that everything is fully in order."

"I would like to examine my colleague's documents, if you please," said Frederico Sanchez.

"The trustees will examine the papers, Señor Sanchez," Castillo replied, passing them first to Señor Alas who quickly perused them and then in turn passed them to Señora Menendez. She took time to read them through, and then without expression returned them to Castillo.

He tapped his fingertips on the table as he carefully read each word and considered each phrase. He examined the impressive red wax seals and the supporting documents. He then took up the documents presented by Frederico Sanchez and read them through again, seemingly to compare the two sets of documentation. "I believe that the beneficiaries are all legally represented here today and that we can proceed," he finally announced. One of the three men in the back row slipped out of the room, no doubt to update their client.

"Is it appropriate to continue while such a mystery lingers as to the whereabouts of one of the beneficiaries?" asked Sanchez. "Surely a short delay while the police establish her circumstances would not unduly inconvenience the beneficiaries? My clients have instructed me not to obstruct any request for a continuance."

"My clients are happy to proceed," said Saboya.

"Are you OK?" Jane asked Charles, who was perspiring and breathing heavily. "Could we have a glass of water?" she asked the assistant. He poured a glass and Jane handed it to Charles, who sipped the water then mopped his face with a handkerchief. Jane was alarmed at his pallor. Charles clutched his left arm.

"I'm not feeling too well all of a sudden," he said.

"Are you having chest pains?" she asked.

"No, but I'm having trouble breathing and I have shooting pains in my arm," Charles grimaced.

"We need an ambulance." Jane said, her normally quiet voice rising sharply. "My father isn't well. It could be his heart."

Castillo nodded to his assistant who jumped up and ran from the room. Jane ripped open her father's tie and the top buttons of his shirt. He was panting and rivulets of sweat were coursing down his cheeks.

"Please, quickly...does anyone here have an aspirin?" Jane asked

Ramon Saboya reached into his waistcoat and produced a silver pill case from which he extracted an aspirin. "My doctor advised me always to carry some," he said, as Charles took the pill with another sip of water.

"I'm sure it's nothing," said Charles trying to wave them all off. "Indigestion probably, too much wretched olive oil and garlic. Just give me a minute to catch my breath and we can continue."

"You should undergo a thorough medical check," Señor Castillo responded. "We can reconvene when the doctors are happy to give you the all-clear. The medical facilities here in Andorra are excellent. The hospital will make you comfortable while they run some tests." His voice was courteous but firm. He did not intend to proceed. "The ambulance will be here in just a moment. They have a very quick response time. Please try to relax until then."

The ambulance attendants wheeled a stretcher into the room without fuss and bent to take Charles's pulse and to listen to his heart. They spoke soothingly to him in English as they asked him some basic questions to test his orientation. Charles had no trouble in repeating his name, age and where he was staying. He also insisted that he had no previous history of heart problems.

"I'm sure it's nothing," said one of the attendants, unconsciously repeating Charles. "But we need to take you to the hospital to be sure."

"I'm his daughter. May I go with him?"

"*Claro*, of course."

As they wheeled her father from the room, the lawyer Frederico Sanchez was on his mobile phone, no doubt advising his client, Jane thought. She dropped back briefly to thank the trustees.

Castillo and Saboya accompanied her to the elevator.

There Castillo's assistant interrupted them. "*Lo siento*, I know this is not a good time, but I have an urgent parcel for Ms Burns."

The three of them looked at a small, square parcel in his hands. On it, printed in large black letters were the words, "SENORA JANE BURNS. URGENT. OPEN IMMEDIATELY."

"When did this come, Jaime?" asked Castillo.

"Not long ago. A personal delivery. The receptionist signed for it, and then wasn't sure if she should wait until the end of the meeting or bring it in straight away."

Saboya took out a Swiss army pocket-knife, casually slid out the blade, then sliced through the masking tape holding down the four flaps of the cardboard box and lifted the lid. Before he could unwrap the layers of tissue paper Jane reached for the box and then suddenly recoiled, dropping it on the floor. The contents slithered out of the box – a black silky snake. As the men jumped hastily back, Jane pounced, her heart hammering so hard, her ears buzzed. When she straightened, the movement released the faintest waft of Channel perfume into the air. The two men saw that Jane was caressing a coil of jet-black hair.

"It's Pearl's ponytail!" she said.

Castillo stooped to retrieve the box. Nestled in the bed of tissue paper was the printed note, "DO NOTHING UNTIL YOU RECEIVE INSTRUCTIONS."

"We should call the police. I don't like this. It's a very nasty situation. It didn't occur to me that the disappearance of Señora Wentworth could involve another person." A frown creased Castillo's face. His hands tightened.

Jane thought aloud, "Let's not be hasty and put Pearl in danger."

"To be cautious is usually to be wise," Saboya agreed. "I'll come with you to the hospital and we can talk about this some more. Ricardo, we'll keep in touch. Don't discuss this with anyone else. That includes the other two trustees. It's best we keep this knowledge between the three of us. Then if there is a leak we will know...." He did not finish the thought.

Castillo slowly nodded. Saboya held out the empty box for the length of hair. Jane drew it softly across her cheek before reluctantly parting with it. Saboya opened his capacious briefcase and placed the box inside.

Jane thanked Castillo again before she headed into the elevator with Saboya. In the street below, the back door to the waiting ambulance remained open. An attendant was bent over Charles's body adjusting an oxygen-mask over his face. Jane gave a wave to Saboya and climbed awkwardly into the back. She took Charles's hand in hers and squeezed it.

The ambulance attendant smiled to reassure her, "Don't worry. He'll be fine."

The Meritxell Hospital was a modern multi-storey building on the edge of Escaldes-Engordany. The ambulance swept into the emergency arrival bay where they received Charles with very little fuss, transferring him to a wheelchair and wheeling him through to the triage nurse who carefully questioned him about his symptoms and previous cardiac history. She took two ampoules of blood, then an orderly helped him into a bed in a small adjacent room. Jane sat by his side until he was wheeled away for tests. She found Saboya near the elevator, an unlit cigar clamped in his mouth. His clothes were rumpled but his demeanour was perfectly relaxed. She looked for "No Smoking" signs but found none. The receptionist was pointedly looking in the other direction.

"I've brought your backpack," Sabayon boomed, holding it up, making no concession to volume despite the fact that friends and families of patients were constantly passing to enter the lift.

"That was thoughtful of you, thank you." Jane drew close to him. "I've been thinking. Maybe we should get an independent DNA test to make sure the hair is Pearl's. There's a hairbrush in her bathroom that would give us hair for comparison. Could you find a reputable forensic laboratory in Spain or France that could conduct the tests, and also take any fingerprints from the note?"

"You are a very sensible young woman," Saboya nodded his approval, his tone unconsciously lowered to model her own. "It's a pleasure to work with you. In many cases, emotion overcomes common sense. I always say that there is no substitute for rational thought. A situation may be dramatic, but the people involved in it are best served if they are not."

"What do you think – about the ponytail? Does it mean Pearl has been taken for ransom? Has anything like this happened before in Andorra?"

"Never. Not in Andorra. We rarely have a serious crime, although I suppose we are afraid that crime will be an increasing problem now we have a large population of migrant workers with different traditions.

"There has been some talk about the Russian Mafia laundering money in Andorra through property deals, but I think that is xenophobia talking, myself. Even if it were true, it wouldn't make sense to turn a safe haven into a hornets' nest by committing a serious crime, like kidnapping, here."

"So what do you think?" Jane repeated. It was the first time anyone had said "kidnapping" out loud. She wished it could be unsaid.

Saboya sighed. "Crime tends to be personal – sometimes for passion, sometimes for money. Then there are the crimes of opportunity committed by people passing through. The victim is in the right place at the wrong time, you might say. But I would think a kidnapping takes a great deal of planning ... unless there's a sexual motive," he added reluctantly.

"I doubt that a sexual predator would send us a note."

"Not unless he gets his pleasure from tormenting others."

"My husband always used to say 'follow the money'. So who benefits?"

"Pearl's will is unexceptional. There are bequests to her mother and siblings, and the remainder of the estate was to go to her unborn child."

"Do you think it significant that Pearl suddenly decided to make a will? Wouldn't it be more usual to make the will after a child was born?"

"No, not at all. It was an entirely sensible precaution. In Andorra, as in Spain, if you die intestate it is quite possible that your property could go to the State or the *Comu* – the Parish in which you live. There was a recent case in Spain, just over the border in fact, where the nephew of a wealthy landowner grew tired of waiting for him to die, and strangled him. Then it turned out the man died without a will and the property went to the *Comu*. The perpetrator inherited nothing. Instead he's in jail for twenty years."

Jane continued to think about the trail of money. "We should ask to review the provisions of the trust. Maybe there's something in there that will provide a motive."

"Yes," Saboya agreed. "It's a good place to start. I know Castillo well. I could see he was very upset by this and I am sure he'll co-operate. I'll call him and set up an appointment for tomorrow."

"It's strange that the other beneficiaries didn't seem to be in a hurry to wind up the trust. They were perfectly happy to have a delay."

Saboya nodded, "I noticed that too."

It was late when they left the hospital. The doctor at Emergency advised that Charles' prognosis was good, but they would keep him overnight for observation. Blood tests confirmed he had suffered a minor heart-attack.

The taxi from *Urgencias* took no time at all. Saboya hummed with approval at Pearl's décor. "*Bonito!*" he said, slowly turning around in a circle to take in the framed photos and the vibrant colour palette. Jane collected Pearl's hairbrush from the bathroom and placed it into a large manila envelope and handed it over.

"Don't send the whole ponytail; we'll have to hand it over to the Police in due course. Just send a few strands."

A deathly weariness was creeping over her, yet the flashing light on the answering-machine told her that there was one more thing to deal with before she could go to bed. Juan-Antonio's voice produced an instant and unexpected reaction. A warm flush suffused her body creeping up her neck and leaving a telltale blush.

"Jane. It's eight-thirty. I didn't think I should call you on your mobile in case you were still in the meeting. I hope everything went well. Call me when you're free."

Jane thought about Saboya's words in the trust meeting. "You should be aware that Llourdes Vendrell is married to Fernando Ribera-Lopez. It seems our esteemed minister for public works is married to one beneficiary and was also involved with another." Juan-Antonio was Fernando's cousin and they were on close terms. He must have known. Yet he had said not one word.

"Here a crime tends to be personal." Saboya's rolling syntax echoed in her ear. Jane felt nauseous. The previous night with Juan-Antonio had been a huge error of judgement. Her index finger pressed the erase button so hard her nail snapped.

"Damn!"' she said. Long into the night she tried not to think of Pearl's silky ponytail slithering out of the cardboard box.

CHAPTER TWENTY-ONE

Friday brought a welcome change of weather. Jane woke to sunshine breaking through the shutters. Outside birds were singing. Jane breathed in the sweet morning air and murmured the steps; her morning ritual. "Step Eleven; I seek though prayer and meditation to improve my conscious contact with God as I understand him. I pray only for knowledge of his will for me and for the power to carry that out." Jane no longer went to church. Embracing God was one of the hardest tenets of AA, or it had been until Jane invented her own version of God. She meditated on God's kindness. Kindness was often underestimated.

In a bid to avoid Juan-Antonio, she decided to vary her routine and hike behind the village, taking one of the well-marked trails that looped up to the Hotel Babot and down the *Coll d'Ordino* road back to the village. Before leaving the apartment she called Harris at the hotel without success, and then tried his mobile phone. The number rang-out without reply. She clipped her mobile onto her waistband and set off.

The trail traced the stream past the old quarter of Segudet. Jane was soon breathing heavily and expelling the air from her diaphragm with a conscious "shush" every other step. As always the exercise helped to clear her mind. She passed a herd of goats munching leafy branches in a noisome pen, next to a yard containing four red hunting-dogs. The pungent smell of goats mingled with the whines and barks of the dogs. On her right, across the stream, a narrow four-storey house displayed lace curtains through a series of small windows. Each window framed a different lacy vignette. The lace curtains in the neighbouring house depicted a bullfight, and the next house had windmills. Pearl should do a photographic essay on lace curtains in a variety of window frames. The differences were charming. This unsolicited thought cheered her up. Her subconscious believed Pearl was alive. They would find her.

The houses segued into fields and Jane quickened her pace as she crossed the unassuming bridge over the stream and started up the rocky path towards the vertiginous Hotel Babot. When she at last reached the bitumen road she paused to stretch her calf and thigh muscles before jogging down the road back to the village. There was no doubt that a night's sleep had restored her sense of purpose. There were things to do today. She would check on Charles, and then go to see Castillo and read through the terms of the trust. Perhaps the person who had sent her the mysterious box would send instructions. The search had quickened. She would examine the documents and shake them until they spilled out secrets. This was her forte. She was good at secrets – both at keeping them and discovering them.

The phone shrilled at her side. Her watch read 8.15.

"It's Victor. We've found Harris. I'm sorry Jane, but we need you to come and identify the body."

"The body?" Jane repeated. Her tongue found it difficult to formulate the words, as if it had swollen like a toad in her mouth.

"Yes. I'm sorry. It seems he had a fall. Two young climbers found him early this morning. They heard his cell-phone ring and climbed down off the trail to see what it was."

"That was me. On the phone. I called him when I got up."

"They used his cell-phone to call 110. Dispatch contacted me after they took the details. They noticed in the log-book that I had notified Pas de la Casa and Porta police to look out for him. The description matched. We'll pick you up in fifteen minutes."

"Twenty. I'm halfway up the *Coll d'Ordino* road."

"*Vale.* OK. Wear some sensible shoes to walk in." He rang off without wasting more of his precious supply of English. Jane ran on, but now the bitumen was a swamp that sucked at each foot. She remembered the photo of a pretty dark girl in Balgo Mission with a baby in her arms.

It was hard to fit the key in the lock. She gulped gusts of air into her lungs and tried to stop her hand from shaking. The power was off again but she barely stopped to throw up the breaker switch before she started tearing off her running clothes.

"Please let it not be him," she begged. Harris deserved another chance in life. Everyone made mistakes. People could change. This belief was central to her life and to the rehabilitation process of AA meetings. She threw water over her face and neck and wiped the sweat off with a towel before pulling a T-shirt over her head. She struggled into a pair of leggings, cursing when they refused to co-operate and stuck to her still damp legs. She was slipping her running shoes back on when the doorbell rang.

"I'll come down," she yelled into the security system. She grabbed her shoulder-bag and closed the door with a bang, then ran back down the stairs into the foyer and slap into the broad chest of the phlegmatic detective. He steadied her with his hand under her elbow.

"*Tranquila*," he said and he didn't take his hand away until she had taken several deep breaths and lost her red face. "Every day there is something to test us," he commiserated, "but if we proceed carefully, *poco a poco*, we win." Jane was close to tears. The swarthy detective gave her a little shake. "*Vale*?" he asked

"OK." she agreed as they continued out to the police car parked on the kerb. Before she had done up her seat-belt, Victor gunned the motor and accelerated back up the road to the col and on to Pas de La Casa.

"*Déjà Vu* all over again," Jane commented – but Victor had a hard time processing that thought. He turned his head and gazed blankly at her while tooling around one of the numerous curves. "*No importa*," she clarified, allowing him to concentrate on the road. "It doesn't matter. Where are we going exactly?"

"Lake Pessons. They're bringing the body down by foot because the helicopter can't easily recover it. Also, there is no need for speed because the man is already dead. We will make a walk up to where he was found and then we would like you to identify the body."

"Wouldn't I normally go to the morgue to do that? ... and didn't you actually meet Harris when he was interviewed at Police Headquarters?"

"According to standard procedures, a relative or friend must identify him – plus we'd like to know what you think." Victor's English was improving rapidly with use, like a backhand at a tennis lesson.

"Think about what?" asked Jane. "Who is 'we'?" But Victor would not be drawn. Instead he increased his speed and they flew down the road, the acceleration pushing Jane back hard into her seat.

CHAPTER TWENTY-TWO

When Victor-Ignacio parked the police car at the Lake Pessons restaurant, Jane noticed a truck bearing the sign "*Bombers*". Seeing Jane's astonishment he said, "Not 'bombers' in English." He waved his hands as if conducting an orchestra and tried to pluck an English note from the air but it eluded him.

"What do you call it? They run the mountain rescue service."

"Bombers?" queried Jane, blinking.

"Not 'Bombers'. How do you call the people who put out the fires?"

"Firemen!"

"*Exactamente.*"

He walked towards a motley group of people standing on the terrace at the water's edge. Jane trailed behind him, musing that if one were to handcuff the entire population they would become mute.

Standing apart from the others, a youth with mountain-climbing regalia clipped to his belt was smoking a cigarette with furious concentration. Victor spoke to him first. It sounded like a gentle interrogation. The young man answered in a slow considered manner, taking his time to think about what Victor was saying to him. Without understanding the Catalan, Jane merely tried to get a sense of the body-language and the tone. Despite Victor's own youth, he assumed a paternal air and laid his hand lightly on the young man's shoulder.

Finally Victor turned to Jane and explained. "This is one of the climbers who found the body. He waited here to guide us to the scene so we wouldn't take a deviation in the trail by mistake. His friend was to stay with the body until the *bombers* reached him. They will remain there to make sure nothing is disturbed until we examine the site of the accident and take some photos." The young climber inclined his head courteously to Jane.

"We will need to hike for about one and a half hours."

Jane looked at her jogging shoes and hoped the trail would not be too slippery after yesterday's rain. "OK. I suppose you know what you're doing."

Victor had a few words to the rest of the group, perhaps giving instructions for the arrival of the body. A man with a crew-cut joined them. The camera slung around his neck and a backpack, with an extendable tripod hanging from it, identified him as the police photographer.

"I came too late to go with the mountain rescue team," he said.

The four of them set off without further discussion. The young mountain-climber drew a telescopic walking-stick from his pack and passed it over to Jane, showing her how to adjust it for her height.

"This will help you with your balance on the steep parts," he explained. The cigarette was a permanent feature in the corner of his mouth. He looked hardly old enough to shave.

The trail began as a flat path over small rivulets, which fed into the lake, but after twenty minutes it began to steepen into a rocky mountain-range barren of all trees. Despite her frequent workouts, Jane found her heart and lungs hammering as she plodded along behind the men. Every fifteen minutes they stopped for a short break to regain their breath. After an hour of steady hiking they stopped to ford a small stream, and all bent with cupped hands to drink their fill. It would be hard to perish of thirst in Andorra. Water sprang out of the ground in fonts and streams throughout the mountains and valleys. Jane fished in her shoulder-bag for sun screen and applied it to her lips, nose and cheeks, wishing she had remembered to bring her cap. Untying the scarf from the handle of the bag, she wound it around her head. It was mostly white and would deflect some of the sun's rays. She then awkwardly fashioned the straps of her bag over her shoulders to create a backpack to stop it banging against her side at every step. The men waited patiently not saying a word until she finished.

"*Venga!*" said Victor, "Let's go!" It was not intended as a rebuke but rather as encouragement, and they continued up the narrow track in single file, Jane once more bringing up the rear. It was well over two hours before they reached the part of the trail where the accident had occurred. An outcrop of solid rock on the right-hand side made the hikers lean away from the mountain. The trail narrowed. At Jane's feet there was a fifteen-metre drop.

"The two climbers heard the mobile phone ring and wondered if a hiker had unwittingly dropped it," said Victor.

"We hammered a piton into the rock-face and abseiled down on our climbing-ropes to investigate," continued the young climber.

"We discovered the body rolled to the back of a narrow ledge."

The mountain rescue team had used the same technique to access the body and now stood huddled to one side, trying to preserve the site until the photographer arrived to take his pictures. Jane wasn't sure if she felt sick because of the fifteen-metre drop, or because of what waited for her at the end of it.

"I thought you could wear one of the rescue harnesses and the team would lower you down and pull you back up, but it's more difficult than I thought. Bringing you here was foolish. There's no need to go down," Victor assured her, but she did not feel comforted. Heights did not agree with her. She had grown up in the flat-lands and beaches of Perth. She retraced her steps to a less precipitous part of the path and squatted on her heels while the police photographer grabbed hold of the rope and swung himself out easily into space and landed with his feet against the cliff, after which he quickly rappelled down to join the others. Victor remained behind and shouted directions as to what he wanted photographed and from which angles.

Jane's phone rang and, thinking of Charles waiting for her at the hospital, she quickly answered.

"Jane. It's Juan-Antonio. I didn't see you on your run this morning and you didn't answer my call last night. Is everything OK?" He sounded concerned.

"Charles is in hospital with a heart-attack, and I'm on the trail to *Portella Blanca* where I am about to go into cardiac arrest myself before I get to identify a dead body."

Before she could add anything else, Victor walked towards her asking, "Is that Juan-Antonio?" and took the receiver out of her hand. They spoke for quite a while. People were always yelling at each other in Catalan, although it didn't seem to mean anything in terms of mood. Victor handed the phone back, and Jane heard Juan-Antonio's anxious voice.

"Jane, are you alright? Do be careful."

"I was born to climb mountains. I have to go now." And with that cryptic statement she signed off. She could almost believe he cared about her. "What was the point of this expedition exactly?" she asked Victor.

"It was an error of judgement. I got over-excited." Victor looked like his pulse had never raced in his life.

"It seems highly irregular," was the best she could manage – trying to outdo him in understatement.

"*Claro*," he agreed. "Juan-Antonio thought so too."

"Did he now? Just show me that harness you were talking about!"

It was Harris. He lay on his side, his body crumpled and so close to the base of the cliff-face that it was impossible to see him from the path above. One arm was under his body and the other flung out. His day-pack had slipped slightly off one shoulder, but was firmly fastened across his chest. The holster for his mobile phone was clipped to his belt but the phone itself was missing. The young climbers probably still had it, or had handed it to the police. The fall had crushed the bones on one side of Harris' face but there was no doubt it was him. The police-photographer had removed his cap and a deep contusion rimmed with dried blood was evident on the back of his head.

"I guess it would have been quick," she said. She looked up at the sheer cliff. There were no protrusions. They were above the tree-line and no stumps or bushes grew in the rocky shale. It was a rocky mountain desert.

"Did you find any blood on the cliff-face?" Jane asked. "It seems strange that he would have damage to both the front and the back of his head. I guess he could have tumbled over and over, but fifty feet isn't far in terms of tumbling."

Victor looked at the *bombers* and then frowned at her, but she had kept her voice low and it was doubtful anyone else had heard. "And if we don't find any blood on the cliff?"

"You should look for something that could have been used as a weapon to inflict a blow to the back of his head. Maybe a rock."

"And why would anyone want to attack your brother-in-law?"

"I have no idea. Perhaps because he was Pearl's husband. Harris lived his whole life outdoors. It's hard to believe this could be an accident."

"You are suspicious, like a good detective."

"I don't believe you brought me because you got over excited."

"I was interested in your reactions."

"And they would be what?"

Victor shrugged – not willing to commit himself to an answer. He looked uncomfortable and would not make eye-contact. In Jane's experience this was usually a prelude to some type of unwelcome news.

"You don't seriously think I have something to do with this, do you?" Her voice rose. "I have an alibi for yesterday remember? You and your colleagues were with me most of the morning. Saboya will vouch for me in the afternoon, as will Charles and the trustees, and then I was at the hospital until nearly midnight for God's sake." Jane was astounded that he might consider her a suspect.

"You have a saying in English. Where there's a will, there's a way."

"I'm not in Pearl's will, actually. She deliberately left me out because I have my own inheritance. And speaking of will, your control over your English seems to come and go at will. Is it a device you use like good cop and bad cop?"

"*No entiendo!*"

"Yeah, I bet you don't understand." She rose wearily to her feet and walked over to the nearest *bomber* and pointed up. Fear of heights suddenly seemed to be the least of her worries.

The trip back was silent. The two young mountain-climbers set off at a clipping pace and were soon out of sight. Jane, Victor and the police photographer walked with their heads down, watching the loose shale and rocks at their feet. The *bombers* had decided they could evacuate the body by helicopter after all and were waiting for its arrival. Victor and Jane stopped at the same stream to quench their thirst but this time there were no words of encouragement. Jane set off as soon as she had finished drinking, without a word. She was pissed off, and didn't care who knew it.

When she arrived back at the restaurant she saw that the tables by the lake were full of lunching patrons. Jane sat at a free table and asked the waitress where Jorge was.

"Barcelona."

That would account for his failure to return her calls.

Not knowing the phone-number of the Meritxel Hospital, she rang the concierge at the Hotel Roc de Caldes and asked for it. On connection it took some time, speaking in her laboured Spanish, to reach a nurse who could tell her that Charles had been released from hospital earlier that morning. She called the hotel back and asked to be put through to his suite but there was no reply. Hell! She hadn't got the number of his new mobile phone. Luckily she had Saboya's number.

"Jane! Your father is fine and he's here in the office with me. We were just about to start on the trust documents. Castillo sent them over first thing this morning. Where are you?"

"It's a long story," she said wearily. "Harris is dead, and I'm out at Grau Roig with Victor. I'm hot, sweaty and upset. I need to shower and change before I join you. I'll tell you all about it when I get there."

Charles' voice boomed from the receiver. "Jane! Ramon had you on his speaker-phone. Are you OK? What happened to Harris?"

"He fell in the mountains, Dad." She was brief. It was a measure of how upset she was that she didn't call him Charles. "How about you, are you OK?"

"It's like John Webster said."

Talking to her father was often like solving a cryptic crossword. Before she could ask him for further clues, Victor's shadow fell upon her.

"Are you ready?" he asked. She simply nodded once, and before she could say a brief goodbye, heard Charles say, "Death hath a thousand doors for men to take their exit." – He was finishing the quote.

"Well that's one mystery cleared up at least."

She followed Victor to the car and as she buckled her seat-belt, the detective said, "I have to explore all the possibilities. That's my job."

"Sure you do," she tried to sound more neutral than she felt. "We have a saying. Follow the money. That's what I think you should be doing now and that's what I intend to do. Why don't you report back to Ribera-Lopez and tell him I'll be doing that. Ask about his connection to the trust money through his wife."

"*Que*? What are you talking about? Señor Ribera-Lopez has nothing to do with the police investigation. We are completely independent. This is a serious matter and your unsubstantiated allegations are not helpful."

"Tell it to the marines. And while you're at it, tell them about your lapse into perfect English just now – and stop bull-shitting me."

Victor gave this his thoughtful consideration. Finally he said, "Jane, the money trail also leads to you. If Pearl dies with her baby unborn, there are two fewer beneficiaries and your inheritance surely grows."

CHAPTER TWENTY-THREE

The drive back to Ordino across the col was mostly silent, except for the squealing of tyres as Victor accelerated over the names of famous Tour de Spain cyclists. – The names had been painted on the road some time ago, before *La Vuelta de España* flashed through Andorra. – Jane projected her unhappiness by scowling. Although she wanted to co-operate as best she could with the police, she was frustrated by their lack of progress and she had questions about their impartiality. Victor in turn had not appreciated her straight-talking and the insinuation that the police investigation was prejudiced. His scowl was equally fierce. When he dropped her off he wagged his finger at her, "We'll be in touch!"

"I'll be holding my breath," she answered, slamming the door of the car so hard it jolted on its wheels. Remorse hit her halfway up the staircase. She needed the good will of the police. To behave so badly went against all her experience in dealing with men in positions of authority. They took it personally (she meant it personally). All the same, she felt marginally better at venting her feelings. Her therapist repeatedly told her she was too buttoned-up.

Uncharacteristically, she decided to call her mother. It wasn't too late. Her mother was a chronic insomniac who never went to bed before midnight. She was often up prowling around the house just four hours later. One thing about her mother, when outside forces ranged against Jane, she was always, unambiguously, on her side.

"Jane, you must be psychic, darling. I was just about to call you. Nanna's had a stroke. I've just come back from the hospital to get some night-clothes. I'm going to stay in her room. They think she may not last the night."

"Oh, Mum, how awful! I'm sorry I'm not there with you." Jane could tell her mother was holding herself together by sheer force of will.

"Do you think you might be able to come home?" Her mother's voice was shaky.

"I don't see how. I'm in the middle of a police investigation. Harris is dead. He fell in the mountains. His death could be linked to Pearl's disappearance, we don't know. There also seems to be the makings of an extortion attempt. Someone sent a package containing a length of hair, which might be Pearl's, and a note saying that instructions would follow. The parcel was addressed to me, so I'm guessing they will contact me soon.

"Also Mum, Charles had a minor heart-attack yesterday, but he's OK – he's out of hospital now. Anyway, the trust meeting was postponed after two new beneficiaries, whom we've never heard of, appeared out of thin air."

Jane's mother was silent while she digested all of this.

"Mum?"

"It's OK, dear. I can manage. There's really nothing you could do here. I'll stay with Nana in case she regains consciousness and is lucid. I need to be with her until the end."

Unspoken between them was the poignant knowledge that, as Jane was an only child, this would be her role one day.

"Take your mobile, Mum. Call me if you need some moral support."

"I'm taking the portable CD-player so I can play Nana all her favourite show tunes. She's unconscious, but all the same, perhaps she'll be able to hear them and they'll bring her some comfort. Music is like taste and smell, it's something you don't forget."

"That's great, Mum. Be strong!"

Jane rang off and walked to the bathroom as if she were treading on broken glass. The soles of her feet were entirely covered by painful contiguous blisters. Wearing cotton socks had been a mistake. A long soak in the bath might go some way towards restoring her. Charles and Saboya were examining the trust documents so there was nothing to be gained by rushing off in such a fragile state. Instead she'd strive to regain some equilibrium. She tried not to imagine her mother playing tunes from "Oklahoma" and "Annie Get your Gun", while her grandmother slowly drifted away. It was too bizarre.

By the time she arrived at Saboya's office, the room was thick with cigar smoke. The two men had stripped to their shirt-sleeves and were pawing through two dusty archive boxes and trying to arrange the contents into some type of order.

"By date," insisted Charles, ever the historian.

"By subject matter," disagreed Saboya.

"By date and by subject matter. We can make as many piles as we like," Jane mediated.

The two men grunted.

"I thought we were going to examine the trust documents first?"

"We already did that. It was perfectly straightforward, with the exception of the new-found family members."

"What about the trust accounts – the record of the money, where it was invested and how it was disbursed?"

"Yes. Yes," said Saboya irritably, pointing at one of the piles in which two large, leather bound ledgers were prominent. "That pile is yours. You're the accountant."

Jane rolled up her sleeves. "What piles are you guys doing?"

"Correspondence from my father," volunteered Charles.

"Catalan, Spanish – and everything else," growled Saboya.

The room quietened as they settled to their appointed tasks.

Charles occasionally interrupted the work to read out his father's letters.

September 1946
Dear Jordi,

It is a great relief to know that you are looking after my affairs. I am trying to wind up my business dealings and to send money to set up a trust as we discussed; however nothing is coming together as quickly as I had hoped. The lawyers I have spoken to recommend setting it up under the laws of England. To be administered in Andorra, but with English jurisdiction so that any disputes are settled in their courts where there are clear precedents. Apparently Jersey is a good place to start as there are tax advantages. For this simple man is appears far too complicated.

My particular concern is for Angel and the child. Thoughts of her are constantly with me. I know the fact she had a baby out of wedlock is a blow to the family. They may be republicans and profess to be socialists, but their view of the family is still very traditional. Their political beliefs are essentially more about economics than anything else. In honesty though, I cannot say I would change the circumstances if I could. I love Angel deeply and not to have taken what happiness we could in such dangerous times would have been madness. When one does not know whether one will live or die, sometimes one risks a consequence that might never otherwise be contemplated.

I am back in Perth with my seven-year-old son and wife. She knows nothing of what happened to me after I was shot down, except that I made my way to Lisbon and from there back to England until the end of the war. Having me home safe is all she cares about and she tells me to put the past behind me now. It is agonising to pretend that everything is as it was before. I wake up with night sweats thinking of our winter trek across the Pyrenees. How cold it was and we all had inadequate clothing. The Tramuntana wind was blowing in terrible weather from the North. I still have nightmares of the American airman we had to leave behind in the blizzard. We simply did not have the strength to carry him. We fought for every footstep over the peak. I argued with the guide, but he insisted that for the good of the group and to ensure the women and children survived we had to leave the American behind. The guide was a real leader of men. I owe my life today to him – although I am sure the guilty dreams will pursue me for a long time. Then the bandits attacked and tried to rob us. It was not war or politics, but greed to prey on women and children who were refugees from what they are now calling the Holocaust. No persons were poorer, more desperate or alone than they were. The bandits at least had food and shelter, rude though it may have been.

My lawyer here is very much against the sale of the gold mine, saying there will be great prosperity now the war is over; however I want to use half of the proceeds to set up the trust and with the rest I have an idea for a new business venture, buying and selling scrap metal, which I think will be very lucrative as countries continue to rebuild infrastructure. It will also give me the opportunity to travel, and during the course of prospecting opportunities to buy wrecked planes and tanks or whatever else, I can visit Andorra and my second family. It will be a different sort of prospecting than the life I spent pre-war, when I was in the outback pegging mining claims.

At this stage, I can't bring myself to ask my wife for a divorce. It is too soon after my arrival home. She has been a faithful wife and a good mother. The months that I was missing and she presumed me dead or incarcerated in prison camp were terrible for her. Please translate my thoughts in this letter and ask Angel to be patient. I will unravel all this and take up my new life with her when I can. I think of her constantly.

Meanwhile I enclose a bank draft for you to disburse for her and the child's immediate needs.

Thanks for your help and my best wishes. Stay well, my friend.

Charles

Jane and her father stared at each other, mute. It was eerie to hear the first-hand account and to begin to divine the chain of events that led to the establishment of the trust. How little they had known of Charles senior and his life.

"When I was growing up," Charles voice was hushed as if he were speaking in church when remembering those days, "My father was never there. Even when he was physically present, he was somewhere else.... Mother would say, 'Don't bother your father, he's working'; and that's what I always thought it was – that he was too preoccupied with his business ever to recognise I'd like some time with him.

"We didn't talk about quality family time in those days. It was enough to put food on the table, and my father was more than adequate at that. We weren't demonstrative. I can't remember either of my parents saying they loved me, or hugging me. It was accepted this might make a little boy unmanly...." He trailed off, and picked up another piece of paper from his pile and peered at it through his rimless glasses, then took them off and wiped his eyes, after which he polished the glasses thoroughly before replacing them.

In front of Jane, the first leather-bound ledger began with the date *1me Agosto 1948* and revealed a journal written in a spidery cramped hand with notations beside each item. Amounts were itemised but no attempt had been made to separate capital items from income and expenses. Instead there were relentless columns of debits and credits. The sale of the gold mine had brought the then not inconsiderable amount of three hundred thousand pounds. Debits to Angel Vendrell had been sixty pounds per month. After Charles's death in 1952, a further one hundred and fifty thousand pounds had been deposited with the trust – obviously from the sale of his scrap-metal business.

Flicking through to the latest computer sheet of balances she noted that this amount had grown to forty-seven million US dollars. Wow! That was a lot of money. She had no idea...! Like Rockefeller had said, compound interest (combined with no taxes) was the seventh wonder of the world. She scrolled down lists of investments, noting triple-A certificate bonds and well-known stocks in various currencies. German industrials such as Mercedes and Siemens were particularly favoured but there were also Swiss pharmaceuticals and Scandinavian shipbuilders plus investments in American icons such as Ford, Exxon and IBM. The scope of investment was thorough and was also an amazing testament to the kaleidoscope of post-war prosperity in Europe, and the success of the Marshall Plan.

Whoever oversaw these investments had balanced a few riskier new stocks with tried and true conservative bonds and stocks in blue-chip companies. Jane was impressed and totally engrossed by the unfolding story laid before her. The fact the notations were in Catalan made no difference to her understanding. Figures and the names written besides the debits and credits spoke a universal language.

"Jane, listen to this will you? Then look in the account book and see if you can match any payments with the time-frame and get us a name?" Charles once more interrupted her chain of thought.

October 1950
Dear Jordi,

What a pleasure it was to see you again after my unsuccessful trip to the Bosporus. To spend several weeks in the tranquillity of Andorra and to see all my old friends again, and once more to stay at the infamous Hotel Mirador, brought back memories of 1942, when I was waiting fruitlessly for the promised authority of a 'safe pass' through Spain (for which I paid an exorbitant sum), while all around me Spanish agents combined the unlikely triple business objectives of contraband, espionage and tourism. Fat cats we call them in Australia, but I was always amused that you called them 'fat cows'.

Without those valuable contrabandistas *and their old tobacco-smuggling routes however, my escape to Lisbon would not have been possible. We are all opportunists in the end I feel. No doubt the*

Jews who escaped through this same route do not regret the gold and family heirlooms they sacrificed in order to stay alive. Commerce is not such a dirty word if it keeps you and your family from a horrible and untimely death.

Which brings me to the point of the letter. While in Andorra, I spoke with one of the guides who smuggled refugees through the escape route from Toulouse to Foix and through Port de Siguer into Andorra. He proposed an interesting business venture between us. I am to be the "venture capitalist" and he is to be "the front man". It is probably better not to use names as I am aware that should this letter go through Franco's Spain instead of France the sanctity of the mail is somewhat of a foreign concept – suffice to say he will make himself known to you and bring you a written introduction from myself. You will be able to verify the signature. Please give him every assistance. I feel this man will go far. He's a bit of a rogue, but a rather polished one – and he certainly showed bravery when it counted.

A bit of fun, with some profit in it. Cut yourself in if you like. Your equity to be commensurate with the capital you invest. I'd be happy to have another partner in situ *to keep things honest (or honest enough). My friend is rather headstrong and could do with a steadying hand.*

My wife continues to suffer from the debilitating effects of the failed pregnancy. She is anaemic and terribly depressed with the still-birth of yet another baby. This is the second in two years. She is a Catholic of course and refuses to entertain the idea of birth control. The doctors say she will never be strong enough to have another baby and that I should exercise more self-control in the future. I'd like to exercise a divorce, but the timing is obviously wrong again. It's a miracle that I have a healthy son here; and of course my beloved son with Angel. How pleased I am that the extended family in Spain makes my absence a little easier as she brings up the little one. I say the little one – but of course he is not so little – as Miguel himself told me in no uncertain terms when I brought him a train-set when he really wanted a pony, or failing that a gun to shoot sparrows! He has the example of his very tough uncles to follow and emulate. I am not sure I measure up.

My best to you, – Charles

CHAPTER TWENTY-FOUR

"Ramon, do you know anything about my half-brother and what happened to him?" Charles asked, carefully adding the latest letter to his discard pile.

"Miguel Vendrell? Yes, I know of him. He was killed in an avalanche around twenty years ago."

"What did he do for a living? Or did he live on the disbursements from the trust?"

Saboya lit another of his pungent cigars and pushed back his chair. He stood, hands on hips, arching his back and pushing his belly forward. Bones creaked alarmingly. Frowning, he paced over to the window and threw it open and considered the street below before throwing the answer over his shoulder.

"He married a woman from Lleida, and they had a daughter Llourdes – now married to Ribera-Lopez. His wife's family had agricultural interests and he spent a good deal of time at the farm. I believe he was also involved with..." (he paused, and – unusually for such a fluent English speaker – appeared to search for the right word) "... transport."

"Transport," mused Charles. He exchanged a glance with Jane. She had looked up from her ledger marking her place on the page with her finger, her mind still on her grandmother and the stillborn children.

"Where was he killed?" continued Charles.

"What do you mean?"

"I mean, where was the avalanche? What was he doing there? Was he with a group of people? Was he the only one who died? Who found his body? When did it happen, exactly? Would there be a report about it in a newspaper of that period? Some obituaries? A report on the funeral and who attended it?"

Saboya blinked at the barrage of questions. He pressed his intercom and called in his long-legged secretary, the one with the insolent face of a Parisian model. She simply nodded when he directed her to trace any newspaper reports of the death of Miguel Vendrell some twenty years ago in an avalanche.

"Check *El Periodico* and *Diari d'Andorra*."

"*Claro.*"

"Señor Saboya, did you send a sample of the hair from the apartment and the ponytail for analysis?" asked Jane, abruptly changing direction.

"Call me Ramon, please. The hair went by courier to France this morning. We will have the results in three working days."

"Not before?"

"It was the best they could do."

Jane continued to page through the ledgers, looking for evidence of her grandfather's business venture with the guide from Toulouse. Finally she said, "This could be it. There was an amount of 5,000 pounds paid to a Señor Alain Bertran-Carrera in January 1951. Another 1,000 pounds was paid out six months later. The following year there appears to be either a partial loan repayment or a 'dividend' from the investment and 195 pounds is recorded against his name.

"Here it is again, 200 pounds paid into the trust eight months later and then 150 pounds after another five months. The payments aren't at regular intervals, but they are frequent enough.

"Do you know of an Alain Bertran-Carrera, Ramon?"

"Never heard of him." He looked over her shoulder. "Maybe it's a pseudonym. Later the payments are simply marked ABC – the initials, you understand? A play on his identity."

"Great!" said Charles, "That's very helpful."

"Anyway," argued Saboya, "It's mostly money coming in. I thought we were more interested in money going out. And it's too long ago. Jane, I think you should be working backwards. Start from the latest figures. We're losing sight of what we're really looking for. I know you're both interested in your newly-found relatives, but it's Pearl whom we are concerned with at the moment."

Chastened, they went back to work without another word. Jane put the old ledger down and picked up the last five years' computer statements. These were now configured in a more conventional manner. It seems that accounting standards had finally reached Andorra. She had to admit the balance of the trust surprised her. The disbursements to Charles, Pearl, Miguel's family and herself had merely been a drop in the bucket compared with the total income the investments had made.

The pert secretary showed her head around the door. "A

gentleman from the Australian Embassy in Madrid is on the line. They are trying to trace Señora Burns. The police gave them our number." Her crisply efficient English belied the sultry, "Madonna" look. Charles looked charmed.

"We'll take it here on speaker phone," Saboya told her. "Yes? Hello, Saboya speaking!"

"Frank Daltry here, Australian Embassy. I'd like to speak to Mrs Burns."

"In regard to?"

"A personal matter."

Jane paused for a moment then, leaning towards Saboya's phone, purred in a deceptively sweet tone "Lose my number did you? I thought you wrote it down." It was hot in the office and she dabbed her forehead with a tissue as she listened to his spiel.

"Ian Wentworth has been in touch with us. The Australian police informed him that his son was found dead in a hiking accident in Andorra and that you identified his body."

"Yes, that's right."

"There's no doubt?"

"None whatsoever," Jane said firmly.

"He'd like you to call him."

"I'll be happy to, if you'd give me his number – but it's late in Australia, I'll call him first thing in the morning."

"I've spoken to Detective Victor-Ignacio and told him that the Embassy will be sending someone up there to see to the details?"

"Oh yes." Jane was bitter. "Glad to see you have your priorities right. The death of a politician's son certainly warrants some action. Perhaps I should have mentioned earlier that my missing sister is Senator Wentworth's daughter-in-law."

Daltry cleared his throat. "Yes. Well. Of course we're very worried about the fact she hasn't been found, and during the time I'm in Andorra – that is, when the person who's appointed to go up to Andorra – is there, he'll also be making enquiries into your sister's disappearance."

Charles interrupted. "Mr Daltry, it's Pearl's father here, Dr Charles Barclay. I'm an old friend of the Ambassador's. Went through university with him. Please give him my regards and tell him I'd like to hear from him while I'm in Andorra. I'm staying at the

Hotel Roc de Caldes."

Daltry appeared to have been struck dumb. Charles gave a wolfish grin.

"I'll pass the message on, Sir, and we'll be in touch." Gone was the supercilious tone. Saboya reached over to switch off the speaker-phone.

"Dr Charles Barclay?" queried Jane.

"I have a doctorate in history. It always impresses bureaucrats."

"I didn't know you were friends with the Ambassador, Charles. You should have told me earlier. I might have leveraged it into getting some action."

"I don't know him, actually, but he's a diplomat, so he'd never be so un-diplomatic as to say he doesn't remember me. I checked his credentials before I left Paris and he certainly went to the same university as me, like thousands of others. It's hard to keep track of them all."

After another half an hour of sifting through columns and making occasional notes, Jane looked up to see Charles staring blankly out of the window. "Did you find something else?"

"I'm not sure. What do you make of this?"

…The investment seemed like a good idea at first, but lately it seems like the tail is wagging the dog. If you can't control him, living in Andorra, how the hell am I supposed to from Australia? It is not as if we have a long-standing friendship. He was simply someone who was around when I was there in 1942. I saw him in various places, mostly in bars with the contrabandistas. *He was known as a larger-than-life character. I always thought half his stories were untrue and the rest were exaggerations, but there was no doubt that in the one instance when he made his name he'd been very brave. There were rumours at the time that some of the* amigos *had actually killed refugees who were in their care and thrown the bodies in the alpine lakes – making off with their possessions – however I never heard any convincing evidence, and there was no suggestion he was ever involved. As you would know, no-one was ever charged or brought to trial on the matter.*

Why don't we simply cut our ties with our friend? See if he'd like to buy us out. He should have made enough to go it alone by now. I got into it for a bit of fun. It was a gamble that might pay dividends but I could easily afford to write it off if it didn't. I was a bit surprised when he did so well. However I now have a legitimate international business and I can't afford to have my good name tarnished by anything shady. More is the pity because he has a great sense for business opportunities.

It's probably a good idea to use the proceeds of the initial investment to start a bank. I wish I'd thought of it myself – but I'm not comfortable with being his silent partner while he dives into ever more shady dealings. I would prefer to put the whole thing to rest. Let him get other backers. A private bank should fly on its own merits. Andorra is certainly ripe for development. I would like to say adios, adieu *and goodbye to our giant. A giant pain in the rear-end is what he is becoming.*

What is your position on this? Are you happy to take your share of the profits to date plus your capital, and quit?

I'll be there in two weeks and then we can discuss it and possibly broach it together. Safety in numbers, so to speak! He didn't get the nickname 'El Gigante' *for nothing. Not that I ever saw him use his size in a show of force – his presence was usually enough to make for a very peaceful night. He would just blink at any troublemaker in a lazy kind of way, as if he were considering how he should eat them – roasted in the oven or grilled over the fire!*

Well. You now know him far better than I ever did. You are the man on the spot and as always I will defer to your judgement in these matters. Let's thrash it around some more when I see you.

As always, I send an embrace to Angel and the boy until I arrive. It's far too long since I saw them last. Miguel needs a father and a strong hand. He is wilful and his uncles indulge him too much. The type of education that he is receiving from them is not what I had in mind. He should be sent away to a private boarding-school, but that would be too cruel for Angel to bear. I blame myself for this dreadful situation I have created.

Here, from the time she lost the first baby, my wife turned to religion for solace. We have priests constantly in the house. Perhaps it is the influence of the partisans and of Angel's family – but I hate the soft tread of their footsteps and their insinuating ways. They appear to be far too familiar with my wife. However she reacts badly to any criticism from me. She has told me she will never divorce me, for divorce is a mortal sin. I often wonder how Charles will grow up; immured in this dreadful atmosphere where I am longing to be elsewhere and Pamela is constantly in the confessional. What sins she has to repent of I don't know – except for the fact that she has tied her husband to her through duty and not through love. She treats Charles more like a pet dog than a son and I know I am always too harsh with him to compensate. Poor child!

I have two magnificent sons and I am a lousy father to each of them. I wonder how my good intentions could have gone so seriously wrong. I am not happy with this life I have, and neither is anyone around me.

You, on the other hand, seem to have life well in hand. My best wishes to you and the lovely Maria. Heartfelt congratulations on your wedding. She is a beautiful woman, and you are a lucky man. I look forward to kissing the bride. Treasure the happiness you have together and don't take it for granted. Looking back at what I had with Angel, sometimes I despair. I speak more frankly than usual, old friend. I must be getting sentimental. It is not the Australian way. Perhaps I am becoming more Latin in my approach to life, and to be realistic, things could always be a lot worse...

Charles looked up and said. "It's dated October 1953. He died three weeks later in a car crash in Perpignan. This is the final letter in the file."

"A coincidence do you think? He writes to his solicitor (who also happens to be a partner in a profit-making venture) and says he'd like to quit, then virtually as soon as he arrives in Europe he dies in a car crash." Saboya moved straight to the crux of the matter while Jane was still stricken by the picture of Charles as a small boy ignored by his father and overindulged by his mother in a household of priests.

"So your hypothesis is: Did my father so seriously threaten the progress of '*El Gigante*' that he was killed? As a would-be banker, this anonymous *Señor* ABC would hold a respected position in the community. More so than as a smuggler; and it's pretty obvious that they were involved in some type of smuggling because that was '*El Gigante*'*s* area of expertise. He smuggled refugees during the war –

presumably for profit.

"My mother had money you know," Charles continued in one of his famous digressions. "My father was a hired hand on her family's sheep-station when they met. He was ambitious, which is probably why I was a premature baby." He gave a wry smile. It took Jane a minute to understand that his mother was pregnant with him when she married. "Now you're telling me my father's fortune is worth forty-seven million US dollars. It seems more than enough to go around. Even with our newly-found relatives there are only five beneficiaries, which translates to just under ten million US dollars each." He smiled at Jane. "I can do math too you know. Maybe you inherited that gene from me."

He started to pace between the desks. "Why is Pearl missing? If it's an extortion attempt why haven't we received some demands? Surely the longer a kidnapping takes, the more chances things could go wrong. If we ignore money for the moment, perhaps exposure could be a motive. Maybe Pearl knew something about *El Gigante*, or some other powerful person, that would affect their current status? She could have stumbled across something explosive from the past...."

Jane interrupted, "She's a journalist, for Christ's sake!" She probably knows everything about everybody. You know how she is. She's never had a normal conversation, it's always an interview. How would we ever be able to work out what was dangerous knowledge and what wasn't? It's probably all dangerous knowledge, if the truth be known, but if she didn't go missing in Bosnia or Bulgaria or any of the other hot spots she's been to and reported from over the years, why would she go missing in Andorra – one of the most peaceful, crime-free countries in the world?"

"Yes. That's a good question." Saboya nodded approvingly. He had been grappling with the cellophane on yet another giant cigar. He lit up and smoked in silence for a while with his eyes closed, his face devoid of expression. Jane wondered if he was simply enjoying the nicotine hit or replaying their conversation. Finally he met her gaze. "You should go back to the *trastero* and look at the photos again."

CHAPTER TWENTY-FIVE

The afternoon dragged on into the night. Saboya made an appointment to see Riccardo Castillo the next morning to interview him about the unknown Alain Bertran-Carrera, the mysterious ABC referred to in the accounts, and also to ask about the nature of the investment with *El Gigante* and the outcome of the attempt by Charles senior to extricate himself from the silent partnership.

The long-legged secretary produced photocopied reports from the newspaper archives, translating them into a few succinct phrases: "Miguel Vendrell perished with his Uncle Pablo in an avalanche below the *Coll de Cabris* on the western border of Andorra and Spain near the ski station of Pal. The snow was abnormally unstable on this north-facing slope. Five people died – three of the bodies were never identified. Miguel's relatives believed there were two different parties caught in the avalanche.

"The three unidentified bodies could have been tourists, although no guests were reported missing from any of the local hostels or hotels. They were all dressed warmly in a well-known Swiss brand of outdoor clothing and had snow-shoes on their feet. However no other equipment or identification was found with the bodies. The police assumed their packs were swept away, but in the spring when the snow melted, nothing was found to identify them. Enquiries with the Swiss authorities revealed that no Swiss nationals were reported as missing. A local man from Pal village found the bodies. He wasn't identified by name.

"The Vendrell family said that Miguel and his uncle had recently taken up ski-touring and had been going out in all conditions to practice. The editorial said it was tragic that this activity had led to their untimely deaths. The funeral took place in Lleida and many local dignitaries from the area and from Andorra attended."

She handed over the photographs, one of which showed a black garbed priest and crowd of people standing by two graves. Another was captioned "*viuda y unica hija*" and was of a forlorn Llourdes aged eleven, her hair in plaits inter-twined with black ribbon, standing with her mother at the door of the church. The photographs of Miguel and Pablo were reproduced from their identity cards. They shared sharp foxy features and were both described as farmers. Llourdes was Miguel's only child. The uncle, Pablo, had never married.

The secretary placed a set of copies of the articles in front of each person before firmly excusing herself for the night. "Excuse me. *Con permisso.*"

Jane called after her with a nod of apology to Saboya, "Could you get us copies of all the funeral notices?"

"*Claro.* Of course. On Monday I will go back to the newspaper archives," she said in her curiously flat diction. "I don't work on the weekend. *Buenas Noches.*"

Charles looked at the photo of his half-brother. "I would like to have known him."

"I've met his grandson, Pedro. He's a lovely boy," Jane said.

"When all this is over, maybe I'll get the chance."

They consulted their watches and saw it was eight o'clock.

"Come and have dinner?" Charles asked Jane.

But she thought of her weary blistered feet and declined. "I'd like to soak in a hot bath and go to bed. Do you mind eating alone?"

"Not at all," her father said. "I'll just order something from room service."

"Are you feeling OK? You look pale."

"I'm fine, just tired. I haven't been sleeping well." His thick blonde hair was sticking up on one side where he had run his hands through it when he was reading the last letter from his father. No doubt he dyed it.

"Shall we share a taxi? I'll drop you off on the way."

Saboya placidly said they should first place everything in the large, walk-in vault before they left, to be sure it would still be there in the morning. "I took over this office from a small private bank. It appealed to me because of the safe. I am a notary as well as a lawyer and I have thousands of wills and *escripturas* for property and goodness knows what else to store after a forty year of practice."

"How do you find everything" Jane asked, interested.

"I have a very sophisticated index system I keep right here," he chuckled tapping his temple. "When I go, it won't be easy for the next man." He seemed to like the idea of the mayhem he'd leave behind.

Jane followed him into the walk-in safe and checked the placement of the two archive boxes. Every shelf was piled high with old documents and ledger books and they found difficulty in finding enough space for the boxes on the floor.

Saboya stepped out and twirled the dial. "We'll start again in the morning around 9.30 or 10.00 if that suits you both, and then go on to the appointment with Señor Castillo?"

"Sure," said Charles, shaking Saboya's hand. "Thanks for everything, Ramon. I appreciated you picking me up from the hospital. It was very kind of you."

No sooner had Jane switched on the lights of the apartment than the telephone by the front door rang.

"It's Juan-Antonio. I'm downstairs."

"Come up." Jane pressed the security button on the phone to unlock the entrance. Juan-Antonio appeared, wearing worn jeans and a pair of high-heeled snake-skinned cowboy boots. He looked uncertain, and hesitated for a moment before reaching out and kissing her on both cheeks. Her tension immediately transmitted itself to him.

"How are you?" he asked, stepping back.

"OK." Jane wondered what tone would strike the right note.

"Have you had dinner?"

"I'm not hungry. My cold I suppose."

"Why don't we go to the restaurant downstairs for something light?"

"If you like," she said, thinking she would prefer to talk to him in a room full of strangers.

They walked the two floors down without speaking, and were shown to a booth at the back, where they silently perused the menu. The crisp blue décor of the restaurant, which looked pleasantly buoyant by day, reflected bleakly on the faces of the patrons under the artificial light at night and mirrored her mood. The woman who greeted them at the door had a German accent. Her hair looked like it had been dipped in concrete. The menus were slapped on the table, and no olives or *tapas* materialised while they were considering the choices. Judging by the lack of diners the woman was probably unhappy at the paucity in revenue, but Jane thought her attitude would ensure business did not improve. The prominence of sangria and paella in an insert at the beginning of the menu showed the target clientele were tourist buses.

"Something is bothering you?" Juan-Antonio finally asked.

She came straight to the point. "I'm upset the police didn't make any attempt to interview your cousin, Fernando, about his relationship with Pearl. And if that isn't enough, it seems his wife is actually my cousin – or half-cousin, I'm not sure what the definition is – and she and her son Pedro are beneficiaries of the trust. So it seems Pearl was having an affair with her own cousin's husband! I know there's no law against it, but I'm sure she would have thought twice about starting the relationship had she known."

Juan-Antonio beckoned for water.

"Was it coincidence that you met me at the sports centre, or were you looking for me? You took me down to the family farm in Lleida for God's sake. And now I'm sleeping with you!" Her voice rose and the other two tables of diners stared at her. "There are far too many cousins in this mixture. Everybody is related to everyone else in this Godforsaken country! Why don't you say something?"

Juan-Antonio took some time to think about his response. He started slowly, "Fernando and I don't discuss personal things – like the state of his marriage, or whether he's involved with anyone else – although in the village it is hard to keep a secret and it was common knowledge that he was seeing Pearl. When you told me she was missing, I didn't take it seriously. The incident about the bottle of champagne was troubling, but it seemed more likely that she had simply gone away for work reasons. You rarely have to produce your passport to enter neighbouring countries so people often forget to take them."

"Go on," said Jane.

"I had no reason to know Llourdes is related to you, or to link her with the trust. I knew she was an heiress to land holdings down in Lleida, and the family talked about Fernando marrying well, but what that actually meant wasn't spelt out. I was never particularly interested anyway. I have so many cousins – first, second and third – that it's hard to keep them all straight.

"Did I tell you my father was also a policeman, and one of my uncles is in the police force as well?" He didn't wait for Jane's response but continued, "This means that if someone in the family were to be involved in illegitimate activities, we certainly wouldn't want to talk about it or acknowledge it."

"What sort of activities are we talking about?"

"Well, smuggling of course. What else?" Juan-Antonio looked surprised. "It wasn't an offence to smuggle tobacco out of Andorra until recently when the EU, and most particularly France and Spain, started to put us under a lot of pressure.

"Even now there is no jail time in Andorra for smuggling. There are simply hefty fines and confiscation of vehicles involved. No-one in their right mind would ever use his own vehicle for smuggling. Usually they 'borrow' one, or use a rental car.

"The *Guardia Civil* found a haul of cigarettes in the French postal van recently. Some enterprising employee thought the *Aduanas* would never bother to search a mail-van! Smuggling is in our blood. Our ancestors took to it in order to eke out a living in what was a very poor country, prior to tourism and ski resorts. The police have managed to look the other way up until now."

Their salads arrived, and spun across the table. Jane put out her hand to stop hers falling to the floor.

Juan-Antonio continued, "It's difficult, because most police-officers have a relative or two who have been involved over the years, so we deal with that by not talking about it. If we heard something we might be obliged to act on it. We've always thought of smuggling as a victimless crime. We're not too concerned about loss of tax revenue in Spain or France."

"How does this relate to Pearl and Llourdes?"

Juan-Antonio shrugged, "I am trying to explain why I wouldn't know that Llourdes is your relative."

"Didn't you know her grandfather was Charles Barclay?"

"Llourde's father's name was Miguel Vendrell. He used only his mother's surname without his patronymic. No-one ever talked about his father because Miguel was illegitimate. Your father and grandfather are named Barclay. Your name is Burns, and Pearl's name is Wentworth. Even if I'd known Llourde's grandfather's name, why would I make the connection?"

"You're a policeman. I'd have thought you'd be more curious."

"Jane, I'm not a detective. I normally handle traffic offences and the odd local crisis," Juan-Antonio sounded exasperated.

They were interrupted by the arrival of their main course. It was hard for Jane to remember when she had been less hungry. She cut into the grilled rabbit unenthusiastically, trying to separate her desire for the words to be true from a more probing doubt.

"Fair enough," she said, "that sounds plausible, but what about the atmosphere when we went down to Lleida? Don't tell me I was imagining it. Everyone was far too interested in me."

"Llourdes knew about Fernando's affair with Pearl. You're Pearl's sister. She considered it a deliberate insult that I would bring you there."

"Why did you then?"

"There were a few reasons," he paused, assembling them. "I liked you and wanted to get to know you better. You were attacked the day before, which made me worry about you if I left you on your own. Since there is a standing invitation for me to join the hunting I thought I'd take you down there. I knew you'd be safe with me."

"But you intended to leave me on my own at the farmhouse."

"You would have been in no danger there; but I was going to suggest you come with me and the hunters anyway...I just wasn't going to give you a gun!"

Juan-Antonio could see Jane was not entirely convinced but he merely tucked into his dinner, not trying to persuade her any further. Jane described finding Harris and her doubt that the death was accidental. Discussing events with Juan-Antonio was cathartic, even while she was guarding her words and being careful not to tell him anything he couldn't find out for himself. Despite her misgivings, she liked being with him. He was a calm and relaxing companion.

At the end of the meal, Juan-Antonio looked at his watch as if he was late for another appointment and bade her goodnight. If he was disappointed not to be invited to share her bed he didn't show it. She thought he probably knew a great deal about human nature. Although she had been determined to reject his advances, she was conversely displeased when there was no need. Not for the first time, she reflected that life was complicated.

CHAPTER TWENTY-SIX

Halfway to the lift, the lights went out. Jane groaned and wondered if this day would ever end. Whoever was in charge of wiring this old building should be shot. She glided blindly along with her hands in front of her until they hit the wall near the lift, breaking another one of her finger-nails – swore – and then slid her feet left until they touched the first step of the stairwell. She continued slowly up the stairs holding onto the hand-rail. When she stepped onto the landing of the second floor she heard a furtive, scuffling sound. A ray of light shone into her eyes blinding her. She froze like a rabbit caught in the headlights of a car, then felt another small animal try to stampede through her chest.

"Who's there?" A childish voice piped.

"Good Grief! Mary, you frightened me half to death. What on earth are you doing up at this hour?" Jane's heart was still beating fast.

"Oh good, it's you. I hoped it would be. Can I sleep at your place tonight?"

"If you promise to go to bed right now. I'm tired and grumpy, and I've got a cold."

Mary took her hand. "The power's off. I tried throwing the master switch, but this time the whole village has gone out. There are no street-lamps but I have a torch. You should always travel with a torch." She drew a figure eight in the darkness, then demonstrated some Morse code dots and dashes.

"I can see that would be handy. Where are Dad and Dave?"

"They said they were going out for an hour or so, but that was ages ago. I don't like being by myself when there are no lights."

"'Course you don't," said Jane, feeling sorry for the child. "I'm glad to have your company."

"Really?" asked Mary. Jane could hear the beam in her tone.

"Yes. I'm not too keen on being alone in the dark myself. We'd better leave a note on the door for your Dad though, so he doesn't worry."

"I don't know," said Mary in her old-fashioned way. "He's keen enough for me to come to visit, but once I'm here we never do the things together that he promised. He just goes off and forgets all about me."

Jane thought she could hear an echo of the mother in the child's tone. How many children go into adulthood bearing the scars of battles fought by their parents? She cuddled Mary to her, and opened the door to the apartment.

"Let's jump straight into bed. I expect you've had your shower already, but I'm going to bed dirty ... just kicking off my clothes and falling under the quilt. I don't like showering in the dark. It reminds me of a creepy film called *Psycho*, which kept me awake at night when I was about your age."

"I should get my pyjamas."

"Don't worry about it. You can sleep in your underwear," said Jane, throwing on a T-shirt that read; "God made us sisters. Prozac made us friends." Mary inspected it with the torch.

"Mum said Prozac's a drug."

"It was a gift from Pearl. She has an interesting sense of humour."

Breakfast was late the next morning, and featured a smorgasbord of styles. Jane was rather alarmed to find her appetite had still not come back. Although she drank three cups of tea, she barely touched any food. Mary, on the other hand, kept up a constant prattle over the noise of the television while devouring everything in sight. Jane absentmindedly watched cartoons on the Andorran TV channel and was amazed to find that she could actually understand a few words. Of course having visual clues helped.

The cartoons rolled into the news and with it reports of a police raid at a local discothèque. It was easy to translate the caption "*droga incursion*" and although the newscaster spoke quickly, "*cocaine*" was close enough to English to be a cognate. A shot of black-leather-garbed men being herded into a police van caught Jane's attention. The light from the television camera glanced off a head of blonde dreadlocks. She didn't see any auburn curls but said casually to Mary.

"Pop next door and see if your Dad and Dave are up yet and want to come over for breakfast."

"The note's still on the door." Mary frowned. "It doesn't look like they came home at all."

"I guess they took one look at the note and thought since I was baby-sitting, they'd go out again and paint the town red. The nightlife starts late here and only seems to wind up around breakfast time. Why don't you have a shower, sweetie, while I clear up the dishes?"

Mary dashed off before Jane could change her mind and ask her to help. Jane looked at her watch and dialled Saboya on his mobile, catching him on his way to the office. "I've got another job for you," she said.

When she logged onto her email, she found a short message from Carol:

I called the hospital and your grandmother is holding on. The nurses think she may pull through, although they don't know how the stroke might have affected her mobility. She was conscious yesterday and humming along to The Sound of Music *but she still doesn't recognise anybody. Its hard to separate how much of that is the Alzheimer's and how much is new from the stroke. The doctors say that a third of people who suffer a stroke recover spontaneously. Your mother is fine, and sends her love. She's too preoccupied to call right now as you can imagine. I'm attaching an article about Harris' death.*

An article from *The West Australian* Newspaper followed.

POLITICIAN'S SON DEAD HIKING THE PYRENEES.
The son of Western Australian senator Ian Wentworth has died in a hiking accident in the Pyrenees. Harris Wentworth fell to his death while attempting to hike across a mountain-range in the tiny principality of Andorra. His body was found yesterday by two mountaineers. He was married to war-correspondent Pearl Wentworth who has recently been reported as missing. They were estranged and have been living apart for a number of years. Harris was a well-known anthropologist with the Department of Aboriginal Affairs. The past five years he has been working in the north-west of Western Australia, cataloguing aboriginal sacred sites. His

colleagues expressed shock at the accident, commenting that he was an extremely able bushman who had spent many holidays trekking in the mountains of New Zealand.

Senator Wentworth announced that he would found a public memorial fund in his son's name to help people suffering from bipolar disease. His son was diagnosed with this condition (also known as manic depression) in his late teens. Senator Wentworth said he was extremely proud of how his son had handled his condition. He graduated from university with honours and went to work in the very important field of aboriginal development and reconciliation. His positive example should prove to be an inspiration to other mental health sufferers, and to their families. Senator Wentworth said that the improvement of mental healthcare was one of his party's major concerns.

Gary Cohen had also been busy on her behalf. She downloaded a large file that contained two photos of Jack Weinstein and several articles from the *New York Times* archives.

Weinstein was around fifty, chisel-faced and frowning, with brown eyes set close together. His curly salt-and-pepper hair looked badly in need of a trim and hung slightly below his frayed collar. Two grooves on either side of his nose to his mouth gave him a melancholy, eastern-European air. Jane would not describe him as average-looking, but then again she wasn't Señor Molina or Jorge, whose attention may have been focussed on Pearl. Men never saw other men the way women did. She wouldn't rule him out as a candidate for the man Pearl met at Lake Pessons. The suit he was wearing in the photos certainly wasn't Armani – or anything close.

She printed several copies of the photos and then turned to the articles.

These chronicled the three decades in which Weinstein had made his name by challenging Swiss banks to make public their records of Holocaust victims' accounts. The funds from these accounts had been absorbed into the banks' asset base when no survivors presented themselves with the relevant provenance for inheritance. Banks had subsequently hidden behind the Swiss privacy laws to thwart claims.

Weinstein was also at the forefront of legal challenges to return land and property confiscated by the Nazis to lawful beneficiaries. A current case concerned the headquarters of Slobadon Milošević, which was currently in the throes of being handed back to Crown Price Alexander of Yugoslavia.

Weinstein's work was funded both by the wealthy American Jewish community and by the ten per cent commission he charged for successful litigation. This money was used to mount future challenges. He took a wage, but was by no means wealthy. He was unmarried and had no family. His parents had perished in Dachau (which would make him older than he looked). His colleagues credited him with a formidable intellect and a ferocious capacity for work.

Gary Cohen had dashed off a quick email to accompany these details:

If this guy has something to do with Pearl's disappearance I can guarantee huge coverage. Just say the word, and I'll do a piece. In a missing-person scenario, there is no bad publicity.

"Should I go home now?" Mary's head appeared at the other side of the desk. Her long thin neck, freckled face and impossibly curly red hair made her look like a sunflower. Her lime green shorts and a yellow T-shirt added to the effect.

"No. Let's spend the day together. I've got a few things to do first, but you can help me later with some stuff like…" Jane had no idea what Mary could help her with. She thought about all the things left undone. What could Mary help with? "…like looking through Pearl's negatives to make a list of what's on them. Do you think you could do that? We can spend the morning at the *trastero* and then have a pizza somewhere for lunch. Here's a notebook and pencil."

Mary looked interested.

"Will this help find Pearl?"

"I hope so."

"My spelling's not that good." Mary looked eager to help, but anxious not to be found wanting.

"Just spell it phonetically and we'll be able to figure out what you mean."

"What's 'phonetically'?"

Jane laughed, although she was furious with Lyn and Dave for leaving Mary at home alone. Bloody men, not taking responsibility for their children. But no sooner had she had this thought, when she remembered Harris proudly holding up the photo of his son, saying he wanted to protect him.

"Hell's teeth," she said. "What time is it? I have to make a call straight away." She caught Mary scribbling in the notebook. "What?" she asked.

"Hell's teeth," repeated Mary. "I've never heard that one before."

Mary was certainly bright enough to write down all the four letter words Jane knew; and she wouldn't have to use phonetics.

Ian Wentworth's secretary took Jane's call and said the senator was already on his way to Europe to collect Harris's body for burial back in Australia. A prominent businessman had offered the use of his private jet as far as Singapore where he'd make the commercial connection to Barcelona. Jane wrote down his cell number. Wentworth answered on the first ring and accepted her condolences gracefully, in turn commiserating with her on Pearl's disappearance.

"Someone from the embassy in Madrid is meeting me in Barcelona."

"That would be Frank Daltry." It sounded like Daltry was on the career path again. "What about Harris's girlfriend Melinda? Has somebody let her know?"

"Yes." Wentworth sounded vague. "We'll have to work something out there."

CHAPTER TWENTY-SEVEN

Greta waved to Jane and Mary from her sun-drenched balcony and beckoned them to come up. The walk from Ordino to Greta's apartment block had been hot and sweaty. A high-pressure system had settled over the Pyrenees that morning, bringing with it another gloriously fine day.

"Come up and have a lemon squash!"

"Thanks." They waved back gratefully and crossed the threshold to the cool, granite-lined entrance.

Mary had started off in high spirits, insisting on wearing her backpack, into which she stuffed a variety of things "just in case," but a thirty minute walk in the sun had taken its toll and her normally pale face was fire-engine-red under the yellow sunhat and matching shirt.

Greta ushered them into her spacious lounge. The expanse of tiled floor was inviting, and Mary sank down onto it, rather than take a plump, scratchily upholstered chair. Between the three of them they made quick work of the freshly-made jug of chilled tart lemonade.

"I've been doing a little research into all the tobacco fields in Andorra, and I've found the one where Pearl took the photos." Greta was boiling with importance. "It's in Pal." She flourished a handful of photos. "I only have a cheap camera, so these are not of the same quality as Pearl's but I think you'll see the similarity."

Jane, with Mary hanging over her shoulder, fanned the photos out on the coffee-table. Although the season was further advanced and the fields were mostly bare of tobacco, the stone walls, the drying shed and the position of the trees were all familiar.

"Fantastic. How did you find it?" Jane asked.

Greta's rosy cheeks glowed and her eyes danced with excitement. "I drove around with my camera and then hiked up and down trails – mostly up. Andorra is all about trails that go up! I decided to do the west side of Andorra first, because Pearl lives on this side. I started with the northernmost Arcalis Valley, and then Arinsal, and ended up in Pal. I knew straight away this was the right place so I marked it on my topographical map then consulted the *Comu* so that they could tell me who owned the land."

"Outstanding!" said Jane, impressed by the audacity and initiative of the small Danish woman.

Greta ran her hands through her short grey basin-cut, and shrugged with satisfaction. "It was easy," she said, not recounting the days of hard slogging up steep stony paths with her lungs raging – nor mentioning the rain and how disheartened she felt after the first two days.

"I told the *Comu* I was interested in buying a secluded piece of land to build a *borda*. They're quite used to enquiries of this nature. The whole country seems to be selling off pieces of their land since the government introduced an annual quota system to limit tobacco production. Anyway, they gave me the name of the owner. – Here it is on official *Comu* letterhead. – There was no phone-number.

"SANTIAGO DE ALMEIDA BARREIRO,
CASA D'OR,
CARRETERA PARTICULAR, PAL, LA MASSANA."

It didn't mean anything to Jane. She gave Greta a hug all the same.

"'House of Gold,'" Mary translated. "How exciting! Is it really of gold?"

"It's just an ordinary stone farmhouse at the end of an unpaved private road. All the shutters were closed. I knocked, then slipped a note under the door with my name and phone-number on it saying I was interested in buying a piece of their land – I didn't say which piece – but they didn't call me. Perhaps they're away at the moment."

"The farmers are still harvesting the tobacco and putting it up to dry so they shouldn't be away," said Jane. "Tractors have been driving past Pearl's apartment in Ordino every afternoon, pulling trailer-loads full of tobacco, and the sheds are full of it, drying in lines."

"We should have a stake-out," interrupted Mary. "We could watch the house until someone shows up."

Jane smiled and ruffled her curls. "You've been watching too many videos! I think we'll get the experts onto it. Señor Saboya can make enquiries. Thank goodness we have a local who knows his way around. He'll be able to get some background information for us."

Greta frowned. "Didn't I hear something unsavoury about Ramon Saboya? Something about him withholding his files when the property laws changed?"

"I'm sure Pearl wouldn't have chosen him if he'd done anything questionable."

"Should we tell the police we've found the place in the photos?"

"When Saboya thinks it's appropriate.... There's no point in having a dog and barking yourself. Maybe the police already know where it is but haven't wanted to tell us. I sometimes wonder if Victor is playing some sort of double game."

The *trastero* had lost its claustrophobic resonance now Jane knew she could free herself by operating the automatic doors. The new globes left no corner in shadow but also did not provide a great deal of light to scrutinise the negatives. After an hour of eyestrain, Greta brought down a retractable desk lamp from her apartment to help speed things up. Even so, the rest of the morning passed slowly as Jane and Greta sifted through the thousands of negatives and painstakingly listed the contents. Mary laboriously made a list of different subjects and concentrated on keeping the slides in order as she worked beside the adults with no complaint. Occasionally Greta or Jane would grimace at the unrelenting pictorial of a far-off war. It was hard to confront evidence of man's inhumanity. Jane wondered how Pearl had the stomach for it. She hadn't shrunk from depicting the worst excesses committed against the aged or women and children. Swollen bodies lay piled on top of each other against a barn door in Bosnia.

Jane was glad they had spared Mary the sight of the photos and given her the task of cataloguing instead. She remembered an excerpt from one of Pearl's letters from the front line.

...Most of the photos have been too horrific to find a publisher. The editors think the public should be protected. Yet how can they possibly understand the nature of the conflict if they can't see the reality and judge for themselves? Photos of dead innocent civilians are a powerful argument against war, and to censor or expurgate them runs counter to journalistic ideals.

I'd like to present the photos without captions – a page or two of them – but apparently images of this nature are against the voluntary press code. I can only say that in sanitizing the photos they insult the average person's intelligence. We should be able to publish the truth and let the public decide for themselves. Of course the generals and the hawks in the US government wouldn't want any propaganda that might influence the doves to vote to decrease the military's sphere of influence.

Strangely though, I am coming around to the argument for a strong military force to act as a deterrent. I could never have contemplated this when I left university. I've just finished reading "The Last Lion", William Manchester's brilliant biography of Winston Churchill during those years of his exile from power, when Churchill was one of the few who argued against disarmament and made a case for building a strong military to deter Hitler. It's a salutary read.

Jane's phone rang, breaking her reverie.

"Saboya here. I found your neighbours. You were right, they were caught up in last night's raid of gay bars in search of drugs. There was no evidence against them so it was relatively simple to have them released from custody. They're on their way home. I put them in the taxi myself."

"Sod taking Mary home now," Jane said to Greta in an undertone with her hand over the receiver. "Let them sweat. They deserve it, the irresponsible bastards."

Greta nodded in agreement.

"Ramon, I need some different information now. Do you know of a Santiago de Almeida Barreiro in Pal? He owns the fields where Pearl took her photo series on the tobacco industry."

Ramon took some time to reply. "Almeida Barreiro is a well-connected *contrabandista*. Any enquiries about him may not be good for my health. I think it may be time for us to lay all these separate threads in front of the investigating detective to see if he and his team can knit them together. If Pearl was investigating this person, I fear she may have involved herself in something that is way beyond her provenance. Men of this type do not take kindly to exposure."

"Wouldn't an enquiry to the police alert him? Surely he'd have family, or paid informants on the force?"

"I have confidence in the integrity of the Andorran police force. This is not some victimless crime that we are talking about but a serious missing-person case, possibly a kidnapping, or worse. The police would never look the other way to cover up a crime of such magnitude. I'll discuss this with your father when I get back to the office. He's still going through the archive boxes. If he agrees I will make an appointment for us to meet with Detective Victor."

At 1.30 they broke for lunch at Can Pere, the local restaurant.

"You promised pizza," said Mary.

"Yes, I know – but wouldn't fish and chips do?" Jane still hadn't contacted Lyn and Dave. She felt bad, but not as bad as she hoped they felt. "We can walk there. It's only half a minute."

The thought of having to walk too far silenced Mary, who was well aware that they still had the return walk to Ordino in front of them, but she complained half-heartedly, "We go there a lot. I was hoping to go somewhere new." Even so she skipped down the street and into the small restaurant, pleased to have a break from her responsibilities as recorder.

Jane and Greta followed more slowly behind her. Greta stopped to say hallo to an elderly couple who were digging up potatoes in their garden.

"They own half of Anyos, but you'd never know it," said Greta as they walked on. "They live simply and don't want to sell any land. When their children inherit I suppose we'll have a building explosion here, like all the other villages."

The village was small and consisted of a hostel, restaurant and five or six apartment blocks of varying vintage surrounding the original core of stone farmhouses. These were separated from each other by narrow cobbled steps and steep slate paths. The fronts of the buildings were pock-marked by age but the profusion of colourful red geraniums spilling from window-boxes and the meticulously maintained streets alleviated any appearance of disrepair. A wicker basket full of exotic mushrooms sat at the entrance to Can Pere. Mary was already sitting at a window table swinging her freckled legs.

A good-looking, thickly-muscled young man in a chef's hat came out of the kitchen to tell them the specials of the day. They agreed on ceps, the fresh local mushrooms the chef had collected in the woods above Anyos that morning, and an omelette. The ceps were cooked simply in olive oil with garlic and parsley and tossed with a curly-leaved salad. Mary stuck with fish and chips. Jane noticed that the menu included old favourites like Steak Dianne that she hadn't seen for twenty years.

Greta barely spoke throughout the meal. She had a hearty appetite and ate with relish, and then mopped up the salad dressing with some bread, downing two tankards of beer in the process. Jane envied her metabolism.

"You've dropped your napkin," Greta said, and bent to pick it up, levering herself upright again with her hand on Jane's thigh. Was that squeeze intentional?

"Time to go," Jane sprang up. "I'd better call Lyn and Dave and tell them what's happened to Mary." She walked over to the bar to pay the bill, leaving a generous tip, and then passed her mobile phone to Mary. "Here you are, kiddo. Better check in."

Jane waited until the connection was made. "Hi Dad, it's me. I'm with Jane helping her with some stuff. We've just had lunch at Can Pere. Oh…" she looked around, "she's not here at the moment, she's gone to the ladies room so she can't talk to you – but we've still got quite a lot to do yet, so I won't see you until later. Bye."

CHAPTER TWENTY-EIGHT

B ack down in the cool subterranean *trastero* and an hour into the afternoon's work, Jane received a call from Charles to ask about progress.

"So far the negatives in the filing-cabinets are all from her work as a war-correspondent" said Jane. "We're cataloguing them as best we can. It's not too hard since Pearl was very methodical. She grouped the work into war-zones. I guess she had her own mental index, but didn't write the key down. It's slow, but with the three of us here we are getting through them at a steady pace. Young Mary has amazing concentration."

Jane could hear Charles pacing up and down on the other end of the line.

"I've been doing much the same spade-work here," he told her. "Saboya's preoccupied with another case, so I've been going through his pile of documents while he is working in another office. I'm using Spanish and Catalan dictionaries to look up key words and just reorganising the paperwork into some sort of coherent theme. If Saboya's desk and vault are an indication of his state of mind, he'd be a good candidate for committal." Despite his *bon-vivant* lifestyle, Charles retained a historian's ordered approach to documentation and any unorthodox methodology or paper haystack made him uneasy. "We're seeing Castillo at six to ask if his father told him anything about ABC – Alain Bertran-Carrera – *El Gigante*. Will you be coming?"

Jane looked at her watch. Six o'clock was two hours away.

"I doubt I can make it. Will you fill me in afterwards?"

"Sure. And we're booked for dinner tonight with Ian Wentworth and Frank Daltry. I had a call earlier. I suggested they stay at the Roc de Caldes, so we'll eat there."

"OK. That sounds fine. Perhaps after dinner the two of us can talk. It's hard to know if we are finding clues or if they are just the loose ends that we all have in our lives. You can argue for a conspiracy in any linked events, but most things are just chance." She sighed, discouraged.

"We have to be patient and check every lead while we wait for the person who sent the ponytail to contact us." His determined voice sent a charge of optimism down the phone line. "If we share our information, no matter how minor, surely we can identify the important parts. We'll work 'til late… 'Midnight shakes the memory, as a madman shakes a dead geranium'," he quoted.

Jane shivered. "Where did that come from?"

"T.S. Elliot. 'Rhapsody on a Windy Night'. Your master's degree left out all the interesting bits in your education, Jane. You may have learned all about finance, but history and English literature would teach you how to think strategically. History isn't a series of unconnected events, although that is often unclear while it unfolds. Anyway – together we have several fields covered and if we pool our knowledge we must get somewhere."

Jane picked up her next set of negatives. The attention, so lacking from her father when she was growing up, was now a warm meal slowly digesting in her stomach. Mary pulled her chair closer as if to bathe in the heat. Jane ruffled her curls absentmindedly.

"Fathers are strange beasts."

Mary was all at sea but unwilling to say so. "I forgot to say that Dad wanted me to say, thanks. I guess he meant for having me to stay for the night."

"It was my pleasure, and thank you for helping me today."

"I like the way you talk to me."

"Well, I don't think anyone should be less polite to a child than to an adult. Sometimes, back home, I see people behave badly towards their families. They use more courtesy towards a stranger. Once, in a supermarket, I offered a guy $20 to stop shouting at his kids. He said I could have a knuckle sandwich for free."

"Most other people wouldn't tell me that. They'd think I was too young."

"Are you too young?"

"I don't expect so," Mary answered. "Mum says I am old for my age, and that it's all Dad's fault, but I don't think being old for your age is a fault, do you?"

"Not if it means you're sensible."

"Exactly! I try to be sensible."

"I wish there were more of us."

Greta laughed. She had been listening to this exchange.

"I think you are both suffering from sugar deprivation. Come up to the apartment and have a biscuit and a cup of tea."

"We get no respect," said Mary, which made Greta laugh harder.

By six o'clock, they were more than halfway through the negatives, but the cruel images of war had become a blur and their senses were blunted by repetition.

"Are you a member of Amnesty International?" asked Greta idly.

"No, but after today, I'd consider joining."

"I would have thought Pearl's work would lead you to join."

"Not really. I wasn't paying much attention to Pearl's career. I've been busy building my own. At university I avoided political groups, and of course being married to a policeman didn't encourage me to question the conservative position. I've always considered myself to be apolitical. If it were not mandatory to vote in Australia, I doubt I'd bother. Still, I read the paper."

"Who are the people leading the debate about Australia's future? Who influences the nation's psyche?"

"Probably the bureaucrats. Political parties are voted in and out, but public servants go on forever."

With that thought they began to pack up for the day. Mary went outside to enjoy the day's dwindling supply of sunlight and warm up after a day spent underground and when they came out of the garage they found her turning cartwheels on the lawn.

"Why don't I give you a lift home to save you the walk?" asked Greta as Jane stretched her arms and shoulders and heard her joints creak. She was slow to move away when Greta reached up and began to massage her aching neck muscles.

"Great," answered Mary for her. "I'll get back in time for my favourite TV programme on Sky."

As they drove down the hill, Greta suggested a deviation. "We could drive by *La Casa d'Or* again and see if anyone is there."

"Sure. Why not?" responded Jane with a quick glance at Mary who was frowning at the choice between missing her favourite show and looking at the fabled house of gold.

Greta accelerated her powerful silver BMW through La Massana and up the valley towards Pal, aggressively changing gears at each curve.

"Nice car," said Jane.

"Yes. Good engineering, but hopeless in the snow without winter tyres." Greta crossed double white lines to overtake a man on a bicycle and a slow truck, narrowly missing a delivery van travelling towards them. Jane shut her eyes but then quickly opened them when there was a squeal of brakes and she was thrown forward against her seat-belt. A bunch of fat horses were ambling down the road, shaking their shaggy manes and setting their bells ringing. At first they appeared to be walking unescorted, but after a moment Jane heard a sharp whistle and a small black dog ran around one side to herd them closer together. At the rear of the horses came a single man leaning on a long wooden stick.

"*Bona Tarda*," he nodded at them courteously. Smoke poured out of his pipe into his weary creased face.

"*Donde va usted*?" Jane asked where he was going, in her slow, careful Spanish. The old man lifted his chin to point down the valley.

"*Millor pastura*."

"Better pasture," translated Greta.

"Ask him about the people at *La Casa d'Or*?" suggested Mary.

Greta offered the old man a cigarette, which he gravely accepted and tucked behind his ear for later use. He spoke quietly, keeping an eye on the horses. Finally he tugged the front of his cap in what may have been a gesture of respect or a casual *adios* and strode after the herd at a pace that belied his age.

"He says they would be bringing in the tobacco harvest until the light fades at around nine o'clock." Greta drove on at a more sedate pace saying, "We'll just drive by there, so you know where it is."

"I didn't know you smoked," said Jane.

"Oh, I have all the usual vices," said Greta in her gruff voice, reaching over to change gears and then turning off the main road in a controlled skid and onto a gravel track, thickly lined with pine trees. The BMW slowed as they bumped along with barely enough clearance to stop the chassis from dragging. After half a kilometre, they reached a clearing large enough for two fenced paddocks, and a rambling stone farmhouse attached to a barn. A giant brown dog of indeterminate breed charged the car, barking vociferously.

"This is a new development," said Greta, unperturbed, driving over the uneven ground until the car was parked directly in front of the wooden front door. Strands of saliva trickled down the car window as the dog sprang up towards the driver's door sharply butting his nose against the glass. Greta tooted the horn. "The noise should bring someone if they're here."

"What will we say to them?" asked Mary, sounding nervous.

"We'll think of something," replied Jane as Greta put her hand back on the horn and left it there for a few seconds. The dog was now throwing itself bodily against the car, "but unless someone appears I don't fancy getting out of the car for any reason." They pulled slowly away, the dog snapping at the tyres all the way to the tarred road.

"It's not even in the sun." Mary looked back through the rear window, disappointed. "The pine trees throw too much shadow. It's not golden at all."

CHAPTER TWENTY-NINE

The taxi turned into the circular driveway and deposited Jane at the grandiose entrance of the Roc de Caldes hotel. Swinging through the revolving doors and turning to her right, she mounted a bank of marble steps leading to the dark clubby bar. Charles was seated before a low coffee-table with two men. Jane's eyes were drawn to a bottle of Johnny Walker Black Label whisky and jug of ice in front of them. She raised her eyebrows at Charles as the men all stood to greet her.

"I'm sorry to see you again under these circumstances. How was your flight?" she said to Ian Wentworth, kissing him lightly on one cheek. He looked exhausted but was well-groomed in a grey tailored suit and muted tie. She had met him only once before, at Harris and Pearl's wedding.

"How do you do." She turned to Frank Daltry and shook his hand, gripping it a little more forcefully than normal. The five o'clock shadow was a surprise in a career bureaucrat, as were the quick blue eyes that swept the room before meeting hers. In his late twenties, he was the antithesis of Wentworth. Daltry sported yesterday's shave and blue jeans. His hairline receded over a high forehead.

"What would you like to drink?" asked Charles, embracing her and kissing her twice. "They've given us the whole bottle. Generous of them."

"Vichy," she replied with a quick grimace at the bottle and the smell of whisky on his breath. She was unnaturally attuned to alcohol and could smell it from several feet away. It was a contradiction to find the fumes repellent but at the same time discover the old desire of wanting to lose herself in a glass. When she sat down she pushed her chair slightly away from the table.

They sipped their drinks in a cavern of silence. Daltry was darting looks at her over the rim of his glass, taking in her expensive wool crêpe slacks and silk sweater. When he spoke to her, he seemed to be addressing her neck. She found it irritating that he didn't meet her eyes.

"I've spoken to Detective Victor. Managed to bring him up to date with a few things he was unaware of."

"Oh yes?"

"I travel in Embassy circles in Madrid and socialise with the other first secretaries. At the functions we talk about work and exchange gossip. About three months ago the Philippine Embassy was investigating a missing-person case that also involved Andorra. After I spoke to you last, I checked the details. A young woman applied to her embassy for the paperwork to renew her passport. It was a routine request and they replied to her address in Andorra with the necessary forms. These were returned as undeliverable and the passport lapsed. A month later the woman's family contacted the Embassy to say that she hadn't been in touch, nor sent the usual monthly remittance.

"The embassy tried to establish the daughter's whereabouts. They made an official request to the Andorran government and the police visited the address where the forms had been sent but no-one there knew anything about her. The Andorrans said the woman had never been issued with a work-visa and there was no evidence of her living or working in the country. They assumed there was some type of snafu. The family is still in regular touch with the Embassy but no-one has any clue as to where she might be."

Jane leaned forward, her heart beating irregularly.

"What makes you think there's any connection?"

"I'm not sure there is. It's just the juxtaposition of the words 'missing person' and 'Andorra' that made me think that there might be a link."

Jane noticed that when Daltry came to the point of his story, his pale eyes met her gaze and held it before dancing off to continue their constant quartering of the room. He perched on the edge of his chair like a game bird ready to explode into the air at the first sign of a line of beaters.

"What did Victor say when you told him?"

"He didn't say anything. He merely wrote down all the particulars and thanked me for my time. This is just a personal observation – but I get the impression that detectives in Andorra don't get many important cases to solve."

"Meaning what? That you think they are giving this their undivided attention or that the whole thing is beyond their experience?"

Daltry shrugged.

"What was the address that they sent the paperwork to?"

"Some place in Pal."

"You're kidding!"

"What makes you say that?" Daltry asked in a conversational tone.

"Pearl took a series of photos of tobacco fields and workers in Pal and I've just been by there to contact the owner of the farm, unsuccessfully as it turns out. Does *La Casa d'Or* ring a bell?"

Charles interjected, leaning forward across the square glass coffee-table. "Saboya thought this man could be dangerous, Jane."

"Well – I assumed we were just going to drive by to look at the house, but there's really no such thing as driving by because *La Casa d'Or* is at the end of a *cul-de-sac*. Anyway, in the end I didn't even get out of the car because there was a large dog guarding the property, so we left without seeing anyone."

"You said: 'We were just going to drive by'. Who are 'we'?"

"Greta and Mary," mumbled Jane, aware that she should not have taken Mary anywhere near the investigation.

"I don't understand any of this, could somebody brief me?" Wentworth said.

Daltry turned to him, "As you know, your daughter-in-law is missing. It seems another young missing woman is linked to a village in Andorra with a connection to Pearl. It's probably just a coincidence."

"There's also a possibility that Harris's death could be related to these disappearances," Jane added. Daltry frowned.

"In what way?" Wentworth sounded bewildered. Jane could see through the polished veneer of the politician to the bereaved father who had lost his only son.

Charles interrupted, to answer him gently, "Harris came to Andorra to see Pearl so he could ask for a divorce. He wanted to legitimise his relationship with his current girlfriend and their son. It may be that while he was here he discovered something about Pearl's disappearance and that his death was not an accident."

"But the police told me that Harris fell while he was hiking?"

"The trail he was hiking was marked on a map the police found in Pearl's car. It heads towards a mountain pass called *Portella Blanca*.

A fragment of a message left on her answering-machine also mentioned *Portella Blanca*. Harris specifically went to investigate the trail to see if he could find anything that might explain her disappearance. His fall could well just be misfortune – but Jane saw his body and observed a wound to the back of his head which she believes may not have occurred when he fell." Charles was succinct.

"You're not a doctor are you Jane – or a detective?" Wentworth was starting to sound angry now rather than upset. Jane took a deep breath, wishing that Charles had left this part out.

"I'm sorry. They took me to identify the body, and – probably because I was married to a detective and heard him talking about crime scenes all the time – I looked at the state of his body. When I mentioned the wound to the back of his head the police didn't want to know. But I'm sure the autopsy will highlight inconsistencies, if there are any."

"Why wasn't I informed of this?" Wentworth turned to Daltry for an explanation but Daltry just gave another in his portfolio of shrugs. Jane could see that her first impression of him over the telephone had been hasty. He wasn't going out of his way to ingratiate himself with a Senator. He was equally disobliging with everyone.

"Perhaps you should take that up with the investigating detective," Charles said, raising his hand in a gesture for the *maître d'* to bring the *à la carte* and wine menus, saying as they arrived, "I can recommend the milk fed lamb," with what seemed to Jane to be a remarkable lack of empathy. A headache began to pound away at the back of her skull. As she rolled her neck, the bottle of Scotch on the table sprang into sharp relief.

"I'm not staying for dinner," she decided and announced in the same breath. "I just wanted to call by to offer my condolences. I'm sure you all want to eat quickly and have an early night. You must be tired.

"Frank, will you give Charles all the details about the other missing woman? We're trying to compile a fact sheet to see if we can glean any new ideas." She knew she was gabbling.

Daltry nodded, one slow movement up and down. "I have the file with me. I'll ask them at reception to copy it for you. Maybe I could sit in with you both and help you review things. A different perspective can be helpful sometimes."

"Thank you. How long will you be here?"

"It depends. I want to make sure that the release of the body goes smoothly. The embassy has authorised me to spend some time on this investigation." Although his words were relaxed, his body was not. Jane wondered if his position as a first secretary was a cover for ASIO, the Australian intelligence service. That might explain his insouciance with the Senator and general public. He seemed too wound up simply to be a low-level clerk in the public service. She stood up and forced a smile around the table.

"Don't get up. Please. Enjoy your dinner. Can I say once again how sad I am about Harris, Ian. When I spoke to him he was very positive and happy about getting his life together. He told me how much Melanie and Freddy meant to him and how rewarding it was to be a father.

"Charles, would you call me in the morning to let me know about your meeting with Señor Castillo?" She sketched a faint wave and headed for reception to order a taxi. Suddenly a night spent with an angry but desolate father plus two men who obviously intended to honour the tradition of a wake and lay waste to vast quantities of alcohol was more than she could stomach.

When the taxi deposited Jane in Ordino, she heard the jaunty refrain of country music drifting down from the village *plaça*. She gave the taxi-driver a generous tip before walking up the uneven cobblestones to see what was happening. A temporary stage was erected beside the Church, and on it a young woman in cowboy-hat, skin-tight jeans and cowboy boots exhorted the crowd to join in a community line-dance. "*Derecha, derecha; Izquierda izquierda!*" the cowgirl piped, moving to the right and then to the left and emphasising the movement by pointing with her hands and giving an extravagant pelvic thrust in each direction. The crowd good-naturedly followed her example, occasionally bumping into each other in their eagerness to comply.

One couple was dragging their Yorkshire terrier to the left and the right with them, causing their neighbours to trip over the lead and to jump over the red jacketed canine as it lagged behind the dancers. Another fiercely moustachioed participant grabbed the woman to his right and began to swing her around so fast that her feet left the ground. The crowd around him parted to make room for his partner's swinging spiked heels. Out of this chaos, three men appeared, their cowboy-hats pulled down over their foreheads. They were dressed in black, with red neck-kerchiefs and flashy silver belt buckles. As they sashayed into a ring cleared of people, they began to dance in perfect synchronisation to the music. Turning out their toes then heels, clapping, turning and gliding in time with each other and the music, they danced to the end of the song with the crowd shouting its approval and whistling "*Olé!*" when the movements became particularly suggestive. To Jane's astonishment, the middle dancer was Juan-Antonio.

A chorus of encores greeted the first dance, and the crowd quickly formed behind them as they began to lead the line-dancing. The enthusiasm was so infectious that Jane slipped into the last row and began to dance, finding it hard to twirl in her rubber soled pumps as she turned to the right and left, backwards and forwards and clapped and jumped and shimmied her hips. Her blonde hair shone like a beacon in a sea of brunettes. As she raised her head from a particularly complicated manoeuvre that had compelled her to watch her feet in case she fell over, Juan-Antonio grinned at her and moved down the lines until he was dancing at her side while his two companions continued to conduct from the front. At the end of the dance everyone laughed when he brought her hand to his lips and kissed her fingers; then, clasping them in his, he nonchalantly walked away pulling her with him to the car park.

"Have you had dinner?" His thumb caressed her palm.

"Not yet," she replied. A chill passed over her shoulders. Her nipples hardened and nudged her silk shirt. Juan-Antonio brushed his fingers over them.

"My place," he whispered in her ear, his breath hot. He helped her up into the Land Cruiser and accelerated northwest, placing his hand flat on the inside of her thigh. Within ten minutes they pulled up at a dimly-lit stone house. Juan-Antonia reached over and kissed her for a long time. They tumbled out of the car and onto a flagstone path that led though a sparse garden to the front door. Here she stopped and, placing her hands on his neck, pulled him close for another kiss. His fingers fumbled with the keys and then slammed the front door behind them. He lent into her, laving her mouth with his tongue. She smelt his singular scent of tobacco and soap as his hands began to caress her under her silky top.

"*Papa, estas tu?*" The hall light went on and a youth appeared at the top of the stairs. Juan-Antonio quickly turned and used his bulk to hide her from view. He sighed heavily.

"*Paco. Estupendo!*" He stood to one side to reveal Jane, who had taken the few moments to straighten her clothes, and then switched to English. "This is a friend of mine, Jane Burns. I was just going to cook dinner. Have you eaten yet?"

"No, and I'm starved," said Paco unselfconsciously. "How do you do, Jane?" He walked down the stairs and shook her hand, kissed his father on both cheeks, hugged him, then pushed him away and regarded his clothes. "Still line-dancing then?" he smiled.

"He's pretty good," said Jane, who had at last found her voice.

"When did you arrive?" asked Juan-Antonio.

"Not long ago. I drove Anna home because her mother's sick. I dropped her off and thought I'd stay the night and spend Sunday with you, then drive back to Barcelona for class on Monday morning." His English was flawless, if somewhat American by accent. He was looking at Jane as he spoke and giving her a thorough inspection. Father and son walked down the hall and into the kitchen, Juan-Antonio's hand lightly over his son's shoulders. Jane followed.

"It's a while since I saw you." Juan-Antonio was inspecting the interior of the fridge.

"Yes. Well – you know. Studies and all."

"How is your mother?"

"Fine. Yeah. She's well."

Jane stopped in the shadow of the doorway and compared them. Juan-Antonio had blunt peasant features and a square blocky physique. Paco was finely built with high cheekbones and slanted eyes. He started to lay the table as his father stacked food on the counter, both comfortable in the well-worn routine.

"Something quick so we can all have an early night?" Juan-Antonio suggested. Jane nearly laughed. No matter how quick it was, this was going to be a long dinner.

CHAPTER THIRTY

At first Jane forgot where she was. The pale light of an autumnal dawn was filtering through the open window but there was no sound of magpies calling, nor was her dog Soda pushing his wet nose into her face, demanding to be let out. She tried to remember if it was a weekday and if she needed to get up early to go to work, but then the realisation hit that she was in Pearl's flat in Andorra. A shroud of dread dropped over her as she swung her bare feet to the polished floorboards. Was Pearl still alive? Would they ever find her, or find out what had happened to her? Thousands of women disappeared without trace every year all over the world. Their families never heard from them again.

She automatically turned on her laptop to boot-up, then headed for the kitchen to start the coffee-pot before washing her face and cleaning her teeth – a well-established morning routine that saved her from having to wait too long to complete any one thing. After she poured herself an aromatic brew of finest Columbian beans, she returned to the computer to download headlines from the Australian newspapers and to open Outlook Express and check her emails.

There were four new emails in her inbox, three from the office and one from an unknown sender with an attachment. She opened the news from Carol first.

Just a note to allay any concern about this end. The doctors say your grandmother can return to the assisted living hostel in a few days. Your mother is back home sleeping in her own bed, so all goes well. You have amazing genes.

Jane smiled, as always pleased with the amount of easy-going, uncritical support Carol gave her, and quickly responded with two paragraphs detailing their lack of progress in finding Pearl.

The next two emails dealt with routine office matters. The Tax Department had just audited one of her clients, Travelling Trinkets, with only one small anomaly found adding up to a fine of $500. The clients wanted to know if they could appeal. Jane emailed back a quick no. Pay it and be thankful. She strongly suspected the business took in a lot more cash than they were declaring.

Carol said that the quarterly business returns were going in late from another client because their computer had crashed. Jane smoothly emailed back, hardly needing to consider her response knowing that Carol was perfectly capable of responding to routine matters and had only checked with her as a matter of form.

The last email was from _embustero_@hotmail.com. The subject header said merely "Greetings Jane" and the message space was blank, but there was an attachment of 344 KB, which could be either a large file or photographs that had not been compressed. She clicked on the paperclip icon. A pop-up screen told her "Some files can contain viruses or otherwise be harmful to your computer. It is important that this file is from a trustworthy source." She contemplated the attachment box, which besides giving the size of the file, also said the attachment was called "greetings". She didn't like the look of it and would normally delete it out of hand, but the heading was directed to her. Who was _embustero_? Anyone, at any cyber cafe in the world, could open a free email account with Hotmail and enter phoney identification details then send an email containing a virus. She opened her Travelpro roll-on airline bag and searched its numerous pockets for her small Spanish/English dictionary.

Embustero, a = adj lying, deceitful   nm/f cheat, liar, fibber.

She slowly returned to her computer and with trepidation, clicked on the attachment box, dragging it to the Norton anti-virus icon displayed on her toolbar and activating a scan for viruses. After only seconds the anti-virus software told her "no viruses detected". Just to make sure, she closed Outlook Express and opened Internet Explorer to update the latest from the anti-virus software site. She repeated the steps to ensure that the attachment was virus free as far as the technology nerds could tell, notwithstanding that there were hundreds of viruses invented and sent out into cyberspace daily. Again, the programme said that no virus was detected.

She felt a paralysis attack her hands, a sure sign of stress. She shook them to relieve the tension and took a deep breath, but before she could click on "open attachment", her mobile shrilled on the bedside-table.

"Are you running this morning? Paco and I thought we might catch up with you at Arans and run down to the gym with you and have breakfast."

Juan-Antonio had reluctantly taken her home after dinner the previous night, staying just long enough while bidding her goodnight to make them both sorely regret his exit.

"An email just arrived," she replied distractedly. "It's from an address that calls itself '*embustero*'. I think it may be something about Pearl. Could you come straight away? I don't want to open it by myself in case it's programmed to destroy itself after I read it, or something. I need a witness. Perhaps I should save it to a file first, before I open it."

"Don't do anything until I get there," Juan-Antonio spoke quickly. "I'll ring Victor and get him to send over one of the detectives who handle computer fraud and he should know how to proceed. I'll be there in fifteen minutes."

He rang the bell within twelve, and was still talking on the mobile phone tucked under his ear when Jane opened the door. Paco was standing behind him in a pair of voluminous tracksuit trousers gathered at his ankles like colourful balloons. She noticed a tattooed butterfly on his forearm. His long sleeves had hidden it the night before.

"He would not be left behind," Juan-Antonio explained, indicating Paco, as he folded the mobile and put it in his pocket, before opening his arms and enveloping Jane in a hug. Paco regarded them uneasily. She drew away and led them to her bedroom where the warning message from Microsoft was still displayed on her laptop's screen.

"I know a fair bit about computers," said Paco.

"You will not touch the computer. It may contain evidence." Juan-Antonio's reply was automatic. Jane's full breasts, swinging freely under the T-shirt that served as her nightie, were distracting him. Jane had pulled on some track pants, but otherwise had not changed for their arrival. "Perhaps you could put on a dressing-gown, Jane."

A flush started at Jane's throat, overtook her face and disappeared into her hairline. Men were so weird, worrying about appearances at a time like this. Still, she obediently went into the bathroom and returned fully-dressed in her asexual tracksuit and sneakers, physicality duly subdued.

"Coffee?" she croaked, and they all had a mug while impatiently waiting for Victor-Ignacio and the IT detective to arrive.

The IT detective was an old friend of Paco's. After introducing himself to Jane and greeting Juan-Antonio, he hugged Paco and they pounded each other on the back – prototypes of the new man; slim-hipped, good-looking and slightly androgynous with their ponytails, even white teeth and tanned faces. When he sat at the computer keyboard, the detective's nails were polished and well-manicured. Jane wondered what it might be like to date a man who had better-kept nails than oneself. Unconsciously she moved closer to Juan-Antonio, who immediately put his arm around her and pulled her even closer – uncaring of the frowns directed towards him by Paco and Victor.

As expected, the 344 KB file took minutes to download on the old-fashioned dial-up system. In the preview box they watched the pixels slowly fill in the background of a coloured photograph until the image became shockingly clear. Pearl stood alone, her hands bound in front of her with masking tape. Her face was indistinct and slightly blurred but the cardboard, handwritten sign that she held was unmistakeable. HELP ME it said in a shaky hand. Wind had blown her waist-long hair across the corner of the sign. Her shoulders were slightly hunched as if against the cold, arms exposed under a sleeveless blouse tucked into a violently coloured batique sarong. The photo was foreshortened, taken from the ground and shot upwards with the cardboard sign in sharpest focus. Behind Pearl, a solidly overcast sky cast a diffused light. Either the camera had been set on a large F setting to compensate for the dull light or the quality of the digital camera or scanner had been poor, because the depth of field was fuzzy.

The IT detective slipped a CD into the laptop and copied the attachment file, pocketing it. Then he enhanced the image of Pearl on the screen, quartering the photo and then examining each quarter first at double the size and then doubled again. Two of the long, blood-red fingernails on her right hand were broken plus the index finger-nail of her left. Her thumbs were behind the sign, but the four fingers of each hand were splayed across the bottom of the sign.

"Defensive breaks of her fingernails," Victor commented. They studied Pearl's face but it revealed little. Her slanted eyes and full mouth were neutral and slightly out of focus. They scrolled down to a second image.

Bare brown feet sporting a silver toe-ring stood on sharp gravel, above them ugly iron shackles were fastened on ankles thick with suppurating ulcers. The sores travelled up the shins until hidden by the flare of the incongruously cheerful hem of the sarong.

Juan-Antonio hugged Jane more tightly to him.

"He's clever" said Paco. "There's nothing in the photos that would identify where they were taken. Cloudy sky. Gravel. Could be anywhere."

The young detective shushed him as he continued to scroll down but there were only two images and no text to accompany them. Clicking on File, Properties, Details, he printed out the minutiae of the path of the email message, saying with a shrug, "Every computer connected to the Internet has what is called an IP address. For permanently-connected computers this doesn't change and identifies the computer uniquely. The guys who hand out IPs to organizations are in Stanford, California, and presumably they have addresses of the installation they are assigning IPs to. Your typical Internet Service Provider will have a sheaf of IPs and assign you one when you connect to the internet, then assign it to someone else when you log off. I could go on – but the upshot is that the computer from which a message is sent is more easily identified than the person using it to send the message.

The computer will probably be registered to some cyber cafe somewhere. Still, having a location would be very useful. I guess he brought his own CD and sent it. In most cyber cafes you can just walk in and sit down at any free computer and start sending or receiving. The computer automatically logs the time you have spent on the Internet, and then you tell the cashier what number machine you were on and you pay cash on the way out, or it could even be a coin-operated system.

"It was sent at 7.30 last night, so that is well within the time a cyber cafe here in Andorra would be open. Received this morning at 6.15am." He directed an enquiring eye towards Jane who immediately felt guilty for not checking her email the night before.

"Should I answer this? Just click on reply and ask him not to hurt Pearl and say that I'm waiting for his instructions?" she asked.

Victor considered for a moment. "Yes, a dialogue would be helpful. Every contact he makes with you means a better chance to get him. You better give us your password. We can then monitor all the messages in your inbox."

Jane wrote it down and passed it over, thinking she'd have to open a temporary hotmail account for her other messages. They then carefully crafted a reply.

"He seems to be toying with us. First he sent us her ponytail, and now the photo to establish the fact that he has her – yet he doesn't ask for anything in return," Jane said. "The photo was taken before her hair was cut so the timeline is out of sequence. Does that mean anything?"

The men obviously thought it was a rhetorical question because they continued a discussion about the email properties; the two younger men explaining to Victor what could and could not be done about tracing the message. Jane's mind raced as she did the math.

"Something doesn't add up here. We received the parcel with the ponytail the day of the trust meeting, Thursday. She was last seen by Lyn and Dave, and by Señor Molina ten days before that. Do you think that ten days is long enough for those dreadful sores to develop and become infected so badly?" The men looked up from their contemplation of the computer screen. "…and the toe-ring. I've never seen her wear a toe-ring. Print out the photos, Victor!"

She could hardly wait to jerk them from the small travel printer and place them side-by-side. She overlapped one on the other, trying to see if the colours in the material of the sarongs matched – but the faint strip of hem on the second photo displaying colours of yellow and red was too small to establish a match.

"We should get an opinion from a doctor – probably a skin specialist – about the length of time it takes for ulcers to develop to that stage, but my gut feeling is that these were taken on separate occasions. Look!" She pointed to the second picture again and a swathe of sunlight in the gravel and a dark-edged shadow. "OK, the sun could have come out from behind a cloud, but the sky looks to be an unbroken grey in the first photo. There's no blue sky or separation of the cloud-cover at all."

The policemen collectively shrugged. They obviously thought she was clutching at straws and not willing to face the evidence of her sister's condition, but Paco looked on and nodded with interest.

"Her face is wrong too. In fact her whole demeanour is wrong. I know Pearl and she's a fighter. She's spent the last ten years in very dangerous situations and she's always looking for an edge. She never gives up. She'd be trying to convey something if she could, with her hands or her features or something."

"Are you trying to say this photo isn't Pearl?"

"No. No, it's her but it isn't like her. Her body-language is too passive."

"She could be drugged and is almost certainly being threatened," Paco said with the tactless honesty of youth, careless of what this might do to Jane's composure.

She turned her face away into Juan-Antonio's broad chest.

CHAPTER THIRTY-ONE

As the men left, taking with them the disc and Jane's assertions that she'd be fine on her own, Victor suddenly stopped and reached into his jacket pocket – producing a mobile phone. "It belonged to Harris. Will you be seeing Señores Wentworth or Daltry?"

"Sure," Jane said, reaching for it. "I'll pass it on."

"We looked at the call register and all the names and numbers that were stored plus messages sent and received, but there was very little activity on it. Just one or two calls to Australia, and a couple of missed calls from your number." Victor smiled as he passed on this information, knowing that if he had not Jane would spend considerable time retracing these steps.

"Thank you," Jane said to his retreating back.

The telephone operator at the Hotel Roc de Caldes put her straight through.

"Frank? It's Jane," she said, not wasting time on preliminaries. "Can we meet this morning? There's a new development and I could do with your input."

"What time?" asked Daltry.

"Say 9.30. We can meet in Charles' suite." She rang off, dived in and out of the shower, then quickly dressed. She called Rosa and asked for a taxi, then replaced her laptop and travel printer in their travel case. As she walked down the stairs, she phoned Greta to say they'd have to postpone cataloguing the slides.

"Shall I continue on my own?" asked Greta, but Jane felt uncomfortable at the thought of Greta pouring over the slides in the silent *trastero* without her.

"No. We'll try and do it together this afternoon."

Rosa put out a restraining hand as Jane attempted to run out of the foyer into the street. Her homely face caught a patch of morning light, illuminating the down on her upper lip as she asked for news of Pearl. The Spanish words appeared like a comic strip balloon from a mouth etched with golden sunshine. Jane shook her head to clear it and said the police seemed no closer to finding her. Rosa exhaled an earthy, "*cabrones*", to express her opinion of the situation.

"Señora, había una carta para Señora Pearl que no cupo en la buzón." Jane quickly scanned the proferred oversized manila envelope before jumping into the taxi with it jammed under her arm. There it crackled, stiffly important, but she resolved not to open it until she was with Charles and Daltry. A taxi was not the appropriate place to examine any new evidence. She tried to push her fear for Pearl further away. She was experiencing an ever-widening ripple of dread.

When Charles ushered her into his sitting-room, Daltry was sprawled on the sofa, one leg crossed over the other. She threw the envelope down onto the table in front of him and announced, "This came in the post." She fanned the two photos that she had printed earlier next to it, "and these were emailed to me last night, although I only picked them up this morning."

Charles picked up the photos, his face grim. He touched Pearl's face gently with two fingers then passed the photos to Daltry who gave them a thorough, unhurried scrutiny. After he returned them to Charles, he contemplated the large envelope. Pearl's name and address were written on the front in black ink in a flowing and elegant script. There was no return address. It had been posted in Paris seven days previously.

"Weinstein," said Charles.

They stared at the envelope as if it were explosive until Charles broke the spell by leaving the room. He returned wearing fine rubber surgeon's gloves and carrying a thin stiletto.

"I use these when I examine old documents for my historical research. Oil from human fingers can damage the paper," he explained as he carefully prised open the flap of the envelope with the knife. He looked inside and drew out the contents – two ten by eight inch sepia photographs. The backs were stamped with the photo studio's name *"24 heures por La Rive Gauche"*. It was obvious that they had been enlarged from smaller, original photos.

The first photo was of a group of eight men dressed in camouflage, some with bandoliers across their chests, carrying firearms. They appeared to be a carefully posed group of hunters. The faces were grim and humourless. Five men held themselves rigidly to attention behind three men seated in upright chairs. The seated men had their hands on their knees above burnished knee-high boots. The men ranged from teens to thirties. The immature faces of two of the younger men jarred with their manly attire. Behind them, the head of a lage boar was mounted over an ornately-carved mantelpiece and brightly burning fire. Impaled on its impressive tusks, a swastika flag hung in folds.

The second photo was a studio portrait of a couple and a small child. The woman wore a patterned scarf covering her hair. Her blouse was buttoned to her throat and fastened with a cameo broach. The left side of her face was turned in profile towards the child, and displayed strong features dominated by an aquiline nose. The man was smaller, older and less striking than the woman. The collar of his shirt was too big for his neck and he gazed fully at the camera from under a crop of grizzled hair. The child – a girl of no more than three – had pierced ears and fair, curly hair. One chubby arm was carelessly thrown around the man's neck and her mouth was open as if in laughter. Her short dress revealed sturdy legs and frilly knickers.

Enclosed with these photos was the familiar letterhead.

Jack Weinstein - Rue de la Réunion
Paris, France.
33 (01) 47422365

Dear Pearl,

Here are the photos. Reinhardt is standing, the third one in from the left. It is the only photo that I can find in the files and I have it only because his Aunt kept it in memory of a favoured nephew before he was posted to the Russian front to die a miserable death. There is no photo of his brother Herman in any of the archives but I hope there will be sufficient family resemblance to allow you to recognise him, or his son if that is who they are.

The other photo is of the Schonbergers. Emile, Ruth and baby Sara.

I hope this helps.

I believe there is no statute of limitations on justice.

Regards

Jack Weinstein.

They studied the young man called Reinhardt in the photo as if willing him to speak across the years. He looked to be in his twenties with dark, receding hair, heavy brow and pale deeply set eyes.

Jane and Charles spoke simultaneously.

"It's so frustrating not to be able to talk to Weinstein. Pearl must have contacted him again while the first letter from him was still on its way. She probably reached him by phone. Does this mean she has met Herman or his son here and recognised them as some type of war criminal?"

"He signed it 'regards' not 'yours sincerely'. Is that significant? To me that seems more personal. Do you think they met?"

"Did she send him the photos he mentioned in the last letter, or give them to him in person? Were they current photos of Herman? If they met, was it here or in Paris?"

"He didn't say that he was going away or where she could contact him if she needed further information."

"Perhaps he'd told her that already, if they got together between the two letters. Or maybe this is all he had."

"Is it the whole Shonberger family that Pearl was interested in, or just one of them? How are they connected to her search for photos of Herman?"

"The statute of limitations for doing what? There is no statute of limitations for murder is there, so he must mean something else. Or is it different here?"

"Stop!" Daltry cut into their rapid-fire exchange of views. "I need to catch up here. Who is this fellow, Weinstein?"

"Didn't Victor tell you about the first letter from Weinstein?"

"He was more interested in what I had to tell him than in giving me a briefing. Here's the file on the other missing woman, by the way." He slipped a manila folder underneath the envelope that had contained Weinstein's photos.

Charles launched into the story of his trip to Weinstein's address in Paris after the arrival of the first letter, while Jane interjected with details about what the IT detective had said to her that morning. Daltry looked from Charles to Jane, his brow furrowed as he tried to keep the two stories separate.

"So these two events, the arrival of both sets of photos, have no connection that we know of?" asked Daltry. "We have two photos emailed from a person whose *nom-de-plume* is "liar" (in Spanish, not Catalan – perhaps this is significant) which appear to show that Pearl is in his custody. We have a separate set of photos relating to some type of enquiry that Pearl was carrying out before her disappearance. These were sent by a man who has a good deal of credibility worldwide, which would seem to eliminate him as a suspect, but not as a source of information. Would that be a fair summing up?"

Jane and Charles agreed that it would.

"Who has your email address, Jane?"

"I gave it to Detective Victor and Juan-Antonio when I reported Pearl missing, and to you when I first spoke with you. Gary Cohen, one of the sub-editors of the *New York Times* who works with Pearl, has it and used it recently to send me some details about Weinstein. Ramon Saboya, Pearl's attorney and the trustees have it of course, but apart from that I haven't given it to anyone. I imagine that anyone could find me through International Directories Assistance."

"That might be harder than you think if you consider that your address is tied to your work. It would be difficult to find you at your address jburns@sentryandparker.com.au unless the person knew you worked at Sentry and Parker."

Jane gave an involuntary shudder at the thought of someone stalking her through the Internet. "Well, obviously the kidnapper could just ask Pearl for it! The police are trying to trace the email to see where it originated from, but they suspect it will just lead to a cyber cafe."

"Well, that would at least give us a geographical point of reference."

Jane, who had been pacing backwards and forwards with agitation since she arrived, sank down into a chair opposite Daltry and let out a huge sigh. Charles picked up the teapot from his breakfast tray and poured her a tepid cup, adding two spoonfuls of sugar and stirring it well before handing it over.

"I don't take sugar," Jane remarked after the first sip.

"Do you good," said Charles, and she made no further protest screwing her face up and drinking it down like medicine.

Daltry scrutinised the photos of Pearl again. Jane explained her doubts about whether they actually matched.

"He's playing some type of game, sending these, but also calling himself a liar so that we doubt that the photos are genuine. He could have superimposed Pearl's face on another photo for all we know. Computer technology makes it easy to doctor photos."

"The long hair blowing across the sign would be hard to fake."

"Let's put these to one side and start from the beginning and go through everything that's happened step by step and see if we can put together what we know for sure and make some type of logical list."

"Where is the beginning?" asked Charles, ever the historian. "Do we start when my father established the trust – because that's why we are all here in the first place? Pearl may have been trying to avoid her problems with Harris by moving here, but she would never have thought of coming to Andorra without the trust."

"Just give me a thumbnail sketch of the trust, Charles, and then let's skip to Jane's arrival in Andorra and the discovery that Pearl was missing."

They went through it all again, with Daltry questioning their memory of events and asking for clarity, not for interpretations. His constant refrain was to tell it "exactly how it was." It seemed to Jane that too often they had no answer to his questions.

"Who owns the last number that Pearl dialled from her home phone?"

"We don't know. No-one ever answered it."

"Who do the police say owns it?"

"They haven't told us."

Daltry snorted and reached for the phone, quickly dialling then shouting some instructions at the operator in Spanish. He listened carefully to the response, then commenced a long, loud remonstration in which Jane could discern the words "*Policia, Cap de Govern, Embajador,*" plus the frequent use of the word sorry. But whether Daltry was saying he'd make the operator sorry, or that he himself was sorry, Jane couldn't tell. Finally he announced with satisfaction.

"The number belonged to the ABC import/export company but it was disconnected two weeks ago. The operator says that all three of their lines have been cut off."

"How did you get them to give you that information, Frank?"

"I behaved so badly it was easier for them to tell me, than to not tell me. Catalans hate to confront bad manners, they are used to people being far more civil." He didn't sound in the least concerned with this breach of diplomacy. "I, on the other hand, think civility can take you only so far." He bared his teeth. One incisor was longer than the other, giving him the look of a lopsided tiger. His tawney-hair and alert body-language added to the image. Jane and Charles laughed uneasily. Perhaps Daltry's officious bureaucrat act was simply camouflage for a far more dangerous species.

"What was the result of your meeting with Castillo, Charles?" asked Jane, realising that she had never followed this up. "Could he tell you anything about *El Gigante* and the Alex Bertran-Carrera in the trust's books because here it is again, ABC, the ABC Import/Export Company?"

"ABC is used pretty commonly as a business name, because it comes up early in telephone listings and captures customers who don't know who they're looking for," cautioned Daltry.

"Castillo didn't know anything about the early investments of the trust. His father was a secretive man and even after his retirement when he was half blind with cataracts, he kept the books of the trust in a strongbox at the family home. It wasn't until Castillo junior was handling the probate of his father's estate, that he found the original books of account and transferred them to the law firm's offices. As the new administrator of the trust he simply accepted the current balance as correct and established that his main objective, together with that of the other two trustees, was to increase the capital and to make a distribution of income to the beneficiaries each year. He never had occasion to speak with his father about the trust or what led to its inception. He described his father as a sombre personality who held his cards close to his chest. He didn't share his thoughts with anyone, not even his only child."

"Castillo looks to be in his late forties or early fifties. When did his father die?" asked Jane

"Two years ago."

"What did he die of?" asked Daltry.

"He shot himself," said Charles.

"He shot himself!" Jane was incredulous. "But you said he was nearly blind, and he must have been in his eighties at least."

"He might have been blind but he could still find his mouth," Charles's voice was dry, "because he put a pistol in it and pulled the trigger."

"Did you ask Castillo if there was a note, or why he did it?"

"I didn't have to ask. He was brimming over with unresolved feelings. I couldn't have stopped the flow if I'd wanted to. It seems that after the suicide, no-one wanted to talk about it. Everyone said it was best for him not to dwell on it."

Jane knew from personal experience how that went. It was the same after Bruce died. Friends avoided mentioning his name.

"There was no suicide note, but Castillo said his father became increasingly depressed after the death of his mother the year before. A woman from the village came to cook and clean for him each day, but his father spent the evenings in the large house alone. He couldn't work without an assistant because of his eyesight. Perhaps in the end he felt there was nothing for him to live for. Castillo invited his father to live with him, but the old man refused. In turn, Castillo's wife did not want to live in the old family home. I sensed there was some friction between the father and daughter-in-law.

"Suicide is an act of anger," mused Daltry.

"Or desperation." argued Jane.

CHAPTER THIRTY-TWO

"Back to the ABC Company. Nearly everything is imported into Andorra so an import company is understandable, but what does the country export?" Typically Charles' thoughts swung onto a tangent.

"Tobacco?" guessed Jane. "Capital? Some of the black money that gets laundered here must go back out again to invest in bonds and the stock market."

"There's no money-laundering in Andorra," dead-panned Daltry. "The government says so at every meeting it has with the European Union. Anyway, what dealings would Pearl have with an import/export business?"

"Perhaps she didn't do business with the company *per se* but with someone who worked there. A friend or a source."

"Well, let's try and find out both what the company did and who worked there." Charles looked enquiringly at Daltry. "You speak the language!"

Daltry frowned and consulted his watch. "I'm meeting Ian Wentworth at noon. They've finished the autopsy and we have to complete some formalities for the release of his son's body. They're really pulling out all the stops, working on a Sunday.

"I'll be driving the Senator to the Barcelona airport while the coffin is transported in a hearse behind us. I want to be on hand to talk with the airline to make sure things go smoothly for the flight to Australia tonight. The coffin has to be off-loaded in Singapore and transferred to a different airline, so there's quite a lot of paperwork to comply with. I don't want Senator Wentworth to have to deal with it. It's upsetting enough to fly home with the body of your only son."

"I'm surprised they'll release the body so soon. Isn't this an ongoing investigation?"

"The autopsy is complete. The pathologist says there are no suspicious circumstances and regards it as an accidental death. The report said the wound to the back of the head was consistent with the fall."

"Did you go with the Senator to collect Harris's personal belongings from the hotel?"

"Yes – after Inspector Victor itemised what was there."

"Could we have Pearl's photo-album back?"

Daltry checked his notebook and flicked over a few pages.

"Sorry. There was nothing like that there."

Charles and Jane exchanged puzzled looks.

"Maybe Victor took it as evidence in Pearl's disappearance. I told him about what happened in the *trastero*." Jane made a note. "What about the digital camera with the photos of the Mercedes and the man outside the dumpster? Maybe there were some photos he didn't give us."

"No. There was no camera either."

"Strange. You'd think he would take it when he hiked."

"Maybe the climbers who found him stole it."

Jane thought about the nice young man who had waited by the body, and the respect the other young climber had shown Victor.

"I doubt it. Will you be coming back to Andorra, Frank?"

"I'll have to check with the office in Madrid."

Jane wondered why she had ever thought the Australian Embassy official could be of some help. It looked like the embassy budget stretched only to helping influential Australians, but beyond that you were on your own. So much for that great fiction, the egalitarian society.

She gave him an insincere smile that was closer to a snarl. "We'll just battle on here without your help. Gary Cohen of the *New York Times* is keen to do an article. At first I thought a media-circus would confuse the issue, but now I'm not so sure. One of the interesting things about the contact we've had with the kidnapper is that the message didn't say 'don't contact the media'."

"I think that's implied. Look, I'll do my best to help. Even when I return to Madrid, I can still make some calls." Daltry touched Jane's arm in an effort to be conciliatory but quickly retrieved his hand when she shrugged him off.

"We'd appreciate that," said Charles.

Daltry loosened his tie and flashed his tiger smile at Jane, apparently not discomposed by her hostility. "Let's keep going with what we're doing so I can make a full report. Perhaps the embassy should request the assistance of Interpol to track down Weinstein so we can at least follow up that line of enquiry and see where it leads us."

After another hour Daltry was satisfied that he had the whole story. He stood and replaced the notebook in his breast pocket. Jane was busy making copy discs of every piece of information they had. After she made the first disc and handed it to Daltry, she copied another and gave it to Charles.

"By the way, did you ever establish if the waiter, Jorge, called Harris in response to your message?" Daltry asked.

"Damn. I left the phone at home."

Daltry looked at Jane in surprise. To date she hadn't displayed any of Charles' propensity to tangential thought.

"Victor wanted me to return Harris's phone to you, to give to his father, but anyway, no, there was no record of a call received from Jorge. When I was at Lake Pessons I asked for Jorge at the restaurant, but they told me he was in Barcelona. He probably didn't get my message."

"What's his last name? I could give him a quick call while I'm down there just in case he was one of the last people to speak with Harris before he died."

"I don't know his last name, but if you call the Lake Pessons restaurant and ask for Señor Molina he'd be able to give it to you, and probably a contact number for Jorge's family in Barcelona as well." Jane flicked open the Andorran telephone book and quickly found the number of the restaurant and scribbled it down on the hotel message pad. In Jane's opinion Daltry continued to be much more interested in the circumstances leading to the death of a politician's son than he was in finding her missing sister. As she bade him goodbye, she continued to flick through the telephone book, looking for the ABC Compania. She found it in the yellow pages, a small listing under *importadoras y exportadoras* giving the address as Edifici Credit Europa, Escaldes-Engordany.

"Charles, the ABC Company is in the same building as Credit Europa. Do you think you could see Señora Menendez about trust matters in general and then pump her for information? Ask her if this is the same ABC that borrowed money from the trust so long ago? Perhaps you could also suggest offering a reward for information about Pearl's whereabouts. The trust could post it, or if the other beneficiaries object, you and I could put up the money; but maybe it would be better if one of the trustees broached the idea to the police?

I was thinking that one million pesetas might produce an informant."

Charles face brightened at the thought of a positive plan of action. He was also not averse to spending time with the intelligent and amply endowed Señora Menendez. Without further discussion he pulled her card from his wallet and dialled her mobile number to ask her to lunch. "Perhaps you would book us into one of your favourite restaurants? I'll call to pick you up in a taxi if you would give me directions." He ended the conversation smoothly. On the speakerphone she had sounded bemused, but proclaimed her availability and her pleasure at the unexpected invitation.

"It's Sunday and she wore a wedding-ring." Jane said as he rang off.

"She's a widow with no children," he assured her. "I asked Castillo about her – just a routine enquiry. Thought it might be an idea to find out all I could about the three trustees. She's a second-generation trustee like Castillo. Her mother held the post before her and was named specifically in the original trust documents. It appears that being a trustee is somewhat like an inheritance, since Señor Alas is also the nephew of the other founding trustee. These Andorrans are discrete and like to keep business in the family, however extended."

"What about shirt-sleeves to shirt-sleeves in three generations?"

"Conversely what about the Rothschild's and the Guggenheims?" Charles said. "It's a different mind-set in Andorra, the antithesis of what we are used to in Australia. It's complete privacy here versus full disclosure back home. I imagine there are arguments for and against. I read a book by the first American to visit Andorra back in the mid-nineteenth century. He wrote that Andorrans were notorious for putting on a dumb-show when they didn't want to answer a question. In fact the phrase 'to play the Andorran' was common parlance for stonewalling in those days."

"I wouldn't mind having full disclosure of all the various family members involved with the trust throughout the last fifty years – specific names and details. Tomorrow I'll go around to Saboya's office and pick his brains. He seems to know all the gossip about who's who in Andorra."

"You may be right, but Castillo told me that Saboya had a run-in with the government over access to his files last year, which doesn't make him a particularly sympathetic mouthpiece to the authorities on our behalf. Who knows? I like him – but he's a maverick, so do be careful."

Jane clasped her head in frustration at yet another person who wasn't quite what he seemed.

"I wonder if Señora Menendez is a natural blonde?" Charles said as he checked his watch.

"You are incorrigible," Jane laughed in exasperation. "Meanwhile, I guess I'll go back and finish cataloguing Pearl's slides," she sighed, not enthusiastic at the thought of another afternoon's exposure to the carnage and casualties of war, "and I should ring Elsa and tell her about the latest developments, unless you'd like to do that?" She hoped he would. It would be hard to find the words to describe the photo of Pearl without greatly intensifying Elsa's anxiety.

Charles squared his shoulders and said, "Yes. I'll talk to her before I go to lunch. Don't forget to have lunch yourself Jane, you're losing weight in front of my eyes. Men like curves you know. All these anorexic women in advertisements are the product of homosexual art directors. Red-blooded men like women who look like women, not those skinny, androgynous teenagers who look like drug addicts."

"Yeah right," she said, as she scooped up the photos and copies of all the evidence and stuffed them in the side-pocket of her computer carry-case, "maybe in your generation, but not in mine!"

They kissed affectionately before they went their separate ways. She was amazed to think that her feckless father was now the only person in her immediate world she fully trusted.

The apartment was fusty when she returned. Jane threw open the door to the balcony and watered the plants, yawning and stretching her arms above her head. Clouds had overtaken the sun and she was suffused with the lethargy that comes with a change in the weather. She reminded herself of the AA's advice to avoid getting Hungry, Angry, Lonely or Tired. To energise herself she downed two glasses of water and vowed to go to the gym and exercise for an hour. Her daily exercise programme had been interrupted of late and the lack of endorphins was dragging her down. Taking a deep breath, she told herself it would be OK to call Juan-Antonio on his cell-phone and ask him if he'd like to join her for a workout. That's what modern women do.

Juan-Antonio was tooling down to Lleida, a passenger in his son's car, when he took her call. He and Paco were on their way to have lunch with his grandmother and family, after which Paco would continue on to Barcelona and he'd catch a ride home with Fernando.

"Lunch with the family on Sunday is a strong tradition here, Jane," apologised Juan-Antonio. Making it obvious that it was one he regretted at that moment. At least they were thinking along the same lines.

"Will you talk to Fernando about Pearl and tell him about the email?" Jane wondered if Juan-Antonio would breach family etiquette to delve further into the mystery of Pearl's disappearance.

"I'm not sure. Paco will probably bring it up if I don't, as long as Llourdes isn't in the room. He is very straightforward by nature and thinks a frontal assault is the only option. It is a type of innocence the young have. I'm not sure if it's endearing or annoying."

Jane decided to say nothing of the latest letter from Weinstein. "Have a good time."

Jane felt close to Pearl. There must have been many Sundays when Pearl was alone, while Fernando spent time with his family in Lleida. It was unsettling to think of her beautiful sister being at the disposal of a married man. No matter how fulfilling Pearl's career was, there must have been times she regretted not having a more regular relationship.

The list of names Jane had jotted down from Pearl's letters home had only two names without checkmarks; Jean-Paul and Isabel. Jane continued to glance down the list until she reached Greta's name and the phone-number she had hastily scribbled beside it. Greta answered the phone on its second ring, and agreed to finish cataloguing the slides with Jane later in the afternoon.

"By the way, Greta, do you know Pearl's friends, Jean-Paul and Isabel?"

"Of course. Jean-Paul is the manager of the sports-centre here in Anyos and Isabel is the daughter of one of the first families of

Andorra. I bumped into them when I was shopping at Ferre's in La Massana yesterday. They've been away on holiday in the Canary Islands and looked wonderfully tanned and relaxed, although Jean-Paul was complaining that it cost him a fortune because Isabel refuses to stay anywhere but the best hotels."

"Do you think Jean-Paul would be at the Anyos Club on a Sunday?"

"I'm sure he'll at least call by to make sure everything is going well."

"Can I work out there, do you think, like I can here in Ordino?"

"Well it's a private club, unlike the other *sportius*, and it is actually attached to an apartment hotel. They have top-quality facilities for private members and there are separate, more standard, facilities for the hotel guests. I've been a member for ten years. I could sign you in if you like?"

"That would be great. Maybe I could speak to Jean-Paul, get some exercise, then have a quick salad at Can Pere before meeting you to finish up in the *trastero*."

"Won't the walk up here be enough exercise for one day?"

"Well, it's pretty muggy but I've got my bathing-suit so I might swim laps to cool down instead of using the weight-machines."

"Then you won't need me to vouch for you. The pool's available to the hotel guests, so I'm sure you can just pay a casual user fee. I'll meet you in the *trastero* when you're ready. Afterwards, maybe we can take another look at the *Casa d'Or*? Perhaps they don't work in the tobacco fields on a Sunday since it's a day for the family." Greta was unwilling to let go of the one piece of information in the investigation she had uncovered without exploring it to its final conclusion.

"Sounds good," agreed Jane. "*Hasta entonces*," she tried out her Spanish.

Greta laughed, "*Hasta luego*," she corrected. "See you later," and rang off.

CHAPTER THIRTY-THREE

By the time Jane reached the Anyos Club she was in a lather of sweat and looking forward to a swim.

"Please shower before using the pool and use a swimming-cap," the young receptionist said as she took Jane's money.

The black and white cap with the Anyos logo cut off the circulation to her head while the swimming-goggles carved semi-circles into her cheeks. In order to reach the pool she walked through four automatic jets of water that drenched her in cold water. The dedication to cleanliness outdid anything she'd ever seen. She dived into the pristine blue waters and began to swim fast untidy freestyle laps, her wake disturbing no-one in the empty half-Olympic-sized pool. Obviously lunchtime was a good time to use the amenities. She didn't count laps, merely ploughed on up and down until the wall clock showed she had been swimming non-stop for forty minutes, by which time her goggles were fogged and her eyes streaming. As she hung from the ladder pulling off her cap and shaking the water from her eyes, an athletic pair of bronzed legs came into focus. Her gaze travelled up to neat hips ensconced in black swimming-trunks surmounted by a trim waist and a chest that had seen its share of weight training.

"I thought it was you." The smile had lost none of its brilliance. Jorge stood revealed as a human hunk. Body tanned golden, and topped with a lazily smiling face. "I was out on the sun deck and wondered who would be crazy enough to swim at this time. It could only be a foreigner. We usually dedicate Sunday lunchtime to the table."

"I didn't realise you were a member here," said Jane in surprise. "Hasn't Encamp got its own sports-centre?"

"I go there too sometimes. It's my passion – the body beautiful. Let's have lunch together and you can tell me what's been happening while I've been away."

"Fine. I want to see Jean-Paul, the manager, too if he's here."

"He's in the bar. Shall we meet there when you're free?"

Jane nodded her head. Andorra was like an island. Sooner or later you bumped into the very people you wanted to see, and no doubt those you didn't. She could see how it could be claustrophobic.

Jorge sat on the edge of the pool and slowly dipped a foot into the water, testing the temperature. He gently placed his toes on Jane's shoulders as she held on to the rail saying, "The temperature's perfect, don't you think?" Suddenly he pushed down hard with his feet, ducking her into the water. He held her there for a moment while she struggled, then all at once let her bob to the surface spluttering and gasping for breath.

"Sorry. I couldn't resist," he laughed.

"What the fuck...," she coughed, taken completely by surprise. Her well-toned arms pulled her up the steps and past him. She briefly thought about taking a swing at him but instead stalked towards the changing-rooms. "Asshole," she muttered. She hated that kind of horseplay. Men seemed to find it funny.

"I get the impression you don't like men much," he called after her. "What's the word for hatred of men? Homophobic?"

"Misandry," she stopped and considered, looking him over, her eyes taking in his perfect body, "but in your case it could be homophobic."

Jorge was talking to Jean-Paul when Jane walked in. After the introductions, Jane considered a thin, intense man with a shaven head and suspicious eyes. He assured her there would be no problem in giving her a moment of his time before she had lunch.

"I was shocked to hear that Pearl was missing. She's been a good friend to Isabella and me. Anything that we can do to help...it's yours. Just ask."

Jane thanked him and moved away from the bar to a corner table for two, compelling Jean-Paul to follow her. She preferred to talk to him without Jorge eavesdropping.

"When did you see Pearl last? We're trying to track her movements in the last few weeks. Did she mention anything unusual?"

"I've been away for three weeks. I suppose I saw her a week or two before that. We mainly talked about my upcoming holiday and how expensive Isabella is to maintain." His smile was wry. "Pearl mentioned you were coming to visit and hoped we could have a meal together one night. I asked if you were the sporty type and gave her a free pass for you to use.

"You didn't pay for the pool did you? Please – I'll have the receptionist refund your money if you did, plus I'd like you to be our guest for lunch." He shouted over at the desk.

"Thank you." Jane rummaged around in her shoulder-bag and brought out a sheaf of letters. It didn't take a moment to locate the one she wanted. "Perhaps you could clear up something in one of Pearl's letters. Here it is!" She read it out.

I've got an idea for an article that I might freelance. What set me off was a casual dinner I had with Jean-Paul and Isabella. He mentioned some rather unsavoury practices that took place here during the Second World War. Isabella emphatically denied that what he was saying was true. … A mystery is always intriguing.

"What did she mean?" Jane asked again.

Jean-Paul was nodding. "I remember the night. We'd had a bit to drink and I was saying that Andorra is not very friendly compared to Spain. As outsiders, Pearl and I were sharing our experiences of trying to make friends with the natives. Isabella, being Andorran, wasn't too impressed with our take on things. I baited her by telling Pearl that during the Second World War some of the families here robbed and killed refugees then threw their bodies into the high mountain lakes. The village of Pal was notorious in this regard. TV3 Barcelona is making a movie for television from the book about this. Isabella is from Sispony – not far from Pal – and she wasn't too happy with me for implicating her neck of the woods. I had to sleep on the sofa that night – a not unusual occurrence in our house."

He grinned and ran his hands lightly over his skull, looking not at all disturbed. "Does this help? Is there some kind of connection?"

"I don't really know," Jane said slowly, her skin prickling at yet another thread leading to Pal. "Probably not, although it's a coincidence because my grandfather wrote a letter about this back in the 1950s." They talked in a desultory way for a while longer before Jean-Paul gracefully excused himself, once again pressing her to have lunch as his guest. She was unenthusiastic at the idea of dining with Jorge after her dunking in the pool, but she tried to make it a rule not to let her feelings get in the way of business. If people only realised what good actors accountants could be.

Jorge was nursing a coca-cola at the bar. They walked upstairs to the pizzeria without much discussion. The restaurant was empty, making Jane apprehensive about the food. When two chefs popped their heads out of the kitchen to advertise the menu of the day, she agreed to it without thought, however Jorge consulted the *à la carte* menu and entered into a long discourse before making his order. She noticed that he ordered the most expensive dishes on offer. The urge to have a drink was huge. To distract herself she ate the entire contents of the bread-basket while Jorge lectured her on the Basque separatist party Batsuna, finally winding down by saying.

"I got your message when I returned from Barcelona yesterday. I heard what happened to Harris and maybe if I'd been with him I could have prevented such a tragedy. I guess he lost his footing. It's pretty unusual to have a fatality in the mountains here."

"You didn't mention that you were leaving Andorra when you gave me your number. I thought you said you'd be around and could give me some help."

"I wasn't planning to go away but my father has a heart condition and my mother needed me because she can't drive." Jorge used a toothpick to worry his movie-star teeth. "Are they any closer to finding out what happened to your sister?"

"We have a few leads."

"Did you find the man who met her for lunch – the one on TV?"

"Not yet. The police are still waiting for the tapes of the News broadcasts."

"Slow, isn't it? – The way justice works."

She nodded, in agreement with him for the first time that day.
"That's how it was when my brother died. It took them forever to interview all the people who were involved, and then they never prosecuted anyone."

"What happened?"

"They found him face down in a swimming-pool after a party. The coroner said it was accidental death. He drowned, but there was evidence of both alcohol and drugs in his blood. No-one was charged with supplying the drugs. Everyone at the party professed to know nothing about it. No-one knew or saw anything – so they said."

"How old was he when he died?"

"Nineteen."

"How terrible for you and your parents."

Jorge looked away. "Yes," he said after a moment. "I know what it's like to lose someone close to me. That's why I wanted to help you."

"Was he older or younger than you?"

"We were twins."

"Were you at the party too?"

"I was at home studying for an exam."

"I'm so sorry." Words are so inadequate, Jane reflected.

The Toreador song from Carmen rang out from Jorge's mobile phone.

"Sorry," he unconsciously echoed back, snapping the phone's cover open and answering with the concise Spanish greeting "*Dime!*" (speak to me!), followed by a drawn-out "*Si, si, si,*" and then, "*No, no, no en absoluto!*" before rapping out a brief farewell. He drummed his fingers on the table and gave her a hard stare. "A friend of yours asked Señor Molina for my parents' address in Barcelona."

"Oh yes?" Frank Daltry hadn't let much time go to waste.

"It was fortunate he checked with me first. My parents do not like to be bothered. They get very distressed by anything unexpected. My father has to be careful about his health."

"I didn't know."

"Yes, well. I've got things to do." He beckoned for the bill.

"It's on Jean-Paul." Jane put down Jean-Paul's card with the scribbled note on the back, together with a 500 peseta coin for a tip, and before she had picked up her bag, Jorge was gone.

CHAPTER THIRTY-FOUR

The steep stone *camì* from the sports club to Greta's apartment snaked through a paddock of cows and on through the centre of the village of Anyos until it came to a fork. The left turn led up rustic stone steps to the postcard-perfect Romanic church on a rocky buff. The right entered a village street so empty of activity during the long hours of an Andorran Sunday lunchtime that you could fire a gun down the street without endangering life. Jane leaned into the incline of the road and headed towards Greta's four-story apartment block. With its windows shuttered against the afternoon sun, the building looked as vacant as her grandmother's eyes.

In the cool of the vestibule, Jane took her time, mopping her sweaty face with a tissue before pressing the doorbell.

"Greta, it's Jane. I'm on my way down to the *trastero*."

"I've made a thermos of iced tea. I'll bring it down."

Bring vodka, thought Jane, after she turned away. She was thinking about Jorge's strong legs holding her down in the pool and wondering what she could have done to break free. McPherson, her quirky psychotherapist, lectured victims of crimes to work out ways in which they could regain the initiative, and then replay this new script in their minds. McPherson also maintained that recovering alcoholics needed to feel in control of their lives so they could break the pattern of using drink to alleviate stress or uncertainty. They argued about this. Jane thought it was her desire always to be in control in a disordered world that drove her to use alcohol to relax; however the unreceptive Scot insisted they continue with the revisionist drills, rescripting significant moments in her life.

She shut her eyes and imagined herself grabbing Jorge's ankles and using her feet to push off the side of the pool. He would either have fallen in, or caught hold of the hand-rail, in which case she'd have kept going backwards and freed herself. Of course he could have fallen backwards and cracked his head open and she would have been arrested.

"Do you think a person would fool around in a pool when his brother drowned in a swimming accident?" she asked, but Greta just shrugged.

"Who knows what people might do, Jane? Everyone is different."

"It seems strange to me. Wouldn't you think he'd be extra careful?"

"Are you sure you are not jumping at shade?"

"Shadows," corrected Jane automatically.

"My mother always told me it was better to trust people."

"I'm not sure I agree. I'm not in a position to trust anyone."

Greta pressed her lips together and looked offended. They started to sort through the negatives in silence. The infinite number of positions a person could assume in death would fill many large coffee-table books, mused Jane, if there were a market for that macabre sort of material.

"You can die a thousand deaths, all of them different." Greta unconsciously echoed Jane's thoughts. "I've lost many family members and friends to different causes: to heart-attacks, cancer, in car-accidents and so on. Is drowning any more unusual, or suspicious, than choking to death on a chop-bone? Of course it is tragic for the family, but do they give up eating meat?

"When I was a child, there was a gipsy girl in my class who gave birth in the girls' changing-rooms one Friday, when the rest of the class had gone ice-skating on the lake behind the school. She wrapped the baby in her red felt petticoat to keep it warm and cut the umbilical cord – but she neglected to tie a knot in it. Both she and the baby slowly bled to death over the weekend. No-one found her until Monday morning when we arrived for the new school week.

"Death is so random. If the baby had come earlier in the week, she'd be alive today. What haunts me is that we never said a friendly word to her. We judged her unworthy. I try not to judge others now. Each life is precious. That's why I joined Amnesty International."

"How old were you?"

"We were fourteen. Young – but old enough to know better."

Another image of death to add to the ones in a pile on the table.

"I don't believe Pearl is dead," Jane said.

"Of course not. Someone has taken her for a purpose. The email and the ponytail were sent to prove the sender is legitimate so he can ask for something."

"I don't know. I just don't know," Jane cried, and the tears she had been holding back all day spurted over her lashes and down her cheeks.

"He must want money," Greta continued. "If it were a random act, or a sex crime, he wouldn't need to be in contact with you."

Jane wiped her eyes with the bottom of her T-shirt.

"I think you are over-tired Jane. Perhaps we should forget about doing the rest of the negatives today. By tomorrow another contact could be made. A ransom demand would give the police something to work on." Greta was following her own theory.

Jane responded wearily. "Everything to date is just supposition." She blew her nose and took a deep breath to calm down. "We need to finish the negatives if only to prove there's nothing here. I'd like to know something for certain, instead of always trying to interpret some obscure fragment and wonder if it's a clue. Assumptions aren't proof. In fact sometimes assumptions are dangerous because they close off another avenue of thought."

"I don't think these photos of heartbreaking and pointless wars have anything to do with Pearl's disappearance." Greta threw down the slide she had been holding. "Do you believe there is room for intuition in an investigation?"

"Bruce always said intuition was the subconscious working out the facts in a logical way. But in most of his cases the spouse was guilty so he didn't need intuition...." Jane trailed off, thinking of both Harris and Fernando, and asking herself once again if she thought either one was capable of harming Pearl. If Harris was involved with Pearl's disappearance, now that he was dead they might never find her.

Greta took off her glasses and rubbed the red mark on the bridge of her nose. "From my reading, I know that statistically a lot of crimes are committed by a member of the family, or a loved one, but there's also a lot of indiscriminate violence involving drugs. These cases are the hardest to solve. However if Pearl's disappearance were totally random, there would be no ponytail and no email. So if you think of it in that way, it's encouraging."

"Encouraging? The longer we go without finding her, the less likely it is that we will find her alive, or at all. Look. Let's stop talking about it for a while. My emotions are swinging so much I feel sick to my stomach. I need to concentrate on something mundane for a while."

The grim roll-call of death and war churned on until they reached the final box of negatives. By then their skins were shining with sweat in the stale air and the 40volt lights washed their features flat so that their eyes and mouths were dark holes. Jane picked up the first in a new series of negatives and wearily put it in the small viewing screen and saw a photo of a young girl in folk costume framed by a stone archway. In the foreground, slightly out of focus, two girls whirled each other around with their hands clasped – leaning back with their hair flying out from under white starched caps while their mouths splayed wide open with joy.

She reached into the middle of the box and pulled out a negative that showed a fiery sunset over an icy mountain lake. Another randomly-selected negative showed shadows made by the brim of a fedora on an old man's face, a slash of sunlight showed his eyes opaque with cataracts.

Jane looked at her watch. 8.00pm. "I think I've found the silver lining at last. These are beautiful shots of people and scenery for her art portfolio. Thankfully, we've come to the end to war and the beginning of life. Speaking of which, it will still be light outside for another couple of hours. Do you feel like a walk to breathe some real air before we knock these off?"

"How about a drive to Pal before the sun sets?" countered Greta.

"Back to the *Casa d'Or*? OK. I'd like another look at Pal; it keeps cropping up in all sorts of different ways. Would we have time to look at the *Coll de Cabrils*? That's where my Uncle Miguel died in the avalanche, or my half-uncle to be precise. I'll take the last box of negatives with me to finish in the apartment. At least these photos won't give me nightmares."

Greta answered by picking up the empty flask of tea and making for the door to the *trastero*. "Thank goodness that's over," she spoke for them both.

Once again the silver BMW flew like a dart towards Pal, taking a shortcut on the wrong side of a roundabout by an etiolated golf course.

"No-one is coming for miles," excused Greta.

"I thought Scandinavians were supposed to be law-abiding."

"We are," agreed Greta in surprise. "We have the lowest incarceration rate in Western Europe, only around sixty prisoners per one hundred thousand of population. Portugal has the highest at around a hundred and thirty. America has about seven hundred and Russia slightly less. The kinds of economic and social disparity that produce violence don't exist in the Danish welfare state. Street-crime is very low."

"You sound proud of Denmark, and your son still lives there, yet you've opted to live in Andorra. What made you decide to move?"

"The weather. Three hundred days of sunshine a year is very appealing. And you must know that Andorra too is an extremely safe place to live." She shrugged at the apparent anomaly of her words and their current activity.

"Were you an English teacher in Denmark?"

"Heavens, no! I worked in the Department of Corrections for twenty years. I suppose that too encouraged my interest in Amnesty International. There are so many countries in the world that don't have an enlightened approach to reform. Denmark believes in the value-shaping effect of punishment, and not in punishment as retribution."

"Did your husband work for the Department too?"

"I never married," Greta said, surprising Jane.

"Lizzie said your son had a legal problem?"

"A copyright issue – but one that is very complicated and expensive to prosecute. If he wins his case, I will be well compensated for the lump sum I gave him. Were you thinking he was a criminal?"

"No. No." Jane hoped she sounded convincing. "Look out for the..." But before she could finish, they were past the on-coming bus and around the corner, leaving the village of Pal behind and speeding on towards the *Coll de Cabrils*.

CHAPTER THIRTY-FIVE

The asphalt road was lined with sections of safety rail separating Jane and Greta from a thickly wooded precipice. To the left, in the distance, a three-pronged ski run looked like the petroglyph of an ancient pitchfork. Above the road, a red gondola linking the Pal and Arinsal ski stations transported a cargo of hikers, who shouted and laughed through open windows. When the bitumen abruptly ran out in a saddle between two hills, Greta skidded the BMW to a stop. A small herd of horses came to investigate. They stood around the car like a welcoming committee, tossing their heads and gently bumping into one another. Jane had to push a piebald mare aside as she climbed out of the car. The cool breeze and dying sun made her shiver. A muddy black stallion moved closer and nudged her shoulder, nipping the shoulder-strap of her backpack with his teeth.

"Ouch!" She jumped.

"He thinks you have food in there. The tourists give them bread so they'll come closer, to be photographed," Greta said.

Jane rapped him on his nose and shooed him and his harem away. The stallion neighed loudly and momentarily stood his ground, but as the mares moved away, he slowly followed suit, stopping after fifty paces to turn and once more neigh in their direction. "Go on," said Jane, picking up a rock and throwing it at the ground by his hooves, but he just stood there, considering.

Greta interrupted the staring contest. "We're standing on the western border. The gravel road from here into Spain used to be a popular smuggling route, using donkeys then, later, four-wheel-drives, but now customs agents patrol the road. These days the smugglers often use human mules to carry heavy backpacks of cigarettes on the hiking trails, where it's harder for the *Guardia* to catch them. I talked to two young men the other day at La Rabassa in the south, and they opened their backpacks to show me the cartons of cigarettes inside.

"That's the *Coll de Cabrils* to our left. Shall we walk to where we can get a better view?" Greta indicated a track leading up towards a rugged bluff.

They walked at a good pace, not talking. The trail was steeper than it looked. The soles of Jane's shoes slipped on the scree from time to time. Greta, with her sturdy hiking boots, had no such difficulty. She was in good condition for her age and wasn't breathing hard. They walked past a fold in the terrain and on a sloping upward course that took them to a large rock-fall. There the path looped back on itself and continued on a diagonal route to the skyline.

"Do you think these rocks are from an avalanche?" Jane asked. "Perhaps we're close to where my uncle died. It would be dreadful to be buried under tons of snow."

"He was probably unconscious and didn't suffer."

"It's strange that they never identified the other three bodies. Three people can't just disappear without being missed. I wonder if they were out here taking advantage of the snowy conditions to smuggle cigarettes on their touring skis."

"Do you mean the three unknown men were smuggling, or your relatives?"

"Either, I suppose. Or both."

"Two smuggling teams? That seems unlikely."

"Yes, perhaps they were working together. The others may not have been from around here so they weren't identified. Saboya said that Miguel was in "transportation". He hesitated for a moment before he said that, so maybe he was using a linguistic sleight of hand to transform an illegal activity into something more respectable, and he really meant my uncle was a smuggler."

"He'd be in good company, then. More than half the so-called first families in Andorra made their wealth through smuggling, and they consider themselves to be highly respectable."

"Sometimes Andorra seems more like a caricature than a real country."

"Yet it is the oldest country in western europe with unchanged borders."

They turned and retraced their path through the twilight to the car, where Greta pulled out a map and pointed out all the potential smuggling routes and unmanned border crossings in Andorra.

"They're called a *Port*, for port of entry, or sometimes a *Portella*. So you see here we are at the *Port de Cabus*, then further up we have the *Port de Rat* – where Andorra constructed half a tunnel through the mountain in the mistaken belief that France was going to tunnel though from the other side and meet them in the middle."

"The Minister for Public Works must own a construction company!"

Greta laughed. "It's more that the Andorrans consider negotiations to be complete before the final wording has been thrashed out and the contracts signed. They act in good faith."

They piled into the car to get out of the wind and wheeled back towards the *Casa d'Or*. When they pulled into the long driveway Greta groped with one hand for a plastic bag at her feet.

"You can deal with this."

Jane wrinkled her nose at the strong smell and looked inside the bag at a slab of evil-looking steak.

"What dog could ignore a big steak?" asked Greta. "I cut a pocket in the middle and tipped in a good part of this month's sleeping pills. If we wait for them to take effect we can at least get out of the car and have a look around. There's a torch in the glove-box."

"Is drugging a dog an offence in Andorra?"

"I doubt it. Is it an offence in Australia?"

"I expect so. Even riding a bicycle without a helmet is an offence."

"Once the dog has eaten the evidence, we're in the clear."

"Great. Good plan. I hope he's hungry," said Jane with little enthusiasm.

The BMW pulled up without the instantaneous display of barking of their previous visit. "Where is he, I wonder?" They sat quietly in the dark for several minutes before Jane cautiously opened her door and slipped her feet outside, making sure she was ready to throw the steak to give her time to retreat if need be.

Greta turned off the car's interior light and whispered, "Don't slam the door."

Jane crept forward, her heart thumping. She tried to steady her imagination along with her pulse. How was she going to switch on the torch when her other hand was immobilised by stinking dog-bait? She pressed the torch-switch against her thigh and slid it down her leg, then jumped when the large pool of light shone on the path at her feet. Her fingers crept down and across the bulb to dim the beam. A breath of air disturbed the hair on the back of her neck and a hand touched her shoulder. She gave a muffled scream as she whirled around, preparing to use the torch to bludgeon her assailant, and in the process dropped the meat. Greta's strongly-planed face was illuminated, her finger to her lips in a shushing motion.

"Bloody Hell!" breathed Jane grumpily, wiping her slimy hand on her trousers. She gestured towards the steak, which she'd dropped and was now covered in pine needles. "You take it. You'd better hope it looks tastier than we do. I'm going to knock on the front door so you can hang back a bit and drop it somewhere inconspicuous if there's someone home. This is the dumbest thing I've done for a long time."

Greta shrugged nonchalantly and, using the plastic grocery bag she'd brought from the car, scooped up the meat. Jane checked her watch. Maybe she'd find the family sitting around the kitchen table.

No light filtered out of the shuttered windows at the front of the house. The front door was a massive construction carved out of a single piece of oak, and looked like it could withstand a considerable barrage. The wood was dark and weathered. An impressive bronze knocker in the shape of a boar's head was set at head height. Jane examined the knocker then twined her fingers in the boar's tusks and knocked four times – hard – wincing at the cannon-shot-like result. An immediate howl answered, followed by the familiar sound of a large dog throwing itself bodily against an immovable object, this time the front door. The sound of bolts being shot was loud in the still mountain air. Greta impulsively reached for the torch, switched it off, then quickly faded around the corner of the house.

As the door opened, an oblong of light struck Jane's face and stole her night vision. She squinted and put one hand up to shade her eyes, trying not to run from the deafening snarls of the giant dog.

"*Callate!*" The command was given with a brutal cuff to the beast's head.

A small figure, not much taller than the dog, held tightly onto its chain-link collar. A further fierce slap caused the dog to blink and sink to a crouch, although it still growled softly and strained at the chain.

"Pedro!" cried Jane in surprise.

"Cousin Jane. *Buenas*. How nice. Do please come in," the small boy responded, with a total lack of surprise and perfect courtesy. "*Yayo!*" he shouted over his shoulder "*Es mi prima – la Australiana.*

La amiga de Juan-Antonio."

"*Oso – aqui!*" The gruff command from the rear of the house caused the dog to prick his ears and whine.

"Bear," grimaced Jane. "Great name."

Pedro cautiously let the collar go and the dog jumped up, thrusting his huge head into Jane's crotch and inhaling her scent with such gusto she felt the lightweight material of her trousers briefly enter his mouth. She dared not move an inch.

"*Oso,*" growled the voice again, and the dog trotted off on tip toes, looking once over its shoulder with a grin that showed off all of its teeth. Saliva fell to the stone floor and pooled there.

"*Adelante!* Come in. We have just finished our meal."

Jane followed without a word. She had nothing rehearsed and had no idea how she was going to explain her visit. She took her cue from Pedro's total lack of surprise. Two could play the Andorran. She arranged her face in what she trusted was a neutral expression and hoped her powers of extemporisation could withstand the interview to come.

CHAPTER THIRTY-SIX

Jane's steps echoed as she followed Pedro down the passage to a badly-lit family dining-room at the rear of the farmhouse. The slate floor absorbed light from low wattage lamps set into unplastered stone walls. In one corner of the room a fire burned low in a simple fireplace, a trivet placed over the coals. On the table, candles cast a soft light on the remains of barbequed duck breasts and torn pieces of baguette on uncleared dirty plates. A half-empty bottle of *rioja* had stained the heavy white linen runner in the centre of the table with a purple ring of wine. The wine was evident in only two of the four adjacent glasses. At one end of the table, a jug of water, slices of melon and a selection of cheese and dried fruit completed the tableau. Eight massive chairs of wood and tooled leather surrounded the weighty refectory-style table.

The room had only one occupant. In the shadows by the fire an old man sat on a rocking-chair. His curled and withered right hand lay on the plaid blanket across his knees while the other exquisitely-manicured hand held a cigarette to his mouth. The long ash of the cigarette was burning dangerously close to the skin. The giant dog *Oso* sat quivering and whining at the old man's feet.

"Take the dog into one of the other rooms, Pedro. He is over excited," the man said. "I'm sorry I can't get up, my dear. I don't move so well these days. Arthritis. Come and kiss your great-uncle. Such a pleasure to meet you at last."

Jane waited until the door closed behind Pedro and the dog before she advanced. The man chuckled, the sound of dry rustling paper.

"You are safe with me. I won't bite. There are no natural predators left in the Pyrenees. The last of the wild brown bears left the Pyrenees many years ago."

He tilted his head to one side. She pecked at it, breathing in a smoky scent. He took her hand in his and brought it up close to clouded eyes, turning it over and examining the palms and the short utilitarian nails. He sniffed her wrist and gave a half growl, half purr.

"Panther by Cartier. A perfume with muscle to match a strong hand."

It was indeed Panther. "You have a good nose."

"My dear. It is one of the family businesses."

"Family businesses are one of my interests."

"And I am interested in you and your family. Where is your father tonight? Why isn't he with you? I would like to meet him."

"He had another engagement," she answered carefully. "He'll be sorry to have missed you. History is his passion, and family history most of all; however he wouldn't expect us to wait for him before we exchange ours."

"No, indeed. It is tedious to wait for the things you want, especially at my age when time is no longer in my favour." He gestured towards the table. "Pour yourself a glass of wine and one for me, dear, then pull a chair closer to the fire. I get cold these days, and need a fire all the year-round."

"Alcohol doesn't agree with me," she said, as she poured him a glass of *Rioja* and herself a glass of water from the crystal jug.

"I heard that about you." He exhaled smoke.

"So was that a test?"

"An old man forgets so much more than he remembers in a life time."

"Your English is excellent. To be so fluent you must practice?"

"I welcome the opportunity to do so. The one thing I was given in my life was education; everything else came with hard work. Education does not wear out with time. The *cura* in my village did at least do that for me."

Above the stone mantelpiece of the fireplace, a large painting of a beautiful girl dominated the room. Her incandescent face was shaped like an inverted triangle. As Jane moved to examine it more closely, the laughing eyes of the painting followed her. Flickering light from the candles on the table reflected from her ivory skin. Glossy dark hair escaped in wisps from the scarf that tried in vain to contain it. A colourful shawl was draped across her shoulders while her hands held out a gathered skirt partially covered with a small apron. She appeared to be bowing to an imaginary dance-partner. Peeping out from under her skirt, one pointed foot was clad in an espadrille with red laces tied at the ankle. Somehow the artist had managed to depict a mischievous girl on the brink of becoming a woman. The childlike face had sensual lips. She was a dancer in need of a partner. Jane drew closer to the see if she could identify the scrawl of signature.

"A minor artist with a special affinity for his subject. I believe this is his masterpiece after endless practice with still life and farm animals. Prize cows and horses were his speciality. Sit down my dear. You are a tall woman and you are looming over me where I cannot see your face."

Jane sat. The man's tone was peremptory and she could see that he was used to giving orders.

"What should I call you? Great Uncle is rather cumbersome. How is it that we are related exactly?" she asked.

"*Tio*, or Uncle, would be convenient," he replied.

"Are you Pedro's grandfather? He called you *yayo*."

"You flatter me. I am eighty-seven years old and he is eleven! *Yayo* is simply an expression of respect."

Jane shrugged. "I only recently discovered the Catalan side of my family. Perhaps you could elaborate."

The old man nodded his head slowly in approval. "You understand that we are Catalan. This is important. To be Catalan is a proud thing."

Jane decided to wait him out. He turned towards the painting of the girl and sipped his wine, his eyes on fire with the reflection from the flames.

"Her name was Angel. From the time she was born she looked just like an angel. How banal that sounds. It is difficult to describe beauty. She was seventeen when she met your grandfather. He was twice her age and despite the fact he was married with a child of his own, he stole her heart from us. We all believed him to be a thief, although she swore she gave herself to him freely. In a time of great danger, fear and romance are often indivisible – especially to a silly young girl who had been cosseted and protected by her family all her short life. What could she know of love and the ways of men?" He cleared his throat and pulled the rug more closely around him.

"When I was young, after the *cura* arranged for me to go to university, I repaid his interest by repudiating the church and loudly proclaiming socialism as my new religion. We dreamed of a new world order, but we did not expect our family to change. Family and honour are the bedrock of our souls. Angel grew up listening to stories of how we were fighting to transform society. She did not understand that the family was sacrosanct and was not to be part of this change."

"She was your sister?" Jane said.

The old man nodded, slowly. "When she was growing up, young men left the village to fight in the civil war and they did not return. Some were killed; some went into exile, and the fate of some we shall never know. The women and the old men were left behind to plant and harvest the crops and to look after the sheep."

He used his crippled hand to indicate the painting that faced him. "Angel was not content to live a quiet life among old men. She wanted more. When the chain of evasion formed during the Second World War to escort refugees across Catalunya on their way to Portugal, she was one of the first to volunteer."

"And this is how she met my grandfather?"

He coughed long and hard, and spat into his handkerchief. "They say he had a halo of blonde hair, like yours, plus of course he was *simpatico*, a hero. You must know that he escaped France by walking across the Pyrenees to Andorra. From here he wanted to make his way to Portugal and return to England. To be fair, he did not simply seek to save himself on the first part of his journey, he helped a party of Jews fleeing from the Nazis."

Jane moved closer to the fire, and looked up at the painting and into the innocent face of her grandfather's lover.

"We Catalans have a special hatred of the Nazis. They were Franco's allies in the *guerra civil*." His voice began to fade and he took a large gulp of wine. "The German Condor Legion used dive-bombers to wipe out an entire town going about their business on a busy market day in Guernica. Were it not for Nazi help, it would have been Franco who lived in exile, and I would have lived my life in a free Spain."

"Well at least you and my grandfather were on the same side!" said Jane.

The old man ignored the interjection and continued, "You understand the forces of the civil war? – How we, the Republicans, the rightfully-elected government of Spain, had to pay the Russians for our arms with our total gold reserves, while Franco was given arms by other nations on credit? – That these same nations blocked the delivery of our lawful arms and sank the Russian boats that carried them?"

Jane nodded her comprehension of his baroque commentary, not wishing to stop his train of thought; glad that one of the books she had thumbed through on the plane was a traveller's history of Spain.

"Ah yes. You are the child of an historian. You would examine our history. You would read Ernest Hemingway and George Orwell and regret the blood of the International Brigade." He said the names with irony.

"Your grandfather was *macho. Un hombre*! How could our Angel resist him? His sharp blade reaped our prize flower. Those were difficult times and the family tried not to blame her. It is unjust to blame the victim. A real man would not take advantage, but act with honour, not only towards a woman, but to her family. This man gave Angel money instead of respect. In his heart he was a phantom and not a man at all."

Jane digested this tirade. Time had not diminished the rage of the man before her. She wanted to defend her grandfather and say that at least he had supported Angel and his child, but she knew this was an inadequate defence. Although Charles – or rather the trust – had supported her, she had felt no less abandoned. "Where were you when all this was happening?" she asked instead.

"Lleida fell in April 1938, then Barcelona in January 1939, but I fought on with my comrades for one more, tragic, month until the final thin line we were holding from Seu through to Gerona at last fell. The Catalan countryside became hysterical with fear at the reprisals that Franco would take. We knew there would be no mercy.

"France was one of our few friends during this period. At the beginning of the civil war the Blum government did nothing to help us, but in the end, France returned to her republican ideals and allowed column after column of us to escape. I was one of the two hundred and fifty thousand troops who crossed the border into France during a five-day period. After two and a half years of civil war we went into exile. Most of us never returned. It is a bitter thing to be exiled from your motherland."

He sipped his wine ruminatively, the claw that was his right hand contrasted sharply with the delicate crystal of the glass. Jane thought it best not to speak. What could she know of the horrors of a civil war? A long time passed before he spoke again.

"When I escaped, Elena – my wife – stayed behind in Lleida with our daughter to help her father after a debilitating stroke. We had defied the family to marry. They were landowners who supported the monarchists. Civil war rips families in two. Sometimes love doesn't conquer all; it is ambushed by duty. Elena embraced her duty to her parents, while I lived in a squalid refugee camp near Perpignan. In due course I joined the Maquis – the French resistance fighters – and like so many other displaced Catalans we fought another, covert, war against the German occupation of France. We had hate enough to spare."

"Did you ever meet my grandfather?"

"I did not." The old man gave her a steely gaze that gave her no doubt as to what his intentions would have been if he had met Charles senior.

"We have a saying … about the sins of the father being vested in the children. Do you believe that?" Jane asked.

"*Depende*," was the ambiguous answer. "The quotation is Greek, from Euripides. The gods visit the sins of the father upon the children."

"What happened to Angel?"

"She is dust."

"What about your own daughter?"

The old man smiled and gestured around him. "Elena, after her mother. A great success story. Her marriage has made life very comfortable for me."

"So Santiago de Almeida Barreiro is your son-in-law? – And what does he do for a living?" Jane asked.

But the old man said, "I am tired now. We must speak again another day. Bring your father next time. We have many things to talk about."

"Did you ever meet my sister, Pearl?" she asked quickly.

"A beautiful woman, but like many beautiful women she brought trouble with her wherever she went. I am sorry to hear she is missing, but not surprised."

Pedro was summoned by three hearty knocks to the floor with the old man's walking-stick, so that he could once again see to the unbolting of the mighty front door. *Oso* the dog who so resembled the vanished brown bears of the Pyrenees did not reappear and Pedro assured Jane she would be safe to reach her car.

There were many questions that remained unanswered. "Pedro, are you here with your mother or father tonight?" Jane asked.

"No señora – I am staying with *yayo* and helping with the tobacco harvest. It is a busy time and I must begin to learn something of the family business."

"The other two place-settings at the table were for...?"

"Uncle Santiago and Aunt Elena – but they left for the airport after dinner. Maria will clear the dishes in the morning."

"Are they flying somewhere?"

"Bogotá."

"Bogotá, Columbia?" The cocaine capital of the world.

Pedro nodded. He stood with one foot tucked behind his calf, while he watched her walk to the BMW. Where was Greta? She saw no sign of her. She slipped into the driver's seat and Pedro waved from the half-moon of light on the front step. The car purred to life and she carefully backed around to drive out of the long gravel driveway. Greta was calmly smoking by the side of the road.

"I thought I'd look around the outbuildings while you kept them busy inside. Then if you didn't reappear I was going to notify the police," Greta said. "What happened in there? Was there any sign that they knew Pearl?"

"They know who she is all right. It seems the *Casa d'Or* belongs to our relatives. Tonight's relative *du jour* was my great-uncle. He must be one of the "tough uncles" Grandfather wrote about, who helped to take care of educating Miguel when he was growing up. There were a series of paintings in the house signed XVO. I suspect my great-uncle was the artist – not that he would be so direct as to tell me that."

"It's odd that Saboya didn't know about the family connection to *Casa d'Or*."

"Saboya can't be expected to know everyone in Andorra. There are over twenty thousand Andorrans after all, not to mention another fifty thousand foreigners living here."

"Good point!"

"So in the end the photos were of the family tobacco farm?" The disappointment was plain in Greta's voice.

Jane was pensive. "The more I find out, the less I know. No sooner do I cross something off my list, than I add several things to the bottom. How did Pearl discover this side of the family, I wonder? Do you think Fernando told her?"

Greta headed the car towards Ordino. "It seems unlikely; perhaps one of the trustees told her." She reached over and patted Jane's hand. "Don't worry, we'll find her."

During the long hours spent together in the *trastero* Jane had come to trust the Danish woman. She always spoke of Pearl in the present tense. It was reassuring. Today marked the eleventh day since Pearl was last seen at Lake Pessons. Jane knew so much more than when she had first arrived, but any link between what she knew and finding Pearl completely eluded her.

CHAPTER THIRTY-SEVEN

W as the man who met Pearl at the Lake Pessons restaurant the same man who dumped the car? A co-conspirator? A different man? Was Señor Molina right about him being on TV? Jane sprawled on Pearl's sofa making lists.

Although it was late, she was too keyed-up to sleep. A cup of chamomile tea had failed to calm her and a craving for something sweet drove her to consume half a packet of caramels she found in the cupboard. She pawed through her shoulder-bag and pulled out the scrap of paper Jorge had given her. 2Jorge@andorra.ad. The good thing about email was that you could send it at any time of the day or night and the recipient picked it up when it was convenient. It was the perfect medium for lonely insomniacs. She plugged in her laptop and copied the two photos of Jack Weinstein, sent to her by Gary Cohen, then pasted them into an email to Jorge, making sure that she deleted Weinstein's name before asking, "Jorge, is this the man Sr. Moline saw with Pearl at Lake Pessons? – Jane."

She looked at the brief message and thought it was probably too short for courtesy. Spaniards used a lot of circumlocution in order not to sound rude. Still email was supposed to be concise. She pressed the send and receive button.

Her message was gone in a flash and Outlook Express reported an incoming message. The police were supposed to be monitoring her emails. Could she receive an email while they also intercepted it? She'd forgotten to open a Hotmail account.

She watched the download rate with misgivings, wondering if she would ever again be able to pick up emails without anxiety. The message arrived swiftly and with her secretary, Carol's by-line. Her relief, knowing it would not contain further disturbing photos of Pearl, fought with the disappointment that there were no messages or instructions from *embustero*:

"The hospital is releasing your grandmother tomorrow. She is recovering well but needs some assistance to walk. Her mental state is still confused and it's hard to know how much is from the stroke and how much from the Alzheimer's, but today she recognised your mother, so there is some cognisance there. She seems to think I am someone called Wendover."

Well they were unlikely ever to solve that one.

The phone shrilled, making her jump.

"I thought you'd still be up," Charles's voice boomed.

"You'll never guess what happened to me!" Jane said, "I met Angel's brother at the *Casa d'Or*. He lives there with his daughter and her husband. It looks like Pearl was taking photos of the family tobacco farm – nothing more suspicious than that. What happened with you and Señora Menendez?"

"A charming woman and a good lunch. I waited until we'd finished a bottle of wine before I asked any questions. Mind you, I think I drank most of it.

"The ABC *Compania* belongs to a consortium of Andorran families, one of whom is Santiago de Ameida-Bareiro – which is another link to the family and the *Casa d'Or*. I have a list of the members but I didn't recognise any other names. Apparently the trust bankrolled the ABC Company in the early days and still gets a very healthy dividend from the investment. There is nothing sinister about the phones being disconnected: the business recently moved to larger premises after changing its name to *Apice Finances* or 'Apex Finance', better to suit the company profile. They are into private banking, insurance, tobacco, retail – in fact, you name it. Señora Menendez didn't seem at all bothered by my questions."

"So that's another dead-end then."

They both sighed.

Jane asked, "Did you ask about Alain Bertran-Carrera and *El Gigante*?"

"Yes. She hadn't heard of either. Perhaps Saboya was right and it was a pseudonym which no doubt morphed into the ABC Company. She didn't know who started the Company, just shrugged and said it was ancient history now, and not important since the families in the consortium had equal shares. I asked if she'd ever heard how the trust was founded, but apparently she never asked and her mother isn't alive. It seems all the original trustees have passed on."

"Someone of that generation must still be alive. Andorrans have the highest longevity in the world according to a recent publication by the World Health Organisation."

"They all smoke like chimneys. Cancer is bound to take its toll." Charles was a militant former smoker. "What about Angel's brother, what did he have to say?"

"He's keen to meet you, but I should warn you that he is still carrying a grudge about Grandfather's affair with Angel, even though it was over fifty years ago."

"We'll have something in common then," Charles said. "Is he angry enough to take his revenge on Pearl?"

"I shouldn't think so. He made it clear that families should be treated with honour; plus he's an old man who can hardly get out of his chair. And I can't see the next generation carrying out a vendetta since Miguel and then Llourdes surely did pretty well out of Grandfather and the trust. We should go out to *Casa d'Or* to see him tomorrow."

"Tomorrow we need to spend more time with Saboya pouring over the old archives. Maybe we could go in the afternoon?"

"Sure, let's see how the day goes. I'd like you to ask the police if there are any developments regarding the email from *embustero* or if they have identified the man Pearl met for lunch from the news tapes. Try to organise regular updates on their investigation."

"OK. Let's plan to meet at Saboya's office at ten."

The phone shrilled again as soon as Jane hung up. She checked her watch and saw that it was well after midnight.

"Your phone was engaged so I knew you'd still be up," Juan-Antonio said with flawless logic. The deep bass tone was welcome in her ear.

"Where are you?" asked Jane.

"I'm in La Massana – I'll soon be heading past your place for home."

"Why not stop by, or are you still with the delightful Paco?"

"He's back in Barcelona." – His voice held a smile. – "But I am with Fernando. He's driving me home."

"Ask if he'd like to stop by coffee."

A twenty-four hour day seemed to stretch to thirty in Andorra, Jane reflected. When did they ever sleep?

Juan-Antonio and Fernando did not look like cousins when they stood side-by-side. Juan-Antonio had what Jane thought of as a cheerfully rumpled look. His jeans were cinched below his belly and hung off his bottom where the tail of his workman's shirt had come untucked. His hiking boots with the heavy soles added another two inches to his height but he was still slightly shorter than she was. By contrast Fernando, although dressed casually, looked like an advertisement for expensive cologne. Give him a ponytail and he could be Paco's father.

"Coffee or a glass of wine?" asked Jane. "There's wine in Pearl's storeroom."

The men agreed that coffee was fine, both taking it black with spoonfuls of sugar. They sat on the leather sofas and Juan-Antonio unabashedly made himself at home by immediately lighting a cigarette then looking around for an ashtray. Fernando crossed his shiny loafers at the ankles, a surprisingly prissy look for such a good-looking man, and pushed himself back in the chair to avoid the smoke.

"Did Pearl know Llourdes was her cousin, and vice versa?" Jane asked.

Fernando coughed, splattering his tan chinos with coffee.

"Jane doesn't practice small talk," Juan-Antonio smiled.

She brought out a bottle of soda water and a napkin so that Fernando could mop up. She was not unhappy to have chipped his perfect façade. Fernando looked at Juan-Antonio who merely turned his mouth down. As signals go, Jane couldn't decipher it.

"Llourdes knew who Pearl was from the moment she moved here. One of the trustees told her, and naturally she told me, so when I was introduced to Pearl at a reception, I gave her my card and offered assistance should she ever need it. I didn't mention the family connection, not wanting a distant relative to presume to have any influence with me, but I was intrigued that my wife's distant cousin should be a beautiful woman with worldwide political contacts." He sipped his coffee and thought a moment before continuing.

"My wife asked me to make sure Pearl didn't get into any trouble, so several weeks later when Pearl called me for advice on getting her motor vehicle licence – which is a tortuous affair here if you are not from a European Union country – I suggested we discuss it over lunch. One has to eat after all."

"How did the relationship develop?" Jane asked.

"We talked for hours that day. I lost track of the time. I turned off my mobile and missed an important meeting. By the time we finally left the restaurant I felt like I had found *mi media naranja* – my soulmate. We began meeting for lunch on a casual basis, and when I stopped telling Llourdes about our meetings, I realised it was serious.

"If Pearl were Catalan, I doubt I'd have felt the same attraction. I've met many beautiful women in my life, but she was different. Our relationship developed slowly because she knew I was married, but eventually it was more than friendship. I married young, and after Pedro was born the intimate side of the marriage faded. I convinced myself that as long as I was discrete, Llourdes wouldn't mind me straying. It was only when Pearl discovered the family connection and became so distraught, that I saw what an unforgivable thing I had done."

"What about Pedro? Didn't you at least concern yourself with your son?"

"Love isn't rational. For a time you are simply possessed."

"I suppose your career wasn't a factor," Jane said.

Surprisingly, Fernando laughed. "This isn't America, where one senator from Texas, when asked if he would have resigned over the Monica Lewinsky affair said, 'I wouldn't have had the opportunity. I'd be lying in a pool of my own blood and my wife would be standing over me asking, "How do you reload this son of a bitch?"'

"If you read the popular press, you'd see that gossiping about the divorce and love affairs of politicians and celebrities is the lifeblood of their sales, but this rarely interferes with anyone's professional life. Having a beautiful mistress in Europe is more likely to boost a politician's career than harm it."

"What about your duty to the baby Pearl was expecting?"

"Pearl didn't tell me about the baby. I had to discover that from the police interview on Wednesday." His tone was bitter. "The last time I saw Pearl, she said that since I had not been truthful there was no future for us. She ran out of the restaurant and wouldn't take my calls. I don't know how she found out Llourdes was her cousin. I guess it was from the same trustee who told my wife about her."

"Señora Menendez?"

"The very same," he said, standing up to take his leave.

"It's strange how history repeats itself," Jane said later, as she lay in Juan-Antonio's arms. "My grandfather was trying to extricate himself from his marriage, to have a life with Angel. Charles left my mother to live with Elsa. Elsa left Charles for Bill, who left her for another woman when Polly was born with cerebral palsy. When Pearl found she was expecting Fernando's baby, instead of being able to pretend she was merely having a harmless short-term affair with a married man, she knew Fernando would have to choose between his current family and a new family. Either way, one child would lose. In therapy they talk about the mirror image; how we hate most in others the flaws we see in ourselves."

"What do you see in yourself?" asked Juan-Antonio.

Jane wasn't going there. "Did your wife leave you for another man?"

"Not that she ever admitted."

"She didn't remarry, or live with anyone else after you separated?"

"No. Just collected the alimony cheques and went shopping." Juan-Antonio pronounced it alley-money.

Jane laughed. "How did she explain leaving you then?"

But instead of replying, he laced his fingers through her hair and pulled her head gently towards his, and after that Jane lost the thread of the conversation entirely.

CHAPTER THIRTY-EIGHT

"It's Meritxell today, our national day," announced Juan-Antonio when the village church bells struck six. "Put your boots on. We have a long hike ahead of us this morning."

Jane struggled out from under the bed-covers to see Juan-Antonio fully-dressed and carrying two steaming coffees on a tray.

"I've barely had a couple of hours' sleep. Why get up so early?"

"Andorra has a holiday today and most shops and businesses are closed."

"A perfect opportunity to sleep in!" Jane pulled the covers back over her head.

"Once a year we honour the Virgin of Mertixell by walking to the National Cathedral from each of Andorra's seven parishes. We celebrate mass, and then have a picnic afterwards."

"I was supposed to meet Charles at Saboya's this morning." Jane sat up and gulped half a cup of black coffee to clear her head.

"No-one works on Meritxell day. I'm sorry Jane, but there's not much you can do today. Call Charles later and he can take a taxi and meet us at the church for mass; obviously he can't walk over the *Coll d'Ordino* with us."

"The *Coll d'Ordino*?" Jane protested in disbelief. "But it must be over a thousand vertical metres to the top."

"Six hundred and fifty metres, if we take the shortcut through the woods and don't walk on the road," agreed Juan-Antonio. "We'd better get started. Do you know if Pearl has a walking-stick, because the descent is quite steep? We're joining Victor and his family for lunch. They have more than enough food to share. They're bringing chairs for us too."

"You've been busy this morning," Jane grumbled. She needed more coffee. Juan-Antonio was wise enough to forego any further conversation until she had some.

About thirty walkers stood waiting at the *pueblo* of Segudet above the village of Ordino for the local *cura* to escort them up the mountain. As Juan-Antonio led Jane to the first steep slope, other walkers greeted him jovially. The range of ages surprised her. Several men who looked to be in their sixties took off and made good time ahead of them, long wooden walking-sticks in evidence. The men were short and wiry; their faces a pattern of vertical wrinkles caused by crinkling up their eyes to avoid the ever-present cigarette smoke emanating from their mouths. None were out of breath.

"Water!" gasped Jane as a comfortably-upholstered grandmother in black steamed past them towing two young girls in her wake. "Jesus. The people here are incredibly fit."

"Quite a few of them do the annual *travessas* and race up the mountain."

"What do they win?"

"A trophy, and the satisfaction of being the best. We're a mountain people, Jane, so we take pride in being at ease in the mountains." Seeing that Jane's chest was still heaving, Juan-Antonio continued, "It was a famous case of mountain ability that brought about the repeal of the death penalty here in the late 1940s.

"Two brothers farmed some land in Canillo – near where we are going – and following the tradition of primogeniture the oldest brother inherited the family property. One day he was found shot to death. The younger brother was away selling sheep in the town of Hospitalet, across the border in France. The police couldn't find the person responsible for the murder and after some time the case was closed, unsolved.

"Months later, the younger brother confessed. People thought grief had turned his mind, because he had ample witnesses to testify he was at the market both the day it happened and the following morning. The young brother swore he had taken dinner in Hospitalet to establish an alibi, then climbed and ran all the way back to the farm, shot his brother and returned in time for breakfast with all the other shepherds. Nobody believed this was possible, but wanting to be thorough – and in fact wanting to confront the younger brother with the insanity of his claim – the police sent their strongest man to repeat the journey. He made it there and back within the time limit."

"What happened to the younger brother?"

"In those days the death sentence was carried out by garrotting, but no-one could be found to act as the executioner. The police chief resigned and his replacement decided to use a firing squad. The younger brother was taken to the square, blindfolded and shot. My father said that many people came to watch, even children. Afterwards the whole population was so traumatised the death sentence was abolished."

"That was very progressive for those days."

"Indeed."

They continued in single file. Occasionally they would pass a man or woman who had momentarily stopped their pilgrimage to pick the abundant wild mushrooms germinated by the recent rains. The fir trees were dense, giving the walkers a pleasant, cool shade. Underfoot, the path was in turns rocky then mossy and sometimes strewn with small pinecones. When stepping on these, Jane thought it was not unlike trying to roller-skate uphill.

"*Cuidado!*" Juan-Antonio caught her arm as she started to fall. "Watch your feet."

She cuffed him lightly. "Slow down then. I'm not a mountain-goat."

The descent went quickly. Jane found the rhythm by bending her knees to control her centre of gravity and taking some of the weight on her stick. She cruised down behind Juan-Antonio to his obvious approval and they began to catch up with some of the walkers who had passed them going up. Always there were friendly greetings and laughter. Andorrans showed respect and friendship to their policemen and didn't treat them like pariahs, as was too often the case in Australia, Jane thought. She remembered some of the more uncomfortable moments with Bruce; like when they moved into their new house and introduced themselves to their young neighbours, only to have them mumble and drift away when they discovered her husband's occupation. People who smoked dope weren't too keen on having a detective for a neighbour – except when they thought he'd be able to quash a fine or a speeding ticket. Only the elderly couple across the road had welcomed them to the neighbourhood.

As the ground began to level out, they reached a road flanked by a large, circular, stone building. The area was jammed with parked cars and people unpacking picnic supplies. They walked on down a four-lane highway, manned by traffic police in their gold-braided dress uniforms, and followed the crowd half a mile up a short trail to a stone bell-tower, which marked their arrival at Meritxel. The scene surrounding the church was one of impenetrable activity. Cars were parked randomly, boxing in others, leaving no room for them to depart. Families milled around searching for missing walkers to make up their number, while others spread blankets on the ground or set up folding tables and chairs. Children ran around unchecked. A toddler squirmed along on his stomach underneath a tunnel of chair legs.

"How do they sort themselves out at the end?" Jane asked, but Juan-Antonio just shrugged. It wasn't his parish or his problem.

"It all works out."

They insinuated themselves into the cool of the Cathedral. The church was a fusion of styles, incorporating the layout of a Greek cross with various elements of Islam and Medieval churches. Juan-Antonio drew Jane's attention away from the geometric figures on the pavement to point out the stone arches and slate, direct copies of the original Romanic church which had burnt down in the 1970s. Instead of traditional stained-glass windows, the architect had opted for clear glass to bring in the surrounding beauty of the mountainside. A statue of virgin and child – with faces elongated and heads squared off – presided over banks of votive candles and lush floral arrangements.

Juan-Antonio squeezed into an already jammed pew, making a six-inch slice of bench available at the end for Jane. She perched a cheek of her bottom on it and hoped the mass would start on time. She hadn't been inside a church since Bruce's funeral. A crescendo of organ music presaged the appearance of the priest and when he stepped onto the altar-steps the choir burst into full-throated voice, but before Jane could lose herself in the theatre of a Catalan mass her mobile phone trilled.

"Sorry," she mumbled in acute embarrassment to the crowd of frowning faces surrounding her, tripping over herself in the haste to flee outside and take the call. Turning off the mobile was not an option until Pearl was found.

Charles's voice boomed in her ear. "I called Saboya and he agreed to open the office for me for a couple of hours this morning. He wasn't going to church so it didn't inconvenience him but when he unlocked the front door, someone had broken in over the weekend and completely trashed the office. Whoever it was forced the doors to locked cupboards and filing-cabinets and dumped the contents out. The papers are fused into a soggy mush because a few buckets of water were thrown around to add to the general mayhem. Poor Saboya sat there with his head in his hands until the police arrived. It's going to take a lot of work to get it ship-shape again."

"Did they get access to the safe?"

"No. There was scorching on the door from what looked like marks from an arc-welder, but luckily it was a bank vault and built to withstand robberies."

"So the archive boxes are safe?"

"Yes. I've taken them back to the hotel and the manager has agreed to store them in the hotel-safe overnight."

"I'll see if I can get a taxi and meet you there."

As she clicked the off button, Victor materialised beside her. His linen trousers and short-sleeved shirt bore no trace of a hard trek over a mountain-top so she presumed he had come with his family by car. In a brief sentence she explained what had happened.

"No need to take a taxi," he said and took her arm to walk her down to the highway where he flagged down the first car he saw. He produced his police shield and asked the driver to take her to the Hotel Roc de Caldes.

"*No problema*," the burly man behind the wheel of the Audi responded.

"Tell Juan-Antonio where I am," Jane shouted through the window as the car sped away. She hadn't said goodbye. The driver floored the accelerator, no longer concerned with speed limits. He was on a police mission. When other cars were slow to respond to his flashing lights he used his horn. The well-sprung car cornered as if on rails. At the impressive entrance to the Roc de Caldes Jane got out of the car on shaking legs. The four-wheeled drift to a screeching stop had seemed particularly unnecessary. The liveried doorman emerged from the alcove into which he had dived for cover and frowned at the rubber the car had left on the driveway.

"*Gracias. Muy amable*," Jane managed, through clenched teeth.

"*De nada*," the driver responded with aplomb, touching his hand to his forehead in mock salute. Jane had to admit that the accommodating motorist had exhibited more enthusiastic support for a police request than she ever expected to see in her lifetime.

Charles waved a distracted hand at her as she let herself into his suite. He was slumped, surrounded by a paper moat of unsorted documents, a fat Catalan dictionary at his side. On the table, the screensaver on his laptop displayed a genealogy chart of Merovingian kings. "*We spend our midday sweat, our midnight oil; we tire the night in thought, the day in toil*," Charles quoted. – "Francis Quarles," he explained.

"How appropriate. What are you sweating over now?"

"I always get my ideas at night; I can never sleep until the early hours. I had the crazy idea that since the trust helped found the ABC Company maybe it founded the Credit Europa Bank as well. What if we owned a bank, but its nominees didn't want us to find that out? What if they kidnapped Pearl to delay winding-up the trust, so they could finish laying down a false paper-trail to disguise the true value of the trust?"

"They've had fifty years to do that Charles. Why be in a rush now?"

"Who knows? It's only an idea."

"What do you expect to find?"

"Anything that would tell us why a delay might be significant. You finish the ledgers and see if there is anything there that doesn't add up. Metaphorically, I mean. Obviously the books will balance in a literal sense."

"Not necessarily." Jane was more experienced with blatant frauds than Charles. She thought of the Italian company that invented a fictitious offshore subsidiary to support its bottom-line. That scam had gone unnoticed for seven years until an eventual incautious merger.

"Sorry to drag you away from the festivities."

"Don't be stupid, Charles. I'm not here for the entertainment," Jane snapped as she picked up the heavy ledgers and set them down on a side-table with a thud. "I just didn't know what we could accomplish today. Juan-Antonio told me everything would be shut for the holiday."

"What if you got a call at Pearl's apartment?"

"I left my cell number on the answering-machine."

"Seeing rather a lot of Juan-Antonio aren't you?"

"You don't think it is handy to have good relations with the police?"

"I didn't say that." Charles was peering myopically at a piece of paper, his glasses pushed onto his forehead, "but he's only a village policeman, not exactly at the heart of the investigation."

"I don't suppose it's the end of the world if I use him to help me understand this weird country."

"'*Some say the world will end in fire,/ Some say in ice./ From what I've tasted of desire/ I hold with those who favour fire.*'"

"Robert Frost," Jane shot back to Charles's evident surprise. "I'm not a complete ignoramus. And I have no intention of talking to you about desire – mine or yours for that matter – let's just concentrate on the matter in front of us."

"Exactly!" Charles nodded as if Jane had just proven his point.

CHAPTER THIRTY-NINE

"He did not wear his scarlet coat, for blood and wine are red,
and blood and wine were on his hands when they found him with
the dead,
the poor dead woman whom he loved, and murdered in her bed."

Charles was standing by the window as he declaimed these words, more to himself than to Jane. She shivered and walked over to join him. The handsome young hotel valet, his cropped jacket and tight trousers reminiscent of a matador, was helping Saboya out of a large black Mercedes. Jane's heart gave a jolt. She looked for the number-plate but couldn't see it from side on. Saboya wore a crimson jacket over wide grey trousers. The stubby cigar in his teeth had long since gone out. A gold signet ring on his pinkie glinted as he made a point to the young employee.

"That's creepy, Charles, and since he is wearing a scarlet coat it's not appropriate. We studied 'The Ballad of Reading Goal' in my last year at school. What on earth made you think of that?"

"Ah yes, my little scholarship-girl. To think of all the money you saved the trust over the years by winning scholarships and depriving low-income children of a leg-up. Honours in every subject from primary-school onwards as I recall, and then *dux* of the school in your final year."

"I failed art."

"Failed art! The mind boggles. I suppose I should have congratulated you for that show of individuality, but your devoted mother made it clear she didn't want me to have a hand in your upbringing, be it for good or ill. Nevertheless she sent me a copy of every school report – I'm sure in an effort to make me regret the family-life I was missing out on. One thing I never had to worry about was you under-achieving."

"Yet each man kills the thing he loves... Is that what you were thinking about?" Jane was still focussed on the poem.

"Was I?" said Charles. "Perhaps it was just the red jacket that brought that piece of doggerel to my memory."

"Oscar Wilde hardly wrote doggerel."

"Not my favourite pederast."

"Jesus, Charles. Where did that come from? You are so intolerant. I would have thought an historian would be more in tune."

"Sticks and stones...." Charles made a boyish face. "I never learnt to share my toys either. An only child doesn't." He patted his face with his handkerchief. "It's hot in here. I'm glad I asked Saboya around for a decent lunch to cheer him up. This morning was a shock to him. We're going to have a drink in the bar first. Are you coming?"

"You go and meet Saboya, Charles. Maybe I'll join you for coffee later after I've had a shower. I'm not sure if sweaty hiking gear is the appropriate dress code for the dining-room at the Roc de Caldes."

"You look fine, dear." Charles appraised his daughter in her loose-fitting Khakis. "I've got several clean shirts in the wardrobe if you want to borrow one. Just roll the sleeves up."

"I'll keep working on this ledger for a bit to see if I can catch a break."

Jane was soon engrossed in the figures. They told a story. In the numeric history that unfolded, heroes appeared to outmuscle their antagonists. Few of the trust's investments had proved to be a poor risk. Less than five percent had been written off, an unusually low number in her corporate experience. The ABC *Compania* revealed itself to be the superman of the trust's investments by constantly returning double digits. Jane couldn't think of a single company she had audited with profits like this that hadn't ultimately proved to be dodgy. Mostly they had turned out to be Ponzi schemes, where incoming investor capital was paid out as interest or dividends until either the perpetrator ran away with the investors' money, or the whole scheme failed in spectacular fashion. Was the trust a victim of such a scheme, or was there was some type of money-laundering going on?

She remembered one of her small clients who had washed the profits from selling amphetamines through his laundromat. Unfortunately math wasn't his strong point. Jane had pointed out that even if all twenty machines were going twenty-four hours a day, at four dollars for a forty-minute cycle, they couldn't possibly support the gross income he declared.

"What do you care? I'll be paying the tax department." The young thug had asked aggressively.

"Your consultation with me is privileged of course, but I have a great number of friends and clients in the police force who take a dim view of drug-pushers so it might be better for us both if you consulted someone elsewhere," Jane snapped. The client reached for his file and fled the office leaving a few choice profanities in his wake. This was one client who practiced money-laundering in a close to literal sense.

Unless the ABC *Compania* had been involved in the all-Andorran sport of smuggling, she couldn't envisage the type of yields that the books revealed. Her comfortable upbringing and current life-style might well have been financed by illegal activities – she, who was careful to purge companies with poor environmental records from her share portfolio.

But money-laundering wasn't an end in itself. Who benefits?

A comparison of distributions to beneficiaries of the trust proved them to be scrupulously fair. Although some beneficiaries had drawn down more in one year, the long-term dispersal of funds had been remarkably even. She scoured the latest computer-generated balance-sheet and noted, interspersed among the endless lists of AAA and AA+ quality international bonds, that funds had been reinvested into securities issued by *Apice Finances*. The balance-sheet recorded the investments as triple-A rated. A quick mental addition told Jane that in contrast to the detailed balance-sheets in the old, handwritten ledgers where no single investment came to more than five percent of the trust's capital base, the sums currently invested with *Apice Finances* totalled sixty percent of the trust's capital.

"Bingo!" she whispered.

The receptionist at the front desk was only too happy to allow her to use their photocopying facilities. Jane made three copies of the balance-sheet before going outside to check the registration plates on the Mercedes. She scoured the parking area but no black Mercedes appeared in the shining ranks of Porsches, BMWs and Audis. There were no cars over two years old. Where did old cars go to die? Certainly not to Andorra.

"*Puedo ayudarle, señora?*" This valet was in his fifties and his stylish matador uniform was worn to ill-effect. The short embroidered jacket was rucked above his well-nourished stomach and a cache of ash from his cigarette was caught in the fold of the material. His breath exuded dead animals. Jane reared back in dismay. The valet switched carelessly to English. "Did you want something special?" His leer suggested impropriety and displayed blackened irregular teeth.

"I thought I saw a friend of mine arrive in his Mercedes – but I don't see it parked? Señor Saboya? Did he leave?"

"I don't know, Madam. I just started my shift."

Whoever employed the man believed in a scorched earth, take no prisoner policy towards guests. His breath could clear a building.

"An S500 black Mercedes sedan. See if you can find it," gasped Jane, trying to speak and hold her breath at the same time.

She found Saboya and Charles in the bar consulting extensive, leather-bound menus. She handed them an envelope each. "The trust has nearly thirty million dollars invested with *Apice Finances*. That is serious money. Ramon, I want you to check this out. How do we get to see accounts for *Apice Finances* if they are not a publicly-listed company? I'd also like to see the maturity dates of these investments. The trust's balance-sheet doesn't follow accounting convention and divide the assets into current and non-current assets, which means I have no way of knowing if the investments are due to mature this year – but I'll bet that they are due soon, or overdue. I'd also like to know what these securities funded?"

"Phew," Saboya whistled through his teeth and gave a smile of undisguised satisfaction, "this will put the cat among the hawks. I'll call Castillo. Together I am sure we can arrange something."

"Cat amongst the pigeons," chorused Charles and Jane.

"The families that own *Apice Finances* are no pigeons," objected Saboya, eyelids drooping over hooded eyes, making him look not unlike a raptor himself.

"I thought you disclaimed any knowledge of the ABC *Compania*, or *Apice Finances*," Janes reminded him.

"Specific knowledge. I had no specific knowledge, but now your father has shown me the list of *socios* – partners – Señora Menendez gave him, obviously I know these families. They are prominent in many aspects of business here, and interwoven in the fabric of Andorran politics and life. They support political candidates. Members of the families work for the *Comus*. There is very little with which they are not involved."

"Where is that list, Charles? I haven't seen it yet."

"In my room buried in paperwork somewhere, I'll give it to you after lunch."

"Excuse me Señor Charles," the *maître d'* interrupted, his usual *savoir-faire* nowhere to be seen. A tic in his cheek caused his jowls to tremble.

"Run out of salmon, Alfons?" joked Charles. "No need to look so glum. There are plenty of other choices on the menu. How's the rabbit?"

The man handed him a note and wordlessly indicated the muted television, set high above the bar. The screen showed two men dressed in the distinctive uniform of the bombers carrying a stretcher towards a waiting ambulance. As the camera panned onto the stretcher they saw it was covered by a white sheet. Standing to one side, a hirsute man wearing only trousers and thigh-high rubber wading-boots responded sombrely to a reporter's questions. As he shook his head vehemently in response to something the reporter said, a small waterfall erupted from his person causing the reporter to take a step back. The *maître d'* produced a remote control from behind his back and pressed a button, then translated the flood of sound in a hushed voice.

"They have found the body of a woman floating face down in the pond at the trout farm at El Serrat, *Señor*. The worker who is being interviewed jumped into the water to pull the body out. He used his pocket-knife to cut away her hair, which was caught in one of the filters. The reporter pointed out that he should have left the body where it was and called the police, but he acted on an instinct to save her life – and even when he could see she was dead, he could not bear to leave her in the water." The *maître d'* appeared to be trying to speak without moving his lips as if to disassociate himself from the news he was imparting.

"Normally the worker would not be at the trout farm on Meritxel Day but he went out drinking with his friends last night and forgot to feed the guard-dogs. When he arrived this morning to remedy the matter, the dogs weren't crowding the gate for the food as he expected. He whistled, but they did not come. He thought they might have dug a hole under the wire fence to escape, so he walked around the perimeter to check. When his view of the trout-ponds improved, he saw that they were full of dead fingerlings, floating *al revés.*"

Señor Alfons turned his palms towards the ceiling to indicate the position of the trout, floating belly-up. "He pulled on his waders and hurried to investigate. It was then that he saw the body, face-down surrounded by hundreds of dead trout."

The television moved to a close-up of the furrows in the worker's cheeks. The tremor in his voice transmitted itself to *Señor* Alfons who unconsciously echoed it as he continued to translate.

"The man, *el Alberto*, pulled the body from the water and wrapped it in a blanket from his the car, and then he called the police from his mobile. The police found two of the three guard dogs dead by a gap cut in the north fence that overlooks vacant woodland. It seems the dogs were poisoned. One dog had vomited part of an undigested meal of meat and was barely alive. The worker says perhaps the meat fell into the trout ponds as well and killed the trout."

The channel switched to an advertisement and *Señor* Alfons once more muted the sound. Charles opened the folded white note the *maître d'* had given him and held it cupped in his trembling hand. Saboya took it from him and flattened it on the table where they could all read the jagged black writing together.

"Call me urgently. Victor-Ignacio. 337800"

The *maître d'* snapped his fingers at the barman who immediately brought a phone. "I'm very sorry, *Señor. Quisiera darles nuestros pésames*!"

"Our condolences," translated Saboya.

Charles stared at the note as if it were written in hieroglyphics. Jane pressed the button for speakerphone and punched in the numbers.

"*Dime*," the gruff voice of Victor-Ignacio answered.

"It's Charles Barclay," Charles's face was slack, "Jane and Saboya are with me. We've just seen the news on TV."

"I am very sorry *Señor*; I wanted to be the first to contact you. I'm at the morgue now. There will be an autopsy of course when the medical examiner returns from Barcelona tomorrow."

"Are you sure it's Pearl?"

In the small hesitation before Victor-Ignacio answered, they heard the sounds of wheels squeaking in the background, and imagined Pearl lying on a gurney under the all-encompassing white sheet as she was wheeled past the detective into a holding room to be stored in a refrigerated drawer.

"Did Pearl have any distinguishing marks, *Señor*? Tattoos? Anything of that nature? I am afraid the face is disfigured and it is not possible to identify her."

Charles looked at Jane in pained enquiry.

"I don't know of any distinguishing marks, but her dentist is a Señora Garcia." Jane quoted the name from her memory of Pearl's checking account.

"Thank you."

"Can we see her?" asked Jane.

"I'm sorry, *Señora*," Victor spoke with infinite regret, "that won't be possible for the moment. There is much to do. The idiot who found her contaminated the forensic evidence. The body has traces of fibre from the blanket he wrapped her in, leaves and gravel from where he laid her down by the pool, his own clothing…" He took an audible breath and broke off. "I am sorry. I assure you we will do everything in our power to conduct a successful investigation. I will call you tomorrow when the medical examiner has finished. Please accept my deepest condolences, *Señores. Hasta Mañana.*"

CHAPTER FORTY

The next hour passed in a blur. The barman brought a bottle of Chivas Regal and set it on the table with a jug of water, ice and three tumblers. Jane poured herself a glass and sat staring deep into it, eyes slightly out of focus.

"Jane…," Charles warned, then shrugged and followed suit, pouring a hefty portion for Saboya and himself. Jane pressed her index finger and thumb into her eyes as if trying to stopper a bottle but the silent tears flowed around them.

"Someone should ring Elsa," Jane croaked finally. She hoped that Charles would volunteer. Charles winced and tossed a third large scotch down his throat.

"There's been no official identification of the body yet," he stalled. "Let Elsa have one more night of peace. To be woken up in the middle of the night with the worst news a parent could ever hear…."

Señor Alfons skated into view on silent shoes; his outstretched arms balancing a tray that displayed a pot of coffee and three expresso cups, a huge platter of delicate, crust-less sandwiches, side-plates and deep burgundy linen napkins, which he placed reverently in front of them. If not quite Holy Communion, it bore a close relationship to a religious event.

"With our sympathy," he said, simply.

Saboya reached forward and took three of the dainty sandwiches and crammed them into his mouth. His cheeks bulged and he snorted through his nose with the effort of chewing and breathing while trying to keep his mouth firmly shut. Showing a surprising dexterity he poured everyone a small coffee and another scotch for himself and Charles at the same time – coffee-pot in one hand, scotch bottle in the other. "A wake, is it not? An English tradition," he said as he demolished a further clutch of sandwiches in a spray of breadcrumbs.

Jane's mobile trilled and she wrenched it from her bag.

"*Hola*, Jane. *Bon dia*. It's Jorge. Where are you?"

"In town."

"I am sorry to interrupt. Are you with friends?"

"Jorge, I don't have any friends in Andorra, remember?"

"I understand. Would it be convenient to meet me after I finish work in about half an hour? I printed out the photos you emailed me and showed them to *Señor* Molina and I have something to tell you. The bus from town leaves for Encamp every fifteen minutes, or you could take a taxi. I'll meet you at the bus-stop."

"Was the man in the photo the man you saw with Pearl?"

"I have to go in case *Señor* Molina overhears. I don't want to lose my job." Jorge pronounced it as "hob" in the Spanish manner. "They're calling for me to finish my tables. We are very busy right now."

"OK. I'll be there." Jane kept it short before Jorge was put to the test with another half-dozen excuses. She shrugged at the two men when she replaced the mobile in her bag. "Something definite to follow up. I'm not good at dealing with my emotions despite years of therapy."

"Shall I drive you?" asked Saboya when she explained.

Jane thought about the Mercedes. "Sure. Thanks."

Charles bestirred himself, his face grey and desolate with grief. "I'll just wash my hands and face and then I'll be ready."

"Why don't you stay here, Charles?" Saboya said gently. "It's not long since your heart-attack. Better to rest up a bit for tomorrow, don't you think?"

Charles waved his hand vaguely. "I'll stay if you think it best, Ramon, I confess to feeling very tired."

The man who got up was not the familiar jaunty father Jane had come to know since the first time she met him, at the twenty-first birthday lunch she had with him so many years ago, but a man infinitely older. He held his hand to the small of his back as if the news had lodged there like an arrow, and picking up the half-empty bottle of Chivas Regal, he shuffled out of the bar. Saboya and Jane exchanged looks.

"He'll be alright," Saboya said, "sometimes men need to drown their devils."

Jane nodded, although the scotch remained in front of her untouched. The curved side of the glass reflected the distorted face of Saboya and displayed his huge open-pored nose with forehead and chin receding from it. "I just need to powder my nose."

A silver Volvo station wagon pulled up to the entrance of the hotel when Jane rotated through the revolving doors. Saboya waved from behind the wheel.

"What happened to the flash Mercedes you arrived in?" Jane asked.

"Oh, I don't own a car, my dear. I usually take taxis. It saves having to park in this wretched country where a good portion of Catalunya is in transit through Andorra *por coche* on a shopping spree on any given day. Last week we were supposed to share a car going to work to halve the pollution. What a failure! There was such gridlock in Avinguda de Tarragona that it paralysed city traffic for two hours. This is the hotel courtesy car. They were only too pleased to lend it to me."

"The hotel's courtesy car is a Volvo?"

"The agent for Volvo is a persistent and likeable man."

"So was the Mercedes a taxi?"

"A client dropped me here on the way home."

"A private client or was it a government consultancy?"

"I believe that comes under privileged information," Saboya smiled. "I've been practicing law for far too long to talk about one client to another. Even the most innocuous conversation has a way of turning into a betrayal of confidence."

"Yet you told me about Pearl's pregnancy."

"I drew up her Power of Attorney, and the will naming you as her executor, so there is no doubt that in her absence I was acting lawfully, and in her interest."

"One of the trustees indicated you were a maverick who tried to extort money from the government. Yet, you claim to be quite the conservative lawyer?"

If Saboya heard the query in her tone, he urbanely declined to respond. He drove the Volvo much as he walked, solidly, down the middle of the road, wheels straddling both lanes.

"So how is your relationship with the government now?"

"Everything was resolved professionally and to our mutual satisfaction." Saboya's skill in lawyerly double-speak was evident. "I prefer the word 'negotiate' to 'extort'."

"Have you ever considered entering politics yourself?"

"I believe my maverick nature would be better suited to the bench. Perhaps as a judge in the court of last appeal, *El Tribunal*

Superior de Justìcia," he said, as if the idea had only just occurred to him. "You are an unusually cold woman," he changed the subject without a beat and without changing his conversational tone, "your sister dead in the morgue, and you on a quixotic quest to discuss the photo of a man who probably has no bearing on your sister's disappearance whatsoever."

"The body in the morgue isn't Pearl until the forensic examination proves to me that it is. And if it's not my sister, then it's all the more urgent to keep on the trail. The body in the pool had long hair, caught in the filter. If it *is* Pearl, whose ponytail was in the box?"

"To be cold and analytical is a trait I admire. I find women who don't display their emotions publicly are unusually passionate in bed. What a pair we could have made, were I younger."

"Now who's inappropriate?" Jane snorted. "It's hardly the way to speak to the bereaved."

"You catch my drift entirely," Saboya's modest grin was that of the cat who caught the canary. He barked a small cough, as if to dislodge a feather from his throat.

"Drop me a little way from the bus-stop, Ramon. No need for Jorge to see you and be frightened off if he has some information for me."

"You suspect Jorge may be dangerous." It was not a question. "Do you plan to turn yourself into a sacrificial goat? If so, I am a meagre resource for backup. I'm elderly and overweight, with diabetes and a bad heart. My mind is the only thing about me that I believe to be unimpaired – and my imagination." He gave Jane's breasts an appraising look.

"Passive acceptance isn't my style."

"Pearl had a Type A personality as well, so take care."

Saboya parked with hazard lights blinking. He made a moue at the policewoman, in her red traffic uniform, who was walking his way; and held a hand to his heart in pantomime. "*Momentito*," he said, as he made a show of flipping open his small silver pill case. As the policewoman held up her hands in surrender, Jane got out and walked to a turquoise Panda, pulled up at the bus-stop. The passenger door opened and a blue shirted arm beckoned Jane inside.

"What's all the mystery?" she asked Jorge.

The Panda pulled out into light holiday traffic. Jane eyed the side mirror and watched the silver Volvo jerk back onto the road in front of a tourist bus. The driver stood on his brakes but could not avoid clipping the Volvo's back fender, but the station wagon did not stop.

"No mystery," Jorge answered, pressing his foot more firmly on the accelerator. "It's something I have to show you, or you won't understand."

"A video of the news report Señor Molina saw?" she guessed.

"Not even close," Jorge was crouched over the wheel, face tense and excited. He turned and looked into her eyes, nodding once as if to confirm something. "It's a breakthrough. That's what they say, don't they? A definite breakthrough."

"Is it about Pearl, or her abductor?"

"I can't explain. I have to show you."

The Panda slipped in front of a gas tanker then quickly turned right. Jane saw that Saboya was blocked and would be unable to follow. She caught the sign *Els Cortals* as Jorge turned right again, slowed by a row of unkempt apartment blocks and turned down a narrow snaking driveway with the evidence of drivers' spatial misjudgements displayed in differing coloured paint on each bend. The small car missed the walls by a hair's-breadth at each turn of the wheel. They parked close to a box-trailer housing a partially dismembered motorbike. Its entrails were spread around the trailer and overflowed onto the ground. Jane stepped over the debris and into a puddle that had pooled under a dripping pipe. Jorge gripped her arm and guided her through the semi darkness to a small, badly ventilated elevator. The last occupants had left behind the unmistakable odour of unwashed clothes.

Jorge pressed the button marked *Planta 4* and the lift clanged into motion, rising in a series of jerks that made Jane's jaw snap. When they stepped onto the threadbare carpet of the landing, Jorge gestured to the door at the end of the passage. Someone had carved the names "Sami and Pablo" under a heart in the scuffed oak veneer. 1973 it said – a testament to decades of neglect.

"*Bienvenido a mi casa!*" said Jorge, bowing in a curiously formal way and waving her through the door and towards a sofa blanketed by a grey woollen rug. "I have what you want in the other room." He backed towards a passage leading off to the left, like a supplicant before a queen. As she sat down Jane felt a hidden spring dig sharply into her buttocks and suppressed an involuntary yelp. She eased sideways, and examined the room behind Jorge's retreating back.

The sofa and a scuffed leather chair faced a portable television set on top of an old-fashioned travel trunk. Behind it a pine table stacked with multicoloured files was pushed against the wall. A hard-backed chair with a frayed woven rattan seat stood slightly askew in front of an outdated Macintosh computer. The curtains behind the sofa had darkened with dirt over the years so the original colour and pattern were now indiscernible. She lifted the hem to see a window framing a dim light-well, about seven-foot square. Washing hung from lines strung between the windows on two sides. Drying clothes waltzed and shuffled in a slight updraft. No laundry hung from Jorge's lines. The wooden window-frame was nailed shut with what looked like six-inch nails. Their gleaming heads stood out in stark relief against the old oak.

CHAPTER FORTY-ONE

"Jane," said Jorge, behind her, making her jump, "Give me your mobile phone." The gleaming pistol in his hand was pointed at her head.

Jane dug into her shoulder-bag. Her fingers touched the pocket where she had put Harris's phone with the intention of posting it to his father, and hesitated before they travelled on. She fished around noisily, jingling the debris in the bottom of her bag until finally she pulled out her own cell-phone. "Your rates must really be exorbitant in Andorra if you have to resort to hijacking mobile phones." Her voice was steady but to her it sounded high and false, as if an unknown woman was using her mouth without permission.

"Put it on the television."

She did, setting it down on the slightly rounded top, so that it slid against the rabbit ears before rebounding onto the floor.

He motioned her back with the gun and picked it up without taking his eyes from her and unlocked the keypad. "The call register says you have a missed call. A Ramon Saboya called five minutes ago. I didn't hear it ring."

"It was on vibrating alert and I forgot to turn the ring-tone back on again." She wanted to reduce the tension between them by speaking calmly. Her gaze stayed on the gun, mesmerised by the ugly threat of it.

"Who's Saboya?" Jorge was curt.

"The notary who handles my sister's affairs."

"Perfect. He's the one I will contact."

"What's all this about, Jorge? Saboya has nothing to do with me."

Jorge went to the front door and double-locked it top and bottom. He slipped the key into his pocket. "It's nothing personal," he assured her.

"You're pointing a gun at me. That feels pretty personal." She moved slightly to a more comfortable position on the sofa, and watched the gun-barrel follow her. "What do you want?"

"*Carpe diem.* Seize the moment. Who said that?" Jorge asked.

Jane was sure she could come up with the answer given time, but today wasn't the day. "I don't feel like twenty questions right now, Jorge. Perhaps if you'd put down the gun I could think more easily.

Surely you don't need it now that you've locked us in. With all the gym work you do I doubt I could overpower you."

Jorge cocked his head and appeared to consider the proposal before gently but emphatically shaking his head from side to side.

"Better to keep every advantage."

"What if I give you my word not to try anything?"

"What is your word worth?" He smiled at that, a small secret smile that didn't show his splendid teeth, "Perhaps quite a lot of money in the end." He turned sideways and motioned toward the passageway. "I have to lock you in the bedroom." He stepped back as Jane passed him, keeping a wary distance between them. "Take the second door."

Jane glanced into the kitchen as she passed the open door. A glossy-white box-freezer was pushed inconveniently against the sink and adjacent stove, incongruous in a kitchen full of dust balls and peeling Formica counter-tops. She opened the second door as instructed, and entered an all-white room. The walls and floor had been completely lined with blocks of Styrofoam, giving it an igloo effect. A neatly-made camp-bed on an iron frame was pushed against the wall. By the bed stood a cardboard box, a galvanised bucket and a plastic gallon container. The single light source came from a utilitarian floor-lamp. It illuminated marks scratched into the Styrofoam by the bed.

"The apartments above and below are empty, so no-one will hear you if you scream. Save your breath."

The door slammed and locked behind him. The Styrofoam squeaked and protested beneath her feet. She undid her hiking boots and slipped them off, then padded towards the cardboard box. It was full of snack food. Packets of nougat, bags of roasted almonds, cheese crackers. The plastic container held water. She thought about drinking some but wondered if it might be drugged. She sat on the bed and ran her fingers over the marks on the wall. What is a five-letter word starting with P? But her eyes had deceived her, it was not Pearl but Petra, repeated over and over again. Petra, Petra, Petra.

Petra? Andorra was a long way from the famous ruins of Jordan.

She padded carefully back to the door and tried the handle. It didn't give. When she put her ear against the wood the silence was absolute. She returned to sit on the bed. Her fingers went to the pouch in her shoulder-bag containing Harris's mobile. It was no surprise to find the battery was flat-lining. She tipped out the contents of her purse. There amongst the coins, the tampons and the tissues was the small adaptor plug she had ripped off her mobile before producing it from her bag for Jorge. Jane connected Harris's mobile to the adaptor. After unplugging the lamp and plunging the room into darkness, she used her fingers to feel for the two holes to connect the cell-phone to the power. The display immediately lit up. She punched in zero for the operator. Muzak exploded in her ear and she guessed that she had been placed in a queue.

"Come on!" She had no idea how long it would be before Jorge returned. It could be minutes or days. "Come on!" she urged again.

"*Digame!*"

"*Policía por favor. Emergencia!*"

"*Momentito.*"

The line rang once.

"*Si,*" the woman on despatch answered with economy.

"I am being held against my will in an apartment in Encamp. Somewhere near the sign to *Els Cortals*, on the turn-off from the main road. The apartment block is old and run down. Please help me!" Jane gabbled as much information as she could into her short sentences. Who knew when Jorge might reappear?

"*Momentito.*" She was placed on hold.

"Jesus!" Jane swore with frustration.

A calm voice said, "Yes, can I help you."

"A man called Jorge kidnapped me. He has a gun. He works at the Lake Pessons restaurant."

"What is your name, *Señora*?" interrupted the calm voice with no discernable excitement.

"Jane!" called Jorge, opening the door to find the room in darkness.

"Jane Burns," echoed Jane as she ripped the plug from the wall and quickly slipped it and the mobile phone under the mattress. She sat quietly at attention. The door slammed and locked again. In less than a minute he was back. This time a torch scoured the room until it found her face.

"Plug the lamp back in."

She didn't move.

Jorge was quick. He covered the distance between them in two strides and slammed the torch into the side of her head.

"*Puta!*" he said.

Something sharp pricked through the material of her shirt. Nausea undulated from her stomach to her throat before she was plunged into a cave of unconsciousness.

Hours later, an eyelid lifted and briefly imposed reality upon her confused dreams. It was very dark. Her head hurt, and she felt unwell. Not as if she would be violently sick, more like her eyes would fly from their sockets if she moved. And that would be a bad thing. Then the dark would never recede. She groaned a little and moved restlessly on the bed, her feet clanging together. She moved again. Her feet clashed as if cymbals had been screwed to her ankles. Perhaps she had died and been reincarnated as a drum-kit. If so she'd been dismantled and put back together so roughly some pieces appeared to be missing. Jane shook her head woozily. Clink, clash, ker-boom. She waved her feet around in a circle. Clip, clop, clap. Now she sounded like a venereal horse. That was pretty funny. For a drum-kit, her sense of humour wasn't bad.

"*Tlot tlot, Tlot tlot! Had they heard it? The horse-hooves ringing clear. Tlot tlot, in the frosty silence.*" No – wait, that wasn't right. She'd missed a bit. "*Tlot tlot, in the distance. Were they deaf that they did not hear? … The Highwayman came riding, Riding, riding….*" Sleep pounced like a hood thrown over her head. Dreams shadow-boxed by, on a brilliant white background. The highwayman lifted his mask and was revealed as …Charles. Of course, she should have known.

Suddenly she was wide-awake. Her mind clear. The room was still in darkness. She rubbed the back of her arm. The muscle was sore and the skin torn from the rough injection. Her fingers took inventory of her body and discovered that a foot-long chain shackled her ankles together. She sat up cautiously and swung her feet over the edge of the bed. After the dizziness subsided she slid to the floor and groped around until she found the galvanised bucket. She peed in it for a long time. It was awkward squatting over the bucket without being able to move her feet more than a foot apart and she was careful not to overturn it and soak her hiking trousers. Her hands were free, so she used one to steady herself while the other held the bucket. She pulled up her trousers, managing not to overbalance, and slid the bucket under the bed to avoid inadvertently stumbling over it. As she lent against the side of the bed she swept the space before her with outstretched arms but encountered nothing. She knelt on the floor and began to quarter the room, crawling back and forth until her knees were chafed. The sturdy hiking boots she had kicked off by the door bruised her right knee. Cursing them thoroughly before putting them on again put her in a better frame of mind. Then she crawled one more time to the bed. The lamp had been removed.

"Please, please be there," she whispered as she reached under the matress for the mobile phone. "Yes!" Her left fist pumped the air triumphantly as she found it tightly wedged in a gap between the wire bedsprings. After some trouble she wrestled it free. It took another few minutes to find the power point. She made sure the lead was connected firmly at both ends. The LED display lit up. Enter Pin number, it said.

"Shit. Shit. Shit." She didn't know Harris's pin number. How had the cell-phone turned itself off? Maybe a delinquent bedspring had connected with the on-off button. Jane wanted to scream with frustration. Instead she started trying different numeric combinations. Birthdays. Both Harris's and Pearl's. Then 1234. 4321. Jane had any quantity of numbers in her memory at a time. She remembered the Perth telephone number for Pearl and Harris. She tried different variations of it. Nothing. She tried their street number, postcode and the number of their apartment. But it was all so long ago. Harris was bound to use a more current number, or more likely, the PIN number was allocated by the telephone company and was entirely random. Jane tried combinations until her fingers and wrist ached. Finally she let the phone fall to her lap. At least the faint glow from the display was comforting.

She sat, not moving for a long time, while her mind roamed. She replayed conversations with Jorge and tried to remember his body-language. What did he like, what upset him? From his first words at Lake Pessons, "Can I help you, *Señora*?" the tape wound on in her mind.

Finally, the door opened. Jorge stood in silhouette, the torch at his side.

"They're coming," Jane said without hesitation. "They'll be here soon. If you want to escape you'd better hurry."

"Jane? You are dreaming." Torch-light stabbed her face. She brought the cell-phone up into the light and waggled it. Jorge reached her in two big strides. She tried not to cringe as he snatched it from her hand.

"I turned it off when you unlocked the door. You won't be able to check the call register. It's Harris's phone and I don't know the PIN number so you can't beat it out of me." She smiled, and although this was lost in the dark, the smile carried into the tone of her voice. "I called everyone – every single person I know here in Andorra – and two in Australia, just in case. They know who you are, and they know where we are. You're going to jail." Jane could smell sweat as he lifted his hand high above his head to strike her. "I have a photographic memory for numbers," she babbled, "so I just kept dialling and dialling. Hitting me won't save you. You're just wasting the time you could use to get away."

Jorge didn't respond beyond lowering his arm and shifting the torch to his left hand. He took a small key from his pocket and stabbed it awkwardly into the padlock on the chain between her ankles. The key turned smoothly allowing the shackles to drop to the floor. Jane immediately swung her feet and caught him a heavy blow with the heel of her boots against his knee. He swore and by reflex grabbed his knee with both hands, dropping the torch, which rolled under the bed.

"*Me cago en tu madre*," he roared. Her mother wouldn't like that activity at all!

Jane ran for the door.

"*Para!*" he shouted. "I have the gun. It's your choice. *Estop* or I'll shoot."

Jane heard a metallic click as Jorge released the safety catch. She dived for the floor, landing on her shoulder and rolling through the door as smoothly as if she had attended self-defence classes with Bruce the weekend before. It took a moment for her to convert the sound of jumping jacks fireworks from her childhood into rapid gunshots. The hall smelt like Guy Fawkes' Night. She wriggled forward on her stomach, using her elbows and knees for traction. A bullet kicked up a shard of linoleum inches in front of her face. She froze.

"In the back. In the back," screamed Jorge. "I'll shoot you in the back." He stomped down the passageway and kicked her under the right breast, using the tip of his shoe like a chisel. "*¡Coño!* Don't try that again."

Jane put her hands behind her head. "You're wasting time," she wheezed, her chin on the floor. "The police are on their way."

The two-tone discordance of a siren penetrated the apartment.

"*Es una ambulancia*," sneered Jorge. "Get up, Bitch. This doesn't change a thing. Whether I hold you here or somewhere else, they'll pay to get you back."

Jorge dragged her upright, then kept the gun pressed to Jane's side. His left hand grasped her shoulder tightly as they retraced their steps to the garage, where he opened the hatchback of the Panda and shoved her in. The limited space in the back of the Panda was not a good fit for her tall frame. It was like trying to fit a giraffe into a coffin. No sooner had Jorge rearranged her arms and torso inside than her legs fell to the garage floor and her feet scrabbled for purchase. As she continued to struggle, he held her down with one hand while picking up a coil of rope with his gun hand.

"If you don't stop resisting I might shoot you by mistake," he said. His voice betrayed no concern. "It makes no difference to me if I ransom a dead body."

If anything Jane increased her efforts. Once she was immobilised there would be little she could do to save herself. Jorge let go of her momentarily and she sprang forward onto her heels and pushed against the back of the seat with her hands, driving her head into a stomach that proved to be rock hard.

"*Porfiada mujer!*" Jorge said in grudging admiration, as he slapped her hard with his open palm. The force of the blow rocked her onto her side. Through her tearing eyes Jane saw Jorge grab his crotch through the cloth of his jeans and make an obscene gesture. He slipped the gun behind his back into his waistband, leaving his two hands free to loop the rope over her wrists. It bit into her so tightly that she screamed with pain. She screamed again, more loudly.

"Help me. Help me. Somebody help me." Her legs flailed around until they found purchase with his thigh. Jorge, unfazed, ran a bit of rope out so it would reach around her ankles. He threw a coil over her thrashing feet and pulled it taut.

"I saw this in a cowboy movie. Pig-tying they call it?"

"Hog-tying, you stupid fuck." Jane said through gritted teeth. "Don't pull it so tight. You're pulling my shoulders out of their sockets."

"*Callate*! I'll decide if it's too tight," said Jorge, but he loosened the rope all the same.

"You're wasting a lot of time, Jorge. Taking me with you will make it much harder to hide. Without me you could change your identity and go anywhere in Europe. It would be hard to trace you. Think of how many illegal immigrants there are without papers. You could get completely away."

"I'm sick of living like that – in a shit-hole. Why would I let you go? Would I throw away a winning hand of poker? A hostage gives me something to bargain with. I only need to change *el sitio* – the place. My father taught me never to give up. He would give me a good beating, just for his bad humour. I would say "*Papa, por favor*!" and he would ask, 'Do you give up?' I was only a six-year-old against a man, but if I said, 'Yes, yes, I give up', he would call me a little girl and beat me harder. I learned to shout, 'Never! I will never give up!' Then he would laugh and take me to the shop for an ice-cream and boast of me to the neighbours. *El culo*." Jorge snorted.

"What did your mother do when he beat you?" Jane wondered how long it would take the police to discover where Jorge lived. She had to delay. Every second spent in the garage was to her advantage.

"She say, 'Obey your father'." Jorge laughed, his English slipping. "That was *El catecismo de* Juan Pablo. Not the pope. Juan Pablo is my father's name. My mother had to recite the catechism of Juan Pablo chapter and verse or she'd be missing some teeth. She was clever at protecting my brother, of course. She say that it wasn't right to knock him around after such an expensive *operación*. He was born with a hair-lip. When my father lifted his hand to him, he always saw the scar and reconsidered. He said that I needed to be taught a lesson, but a disability gives *disciplina*."

Jorge finished tying her ankles loosely together. "Your *abogado* – your lawyer – didn't answer his phone, but I left a message. I'm sure we'll hear from him soon."

"Too bad the police will be in touch first."

"We'll see." Jorge slammed the hatch of the Panda down, catching her elbow a terrible blow. The pain made her gag and she had to take small panting breaths to avoid throwing up.

'Victims should do anything to stay alive and try to forge a bond with their assailant.' Bruce's voice played like a recording in her mind. 'She got away by making him trust her. She stayed alert for any opportunity to escape. She was smart. Not many young girls are. They are too paralysed with fear.'

Fat chance she had to escape; hog-tied like the victim she's vowed not to be, Jane thought. She had to be smart and use her mouth. It was the only thing not under restraint. She heard Jorge's steps receding. Although bent into an inverted bow she wriggled around in the tight confines of the car scraping her knuckles as she tried to find a side-pocket that might open under her weak ministrations, but the sound of the hatchback opening and Jorge's quick reappearance made her freeze. He held a hypodermic needle and tapped it professionally before he pushed the point smoothly into the fleshy back of her upper arm.

"Now you are undercover," he said with satisfaction. He bent to pick up the grey blanket that had covered the sofa and threw it over her. As it floated down over her face, Jane saw a rust stain that proved to smell sweetly metallic. Her brain kept trying to erase this image as the Panda revved into life and drove carefully up the twisting driveway and bumped over the gutter into the street.

Why would Jorge need a giant freezer? The kitchen had shown no sign of use. Is that where he had put Pearl? The Panda itself was not unlike an ice-box on wheels. But it had tail-lights, she reminded herself. Maybe she could damage them before the drug made her pass out. She prayed that Saboya had taken down the car's number plate and was even now talking with the police and they were keeping a watch for it. How long would it be before Saboya discovered Jorge's message?

'It's always about money,' Bruce's voice said in her head, 'when it's not about sex or power'.

CHAPTER FORTY-TWO

It was the smell that Jane noticed first, a wave of strong ammonia and the simultaneous sound of a steady stream of water hammering the ground. It was the smell of barnyard animals. She opened her eyes and saw she was in a barn of sorts – the type that Andorrans called a *borda*. Light falling from a high barred window opposite a hayloft displayed walls of stone roughly held together with cement. Exposed hand-hewn beams made from the boughs of aspen trees provided a frame for the rough slate roof. She was lying on packed dirt next to a yellow tractor and a slew of cultivating equipment. Someone had backed the tractor through the double wooden doors and left it facing out for easy removal. The strong odour was coming from an adjacent stall where something moved.

She was relieved to find she was no longer hog-tied. Instead the familiar grey blanket from Jorge's sofa had been tucked tightly around her, restricting her movements. She rolled awkwardly out of its tight embrace and got to her feet. Her side ached and she wondered if Jorge's kick had cracked a rib.

Once past the tractor, she was not surprised to find the doors locked. A plastic shopping-bag hanging from the tractor's gear stick caught her attention. The dozen stunted apples inside prompted her stomach to flip-flop. She slung the bag over her arm and plucked out a tart green saviour. Her mouth puckered as the juice from the apple ran down her chin with her first bite.

Peering thoughtfully at her from the entrance of the next-door stall, the dark head of a broad-faced horse showed equal interest in her and the apple in her hand. It tossed its head a few times as it shuffled forward, the movement causing the bronze bell around its neck to toll. The horse's belly barely made it through the opening.

"Nice horse," said Jane, regarding it equally thoughtfully. It was a shame that horsemanship had never been one of interests. She had no idea how to approach a horse. The horse had no such inhibitions and continued towards her tossing its head up and down in a parody of an emphatic "yes". Jane backed away. The horse daintily reached out and plucked the remains of the apple from her hand. If a horse could be said to beam, it beamed. Jane checked between its hind legs. Being shut up in a small space with a stallion probably wouldn't improve her chances of survival, but the gelding put his soft muzzle into her hand and nuzzled. "No more," she said and tied a knot in the top of the bag. Her stomach protested.

She edged past the horse and moved into the stall where a feeding-bag with a few stray oats clinging to the bottom hung next to coils of rough rope and a trough of water. Cupping her hands together she drank until her thirst was quenched. The water was clear and ran through the trough, entering from the left and exiting right. The stall was a-flood with urine, hay and manure and this malodorous cement caked thickly onto her hiking boots. The horse stood barring her exit and showing the whites of his eyes. There was room for them both in the stall but the idea of close proximity to the four large hooves and the strong hind-quarters was not a happy one. Horses kicked. She'd heard somewhere you shouldn't walk behind a horse on the strong likelihood that it would be tempted to go for a goal.

"Shoo," she said in a half-hearted way. "Go on. Shoo," she said again with more conviction, and this time lifted her hands palms upward from her side. To her surprise the horse backed obligingly out of the way. She crept past him and made her escape up the rickety wooden ladder that led to the loft.

The loft provided not only a refuge but a window onto the world. By lying on her stomach, she could see an unpaved road running through wild grasses to a wide valley, and from there to the foot of a mountain range. Here the road – now a thread of ochre – climbed until it was out of sight. Near to the *borda* a silver creek flowed under a narrow bridge. There were no vehicles on the road, nor any dust in the distance to indicate a vehicle in progress. The lack of long shadows by the sparse trees nearby showed it to be midday. Noon of the following day she surmised, because her hunger didn't seem to correspond with days of starvation. She ate another apple and ignored the eager breathy snorts that accompanied the tolling of the horse's bell below her. The view from the window was mesmerising. The sun moved further west warming her face and a patch of wall in her stone prison.

On either side the river lie
Long fields of barley and of rye,

That clothe the wold and meet the sky;
And thro' the field the road runs by
To many-tower'd Camelot...

'Tirra Lirra', by the river
Sang Sir Lancelot.

And where was Sir Lancelot when you needed him, Jane wondered? Her restless mind drifted near and far without any attempt on her part to rein it in. Fragments of her life with Bruce mixed in with the wreckage of the past two weeks. Her thoughts flowed past this flotsam until the yellow tractor swept into view. It had a small blade at the front for levelling ground or clearing snow. Jane climbed down the ladder and up into the driving seat. The key was in the ignition. She climbed down again and opened the fuel cap. The tank was half empty, or half full – depending on your point of view. She filled it using the fuel can and funnel stored by the cultivating equipment. Finding something to put water in was more difficult. Eventually she gave up, merely drinking as much water as her stomach could hold. Perhaps she would come across another stream.

She jammed the bag of apples under the seat and tied the folded blanket and fuel can in front. Back on the tractor she pulled out the throttle, switched on the ignition and revved the accelerator. The black-faced gelding screamed like a factory whistle at knock-off time. "Time to go," she agreed, letting out the clutch and tramping on the accelerator. The tractor shot forward and crashed into the solid wooden doors and bounced backwards. Jane's head snapped back so hard she saw stars. Perhaps a slow pressure would be better. She raised the blade to the height of her seat. This time she braced herself, rounding her back and clenching the wheel with a white-knuckle grip as she slowly increased the revs and pushed the blade against the door. The wood around the lock splintered and the doors burst open. She broke through into the sunlight with the horse at her wheels, bucking and kicking as it bolted past her, arching its back and lifting all four hooves off the ground. The bell around its neck tolled unceasingly as it took off down the road. Jane headed in the opposite direction towards the hills. The top speed of the tractor was about twenty miles an hour. Faster than walking.

Her target was the ochre road she'd seen from the hayloft. She estimated that it would take no more than half an hour to reach it. Squinting at the sun and making a rough calculation of the time, she blessed the Spanish and Catalan habit of long lunches, that meant, with a little bit of luck, the road would be empty until she got to the protection of the wooded mountainside. From there it would be better to hide the tractor and hike up one of the many animal tracks she was sure to find.

The sun was scorching her left shoulder, and since it would be setting in the west her face was oriented towards the north. Of course it was a disadvantage not to know where she was setting out from. But she didn't consider turning the tractor south and driving it across the plains. She'd be too easy to spot. Heading north involved a half an hour of risk followed by the shelter of the woods. Unless there were dogs.

Why would there be dogs? She cursed her imagination.

The dirt road up the mountain was narrow and rutted by erosion. Jane wondered how cars passed each other on a track barely wide enough for one. Probably there were places to pull over and pass. She could leave the tractor on one of those although it would be easier to spot. She weighed the attraction of making a few more miles against hiding the tractor in the woods. She put the tractor in neutral and climbed down to check whether there was a safe route into the scrub. There were no ravines or holes that she could see. She swung back up into the seat and backed the tractor off the road and up the incline, pulled the hand brake up as far as it would go, undid the fuel can, then jumped down to jam it quickly under one of the back tyres to ensure the tractor didn't roll back down the hill. She rolled the blanket up and put it over her shoulders and ate another apple. The pine needles in the undergrowth made keeping on her feet difficult and she slid the last few metres on her bottom and scuffed her palms.

"Shit!" she said after coming to a stop in an untidy heap on the pointy stump of a fir tree. She rubbed her hip. There were not many parts of her body that didn't hurt.

The gloom of the woods and the dense scrub made it hard to see the tractor from the road but if you knew where to look, you could see the outline of a tyre, a perfectly round shape that nature rarely produced. She raked up some the flattened grass where she had driven off the road, then stood back to see the effect. "Good enough," she decided. Before taking a small track leading into the woods, she looked back one last time. The *borda* was an irregular smudge on the horizon of the dry grassy plain. Dust whirled up from the road with a sudden wind. The sun went behind a cloud. Above her a raptor swooped on a gust of air. A small animal, possibly a field mouse sensing danger, scrabbled to safety in the undergrowth.

CHAPTER FORTY-THREE

At the top of the dirt road, where it met the asphalt, the horses were congregated in a circle around the black stallion – their attention fixed as if on an evangelist during a Sunday preaching. Spellbound, the mares and geldings moved only to twitch away a marauding fly. The bells around their neck tolled sporadically. Jane rubbed the rain from her face with a corner of the blanket. Was it only days ago that she was here at the *Port de Cabus* with Greta? The stallion eyed her and pawed the ground.

"I have one apple left," she said. "It's yours." She tossed it at his hooves where it rolled on, over the edge of the road and down towards the unpopulated *pueblo* of Seturia a kilometre downhill. A brown gelding made a dash for it. The stallion stood its ground.

Jane was surprised when she breasted the hill to discover herself back in Andorra where the road from Pal met the old smugglers' route to Spain. The trek up the mountainside had been unrelenting, but the cloudy sky and sudden squalls of rain had kept her thirst in check. She had blessed the downpour as she trudged ever upward with Jorge's blanket wrapped around her shoulders. It would obscure the trail on the road from her *borda* prison.

A silver RV was parked to one side of the col. The registration showed it to be German. Jane tapped on the door. Germans usually spoke good English.

"Do you have a mobile phone? I need to call the police!"

The handlebar moustache of the man at the door was impressive.

"Is there a problem?" his voice boomed making the stallion shy away.

"Yes. Well, no. There was a problem. I guess there still is a problem, but if you'd let me use your phone to say I'm safe?" Jane was unusually incoherent. "I am safe now, aren't I?" It wasn't rain on her cheeks now, but tears.

"Safe? In Andorra? I would say you are safe. You are safe with us. Come in, come in and my wife will make you a cup of tea. Are you English? Your accent is English. Don't cry. Hush. Don't cry."

"I really need to call the police," she sobbed. "It's a long story."

"We have all the time in the world."

Victor said he'd send a car for her, but the German couple wouldn't hear of it. Why wait for a car to arrive when they could drive her to police-headquarters in half the time.

"Rest in the back. We'll drive you straight there. I have a GPS. Don't you worry; you'll be very safe with us. We won't leave you until you are happy in the arms of the police."

The back of the RV was warm and womb-like. No-one could see her through the high-curtained windows. She had re-entered Andorra with only the horses and the German tourists as her witness. As they set off down the road she wondered for a moment who was at home in the *Casa d'Or*, but the anonymity of the tourist vehicle felt more comforting than stopping to wait for the police with Pedro and his grandfather. "*For secrets are edged tools,/ And must be kept from children and from fools.*" ... Hell, she was getting to be more like Charles every day. – Spouting fragments of poetry with her mind wandering in all directions. – She had to focus. The kidnapping was over. She was safe. Safe was a mantra she could not repeat often enough.

The RV pulled up with maximum inconvenience to traffic outside the concave entrance of the massive police-headquarters.

"We will walk in with you," the Germans insisted, and she was gently frog-marched into the reception area where they stepped forward to say, "We are expected."

Jane glanced down to see if the husband had clicked his heels together. She nearly giggled but reminded herself that stereotypes were politically incorrect. Perhaps she was becoming hysterical.

"*El detective*, Victor?" she said.

The young policeman nodded and pressed an intercom, murmuring something in Catalan. Victor appeared through the double-doors behind the desk. He introduced himself to the German couple, shook their hands and thanked them for their help, asking them to leave their name and contact details at the desk in case they were needed as witnesses in any future court case.

"Pleased to help. You haf a beautiful country," said the German through his handlebar moustache. Maybe he belonged to a moustache club, or sang Gilbert and Sullivan. She visualised a chorus of robust Germans in tights twirling their moustaches. Or rather, she supposed, Germans would sing Wagner.

"Are you OK, Jane?" Victor asked with concern, noting her glazed look. "Would you like to see a doctor before we talk?"

"I feel kind of strange. A little removed from everything. Maybe it's the drugs he gave me, or perhaps it's shock." She paused for a moment and listened to herself breathing in and out. "Have you called Charles to let him know I'm OK?"

"Yes, as soon as I got your call. And Saboya. Your father's in Barcelona waiting for your mother to arrive. She's flying in today. She got the first available flight when she heard about your disappearance."

"I should have driven the other way," Jane said gloomily.

"*Qué?*" Victor was surprised.

"Never mind, we have other stuff to talk about."

"Of course. If you feel well enough. Would you like to call your father first?"

"Not really. As long as he knows I'm alright."

"*Muy bien*, come to the interview-room."

"Did you arrest Jorge?" Jane asked.

"The Spanish authorities are on the lookout for him and his car. His photo's in the paper and on the television news, described as someone we want to interview in regard to your disappearance. We don't believe he's still in Andorra. There's an unmarked police car stationed outside his parents' home and we're also keeping his apartment under surveillance, although we doubt he'll return. You were gone when we got there, but the IT detectives started searching through the hard-drive on his computer straight away.

"The room he kept you in, Jane," Victor paused, "the strange white room; it must have been pretty grim."

"Your English improves in quantum leaps, Victor. 'We are keeping his apartment under surveillance' sounds like an American television series. By the way, 'grim' isn't a word we use much." She didn't want to think about her time alone in the all white room. "How much ransom did he ask for me anyway?"

"Fifty million pesetas in unmarked notes. Small denominations. No dye packs."

"Dye packs? Andorra has dye packs?"

"I'm obviously not the only one who watches television."

"The box-freezer, did you look inside?" Jane gave an involuntary shudder.

"It was empty."

"Yes. I thought it would be," Jane whispered. "I imagined it was intended for me. Even the thought that he would probably kill me first wasn't as frightening as thinking about ending up in the freezer. An unbridled imagination is not always something you should ever aspire to."

"Your English isn't exactly the everyday sort either, Jane."

"It's getting weirder since I spent time with Charles."

Victor led her into a plain white room containing a desk, recording-machine and several chairs.

"No two-way mirrors?"

"It's good to see you are becoming yourself again!" Two uniformed police-officers joined them and silently sat against the wall.

"Let us begin."

They went over it again and again. From time to time one of the silent policemen would leave the room. Jane wondered if he was organising Spanish policemen to storm the isolated *borda*. Or maybe they would hide and wait for Jorge to turn up to give the next injection. Presuming he hadn't run for it. If he found her gone, would he try to follow her or worry about his own escape? Perhaps he had an accomplice? How long did an injection last? Of course the policeman could have just left the room for coffee. Or maybe he had a problem with his prostate, although he looked too young.

Thinking about coffee made her remember to ask for some, and for a baguette. When it came her first bite was so large that she could hardly chew. She swilled it down with coffee and took another super bite.

"The food will help your concentration, Jane. You seem to be drifting off every now and then. I know it's tedious, but sometimes the small, seemingly insignificant things lead to a breakthrough, so let us go over it one more time." And they did. They went over and over it until there was nothing left to say.

"*Muy bien*." Victor pushed back from the desk and turned off the recording-device. The two silent observers left the room. "Now, I have some news for you. The medical examiner completed the autopsy yesterday...."

"Yesterday?" interrupted Jane. "Wasn't yesterday Mertixell Day?"

"It's Thursday today, you've been missing since Monday."

Jane rubbed her arm. She started to tremble. "I was unconscious for three days? Do you think...?" It was hard to express the thought. "Perhaps a doctor should examine me after all," was the most neutral way she could express her fear.

"Of course, Jane. I'm sorry I didn't take you straight to the hospital." Victor's voice was gentle. "I was anxious for details to feed to our investigative team. It was thoughtless. The normal procedure is to take you to a doctor first. I was thinking about catching Jorge as soon as possible...." He stopped, lost for the right words.

"He has my mobile phone. Have you tried calling him?"

"Jesus!" Victor rushed out of the room after the departing detectives.

"What were you going to tell me?" Jane asked when he returned.

Victor was blunt. "The body isn't Pearl's. The blood-type doesn't match. She was B-positive. The body had type-O blood. And another thing, it seems that *embustero* is Jorge – the photos were in his computer – but the woman in shackles is not Pearl. He superimposed a photo of Pearl's face on another woman's body."

"Who is Petra?" Jane said, thinking of the name scraped into the wall beside the cot in her white prison. "Oh God! Then Pearl is still out there somewhere. We have to find her." Her throat constricted and she had trouble squeezing the words out. "Have you received a ransom demand for her or had any further contacts since the last email?"

Victor shook his head. "A ransom demand would be a positive development."

"Do you know who the dead woman is?"

"We're working on it. Her face was disfigured but her hands were intact so we were able to send her fingerprints to Interpol; and we know that her dental-work is American."

Jane was bewildered. "Where does a missing American fit into this?"

"That's just one strand of the investigation. We're working on a murder, a kidnapping and a missing-person's case." He shook his head in disbelief. "It gets more complicated at every turn. Every available detective is working on some aspect of the case. I shouldn't say the case – as if there were only one, it could be several cases that are totally unconnected – as preposterous as that sounds when I say it out loud. Although it does seems unlikely that a crime wave should suddenly hit Andorra for no reason."

"Was there DNA evidence to link the dead woman with Jorge? Any hair in the apartment? Or DNA evidence from Pearl?" She remembered the rust stains on the blanket. "Shit! I left Jorge's blanket in the German couple's RV – the blanket from the sofa that he wrapped me in. It was stained."

"The front desk will call them. As for samples from the apartment, we have no results yet, but Saboya faxed the report from the forensic laboratory in France confirming the ponytail belonged to Pearl." He looked like he was about to remonstrate with Jane for not handing over the ponytail but just then, as he reached for the intercom, his mobile phone shrilled. "*Si, si, si!*" He looked at Jane, "I told Juan-Antonio you were here. He wants to come in."

"Maybe he could meet me at the hospital and take me home." Jane did not want to go home alone. Jorge knew where she lived. Possibly everyone in Andorra now knew where she lived. It was a small country. "Home to Charles's room at the hotel," she amended. "I can wait there for my mother. I don't think I can be on my own right now. I need people near me to help me feel safe."

"Juan-Antonio is a good man," said Victor Ignacio. "I would feel better myself if he were to stay at the hotel with you."

"And he's kind," said Jane firmly.

Victor smiled. "Kindness is a quality we could all use."

The uniformed policewoman who was assigned to escort Jane to the hospital parked with blue lights flashing near the emergency entrance and crowded Jane into the elevator to make their way up to the third floor. The policewoman held her arm lightly by the elbow and drew curious looks from the other occupants of the elevator. Jane flicked a self-conscious glance around and saw that an elderly man's attention was fixed on her.

"You are the missing Australian," he said. "They found you."

"Yes." Jane answered.

"I thought they would," he said, and turned to tell his wife about her in rapid Catalan. Everyone in the elevator started to nod and smile at her in recognition. A young man took out his small camera and held it up to take her photo.

"*Basta!*" The policewoman said, frowning at him.

He sheepishly returned it to his pocket, but not before Jane heard a soft click. Suddenly she was public property. People she had never met knew who she was and were talking about her. They hurried out of the elevator toward a suite of rooms with frosted glass doors and entered an empty examination room. Folded pink hospital gowns were stacked on one of the chairs.

"Take off your clothes and put on a gown while I get Dr Rodriguez." The policewoman was obviously well versed in hospital procedure.

The room faced north and Jane shivered with cold in the thin gown as she waited with her hip perched on the examination couch. She left her socks on, although she took off her mud-encrusted hiking boots. Her feet were the one part of her body that she was pretty sure had not been abused.

Dr Rodriguez and a young nurse bustled in.

"You're a woman," Jane said thankfully.

"I hear that a lot," smiled Dr Rodriguez. Her wiry black hair sprang from a high forehead and seemed to crackle with electricity. "*Venga*. Let us see what we have here."

Her examination was slow and thorough. The doctors' hands were warm and Jane did not move or flinch as she pressed on bruises and took photos with a small digital camera, explaining that these would be used in any future court-proceedings. When it came time for the internal examination the doctor said;

"I'll take some scrapings, but it doesn't appear that you have been raped. There is no sign of contusion or interference at all."

"Thank you for being so straightforward."

"There is no room for euphemisms in medicine. Especially at a time like this when you are feeling vulnerable."

"The worst part is that I wasn't able to resist. The idea of him undressing me, or touching me while I was unconscious feels like such a violation…." Jane couldn't continue. As always when she was uncomfortable talking about the personal, she deflected the subject towards the general. "Do you see many cases of rape, or violence against women in Andorra?"

"The figures are escalating every year, and are probably understated. There's no specific law against domestic violence here, as there is in other countries in Europe but other laws can be applied. Rape, including spousal rape, is of course against the law." Doctor Rodriguez judged that Jane was ready to move from the general to the specific. "Would you like to have a hot shower, now that I have finished?"

"That's just what I need."

Jane looked through the window of the hospital waiting-room. Andorra la Vella was spread below her. Traffic was heavy and low cloud had trapped the emissions causing a brownish smog to obscure the mountains beyond. Juan-Antonio was speaking in a low voice with the policewoman, no doubt going through some type of hand-over formality. Or perhaps she was reassuring him that Jane had not been harmed in any way that showed. Whether her psyche was damaged no-one could tell. Not right now, and maybe not for a while yet.

A familiar ginger frizz bobbed into view above the thicket of indoor plants.

"Mary?" ventured Jane.

Mary appeared from behind a potted palm followed closely by Dave wearing full leather gear. His amiable grin and sharp eyes took her in.

"We heard you were here on the car radio. Mary insisted we come straight away. She thought you might need us."

The man in the elevator had wasted no time in contacting the news media.

"I've been so worried," Mary's voice piped over the top of Dave's. She stepped into Jane's arms and hugged her hard. Her red curls gave off the sweet fragrance of baby-shampoo.

"I hope you won't be travelling on the plane to England on your own." Jane was having trouble navigating where her thoughts would take her next. "Does the airline send someone with you to take care of you?"

"She hasn't let us turn off the television since she heard you were missing," Dave continued, "and she's had us out scouring the countryside for a turquoise Panda day and night – with no luck, needless to say."

Jane hugged Mary some more. "Thank you."

"No, we still haven't thanked you for sending Señor Saboya to help us with bail. The least I could do is to come by to see if you needed any help."

"What's bail?" asked Mary.

"Never mind!"

"Shall we go, Jane?" Juan-Antonio had materialised at her side and was pulling her gently away from Mary's embrace and trying not to frown at Dave's dreadlocks and tattoos.

"No, seriously. Perhaps I can help more than you think." Dave flashed his wallet and showed them an embossed plastic ID. A square-jawed, blonde all-American boy stared out of a card that simply said. "Dave Warner. Interpol." He grinned at their surprise. "I work for Interpol in the unit that helps co-ordinate drug investigations involving two or more countries. Lyn was part of my cover the night we were arrested at The Green Door. I was following a lead to a South-American drug-cartel. I felt bad that we couldn't explain that to your Señor Saboya. It didn't occur to us that there would be a police raid while we were gone and that Mary would be left on her own."

Juan-Antonio and Jane looked blank.

"So your relationship with Lyn is…"

"Real enough. We're partners."

"In the sense that you both work for Interpol?"

"No. In the more personal sense."

"Are you allowed to tell us this when you're undercover?"

"It's my call."

Mary was frowning trying to follow the exchange. "Can I tell my Mum you work for Interpol? She asks about you."

"If you need to, sweetheart." Dave smiled fondly at her.

"Are you working in co-operation with the Andorran police on this matter?" Juan-Antonio was wearing his policeman's face.

"The two countries involved in the drug deals are Columbia and Spain."

"And you are in Andorra instead of Spain… because…?"

"Because of the money-laundering."

"There's no money-laundering in Andorra." Jane and Juan-Antonio chorused.

"We've signed the charter against money-laundering with the EU and the banks are very vigorous in pursuing any irregularities," said Juan-Antonio.

"The banks, yes – but it might not be in the bank's interest to pursue these matters aggressively," argued Dave.

"You should have contacted the authorities before operating here without their knowledge and approval." Juan-Antonio was curt.

"When you're undercover you can't go around telling all and sundry who you are. That won't work! And before you tell the authorities about me, you should call Interpol headquarters in Lyons. Perhaps they will dissuade you."

"Why should they?"

"It's a sensitive matter. Call them and you'll see."

"Maybe you could find Jacob Weinstein for us." Jane said, her mind still unable to track any one thought for any length of time. "The Australian embassy was supposed to ask if Interpol could locate him for us."

Dave took out a small notebook and wrote the name down.

"Let me take you back to the hotel, Jane. You need some rest." Juan-Antonio looked tired of Dave and his Interpol connections.

"Just one more thing, Jane! What happened to the expensive jar of bath-salts we stashed in Pearl's apartment? It wasn't there when the police inventoried the apartment. We didn't want to keep it in our apartment while Mary was there."

"I didn't realise it was on loan. I do love a bath." Jane smiled.

"Don't tell me it went down the plug-hole!" Dave groaned.

"*Que*?" said Juan-Antonio, all at sea.

"Cost a friggin' fortune too. My bosses aren't going to be too happy to hear I've blown all that money for no return. I was trying to set myself up as dealer to give me some credibility on the street, but after you changed the key to the apartment I couldn't get back in again to retrieve it. I've never been any good at breaking and entering. Did you enjoy the champagne?"

"Well, that's two mysteries solved."

"*Que*? What bath-salts?"
Jane kissed Juan-Antonio on the lips, lingering just a touch too long.
"I'll explain later."

CHAPTER FORTY-FOUR

J uan-Antonio parked his Landcruiser next to a taxi in the hotel parking lot and they continued down the driveway. He hadn't let go of her hand since they left the hospital. The halitoxic hotel porter was on duty again but today he also had a certain wild-eyed look. He did a double-take when he saw Jane and stepped forward a few paces, before retreating in the wake of one hard glance from Juan-Antonio.

"Señora Jane," the porter said. "There's a gentleman waiting to see you in the foyer. He would not be dissuaded." Juan-Antonio came to an abrupt halt, stepped in front of Jane and measured the distance back to the car with his eyes. "He seemed upset. It would be better to wait outside until the police arrive."

"Stay here, while I investigate," said Juan-Antonio but Jane stormed into the revolving doors, stumbling on the slick marble floor as she was abruptly expelled. Before she regained her footing she found her wrist taken in a firm grip.

"*Tio*!" she said in surprise. The old man was slumped in a wheelchair at right-angles to the entrance, a shotgun across his lap. Pedro stood behind him in attendance. To one side in one of the hotel's luxurious chairs, a small man in the livery of a taxi company sat bolt upright with the dog *Oso* at his feet worrying his shoelaces. The receptionist stood to attention at the reception desk, her eyes a mirror image of the porter's.

"We took a taxi," said Pedro, "*Yayo* does not drive, and I couldn't manage the manual gear shift on Mama's car."

"I should think not," said Jane.

"The driver wasn't happy to bring *Oso*, but *Yayo* persuaded him," said Pedro, the satisfaction evident in his voice. "It was hard to fit the wheelchair in the boot, so I tied it in with a piece of string. I used a slip knot with a double hitch so it wouldn't come loose."

"How did you know where to come?" asked Juan-Antonio. He had entered quietly through the double side-door, eschewing the drama of being bodily ejected from the revolving door after Jane.

"*Hola*, *Tio* Juan-Antonio!" said Pedro happily. "It was on the radio. They said Cousin Jane had been found and she was being examined at the hospital. *Claro*. She would come to see her father afterwards. Andorra TV interviewed him on Monday outside the hotel. *Yayo* said we should come immediately. *No debemos perder tiempo.* We should lose no time," Pedro quoted.

So far the old man had said nothing, content to let Pedro do the talking; nor had he let go of Jane's arm. His unwithered left hand was remarkably strong. The arthritic gnarled right hand grasped the shotgun.

Juan-Antonio raised his eyebrows in silent question to the receptionist who nodded back; the police were on their way.

"We won't need the taxi now," said Pedro. "We can go home in your Land Cruiser. It will fit the wheelchair quite well. *Usted puede marcharse*," he said to the taxi-driver carelessly. But the man refused to move, his eyes on the dog.

"*Venga, Oso,*" bade the old man. The dog slunk towards Jane – grumbling, his belly on the ground. Automatically, she held out her hand, fingers splayed. *Oso* rose and placed his nose deliberately in her palm and sniffed. Jane slowly tilted her hand until her middle finger reached the dog's ear. She ran her finger gently through the wiry curls from ear to jaw. The dog pressed against her hand, and when she started to scratch him behind the ear he sighed heavily and stood transfixed.

"He remembers you," said Pedro.

"What are you doing here, Uncle?" asked Juan-Antonio.

"*Som Catalan. Parlem Catalan!*" The old man responded.

"Jane doesn't speak Catalan," Juan-Antonio reminded him. The taxi-driver had found the courage to sidle over to the receptionists to ask if the bar was open. The handicap ramp enabled him to back slowly out of the room towards a stiff brandy, away from the menacing dog and old man with a shaky grip on a shotgun obviously dating from before the Second World War.

"Let us go home to *La Casa d'Or*. This is a family matter and should be resolved without outside interference," said the old man.

"The hotel staff has called the police, *Tío*. I believe we will have to wait for them."

"You are the police," the old man pointed out.

"My jurisdiction is confined to Ordino. I cannot help you here. It is a serious matter to use a shotgun to menace the public."

"We'll have to go home soon or Mama will be very angry,"

interrupted Pedro. "*Yayo* locked her in the cellar and it's cold down there."

"Why put Llourdes in the cellar?" asked Juan-Antonio, but on this question *Tio* was stubbornly mute. Instead he relinquished Jane's wrist allowing her to sink onto a wicker chair with the great brown dog panting at her feet. Juan-Antonio sat as well and Pedro turned the wheelchair so they were all facing.

"In a question of family honour the police should not interfere."

"Those days are in the past, *Tio*. Today the police involve themselves in violence in the home and things of that nature."

"I used no violence. I merely locked the door after her for her own good."

"Arriving at the hotel with the shotgun concerns the police."

"But it was for Cousin Jane's protection," protested Pedro.

"All the same, I'm going to call Fernando."

"No!" roared the old man. "*Ese cabrón*! He is part of the problem, not the solution. If he had kept to his wedding vows and thought more about his wife and son we would not be in this situation."

"What situation exactly? Jane's kidnapping, or Pearl's disappearance?"

"Pedro!" The old man waved his hand in a circle to indicate Pedro should take the floor. Pedro tucked his chin into his neck. The verbal attack on his father, calling him a bastard, made him reconsider his zeal in joining forces with his great-uncle. He was beginning to understand this was not a game.

"I was playing in the barn. I wanted to use an old door to make a cubby house but it was too heavy. I thought perhaps the wheel jack from Mama's car would help me lift it. I tipped the back seat forward to get to the spare wheel and there was a laptop jammed under it. It had a label stuck to the outside that someone had tried to rip off, but I could see that it said 'Ordino'.

"Mama was out in the fields giving *onces* to the workers so I took it to *Yayo*. He asked me to open it up. I turned it on and showed him how to go to the email files and click on the messages to read them. He told me not to say anything to Mama and that when she came back we would play a joke on her."

"The emails were in English," the old man continued, his voice weary. "Pedro recognized his father's email address. There were many emails to him. The language was playful and provocative. Inflammatory to a faithful wife. I sent Pedro back to the barn and waited for Llourdes to return. She came in flushed and laughing from the fields – one of the workers had been flirting with her – but her face changed when she saw the computer. 'Now you know,' she said. I asked what had she done, and she exclaimed – 'I? What have I done? Ask Fernando. I have done nothing.'" The old man stopped and reached into his shirt pocket to pull out a leather wallet. He extracted some colourful notes and gave then to Pedro.

"Go to the bar and pay the taxi-driver and ask the waiter to bring us coffee, and a coca cola for you." He watched the boy until he disappeared up the stairs. "I cannot protect the boy for ever, but I can postpone the pain for a little while," he said and took Jane's hand once again in his own, this time with tenderness.

His clouded eyes suddenly turned away. Pistol drawn, Victor came silently through the side door backed up by the same two policemen who had sat in on Jane's interrogation. Both men were armed with automatic weapons. Using his broad back to block their sight of the wizened man in the wheelchair, Juan-Antonio leaned forward and took possession of the shotgun. Victor issued a curt command and held out his hand. His adjutants froze. Juan-Antonio silently handed over the gun, which was passed from man to man and through the door to unseen hands outside. A crash presaged the whirlwind entry of a small figure who threw himself between the policemen and the old man. Coffee erupted from a dropped silver coffeepot, flowing lava like around their shoes, past broken cups and into the four corners of the foyer. *Oso* jumped to his feet and frolicked around the boy and the old man, barking furiously in sudden animation.

"*Dios mio!*" Victor took a step back, "Are you alright, Jane?"

"Yes. Umm, this is my great-uncle."

"What was the gun for, Uncle?" asked Victor.

"*Protección!*" The response was half sullen, half indignant.

"Señor Xavier Vendrell Oliarte – my cousin Fernando's wife's great-uncle." Juan-Antonio shouted introductions, above the dog's pandemonium. "For gods sake, someone do something about the dog."

Pedro cuffed the dog over the head and grabbed his collar. The dog quietened but turned its baleful eyes upon Victor who took another step back.

"He's everyone's great-uncle then?"

"Not everyone's," corrected the old man, "but I have some connections."

"So it seems," said Victor, putting his pistol away in its holster. His two subordinates held their automatic weapons more loosely but kept a watchful eye on the salivating dog. Pedro pulled an insubstantial-looking coil of string from his back pocket and tied the dog to the door handle, demonstrating his efficient use of authentic-looking knots.

"Do you think it will hold?" Victor was dubious.

"Of course. I know knots." Pedro assured him. "*Abajo*, *Oso*!" The dog dropped obediently to the floor but continued to oscillate his impressive head between the standing policemen.

"Pedro found Pearl's computer in Llourdes' car. He took it to show *Tio* Xavier and when they heard about Jane's release on the radio they rushed over here, but first *Tio* locked Llourdes in the cellar. We had better go and sort this out...." Juan-Antonio's explanation tailed off and he put his hand to his forehead.

"How is Señora Llourdes involved?" asked Victor, looking to the old man for an explanation – but *Tio* pressed his lips together and refused to speak, merely shaking his head. The increased tremor of his warm hand in Jane's was the only suggestion of his agitation.

The detective motioned towards the door and they crowded out of the hotel together – Pedro pushing the wheelchair while Jane strode alongside, still holding the old man's hand. Juan-Antonio kept close behind, manhandling a boisterous *Oso*. The policemen brought up the rear. Victor was talking on the phone to the IT detective, asking him to meet them at the *Casa d'Or*.

"*Está bien?*" asked the valet, looking to see if anyone was in handcuffs.

The three cars turned into the long gravel driveway of the *Casa d'Or*. *Tio* had said not a word since he left the hotel but when they reached the step to the front door he cleared his throat and asked for the return of his shotgun.

Juan-Antonio shook his head.

The heavy oak doors were locked. Without discussion *Tio* drew a bundle of keys from his pocket and handed them to Pedro. Pedro opened the door then ran ahead calling:

"Mama, *no te preocupes*, we're coming!"

Juan-Antonio dropped his hold on *Oso*'s collar and hurried after him. The dog immediately wheeled to block the passageway, showing his teeth. Jane was sidling towards it whispering placatory words when she heard the scream. The dog whirled once more and with Jane close on its heels they ran down the passage. Juan-Antonio cried out;

"*Aye no! Dios mío! Dios mío!*"

The policemen thundered past Jane, pushing her hard against the wall and when the dog turned on them, one of the young policemen shot it without hesitation. They hurdled its body, adrenaline giving them a foot to spare. *Tio* remained outside in his wheelchair, unable to negotiate the step to the front door.

"*Ayúdame, ayúdame!*" he called for help, but no-one listened in their rush to negotiate the steep stone stairway to the icy cellar.

Llourdes's body hung from a sturdy oak beam. The hangman's noose was crafted expertly from a coil of half-inch oiled rope.

"Mama," cried Pedro brokenly, his arms clasped around her knees, trying to lift the weight of her body from her broken neck. Juan-Antonio had righted the wooden stool and was standing on it with his fingers against her throat, searching desperately to find a pulse below the ghastly mottled face that stared down at them. Jane retched even as she threw herself to her knees to hug Pedro. "Mama!" he sobbed again. "*Lo siento!*"

"It's not your fault, Pedro," whispered Jane.

"It's my rope! I made the knot!" screamed the child.

Tio's interrogation took place in the dining-room under the gaze of his masterpiece. Angel's ghostly presence did not distract the policemen. *Tio* refused Victor's offer to call a lawyer. The involvement of more strangers was unbearable to him. The IT detective set up his laptop and web-cam to record the interview. One of the young policemen used his initiative to make coffee. Outside Juan-Antonio sat in the sun with Pedro cradled on his lap waiting for the police escort to deliver Fernando from his parliamentary office. The boy hiccupped every now and then with his face buried in Juan-Antonio's shoulder. The storms of tears had subsided, replaced by a dull shock. A black cat crouched in a patch of sunlight, watching in vain for an opportunity to spring into the boy's arms. Jane went back inside. *Tio* stopped talking and turned to her.

"Your sister is dead. I cannot tell you where her body is buried. Llourdes hired an assassin to kill her. She asked him to cut off Pearl's hair and bring it as proof of her death, together with a photo of the body before she would pay. The man brought her the computer as well." *Tio* shuddered. "She was not in her right mind, Llourdes. She paid the man a great deal of money to do this evil thing."

"Llourdes paid Jorge to kill Pearl?" Jane's voice was tight.

Victor interrupted. "No. Not Jorge. *Tio*'s son-in-law, Santiago gave Llourdes the name of a man who could eliminate the problem she had. Santiago de Almeida Barreiro has many connections. The name he gave her was Russian."

"Why? Why would *Tio*'s son-in-law do that?" she slammed her palm against her quivering lips to quell the hysteria. She needed to stay calm for Pedro's sake. He also was a victim. There was nothing more she could do to save Pearl – this thought would haunt her – but right now her concern was for the boy. Time enough to grieve when she was on her own.

"Llourdes convinced Santiago they needed to kidnap Pearl to delay the payment of the trust capital until the *Apice Finances* group could overcome a certain solvency problem. Almeida Barreiro is a partner in the group. It was in his interest to help find a solution. Normally he is careful not to shit where he lives, but he wouldn't expect Llourdes to dishonour the family, and especially not to kill Pearl. The Russians promised they would handle the kidnapping discretely. In turn Llourdes promised to use her influence with Fernando to unblock a stalled planning-application to build a tourist *aparthotel* using Russian money."

"The Russians have all the money these days," *Tio* interjected.

Jane thought about the dishevelled tear-stained boy outside.

"How could she do it?" she asked.

"How could she not?" said *Tio*.

EPILOGUE

"Where did Jorge fit into this?" Jane's secretary asked, as Jane queued – mobile pressed to her ear – in front of the Lufthansa desk to check in to her flight to Perth.

"It seems he took an opportunist approach. Pearl's disappearance gave him the idea to kidnap me and hold me for ransom. The news reports said I would be a wealthy woman when I received the money from the trust."

"Well you won't be so wealthy if *Apice Finances* goes bust."

"I'd end up pretty well the same because now there are only three beneficiaries."

Carol digested this in silence before saying, "That seems a bit rough on Elsa. I'm sure Pearl would have used the money to look after her, and Polly and the boys."

"You don't have to worry. Charles and I are founding a trust for them."

"Another trust! You already have a trust for Bruce and Mandy's daughter. Don't you think too much money can ruin someone's life?"

"Sometimes it does, but life's usually better with money than without it."

"And what about the woman they found in the fish farm?"

"DNA evidence linked her to the freezer in Jorge's apartment and to the grey blanket he wrapped me in. She's a Filipino maid who went missing here several months ago."

"Her name was Petra," guessed Carol, sadly.

"Yes. She scratched her name on the wall when he held her prisoner. The police are now linking Jorge to the disappearance of several Asian women. The Thai embassy in Madrid has asked them to make enquiries. Jorge was advertising on matchmaking sites – but not for brides. The police are reopening the case into his brother's death too. Apparently he fits the perfect profile of a serial murderer."

"You were lucky."

Jane thought of Pearl in her unmarked grave and shuddered. "I was!"

"Have they any idea where Jorge might be?"

"Not so far."

"What about Santiago de Almeida Barreiro and the Russian?"

"Columbia doesn't have an extradition treaty with Andorra, and without Barreiro's evidence, no-one knows anything about the Russian. At the moment the Andorran Foreign Minister is conferring with his counterpart in Bogota and asking for access to Barreiro at least to interrogate him."

"Was it Barreiro or the Russian who attacked you in the *trastero*?"

"Who knows? Victor says there is no Mercedes S500 with the matriculation plates Harris photographed. Charles thinks he's lying through his teeth."

"What do you think?"

"I suspect the partners of *Apice Finances* would try anything to delay the winding-up of the trust, but I also wonder about Barreiro's tobacco-smuggling activities and whether Pearl was planning some type of exposé with her series on tobacco."

"I suppose the other missing link is Weinstein and the photos."

"Dave tracked down Weinstein in no time. Apparently Pearl went to an exhibition of photos taken in Andorra in the 1950s and saw a photo of a Herman Berg, formally Beike. He's on the Nazi most-wanted list for butchering a Dutch art-dealer and his family during the early days of the German invasion and stealing the inventory, including a Vermeer. Looks like he fled to Andorra and started a new life. The Dutch authorities are starting to process the extradition request now.

"Pearl read an article about Beike and the missing Vermeer in the *New York Times Magazine*, and recognized his photo. She was lining up the evidence for a huge journalistic coup. Gary Cohen promises to give her a *post-mortem* by-line."

Jane reached the head of the queue and handed over her passport and documentation. "Gotta go," she said. "I'll call again when I change planes."

"Say hi to your mum."

"She's not with me, she decided to visit some old friends in the UK. While I'm in Perth I can keep and eye on Nanna. Charles and I will get together again in a couple of months when we finally sort out the trust investments. Saboya's keeping an eye on things for us, plus the trustees will be emailing updates."

She switched off the phone and apologised to the agent at the desk.

"Ms Burns, you've been upgraded to first class."

"How nice. Thank you."

Jane went through the exit marked "A" and turned towards the front of the plane. A stewardess took her carry-on bag and placed it in the overhead locker.

"Excuse me, you're in my seat," Jane said to the man bending down to take off his shoes. He sat up and turned towards her.

"Juan-Antonio!"

He gestured for her to sit down. "I didn't think you'd mind if I took the window-seat. I've never been to Australia."

"And where will you be staying?"

"I have a friend there who might put me up."

Jane smiled a slow smile.

"No, thank you," they said to the hostess as she offered them a complimentary glass of champagne before takeoff.

"Did I tell you that Paco's girlfriend works for one of the biggest travel agents in Barcelona?"

"No, but it's a long flight so I'm sure you'll get around to it."

"And will we see kangaroos?"

Barcelona lay at their feet. The plane dipped its wings and offered a view of a wide blue sea. The sixteen-hour first leg of the flight via Hong Kong lay ahead of them with plenty of time to talk, but for the moment Juan-Antonio took Jane's hand and held it tight.

Early Responses to *Death Has A Thousand Doors*

Patricia Grey's *Death Has A Thousand Doors* is a stunningly suspenseful novel set in the little-known principality of Andorra. It keeps the reader constantly curious, as we are led on an intriguing hunt for a missing photographer. The novel travels not only through the mountains, villages and history of Andorra but also through the histories and stories of its characters as a family comes together to search for its missing sister and daughter. Grey obviously knows Andorra well and is not afraid to explore the murkiest parts of its national history. When it comes to families and the secrets they nurture there is nothing which is not possible. She keeps her readers engrossed throughout with her cunning use of plot and story-telling. Each newly introduced character quickly becomes a suspect. The ends do become tied up as the novel draws to a close, although it was not quite the ending I believed I saw coming. – Grey had me there!

— Rebecca Tomasis, author of *Mishpacha – Family* (Joint-Winner, inaugural Proverse Prize 2009)

"The works of English speakers who came to visit Andorra in the last two centuries are an essential part of our literary heritage. With precise prose, and a sharp sense of observation, pioneers like Frederick Harold Deverell, Hepburn Ballantine, Bayard Taylor and many others, have offered us a very personal vision of our country. Patricia Grey's book is a step forward, a new milestone. From the premises of contemporary fiction she offers us a new perspective of our little world, so close, so complex, so unknown."

— Albert Villaró, Andorran writer, author of *Blau de Prússia* (Carlemany Prize 2006)

THE PUBLISHERS

Proverse Hong Kong (PVHK), founded by Gillian and Verner Bickley, is based in Hong Kong with long-term and developing regional and international connections. Proverse has published novels, novellas, non-fiction (including autobiography and biography, diaries, history, memoirs, sport, travel narratives), single-author poetry collections, children's, young adult, and academic books. Other interests include academic works in the humanities, social sciences, cultural studies, linguistics and education. Some Proverse books have accompanying audio texts. Some are translated into Chinese.

We welcome authors who have a story to tell, wisdom, perceptions or information to convey, a person they want to memorialize, a neglect they want to remedy, a record they want to correct, a strong interest that they want to share, skills they want to teach, and who consciously seek to make a contribution to society in an informative, interesting and well-written way. Proverse works with texts by non-native-speaker writers of English as well as by native English-speaking writers.

The name, "Proverse", combines the words "prose" and "verse" and is pronounced accordingly.

YOUR RESPONSE

We are interested to read your response to Patricia W. Grey's novel, *Death Has A Thousand Doors*. If you would like to do so, please give us a few sentences which you are willing for us to publish, describing your response to this book, sending them to <info@proversepublishing.com>.

If your comments are chosen to be included in our E-Newsletter or website, and if you send us your mailing address, we will select another title published by Proverse and send you a complimentary copy.

Unless you state otherwise, we will assume that we may cut or edit your comments for publication.

We will use your initials to attribute your comments.

FICTION PUBLISHED BY PROVERSE

Those who enjoy Patricia W. Grey's novel, **Death Has A Thousand Doors**, may also enjoy the following novels, short story collections, and novellas.

SHORT STORY COLLECTIONS

Beyond Brightness, by Sanja Särman. 2016.

Odds and Sods, by Lawrence Gray. 2013.

The Shingle Bar Sea Monster and other stories,
     by Laura Solomon. 2012.

The Snow Bridge and other Stories, by Philip Chatting. 2015.

NOVELS and NOVELLAS

A Misted Mirror, by Gillian Jones. 2011.

A Painted Moment, by Jennifer Ching. 2010.

Adam's Franchise, by Lawrence Gray. 2016.

An Imitation of Life. 2nd ed, by Laura Solomon. 2013.

Article 109, by Peter Gregoire. 2012.

**Bao Bao's odyssey: from Mao's Shanghai
     to Capitalist Hong Kong**, by Paul Ting. 2012.

Black Tortoise Winter, by Jan Pearson. 2016.

Bright Lights and White Nights, by Andrew Carter. 2015.

cemetery – miss you, by Jason S Polley. 2011.

Cop Show Heaven, by Lawrence Gray. 2015.

Curveball, by Gustav Preller. November 2016.

Hilary and David, by Laura Solomon. 2011.

Hong Kong Hollow, by Dragoş Ilca. Scheduled 2017.

Instant messages, by Laura Solomon. 2010.

Man's Last Song, by James Tam. 2013.

Mila the Magician by Zhang Jian (Catherine Chin). 2014.
(English/Chinese bilingual edition.)

Mishpacha – family, by Rebecca Tomasis. 2010.

Paranoia (the walk and talk with Angela),
by Caleb Kavon. 2012.

Red Bird Summer, by Jan Pearson. 2014.

Revenge From Beyond, by Dennis Wong. 2011.

The Day They Came, by Gérard Louis Breissan. 2012.

The Devil You Know, by Peter Gregoire. 2014.

**The Monkey in Me: Confusion, Love and Hope
Under a Chinese Sky**, by Caleb Kavon. 2009.

The Perilous Passage of Princess Petunia Peasant,
by Victor E. Apps. 2014. (Young adult fiction.)

The Reluctant Terrorist: in Search of the Jizo,
by Caleb Kavon. 2011.

The Village in the Mountains, by David Diskin. 2012.

Tiger Autumn, by Jan Pearson. 2015.

Tightrope! a Bohemian tale, by Olga Walló. 2010.
Translated from Czech by Johanna Pokorny, Veronika Revická & others.
Poetry translated by Justin Quinn and Veronika Revická. Edited by Gillian Bickley & Olga Walló, with Verner Bickley.

University Days, by Laura Solomon. 2014.

Vera Magpie, by Laura Solomon. 2013.

FICTION – CHINESE LANGUAGE

The Monkey in Me, by Caleb Kavon.
Translated by Chapman Chen. 2010.

Tightrope! A Bohemian Tale, by Olga Walló.
Translated by Chapman Chen. 2011.
Chinese translation supported by the Ministry of Culture of the Czech Republic.

~~~

FIND OUT MORE ABOUT OUR AUTHORS, BOOKS, LITERARY PRIZES, AND EVENTS

Visit our website:
http://www.proversepublishing.com
Visit our distributor's website: <www.chineseupress.com>

Follow us on Twitter
Follow news and conversation: <twitter.com/Proversebooks>
OR
Copy and paste the following to your browser window and follow the instructions:
https://twitter.com/#!/ProverseBooks
"Like" us on www.facebook.com/ProversePress

Request our free E-Newsletter
Send your request to info@proversepublishing.com.

Availability
Most books are available in Hong Kong and world-wide
from our Hong Kong based Distributor,
The Chinese University Press of Hong Kong,
The Chinese University of Hong Kong, Shatin, NT,
Hong Kong SAR, China.
Email: cup-bus@cuhk.edu.hk
Website: <www.chineseupress.com>.
All titles are available from Proverse Hong Kong
http://www.proversepublishing.com
and the Proverse Hong Kong UK-based Distributor.

We have **stock-holding retailers** in Hong Kong,
Singapore (Select Books),
Canada (Elizabeth Campbell Books),
Andorra (Llibreria La Puça, La Llibreria).
Orders can be made from bookshops in the UK and elsewhere.

Ebooks
Most of our titles are available also as Ebooks.

Death Has A Thousand Doors 311

www.ingramcontent.com/pod-product-compliance
Lightning Source LLC
Chambersburg PA
CBHW051333020726
47501CB00007B/2053